RETURN FROM DIVALIA

RETURN FROM DIVALIA

KYELL GOLD

Return from Divalia
Production copyright FurPlanet Productions © 2022
Text copyright © Kyell Gold 2022
Published by FurPlanet Productions
Dallas, Texas
www.furplanet.com

Cover art by Sara "Caribou" Miles
Interior design by FurPlanet Productions

ISBN 978-1-61450-579-2

First Edition Trade Paperback

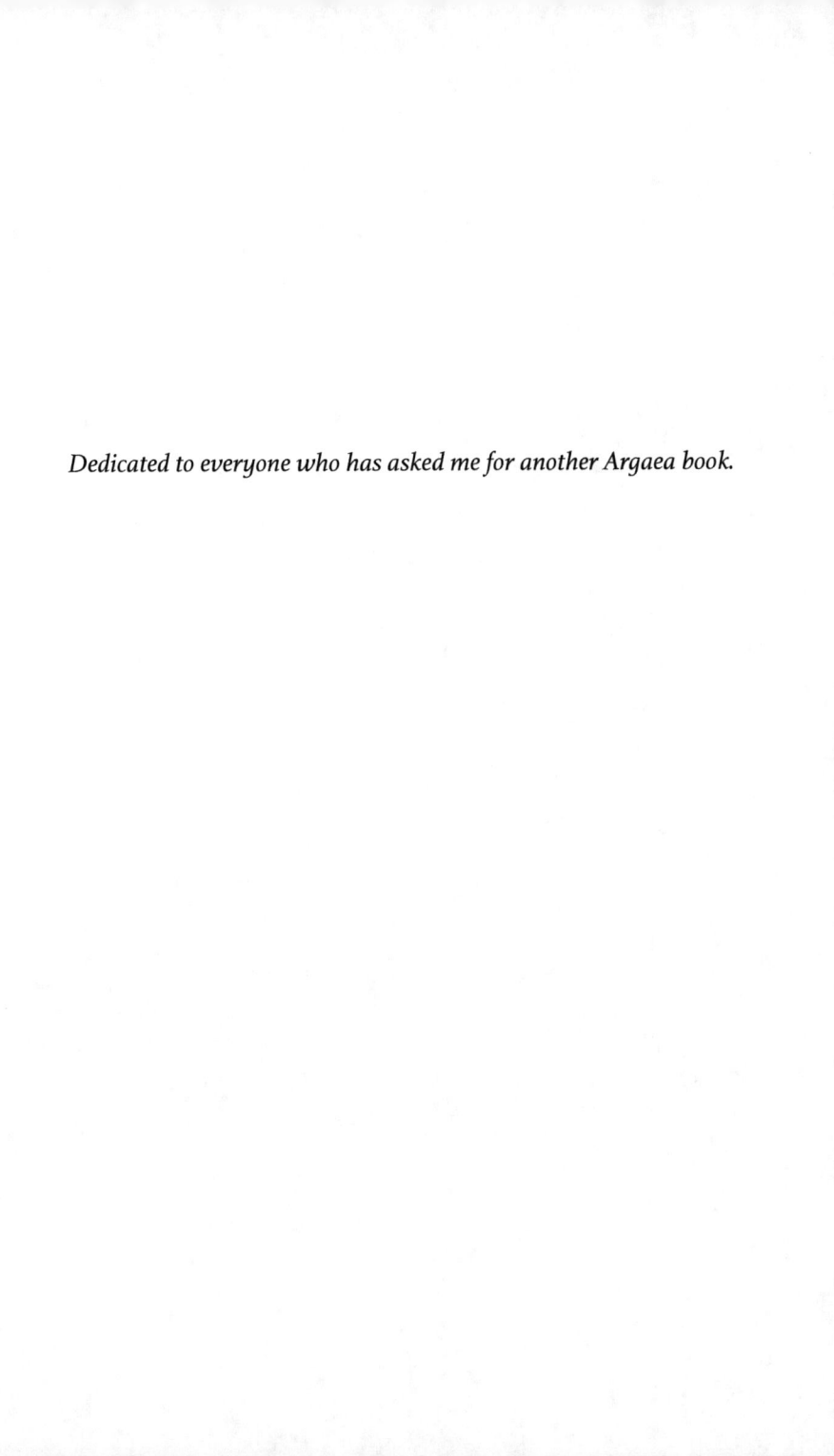

Dedicated to everyone who has asked me for another Argaea book.

CONTENTS

PROLOGUE

Stolen Away

Coryn picked another one of the reeds that sheltered the bottom of his father's stall from the driving rain and wove it into the shape he held in his paw. The weave of the concave shell was not simple, but his fingers took care of it while his mind recited once more the list of things he'd hoped to do in Divalia that had not happened and did not look likely to. Try an exotic drink in a tavern. Take a ride on a boat in the river. See the Great Cathedral. Meet a noble (even the lord of his own land of Deverin would do). Witness a master thief in action.

The only one that seemed remotely likely at this point was the last, and that only if a master thief were desperate enough for food to try to steal a loaf of barley bread or a pawful of raw barley. In the pouring rain. Coryn's father, of course, did not see it this way. "This is the weather thieves love," he'd snarled.

"They come out when honest folk are cozied up in their beds, when nobody expects 'em to be out."

And though he knew better, Coryn had argued, accomplishing no more than to be sitting under his stall with a bruised muzzle. The oilcloth he was sitting on had flooded twice, leaving his tail and rear soaked. None of the other merchants they'd traveled with had made their sons or daughters guard their wares at night. After all, there was a city guard posted at the end of the street. That was good enough for everyone except for one stubborn old wolf, and Coryn had the ill fortune to be that wolf's son.

But at least he was keeping the barley as dry as he could, by making sure the wind didn't blow the oilcloths up from under the wooden pallets. Drier than I am, he thought, holding up the little boat he was weaving. While Father sits in his room at the inn, all snug and warm and dry.

A gust of wind drove through the stall, chilling his fur and spattering him with rain. He huddled under his saturated cloak and folded his ears back, trying to curl into a warm ball. He wanted to close his eyes, but he had to stay vigilant. The only thing worse than being sentenced to sit here all night would be to sit here all night only to find they'd been robbed anyway.

Outside the front of the stall, a veritable river ran through the gutter. Coryn weighed the boat in his paw and then leaned forward. "I Howl thee the Adventure of Divalia," he said. "Sail under the eye of Canis."

It was gone a moment after he dropped it in the water, swept away by the raging current. He imagined the gutter spilling into the Lurine, and the great river bearing it southward to the sea and to the lands beyond. Who knew what adventures it would have while he sat here in the rain? He pulled his cloak tighter around himself and sneezed.

"This yours?" He jerked his head up. A brown pointed

muzzle pushed under his stall, teeth showing in a grin below two soft brown eyes. The water coursing through the rat's fur and around his small round ears didn't seem to bother him one bit. Below his muzzle, one small pink paw held out Coryn's boat.

"Y-yes," Coryn stuttered, as much from the chill in his jaw as from the unexpected visitor.

"Thought I saw it slip out from this here stall," the rat said, dropping the boat in front of him. "You'da lost it right quick if I hadn't snagged it. Oughta be more careful with it. Wouldn't wanna lose a nice boat like that."

"It's j-just a little th-thing," Coryn said. He didn't move to pick it up, focused on the rat's muzzle. The rat was really looking right at him, seeing him. He'd noticed the boat and complimented it.

"Well, cheers," the rat said. "Got things to do and the weather's a touch, well, you know." He pulled his muzzle back.

"Wait!" Coryn yelled. He scrambled forward and almost smacked his muzzle into the rat's nose as the rat poked his head back under the stall.

"Hey, look, there weren't nothing in it when I picked it up," the rat said.

"No, it's not th-that," Coryn said. "I j-just wanted to s-say, thank you."

"Oh." This appeared to perplex the rat. He nodded. "Well, that's nice of you. And now, I really have to—"

"It's my first time in the city," Coryn said, all in a rush. He was aware that he was still shivering under the cloak, but for the first time that night, he didn't feel cold.

"Zat so?" The rat grinned. "Coulda fooled me." He took a closer look around the stall before letting his eyes come to rest on Coryn again.

Coryn's ears flattened further. "Sorry." He sat back. "Just don't take anything."

The rat sniffed. "Barley? Nah, not t'my taste. Nothin' here really worth taking. Cheers." And he was gone.

"Wait!" Coryn called out.

No answer came. The young wolf picked up the boat and turned it over in his paws. "Some adventure," he muttered. Without any ceremony, he tossed it at the front of the stall, near the gutter. It landed on its side and slipped into the churning water, tumbling end over end and out of sight.

His eyes were closed, muzzle down against his chest, when he heard a high-pitched voice. "I reckon maybe I was a bit hasty back there."

Coryn looked up into the sharp brown face, water dripping from the rat's whiskers. "You can have the barley if you want," he said. "I won't stop you. The bread's pretty good."

"Oh, not about that." The rat flicked his whiskers, spraying water. "Seems there might be a thing or two worth havin' here, after all."

Coryn looked at the sheaves of barley, stacked under oilskin, at the loaves of bread wrapped in cloth, and then back at the rat. "Please don't take the oilskins. The barley'll be ruined."

"Wouldn't dream of it." A small pink paw reached out to him. "I was speakin' of the young wolf on his first visit to the city. Seems like a terrible waste spendin' it soaked under a smelly stall."

Coryn's eyes widened. "M-me?" The rat nodded. "I can't, I mean, my father..."

"Left you here to guard the wares while he stays nice an' warm in a cozy tavern, no doubt. Ale in one paw, attractive barmaid on th'other, what?"

"My father wouldn't!" But Coryn remembered the smell of the female raccoon in their chambers, and how he'd just assumed the servants had come around to clean. And how his father had never allowed his mother to come along while she was alive. "He wouldn't," he repeated.

"Course he would," the rat said. "Anybody'd seek out company in this miserable weather, ay?"

The smell of the rat's wet fur insinuated itself into Coryn's nose, through the strong smell of wet garbage and damp barley. He flicked his ears and managed a small smile at the rat's bright expression. "Aye?"

"That's the spirit! Come on, this stuff'll be safe 'nough 'til morning." He shimmied back out of the stall and called, "Shake your tail, there!"

To stay now would be cowardly, and rude besides. Coryn climbed slowly out of the stall after the rat, putting one paw squarely in the icy water of the gutter as he did. He yanked it up and shook it, though the reflexive motion did little in the steady rain.

The rat was already three stalls down and walking briskly away. "Hey!" Coryn called, taking two steps and then stopping. He folded his ears down to keep the insides dry.

The rat stopped and turned. He held aside the collar of his threadbare cloak so he could look at Coryn. "I'm keen to get outta the rain," he said. "C'mon."

"You sure..." Coryn looked back at his stall.

The rat grinned and spread his paws. "You see anyone else guardin' his stall?" he called loudly over the hiss of the rain.

He had, in fact, seen a raccoon down at the other end of the market, but there was nobody in sight now, not all up and down the twenty stalls of this side street, nor on the few stalls he could see on the main street. And some of them, he knew, had more valuable stock than barley. Well, on the off chance that anyone did steal their bread or grain, he'd just get back before his father showed up, and he'd claim he'd thrown out some rain-damaged stock.

His paws splashed through the puddles in the cracked paving stones, catching him up to the rat, who was setting a brisk pace again. "There's a guard," Coryn said, as they approached a stall where a fox kept a wary eye on them amidst a small cloud of hanging bronze lanterns. The few that were still lit cast eerie light and crooked shadows over the fox and the nearby street.

"Got valuable stock," the rat said. "Trust me, no thief'll come down here in this weather."

He said it loudly enough that the fox's ears flicked toward them. Coryn saw his snort and his intent gaze as the two of them passed. "You sure?"

"I know most of 'em. Hate the rain, they do."

Coryn looked at the rat's little pink paws, not curled up against his sides like Coryn's were, but spraying droplets of water from the tapping fingertips in front of him, as active as the rat's eyes darting from side to side. "But you're out in this weather," the wolf said.

"Ah, well, I'm a special case, ay? There's things in the rain that's overlooked by most." His whip-thin tail smacked Coryn in the back of the leg.

They'd reached the end of the market, the last two stalls with their brown oilcloths dripping over wooden tables empty of their wares. Beyond them, a pair of taverns shone through the weather, windows bright with lanterns and roaring fires. Coryn gave them more than a glance, aware of the chill in the rain and the emptiness in his stomach. Then he realized that his father might be looking out any of those windows, and he hurried ahead to catch up with the rat.

"Where are we going?" he said.

The rat didn't pause, leading Coryn around a corner and past another tempting tavern, so close that Coryn could hear the laughter and talk from inside. "Well, tell me, a young wolf, first visit to the city, what would he like to see?"

"The Great Cathedral," Coryn said.

"Sure, we can go by there." The rat ducked into an alley and pulled Coryn with him. "Quicker this way. But how about the house of a noble? Wanna see how the upper crust live?"

"Oh, yes!" Coryn squinted. "Wait...you're a noble?"

"Well," the rat said, "let's just say I'm owed a debt by a noble an' I choose tonight to collect."

"But..." Coryn stopped, then hurried forward again, tugging at the patched tunic clinging to his fur. "I'm not dressed...I'm soaking..."

"Oh, not t'worry," the rat said, humming as he slowed his pace toward the end of the alley. "He won't be there. Would make things a bit awkward."

Won't be there? Coryn had just figured out what that meant when they emerged into a large open street, the rat striding boldly out while Coryn hung back, staring to his left. Over the tops of the buildings, beyond the end of the street, the large dome of the Great Cathedral rose against the sky.

He'd never seen a building so tall. It seemed to reach to the clouds with a seven-fingered paw, six dark spires that were merely breathtaking circling the central spire, which disappeared into the lower layer of clouds. Above that, even in the night and rain, a gleam of gold shone through. He thought at first that it was Gaia herself, looking down on the Cathedral, but it didn't move, and after a moment, he realized that it was the tip of the central spire.

A paw tugged at his sleeve. "Hey." He turned to see the rat there, following his gaze. "It's a wonder, innit?"

"I've never seen..." He groped for words.

"Ay, I know. But it'll be there still in an hour, an' we'll be enjoyin' the view with full bellies an' a warm fire. C'mon."

The rat tugged at his sleeve. Coryn took one last look at the marvel of the Cathedral, then turned to follow the rat's brown cloak through the light crowd of people hurrying to get home through the rain. They walked quickly past two more side streets, and then the rat ducked into the space between two houses. Coryn hesitated, looking around at the crowd to see if anyone was watching him. A beaver, walking more slowly than the rest, gave him a curious look, so he pretended to be waiting for someone until she'd passed. Then he strolled into the alley.

"What kept ya?" the rat hissed, though he wasn't looking at Coryn. He was near the back corner of the building, looking up at a window about two feet over his head.

"Wanted to make sure nobody was looking," Coryn said. He craned his neck to see what the rat was looking at, but the window was dark.

"Look," the rat said, "you want to get caught, best thing to do is stand around thinkin'. Do it fast, do it right, no chance of anyone seein' ya."

"You're standing around," Coryn pointed out, stung.

"Waitin' for you." The rat nodded up at the window. "Them bears like it cold. Leave the window open to get a bit of air." He set his back to the wall and grinned at Coryn, holding out both paws linked together, forming a kind of stirrup. "Come on, then. Up ya go."

"Me?" Coryn said. "But I don't know..."

"Quite simple," the rat said. "Just get up there, open the window, push yer way in. It's a sitting room, or I miss my guess. You'll be lookin' for the dining room, a cabinet all fancy-like. Anythin' silver you see in there, just help y'self and drop it out the window to me."

"Me?" Coryn said again. "But why don't you...I mean, you're the one..." Following the rat had been exciting, a lark, but faced with the prospect of actually thieving, his heart quailed. What if he were arrested? What would his father say?

"Look, i's perfectly safe." The rat nodded up. "I happen t'know the whole family's gone for th'week. Hates the crowds on market days. Most dangerous part is standin' here in th'rain. You rather do that, I'll happily go in where it's dry and out of sight of the guards."

Coryn's tail curled down. As much as he was worried about breaking into a home, the thought of standing out here alone in the rain was worse. He glanced nervously at the mouth of the alley, where he could still see people passing, then up at the window, which did not look open. "Do we have to…"

"I thought you wanted an adventure," the rat said sternly. "If I was wrong, I'll just scamper up an' take care o' this meself, and you can swim on home. Make y'self another reed boat."

"No," Coryn said hurriedly. "I'll go." Before he could second-guess himself, he lifted his foot into the rat's linked paws and stepped up to the window. Up at its level, he now saw that the window didn't open outward like all the windows he'd ever known. The window frame could slide up and down, and the little gap at the bottom where the window'd been left open was invisible from the street because of the broad stone sill. He rested his knee on the sill and worked his paws under the frame to pull it up.

It slid up with surprising ease. He swung one leg inside, then the other, his wet tail splashing against his leg. Water ran off it in streams, and before he could stop himself, Coryn shook just as if he were coming into his barn at home. Guiltily, he looked around at the room he'd just sprayed with water.

An elegant writing desk, half again as large as his father's and probably worth their entire farm all by itself, sat against the window in the wall to his left. The oil lamp on the desk had silver filigree around the glass bowl, so pretty that Coryn took a step toward it, wanting to run his fingers along the silver patterns.

Motion caught his eye from across the room. He froze, flared his nostrils, and perked his ears, but the overwhelming scent of bear still smelled old, and no sound reached him except for a slow drip of water from his tail. Slowly, he turned to look at the wall, freezing when he saw movement once more.

In the dim light, his wide-eyed face stared cautiously back, as if unsure who he was, from a mirror in an ornate silver frame. He relaxed and lifted his nose again to smell the room, making sure there was no fresh scent.

Avoiding the fine wooden chairs, his paws tracked water across the soft carpet in the middle of the room. Two doors in the opposite corner from the open window led out; one led to a hallway, where stairs led up past portraits of bears on the wall. Stepping through the other, he found himself in a large room decorated around the wide, polished table in the center. A cabinet to the right bore three candlesticks, neatly pressed back against the wall and unlit. Coryn skirted the chairs to reach the cabinet, and then saw a second cabinet, larger, nearer the door he'd come in by. He'd been looking across the room and had missed it at first.

Both cabinets came up only to his stomach, and both were identical polished dark wood, the doors carved with elaborate floral patterns in relief. Coryn crept toward the one bearing the candlesticks, reached out, and then stopped, his paw inches away.

He fancied himself an apprentice thief of sorts, had taken many a fruit from old Baggarly's orchard each fall and some-times eggs from Winnit's or Delvar's henhouses. But this was something different. He didn't know these nobles, and the candlesticks were much more than eggs or fruit.

Still, the house was so wealthy. They could easily afford to replace one candlestick, at least. He grasped it in his paw and lifted.

It was not as heavy as he would have thought. The silver felt smoother than any metal he'd touched, smoother even than his mother's cherished silver locket. He stood there for a moment, sliding his paws over it, and then he held it to his chest and hurried back to the window.

The rat was nowhere to be seen. Coryn craned his neck further out the opening, banging the candlestick against the stone sill in the process. "Ey!" came a soft voice from below. "No call t'wake the street."

There was the rat, below him. He'd turned his cloak around and was holding the ends out in front of him, forming a kind of sling. Water glistened at the bottom. Under the cloak, he wore no tunic, only a grey vest laced at the front. "What'cha got? Toss it down."

Coryn dropped the candlestick. It landed in the sling with a squelch. As he clambered over the sill, the rat looked up at him. "Whoa, what ya doing?"

"I got the silver." Coryn stopped, puzzled.

The rat chuckled. "Oh, sweet thing. There was more than one of these in there, ennit?"

"Sure, but..." He gestured. "Isn't that enough?"

Slowly, the rat shook his head. "When we've got the rest of the candlesticks an' you've had a nice look through them cabinets, then we'll talk about enough."

Coryn's heart pounded. The rat smiled. "Yer doin' fine," he said. "Look, i's only another fifteen minutes. Nobody's gonna come by. Just help me out with this, an'..." He tilted his head as if thinking. "Tell yer what...Cathedral's all closed up, but I know a way in. Could take ya in there."

"Inside?" Coryn bit his lip. He looked back again at the fine sitting room, all the elegant furnishings.

"Aye. Been meanin' to go back m'self," the rat said. "Been too long since I seen all those lovely glass windows, an' the statues... the shrine of Canis, oh, it's a wonder, it is." He sighed. "But, if you wanna stop, I'll just walk ya back to yer stall. No harm."

It wouldn't really be so bad, would it? The family that lived here could afford lots of silver. And they had so many nice things. In his mind, Coryn saw again the spires of the Cathedral and the golden sun of Gaia atop it. The memory of the golden gleam gave him a guilty start. He'd wanted to see a master thief in action, not be party to some cutpurse's nighttime raid. Gaia wouldn't look too kindly on stealing.

But surely, the lessons he remembered from church were about stealing necessities—"thou shalt not take from another what he needs to survive," and so on. He never stole more fruit than a pawful at a time, never more than a couple eggs. And he knew the consequences, if he were caught. Perhaps it was not knowing the consequences that was giving him pause now. Would he be thrown in jail? Executed?

Below him, the rat sighed. "Ah, a'right then. Hop on down an' we'll nip back to the market. 'Sbeen a fun evenin'. I hoped for more, but..."

"No," Coryn said. "I'll be right back."

He slid back into the house, ears perked, and returned with the other two candlesticks. The rat had placed the first one on the ground so that the others wouldn't make any noise when dropped. "Now see about them cabinets," he said.

Coryn didn't hesitate this time, emboldened by the silence and the ease with which the candlesticks had been extracted. He made his way into the dining room again and set his paw to the cabinets, but the doors didn't move. There was a small keyhole at the top of the rightmost door, but no key in evidence, of course. He rubbed his wet muzzle, examining the cabinet, now trying to think like a thief. Where would the key be hidden?

There was not much place to hide it in this room; other than the two cabinets, the chairs, and the table, the only other furniture was a tall standing clock, silently watching him from beside the opposite door.

Think, think, he told himself, and then his eyes returned to the clock, and the small door beside it. It was the size of the doors in his house, where the rest of the doorways were all massive enough to accommodate bears. Even a small bear would have a tight squeeze through that door. Curious, he padded over to it, and on the way over he realized that it must be the servants' door.

It was unlocked, and beyond it was the kitchen. And hanging on the wall just inside the door was one dark key.

Tail wagging, he grabbed the key and returned to the cabinet. It fit perfectly, opening the doors to reveal row upon row of silver eating utensils. Heart pounding with excitement and pride, Coryn grabbed as many as he could in both paws and ran back to the window. "There's lots more," he panted, dropping the silver with a clatter into the waiting cloak.

"Careful!" the rat called, but Coryn had already run back to gather another load. He returned to the window and held his paws out, but the rat called, "Wait, wait!"

"What?"

"Find somethin' to wrap 'em with! Napkin or something, makes less noise."

"Oh." Coryn's ears flattened. He should've thought of that.

The other cabinet revealed rows of bone-white plates, and, on the second shelf, a stack of cloth napkins. Carefully, Coryn wrapped batches of the silver forks and spoons in cloth parcels, finding that he could carry more that way. When he dropped them to the waiting rat, they fell without a sound. "Nicely done," the rat whispered, and Coryn's ears flushed with pride.

"Last batch," he called, dropping it.

"Beautiful," the rat said. "I s'pose that's a nice haul for a night."

"Wait." Coryn grinned down. "One more thing."

He'd seen a large silver serving dish left out in the kitchen. Quickly, he ran back for it, rather surprised to find that it was heavier than any of the candlesticks had been. He kept it in one paw as he clambered out of the window, and was about to drop to the street when the rat said, "Close the window, ay?"

"Oh, right." He held the serving dish down for the rat to take, then pulled himself back up to the sill and pulled the window shut.

"This way," the rat said, jerking his head as Coryn landed beside him. He'd removed his cloak and bound it around all the silver except for the dish, which he handed to the wolf. "An' stick this under yer cloak."

Coryn held onto it, not even minding the steady rain that soaked his fur anew. "I found the key," he said in a low voice. "The cabinet was locked, but I didn't want to force it open, so I thought, where would the key be, and I found the servants' door, and I thought, the servants would need to open the cabinet, right, so I went in there and the key was hanging right there!"

"Nicely done," the rat said again, absently, scanning the street in front of them, holding Coryn back with a paw. "Now, we're goin' to that alley over there, but not together. I'll go first an' then I'll wait for you, got it?"

"Sure." Coryn blinked water from his eyes. "How long should I wait?"

"Count to twenty," the rat said. He looked to his left and right. "An' don't come across if you see a guard. But you won't. But don't, if you do." And before Coryn could say anything, the rat was walking briskly across, splashing his way through puddles without appearing to hurry any more than was warranted by the rain.

The serving dish seemed to be getting heavier. He watched the rat disappear into the alley, and then counted.

At five, he was still feeling the flush of the successful job. The serving dish was his trophy, the proof that he could be really useful.

At ten, he was staring at the alley, where there was no sign of the rat. A cloud moved in front of the moon, deepening the shadows. The dry goods store next to the alley was dark and lifeless.

At fifteen, he began to wonder if the rat were still there waiting for him. The rain had soaked back into his clothes, and he wasn't sure which way the market was. All he knew was that the Great Cathedral rose into the clouds off to his left. He actually took a step out into the street, thinking that he could maybe still catch the rat, but then he thought, if he *is* there, he'll know I didn't count to twenty.

At twenty, he took a step out into the street, looked around to see whether any guards were watching. Apart from a bedraggled mouse trudging away from him, nobody was within fifty feet. He walked across slowly, almost dreading the dark alley ahead, because if he reached it and the rat was gone, well, he didn't know what he'd do then, alone in Divalia in the pouring rain with a stolen silver dish.

The mouth of the alley loomed in front of him. The rain washed away any scents he might have gotten; for all he knew, there could be a whole squad of guards waiting, or the alley could be completely empty.

He stepped into an array of discarded wooden crates, the stone under his paws slippery with dirt. Apart from the crates, there was nothing in the alley, all the way down to the next street.

"That was a lot longer'n twenty," the rat said, stepping out from the shadows. The makeshift sack slung over his shoulder jingled as he walked.

Coryn felt a wash of relief, enough to lift his sopping tail. A grin spread across his muzzle as he followed the rat, hopping over boxes to the end of the alley and across the narrow, less busy street beyond.

The sound of the rain grew louder, though it didn't feel any harder. The rat skipped through the street and around what looked like an old warehouse, into another alley that sloped downward. He wasn't looking to see that Coryn was following him, which the wolf took to be trust that he could keep up. He clutched the silver dish more tightly, determined to live up to that confidence.

At the end of the alley, Coryn saw that what he'd taken for a building across another street was a gatehouse on a bridge. And below it—

The sound he'd heard was not the rain growing in strength. It was the rain falling on the broad expanse of the Lurine River, as wide as one of his father's fields. He stood and stared at the boats, the ripples in the water, the pattern of the rain falling, and then the high, majestic bridge with the gatehouse and the smaller stone bridge to his right.

He didn't have much time to admire the statues atop the high stone towers of the gatehouse, nor the broad stone bridge beyond it. The rat had turned at the head of a narrow stair and was beckoning him forward.

Coryn hurried to join him, down the narrow stairs to the walkway beside the river, toward the gatehouse bridge. "This is the Palace Bridge," he said, gesturing upward. "An' this is our friends."

He led Coryn under the bridge. Beneath the wide span, a squat houseboat floated, tied with a single rope to a post on the bank. As Coryn shook water from his head and tail, glad for the shelter of the rain, a cougar emerged from the cabin of the boat and leaned over the rail, watching them closely. The rat raised a paw to him, and he nodded. "Evenin', friend," he said, his expression neutral. His eyes flicked to Coryn and then back to the rat.

"Found my way by the light of the moon," the rat replied casually. He hefted the sack, so that its clinking sound carried through the night.

"She lights the way of friend and foe alike." The cougar's ears had perked up, but otherwise his posture remained unchanged.

"Aye, but the foe follows fruitlessly, while the friend finds," he let the sack drop to the ground, "fortune."

The cougar smiled broadly. "We wondered if you'd be turning up, Two-Claws. What have ya for us? And who's this strapping young fella?"

"Tourist from the farms," the rat said. "Here to take in the sights of the city and lend me a paw."

"I'm from Doubleford, in Deverin," Coryn said. "My name's—"

"Ah, ah!" The rat cut him off. "We call 'im 'Legs'," he told the cougar.

"Legs it is. Welcome to Divalia. I'll fetch the measurer." He raised a paw again and disappeared into the cabin.

"Why did you call me 'Legs'?" Coryn asked.

The rat reached inside his cloak and took the dish. "Cause I noticed when you went through the window that you got a lovely pair." He added the dish to the pile on the dock and looked around, humming under his breath.

Coryn's ears flushed. He rubbed his paws over them on the pretense of trying to dry them, looking at the rat in a new light. He'd played with both boys and girls back on the farm, and if he was all but betrothed to Kika (daughter of Kulic of the Whitefoot family), that was more of a business arrangement than a romantic one. He hadn't even been thinking of the rat as a potential lover, not until that remark, but now he studied the rat with a different eye.

The rat's shoulders, left bare by the repurposing of the cloak, showed lean muscle under the slick, wet fur. His vest, dark with rain, was laced tightly around a narrow chest and a stomach that Coryn thought he might be able to circle with both his paws. He'd never been with a rat, though there was a squirrel back home who'd spent a very pleasant afternoon with him three or four summers back. The rat was leaner and more fit than the squirrel, for sure, and much more confident. Coryn felt his sheath stir beneath his sodden clothing. Once he was betrothed, which would probably happen when Kulic paid the bride-price at the end of this season, his days of playing with boys would likely be over, or at least relegated to infrequent stolen moments. The possibility that this adventure might not end with a tame sightseeing walk was more than he could have hoped for.

"Wait 'til you see how much gold they turn this silver into," the rat said. "Then that tail will *really* wag."

The cougar re-emerged, followed by a fox wrapped in a thick black cloak. While the cougar resumed his position at the rail, the fox leapt over it lightly, letting the cloak billow out to reveal a white tunic and dark vest underneath. He alit on the stone balustrade that lined the bank, hopped down to the walkway, and studied the pile of silver without a word.

He picked up the silver dish first, shook water from it, and then turned it over. He gave it one approving nod and then set it aside. In a matter of seconds, he had undone the cloak-bundle and reached in, finding first the candlesticks, then the napkins rolled around the dinnerware. The dinnerware he set on the tray; the candlesticks he set to one side, and each piece he moved, he hefted in his paw, his muzzle dipping in a quick mental measurement before he set it down.

When all the silver was on the dish or beside it, he stood and beckoned to the cougar, who leapt from the boat to the bank. The fox reached to a pouch at his waist and walked over to Coryn and the rat. "Twenty pounds silver. Quality looks good. Twenty Royals."

He started to count out money into his paw, while Coryn gaped. His father would be ecstatic if they returned to the farm with ten Royals. But the rat cleared his throat. "Beggin' your pardon, but have you seen the fine work on the candelabras?"

The fox raised an eyebrow. "All looks the same in the furnace," he said, but he stopped counting.

"Oh, my friend, what an opportunity you're missing," the rat said. "The serving dish, aye, that's got names, but the candelabras, that lovely detail, you could sell those for five gold each. Surely they're worth an extra two apiece."

"Hmph." The fox held three neat rows of five coins in his paw. He added another row of five, and then two more. He held out his paw.

"Surely you can at least give me twenty-four?"

The fox stared for a moment and then added just one more coin. The rat sighed and cupped both his paws to accept the gold. "May Canis smile on your generosity."

"May Rodenta bless your fingers." The fox waved to the cougar, who picked up the dish with the silver on it and carried it back to the boat. The fox took the candlesticks and followed, examining the reliefs on their base as he walked.

"C'mon." The rat retrieved his cloak and tugged on Coryn's sleeve, pulling him to the other side of the bridge. The coins had vanished from his paws, but if Coryn focused, he could hear a soft clinking under the loud hiss of the rain. Just inches from the edge of shelter, sprinkled with the splashes of raindrops on stone, the rat pointed to a stair in the bank. "Need to drop this off in a lockbox before we go to the Cathedral. You want to wait here? Ah, thought not," at Coryn's headshake. "Right, then, up those stairs, follow me."

He took off at a trot, considerably faster now that he wasn't burdened by the sack of silver. Coryn cast one last glance back at the faint outline of the houseboat through the rain. The fox and cougar had gone inside, leaving the houseboat apparently deserted, bobbing slowly on the river in spite of the storm. The young wolf sighed, and then hurried to catch up with the rat, who was already at the stairs.

"Thought you didn't wanna wait," the rat said at the top. "Don't stay night f'rever, y'know."

"Sorry," Coryn said, water streaming through his fur again. "The boat was pretty."

"That? She's okay." The rat scampered across the street, Coryn right behind. He kept going down another alley without pausing to look around. "We shoulda got thirty gold for that lot."

"Are the candlesticks that nice?"

"Nah. They'll melt 'em down too. But that's a lot of silver. They'll prob'ly get forty."

"You got three extra gold."

"True 'nuff, and from the Vergies, that ain't bad." He slowed to pad across another street, turning onto it and walking quickly. This narrow street was lined with apothecaries and two metalworkers, one copper and one tin. It smelled like scorched metal even through the rain, which might be one reason it was deserted.

"They were Vergies?"

"Aye." The rat slowed, scanning the houses. "Don't stay put, always sailing up an' down the river, or some tribes just wander the country in wagons."

"I know what they are," Coryn said. "They sell second-hand clothes and pots in my town sometimes."

"Aye. There's always one group or 'nother around, an' they

like to anchor under that bridge. Why I did the job tonight is, I knew that fox'd be there. Ah, here we go."

He stopped at a narrow doorway. His body hid what he was doing, but Coryn heard the door handle jiggle, and then the door swung open. "Jus' a quick stop," the rat said, stepping inside. "C'mon in and get dry."

Coryn followed him into a cramped room, with a door at the back and an unsteady-looking wooden staircase leading up. "Wait 'ere," the rat said. "I'll be back in a mo."

He was up the stairs before Coryn got the word "Okay" out. So the wolf leaned against the wall and listened to the rain fall outside, his sodden tail thumping the wall. This was as good an adventure as he could have asked for, and it wasn't yet light. He'd be tired tomorrow, but he would still have time to see the Cathedral, maybe spend some time with Two-Claws, and get back to the market stall before his father knew he was gone. This whole night could be a wonderful secret, something he would tell his sister Ki one day.

It was only when he heard a thump from upstairs that he realized that it had been a little while, and the rat was still gone. He sniffed at the air, but his own wet fur overwhelmed the scent of the rat's. "Hullo?" he called cautiously up the stairs.

He took two steps up and listened. "Hullo?" he called again.

He'd just put his foot on the next stair when the rat appeared on the landing, fastening a light tan cloak around his neck. "Where you headed? I'm comin', I'm comin'." The rat skipped down toward him as Coryn backed up toward the front door, his chest swelling with relief.

He groped for the door handle, but the rat held his wrist. "Just a mo." Turning his paw upward, the rat dropped two gold coins into it. "Fair pay, aye?"

Coryn gaped. The rat had to close his fingers around the coins. "Thank you," Coryn said. "Thank you!"

"Well," the rat said, "Y'did carry that dish. You deserve a li'l something for the trouble. Now on to the Cathedral?"

The weight of the gold in his paw made his tail wag. "Oh, yes!" he breathed.

"All right, then." The rat gestured to the door. "One more wet run?"

Coryn pulled the door open. Outside, the rain hissed down. The rat rested one paw on the arch of Coryn's tail. "Which way?" Coryn said, wagging under the touch.

"Left," the rat said, "an' then just follow me." His paw slid down, with the briefest touch on Coryn's rump, and then he was out the door.

The rain felt just as heavy as ever, but Coryn barely noticed it. He splashed along at the rat's side, and now the rat was more talkative. "That there's the best brothel in Divalia," he said. "Might be able to afford m'self a night there, now."

Coryn looked up at a hanging sign with a picture of a fox-like person, his naked erection huge. Under it, he barely made out the words, "Jackal's Staff." Then they were past it, and that's where Coryn looked to his right and saw the palace for the first time.

Its wall rose up to his right, pitted but solid stone two stories tall. Opposite him was the main gate, a metal fence between two small guard houses from whose shelter gleaming eyes watched him. And through the fence, through the sheets of rain, he saw the front gate of the palace. It rose in a majestic arch over two wooden doors, above which two more floors of windows rose, irregular shadows in the wet night. Between the doors and the gates, rows of flowers and trees shuddered under the water and wind, their colors faded to grey.

Coryn wanted to stay and stare at it, but the eyes in the guard houses worried him. He closed his paw tighter around the two gold pieces and walked on, slowly, fixing the image of the palace and the gardens in his mind. Then he had to run, because the rat was already nearly at the corner where the long palace wall ended.

He caught up just beyond the corner of the palace. The wall bent around to the right, and up in front of them was the vast expanse of the Great Cathedral.

Up close, even through the rain, he could now see the intricate reliefs lining the walls of the Cathedral. They must be on the Mustela side, because weasels and skunks, mink and otter, all adorned the wall, where Mustela herself surmounted the column of sculptures. To either side, narrow stained glass windows were black slits in the stonework. To the left, several plain columns rose, and beyond, he could see another column of reliefs.

The rat looked to either side and then made his way around the Mustela column, away from the large front doors. Over here, sheltered by the bulk of the church, the rain didn't beat down as hard, and Coryn could take time to look more closely at the stone, so ancient, so sacred.

Below the narrow stained glass windows, they passed a small wooden door in the side of the wall. The metal plate around the latch was more formidable than he'd seen on any other door in the city; he supposed it made sense that the Great Cathedral would be more securely locked up than any other place. Hopefully the rat could get through one of those doors. But they passed another one, stopping finally at the base of a column of reliefs of rats, mice, squirrels, and porcupines all reaching up to Rodenta, who smiled down with a pair of prominent front teeth. The rat put his paw in the nearest statue's and hoisted himself up. He grinned down at Coryn. "How's yer climbing?"

Coryn put on a brave face. "I climbed the big needle-tree back home, I can climb that." He looked doubtfully to the top of the column, at least twice as high as that tree. Maybe three times.

"Nobody else in the city can do this," the rat said. "But I know the pawholds. Jus' watch me." And he set his foot on the head of the lowermost mouse, reached up for the foot of the squirrel above, and pulled himself up.

The stone was only slightly slippery from the rain, not as much as Coryn had thought it would be. The rough limestone held his paws well, though twice he would have been stuck had he not seen where the rat found a hold. He resisted the urge to look down, though the wind was now rushing in his ears and his head felt a little dizzy. He did look to the side and thought he saw the awnings of the market a mile or so away in the city. Had they walked that far? He supposed they had.

The climb took a long time, but Coryn watched carefully and put his paws where the rat did. When they reached the statue of Rodenta at the top, her outstretched cloak and arms presented little difficulty to the rat, who swarmed around them with what Coryn would have sworn was magic. While he was studying the sculpture, trying to see where the rat's paws had gone and whether he, Coryn, could also be lighter than air for as long as it would take to get up there, a pink paw came down around the cloak.

Coryn grasped it, and it yanked him so hard he lost his balance, hanging on to the rat with one paw and Rodenta's arm with the other. And then he looked down.

The street swayed below him, fifty feet, a hundred, two hundred. He whimpered and then steeled himself, just as the rat said, "Don' look down, jus' hold on."

"I know," Coryn yelled back, staring up at the smiling muzzle of Rodenta, twice as tall as he was. It hadn't looked like there were more than two or three people in the street below, all either hurrying along with their heads down or holding something over them, but he still felt exposed. "Hurry!"

The rat pulled, and Coryn struggled, and between them, they managed to get him up onto Rodenta's back. Panting, the rat sat back against the wall, ignoring the stronger wind. "Nice view up here, innit?"

Coryn huddled in his cloak. The patchwork of red ceramic and grey stone all the way out to the city walls shimmered with life, even though most of the streets were deserted. The palace lay behind him, but he could see the market, the curve of the Lurine around the heart of the city, the South Gate through which they'd entered, and a hundred other buildings he didn't know. "It's nice," he said, trying to keep his teeth from chattering. "Are w-we staying up here all n-night?"

"Nah," the rat said. "Jus' a nice view from here. Little bit o'climbin' left t'do." He stretched and slid back to the wall, where a ledge extended from Rodenta's cloak. "This way."

Wind hissed past his ears, drenching them. Coryn saw again the spinning ground below him and hesitated. The tall branches of the oak tree above his house weren't this tall, and he hadn't been up there at night, nor in a storm like this, true. But the rat was six, eight feet along already. He lifted his sodden cloak and faced the building.

The wet limestone smelled like the cemetery. Up close, the stained glass was filthy, dirt in all the crevices. Even in the rain, insects scurried away from his fingers as he edged along the ledge, which was not as narrow as it looked. He took a step, then another, gaining confidence with each one. Then he looked to his right, and the rat was gone.

Panic seized him just as a gust of wind came along, driving rain into his face, trying to push him away from the wall and down to the cold stone below. He leaned in against the stone, heart racing, and the weight of the water in his clothes helped press him safely to the Cathedral until the wind had calmed again. He eyed the statue of Rodenta, and began to edge back toward it, not looking forward to the climb back to the ground.

"Ay!"

He turned. The rat's whiskered face poked out of one of the windows, staring at him. "C'mon," he said, beckoning with a paw.

Coryn edged toward him. He saw, now, that one of the windows opened inward. It took him a good five minutes to make his way there, and then, because the bottom of the window was at his waist, another minute to get up the courage to leave his feet and jump inside. But he'd come this far, and the alternative was not very appealing, so he rested his paws on the bottom of the window, lifted himself and hung in mid-air for a moment before pushing himself forward into darkness.

He landed on a carpet thick with the scents of hundreds of people, mostly porcupines and mice. Some of the scents were only a few weeks old, but he caught some that might have been lingering for years. His head spun, all his attention on the smells now that he was out of the wind and rain, its driving hiss comfortingly remote though the window was only three feet from him and rain continued to spatter the carpet.

Light bobbed into the room, a candle and the smell of burning wax preceding the rat from the hallway. He eased a door shut behind him, and Coryn, sitting up, could now look around the room he was in.

Three old wooden chairs, mismatched, lined one wall, a nondescript cloak tossed over one of them. Two ancient wardrobes faced them, on either side of the window Coryn had fallen in through. The doors of the right-hand one were open, revealing its empty interior. The door the rat had come through was the only one, and beside it stood two old wooden trunks whose leather bindings were coming apart. It was over these trunks that the rat tilted the candle to drip some wax. He set the candle firmly down in the soft wax and walked to the window.

The burning, waxy scent overwhelmed the others. Coryn rubbed his nose, still staring around at his surroundings. They seemed quite neglected, not at all as he had imagined.

The rat closed the window with a scrape of metal, leaving an inch gap. "Doesn't close all the way," he said. "Never did, from the time I was a kit."

Under Coryn's paws, he could make out faintly a design, stylized wolves and weasels carrying some golden statue. Threadbare patches erased their destination, but from the golden circle, he guessed it was Gaia. "You served here?"

"Oh, aye." The rat unfastened his cloak and tossed it beside the window. "Mam wanted me raised proper. Course, that didn't help feed us, did it?" He started unlacing his vest. "You plan to soak in them wet things all night?"

"Uh." Coryn pulled his cloak off. His clothes and fur were clammy and cold, and the room wasn't heated. But it wasn't as cold as the wind outside had been. He lifted his tunic off, and when he'd pulled the wet cloth over his head, he saw that the rat was already shimmying out of his pants, and that he wasn't wearing anything underneath.

"Don't worry," the rat said cheerily, hanging his pants in the wardrobe. "Won't nobody come up here before daybreak, and likely not for many days."

"How long is that? Until dawn?" Coryn's fingers hesitated near his pants. The problem now was that he couldn't take his eyes from the rat's slender build, the way his chest tapered to his waist and then broadened slightly at his hips. And of course, at those hips, a nicely-sized sheath, made far less modest by the rainsleeked fur around it.

"Loads o'time. Two, three hours. This is storage, folk don't come here often." The rat ran his paws through his fur and shook them, spraying water around. He started rubbing down his fur, squeezing water from it, and when he got to his hips, his pink paws on either side of his sheath, he looked up and saw Coryn, paw still resting on his trouser laces. "I got quick fingers if them knots got wet."

He'd crouched down next to Coryn before even finishing his sentence. "No!" Coryn scooted back on the carpet.

The rat stared bemusedly, elbows on his knees. The white sheath bobbing between his legs now showed some pink at the end. "When I said we'd plenty o'time," he said, "I was rather thinkin' we'd be spendin' it in more enjoyable ways than just lookin'."

"I don't even know your name," Coryn said desperately, now trying to hide both his staring at the rat's arousal and the bulge of his own.

"You can call me Two-Claws if you like, Legs," the rat said. "Is as good a name as any, ay?"

Coryn didn't move to touch his pants. The chill of the room crept into his fur, but the smell of the rat was overwhelming and immediate. "Why do they call you that?"

"Cause it don't take me but two claws to get into a lock." The rat wiggled his right paw. "Or a pair o'pants."

The matter-of-factness of it, here in a room in the Great Cathedral, felt wrong to Coryn, and the shadows coming over the rat's muzzle didn't help. "Can you show me the Cathedral first?"

The rat tilted his head. "Looks better when sun's up. Look, what's with yer? Why'd I bring ya all the way here if yer gonna keep yer clothes on?"

"Sorry," Coryn said automatically. "I'm just curious." Slowly, he moved to undo his pants.

"I don't do this often, y'know," the rat said. "Don't pick

anyone off the street to do a job or show 'em how to climb the Cathedral. Haven't brought anyone else up here, not ever."

The flickering candlelight cast annoyance in shadows over the narrow muzzle, but perversely, the remark made Coryn feel better. He undid the last of the laces on his pants. The rat had one paw between his legs, cupping his sheath, stroking his growing erection, and that plus the smell of musk and the removal of his clothes did a good job overriding Coryn's reluctance. He worked his pants off and tossed them aside, then lay back on his elbows, showing off because he couldn't bring himself to make the first move this time.

He needn't have worried. His sheath might have been made of silver for as quickly as the rat found it. His pink fingers were cold at first, but his touch was gentle and light. "We'll warm up quick enough," he said, climbing over Coryn's legs to straddle him, one paw around each sheath.

Coryn sat up, putting his larger paws on the rat's legs, holding him at the hips as the rat rubbed life and warmth into his cock. He closed his eyes, breathing in the rat's scent but unable to filter out the smell of the Cathedral and the rain outside. As he relaxed, he felt his tail wag, brushing water back and forth along the carpet. The rat—Two-Claws—didn't make much noise, unlike the breathy, moany boys Coryn had played with before, which only added to the feeling that this was more than just a diversion on a lazy summer afternoon.

And when Coryn looked up, the rat was looking back at him with a faint smile under intently focused eyes. Nobody had ever held him so strongly with a look; nobody had ever met his eyes and seen him like that. When his father ordered him to do things, he saw an apprentice. He and his older sister Ki didn't have much time to themselves, with so much work around the farm since their mother'd died and then Ki's betrothal. They shared a room, which is how he knew she was pregnant and how she'd known about Kika, but they didn't spend much time talking. When she married, she'd move out. To the other field hands, he was the farmer's son; when he played games (clothed or otherwise) with his friends, they never opened up to each other. He was Coryn of his father's farm, always. But Two-Claws here had no idea where his farm was. He didn't even know Coryn's name. He just knew Coryn, and that was special.

He didn't seem to be in much of a hurry to get to know Coryn better. His paw kept moving with nice, even strokes, not the quick jerks of the boys on the farm or the uncertain touches of the girls, who sometimes seemed frightened of his erection when it emerged from his sheath. Two-Claws, belying his name, held Coryn's shaft in all five fingers, holding it against his smooth paw pads while his thumb tweaked the tip in a way Coryn had never felt before. He squirmed delightedly under the weight, holding the rat's hips down to his legs, which were tingling and jumping already.

"Eager, ain't we?" The rat looked down at him with a wider smile, one that showed off his prominent front teeth.

"Sorry." Coryn's paws rubbed around the rat's waist, finding it as slender and muscled as he'd imagined. He tried to relax, but the rat wasn't stopping his strokes, and as each movement of the small paw sent more and more intense shivers through Coryn's body, he twisted and bucked harder.

"No worries," the rat said. "But I'll ask ya to take charge of this here, while I devote my attention to you."

He guided Coryn's paw to his own sheath, closing the wolf's fingers around the long, thin length protruding from it. Coryn did his best to match the rat's strokes, sliding his paw up and down. At first, overcome by his own sensations, he moved as jerkily as the farm hands he'd just been thinking scornfully of. Hard as it was to get himself back under control, he forced himself to relax, or at least, he forced his right arm to relax.

He managed it, or hoped he did, but the rest of his body was passing beyond his control. His hips jerked upward under the rat's caresses, his breath coming in short pants through his teeth, then moans as the sensations built and grew. His paw, the one not wrapped around the rat's shaft, clenched around his hip, and he shut his eyes, breathing in the scents of the stone, the candle, the rain, and above all, the mingled musks of himself and the rat, all of it working its way down his muzzle to his chest. There the scents met the surge of blood from his groin, and as his body surrendered to the delight of climax, his voice burst forth in a loud moan that rang against the walls of the small room.

His muscles felt as hard as the stone beneath the carpet, tight and tense and spasming as he emptied himself on the rat's paw and his own stomach. His moans died down to breathy panting, the shudder of his orgasm fading similarly. The first thing he did was start stroking the rat again, because his paw had stopped when his climax had started.

"Ah, y'don't need to keep up wi' that now." The rat grinned. "Jus' lie back and relax, an' open yer muzzle."

"My..." Coryn let his paw be removed from the rat's shaft. The rat scooted up his body, rubbing wet fur past his sheath and spent shaft, no doubt getting himself sticky as he settled on Coryn's chest. He leaned over and lifted Coryn's head, bringing the wolf's nose right up to the tip of his pink shaft. Streaks of pre smeared the tip, and another drop swelled as the rat settled into position.

"Yer okay, right?"

Coryn was more afraid of performing badly than he was of having the rat in his muzzle. "Sure," he said, and craned his head forward.

"No teeth," the rat said as Coryn parted his lips, tongue already lapping at the tip.

"Mm-hmm." Coryn closed his lips as the rat pushed his hips

forward, the shaft sliding along his tongue. He did his best to keep his lips closed and his teeth out of the way as the rat rocked back and forth. Because his paws didn't seem to be doing anything else, he brought them around the rat's hips and pressed them to the wet fur, riding along with the motion rather than helping it.

"Ooh, that's the stuff," the rat said. Up past the white expanse of his stomach and chest, his pointed muzzle was bobbing up and down in time with the movement of his slender hips. The rat's other paw had moved behind Coryn's head as well, supporting it as he pushed his shaft between the wolf's lips and back, forward and back.

As his hips moved, his tail slid back and forth against Coryn's sensitive sheath, making the wolf squirm, but he held himself as steady as he could. He was enjoying that the rat was enjoying his tongue, but also the feeling of another's shaft between his lips and the taste of the musk. He couldn't help imagining his own hardness pushing up under that tail and into the rat, which made him squirm even more despite the fact that his seed hadn't even dried from his first orgasm.

The rat's hips jerked faster, his musk stronger now. Coryn circled the shaft with his tongue, and the rat liked that, moaning loudly and throwing his head back. His paws grabbed at Coryn's fur behind his ears, shoving his head forward onto the trembling shaft, and Coryn obliged as well as he could, thankful for his long muzzle. Any shorter and the rat's long member would be well in the back of his throat.

At the rate he was going, it felt like it might get there anyway. The rat's balls swung against his lower jaw, the hips pushing into his muzzle with more and more force. "Oh, wolfy, yeah...yeah... unh!" With a loud grunt, the rat shoved Coryn's muzzle all the way into his groin. Coryn closed his lips and sucked hard on the long shaft, feeling it shudder against his tongue, and a moment later warmth splashed the back of his throat. He swallowed, holding the rat's shaking body as tightly as the rat was holding his head.

Even when the rat finally relaxed, he didn't pull back right away, looking down at the wolf's muzzle instead. "Ah, that's a lovely sight, it is," he said, a dreamy smile stretching to both corners of his muzzle. "Downright angelic." His paws released Coryn's head and stroked up his perked ears.

"Mmf," Coryn tried to say. His tail thumped the carpet.

"Good lad." The rat slid his hips back, giving his rear an extra wiggle over Coryn's sheath. Coryn smacked his lips as the long member slid out of it, his head dropping back to the carpet. He stared up at the cracked stone ceiling until the rat's head came into view. "Wait right 'ere," he said. "I'm gonna fetch us a li'l something."

Coryn had no idea what he meant, but he didn't much care. His eyes were drifting shut now that all his energy was expended. "Mm, 'kay," he said. The stone ceiling became the ceiling of the small house he would share with the— with Two-Claws. They would steal just enough silver to live, and they would climb around the great buildings of Divalia, dancing on rooftops, drinking...

"Honey wine."

"Uhh?" Coryn turned his head, getting up on his elbows.

The rat, still naked and half out of his sheath, set two pewter mugs down on the carpet. "Compliments of the Great Cathedral. Reserved for special 'casions." He sat across the mugs from Coryn, cross-legged. "This felt special, ay?"

"Yeah." Coryn struggled to sit up, realizing he was thirsty. The rat already had one mug in his paws, raised in a toast. Coryn took the other and lifted it.

"To a night of..." The rat tilted his head, searching for a word.

"Adventure," Coryn said.

"Ay."

"New horizons."

The rat clinked his mug to Coryn's. "All that. Your health."

"And yours." They drank at the same time. The wine was sweet and rich, pouring over his tongue and lighting his throat and belly with a soft, growing warmth. He took another drink, and another, and then the mug was empty.

The rat's nose brushed his. The scents blurred together, the noise of the rain more distant now. "Got time for a little rest, Legs," the rat murmured.

"My name's Coryn." His tongue felt thick and heavy.

"Ay, Coryn of Doubleford in Deverin." The rat sounded sleepy himself. "An' I'm Two-Claws of Divalia."

Coryn's head felt heavy. "Wake me when the sun's up."

"Course."

And that was the last thing he heard the rat say for many, many years.

* * *

Sound and light made their way into his dreams. He was standing on the roof of his neighbor's barn, naked, and the sun warmed him all over. There were people over on his farm, and they were talking about him, but he couldn't hear what they were saying. His father and Aryss of the Whitefoots were talking, and Two-Claws the rat was there, too. He thought about calling to them, but then he thought it might be best if he just lay down on the roof.

When had they put carpet on the roof? he wondered. It smelled old. It smelled like the time he'd visited the Great Cathedral. He opened his eyes and saw the threadbare patches in the carpet, dust motes drifting through rays of colored sunlight streaming through the window.

Slowly, he pushed himself to his feet. The stained glass painted the room in brilliant colors: the guttered candle atop the trunks, the open, bare wardrobe. All that remained of Two-Claws was his scent and the two pewter mugs lying empty on the floor.

He'd probably gone to get breakfast. Coryn's stomach growled at the thought. He got to his feet and checked his clothes. Still wet. He had to get back to the market; his father would be furious. But he didn't want to leave without saying good-bye to Two-Claws.

His ears perked at the sound of voices. So they hadn't been only in his dream. Coryn should stay here, he knew. But out there, out there was the Great Cathedral. This might be his only chance to see it.

He eased the door open and stepped out into a hallway lit very faintly from above, his paws on cold stone rather than carpet. On wooden shelves, at the height of his chest, small books were stacked, old and identical. The voices he heard weren't coming from the other closed door, nor the spiral stair at the open end of the hallway; they came from a door to his left which stood ajar, light visible through the crack. Coryn padded toward it and, after listening to make sure the voices were too faint to be immediately on the other side, peeked through.

An open room, empty, but much brighter. He couldn't see off to the right, where the light was coming from, so he stuck his nose through the door and pushed it a little further open, keeping his nakedness well behind it, just in case.

This room, too, was empty, but the murmur of voices had grown much louder. The light came from the main space of the Cathedral, which this room overlooked, separated from it only by a waist-high wall. Coryn could not resist; he stepped up to the wall and peered over.

It was the largest building he'd ever been inside. Its walls might have bounded any one of his father's smaller fields. Where his church had one place for the congregation to sit, this Cathedral had six sets of pews, all three times the size of the church in Doubleford, each with its own altar, and shrines off to the side. The section devoted to Canis lay to his left; he could tell by the silver star within a silver circle. And that was where the voices were coming from.

Of course, today was Caniday, and there would be services for Canis. He searched for the cantor and saw a slender fox at the altar, his paws gesturing. It was his voice Coryn was hearing, mostly, and the crowd when they murmured in response. But he couldn't make out the words.

He turned his eyes to the splendor around him, the sun streaming in through the stained glass, illuminating the portraits of Canis, of Fox and Coyote and Wolf, of Felis next to them, and Mother Gaia in the glass of the domed roof. His eyes drank in the beauty of it all, the golden circle suspended from the ceiling, the ornate decorations and tapestries hung all 'round, the air of sanctity and peace they filled him with.

He wanted to close his eyes as he listened to the murmur of worship, but then he wouldn't be able to see the beauty all around him. Everywhere he looked, another beautiful ornament caught his eye: a gilded statue over in the Herbivora area, a stag in robes; a pink marble sarcophagus in the Mustela section below him; a glittering tapestry that he realized after staring at it for minutes must be inlaid with jewels.

And then the service ended, and the congregation lifted their voices in a howl, and then Coryn had to close his eyes. It took a great effort to restrain himself from joining in. He settled for howling in his throat, keeping his muzzle closed, and though it wasn't the same, he could still feel the joy of Canis in his heart. Especially here, in this sacred place, it seemed magnified, as though Canis himself, with Gaia looking over his shoulder, were staring down through the roof at him and smiling.

When the howl ended, he didn't open his eyes right away. There was murmuring from below, but nothing different from the usual talking at the end of services. At least, he didn't think it was different, until his stomach rumbled and he thought he should get back to the room, to wait for Two-Claws. Then he opened his eyes for one last look around.

Below him, the upturned muzzles of foxes, wolves, and coyotes stared at him, and the cantor in his white robes walked briskly across the floor.

Coryn darted for the door, closing it behind him and then running back to the room with the loose window. He shut that door behind him as well, pressing his back to it. But he wouldn't be able to keep people out. He had to escape, even if that meant climbing down the Cathedral wall in daylight. Even though his fur was almost dry, he ran to the pile of clothes and started to pull them on. He could maybe get out the window, move along the ledge at least to the statue, wait until Two-Claws came back to help him down. Or maybe when the people came to check the room, if they found it empty, they would leave again.

His paws fumbled with the damp laces, trying to do up his trousers. One of the doors outside opened. He tied the laces hastily and grabbed at his tunic and cloak, tucking them in a dripping bundle under his arm. Another door opened outside, then closed. He fumbled at the window, pushing it harder, but the cloak and tunic kept slipping from his arms. Panting now, he levered himself up to the window ledge and got half of his torso out. The metal dug into his bare chest, but he kept pushing.

The door to the room opened. "Ho there," said a light voice, firmly, but free of malice.

Coryn froze, then tried desperately to push himself out. A paw grasped his arm and pulled him back in, and though it was a slender paw, it had more leverage than he did. He half-tumbled back into the room and looked up into the concerned russet muzzle of a fox in white robes. "Were you thinking to dash your head on the flagstones below?" the fox said. "Canis does not look kindly on those who would so casually dispose of their good health."

"No, I..." He couldn't think of a way to explain the ledge without admitting how he'd gotten in.

"What are you doing here? The services are downstairs, and there's little of value to steal up here." The fox folded his arms, looking down and then up as Coryn straightened to his full height.

"I was...I'm from Deverin. I wanted to see the cathedral." He paused, awkwardly. "It really is great."

"Indeed." The fox seemed amused, and then his nose twitched and his eyes widened. Coryn became acutely aware of his matted stomach fur, the smell of sex still musky in the air, and dropped his cloak in his haste to throw his tunic on. When the fox spoke again, his voice was amused. "I will show you to a less perilous exit."

"Sorry," Coryn mumbled, following the fox out of the room. They walked without a word down the hallway to a tight spiral stair. The fox's tail swung back and forth in front of Coryn as he set his paws carefully on the worn stone. The ancient stones smelled even stronger here, more than the fox's musk, more than Coryn's musk, but instead of filling him with peace, it made him ashamed now. He'd broken into a church—the Great Cathedral!—and what had he done? Pray? No, he'd pleasured himself with someone else. And yet he still worried about Two-Claws, what the rat would think if he came back and found Coryn gone. His father would be angry and there was nothing he could do about that now, but what if he never saw Two-Claws again?

Two coyotes from the congregation, dressed in brilliant blue finery with gold trim, stared at him as he followed the fox across the floor of the Cathedral. His shame kept his ears down but couldn't keep his head down; there was too much to look at. Even the pews were polished dark wood, almost black, and on the back of each was a silver star in a circle. The pews in Doubleford were plain oak wood and Coryn remembered when they'd been replaced; these must be a hundred years old or more.

When they got to the open double doors of the church, an elderly vixen in a thick maroon dress was waiting there. The lace trim on her sleeves shook as she pointed at Coryn.

"I called the guard," she said, glaring. "I called them right away. They're waiting outside."

"Thank you, Madame Calari," the cantor said. "I am not sure there is any need of that."

"They'll take care of him," she growled, moving aside to let Coryn and the cantor exit.

Coryn hesitated, seeing the bright red uniforms of a bear, who was stifling a yawn, and a porcupine, whose eyes were drooping. The cantor pushed him in the back. "Go on," he said. "Worst that happens is you get to spend a night in a warm, comfortable jail."

At that, the bear gave a snort of laughter. The porcupine didn't seem to have woken at all.

When Coryn stumbled out into the light, his paws splashing in the still-wet street, he felt as though the entire city were staring at him. His ears folded back and his tail tucked down, he stammered, "I'm sorry. I'm new in t-town. I'll go b-back to my father."

And perhaps, had he simply walked off then, they would not

have followed him. The cantor had already turned and walked back into the Cathedral, leaving the elderly vixen to stare at him. The guards did not seem particularly animated, but Coryn waited for their permission. The bear had even raised his paw, and the porcupine looked up to the spire of the Cathedral, then back over his shoulder.

Then the bear paused. "Young wolf," he rumbled, and stepped forward, taking Coryn by the wrist. "Why don't you come with us?"

"Huh?" The porcupine squinted, then said, "Oh." He reached to his belt and took out a length of rope. Before Coryn could do anything, the porcupine had looped the rope around one wrist and pulled the other into the same loop.

"Hey," Coryn said as the porcupine tied the rope tight. "What..."

"Had a complaint," the bear rumbled. "Wolf scent at the scene of a burglary. Just taking you to the guard station to check you out."

Coryn felt colder than he had out in the wind and rain. They were going to match his scent and then he would go to jail. The enormity of what he'd done throbbed in his chest; he could feel the pressure of it against his nose and eyes. Heads turned toward him as he marched behind the guards, too many eyes for him to avoid. He looked down at his feet, at the wet flagstones, and then realized that if Two-Claws were to pass by coming back, he might not see the rat. So he had to look back into the faces of the crowd, to see the pity, the scorn, the disgust on their faces as they met his eyes and then went on about their day.

"What's your name, son?" the porcupine said, holding the other end of the rope that bound his wrists.

"Legs," he said after a moment.

He immediately regretted it. "Ooh hoo hoo," the porcupine

said. "Good thing we got him tied up here, eh, Morrow? Otherwise he might take out those legs and leave us behind."

The bear snorted a laugh and kept walking. "What's your real name, son?" the porcupine asked.

When Coryn remained silent, the porcupine shrugged so that his quills rattled. "All right, you don't have to say. But it looks worse if you don't."

"Who but a thief would hide his name?" the bear said over his shoulder.

A cub hoping he can get back before his father finds out about this, Coryn thought. By now his absence from the stall would have been discovered for certain, but if only he could get away from the guard station soon, he could run back and make up some story, any story. If the worst he got for this was a beating, he'd count himself lucky.

The walk to the station seemed to go on forever. By day, the city looked much different than it had at night, dingier and less romantic. He could see the dirt on the flagstones and on the walls of the buildings, smell the thick smells of garbage and waste that had been hidden by the rain, and hear the bustling crowds hurrying by, all of them part of this city. He no longer had it to himself and the rat, and in fact the whole night was taking on the quality of a dream.

Part of him hoped it was a dream, that when they brought him to the station, they would find that the wolf scent was a coincidence, and he would be free to go. But part of him wanted desperately for it to be real, for his rat to be a real thief who had seen something in him and taken him out of the market to a new life. If it were, he swore, he'd show Two-Claws that he was someone reliable.

The guards took him along a large boulevard and then entered into a discussion about whether they should go directly to the smaller station that was nearer the scene of the burglary, or whether they should check in with someone named Feric first. "Come on," the bear said finally, "I want to get my breakfast." He led them off the main road, down a smaller street. Busy looking at the crowd, although he was beginning to realize that for the rat to find him here would be a miracle, Coryn didn't notice right away that the street they were walking on paralleled the main market street and intersected the street where his father's stall was located.

The temptation to look down the street as they approached the corner tore at him. Perhaps his father could help him. But then he'd be facing the consequences of his desertion, and for a fleeting moment he thought longingly of the safety of a locked jail cell. And yet, the reassurance of the stall, knowing their bread hadn't been stolen even though he'd abandoned his post, would boost his spirits just a little.

And so, as they walked along past the corner, he slowed and turned his head just slightly, enough to see his father's stall. It was four down along this side of the street and it was still there, although there didn't seem to be anyone behind it. The oilskin had been moved, but he definitely saw sheaves of barley and loaves of bread, so nothing had been stolen. He exhaled, turned his head again, and stopped dead.

His father stood there staring at him, a length of rope in his arms. In the last year, Coryn had matched his father's height, and his similarity to his father's markings sometimes gave him the feeling that looking at his father was looking at a greyer, more muscular version of himself. But he did not feel that now.

Neither of them spoke until the rope binding Coryn's wrists pulled taut, jerking Coryn forward. He took two stumbling steps, almost lurching into the porcupine's quills, as his father said, "Coryn?"

The porcupine stopped, turned, and then called over his shoulder to the bear to stop. The guards watched Coryn's father approach him slowly. "Father," Coryn said, but couldn't think of what to say next.

His father's eyes fell to the ropes holding Coryn's wrists, then to the guards.

"My name's Porlin. I'm a farmer with a stall at the market, and this is my son. What's he been doing?"

"Found sleeping in the Cathedral," the bear said.

Coryn's father's eyebrows raised. "He did want to see the Cathedral. I hadn't realized vagrancy laws were so strict here."

"Well." The bear scratched his muzzle. "Er, there was a report of a theft...wolf scent at the scene...but it was much earlier. Middle of the night. If he was with you...if he just went off this morning, then we'll be happy to release him."

The older wolf stared at Coryn, and Coryn felt the warm flush of shame all over again. But this wasn't like the apples, when his father had caught him with juice on his muzzle and the smell of the stolen fruit on his breath, nor the time he'd caught Coryn and Sukan behind the barn when they were supposed to be working. He had to trust Coryn, didn't he? "What kind of theft?"

"Burglary," the porcupine chimed in.

"Surely there are many wolves in the city."

"Oh, aye," the porcupine said. "But not so many breaking into buildings."

"Indeed." Coryn's father stroked his chin, his eyes narrowed. "No, the cub has been gone all night. I have no idea where he has been. Let us go and see if he has been stealing."

Both guards looked taken aback. Coryn's ears flattened. "Father," he said.

"Well?" his father asked. "Were you stealing?" When Coryn didn't respond, he went on. "I come back in the morning, the awning's collapsed, the barley is soaked. I thought you'd just run to get help, maybe you'd fallen asleep. But now I don't know what to think."

"Sir," the porcupine ventured, "it's not likely to be him. We didn't realize he was the son of a tradesman at the market."

"Why not?" Coryn's father's gaze rested on him even when the guards were speaking. "Didn't he tell you?"

"Just said he was new in town," the bear said. He was eyeing Coryn now with an expression that indicated he didn't share the porcupine's faith.

"All right, then," Coryn's father said. "Let's go. I'm as anxious as you are to see what he's been up to, since he doesn't seem inclined to tell any of us."

Coryn opened his muzzle to plead again, but he knew better than to argue with the stony expression on his father's muzzle. The older wolf walked ahead with the bear, while the porcupine remained back with Coryn.

In this manner, they arrived at the small guard station. Out front, a wolf and a stag in red uniforms interrupted their conversation to greet the bear and porcupine. Coryn kept his head down, only half-listening to them. Ahead of him, his father was silent, but he was certainly thinking about his ruined stock, and what disgrace Coryn had brought on him. Would he let Coryn go to jail if he were found guilty? Most likely. What would he tell the guards if they recognized his scent? His mind started to turn, slowly, still weighted down by fatigue. He'd thought of a story to tell; not a good one, but, he thought, a workable one.

His ears perked when the guards talked about the burglary.

"Why's this all over town so early?" the porcupine asked.

"Reward," the stag said. "Two gold if the thief is caught, another two if the stuff's recovered. Especially a big serving dish."

The bear and porcupine looked back at Coryn. "They didn't tell us that," the bear said.

"Glad we didn't check in with Feric. He'd have brought him all by himself. Cheated us out of our share."

"We'll stand you two a drink tonight, if it's him," the bear said.

"Right." That brought a smile to the stag. "Go see if he's done with old Halinnen yet."

He'd spoken to the wolf, who nodded and jogged up the stairs and into the small square building. Coryn looked from the uniformed stag to his father, who stared fixedly at the row house opposite the guard station, pointedly not looking at his son.

"Father," Coryn started. "I didn't mean…"

"Twenty-eight silver, if we sold the whole lot," his father said. "Gone now. And what have we to show?"

Coryn remembered, then, the two gold pieces. He checked to see that the guards weren't looking at him, and then hissed, "I have something to show. Quick, open your pocket."

His father stared at him. "What?"

"Shh." Coryn looked at the guards. "Please."

His father looked dubious but reached down to the pocket of his cloak. Coryn reached into his at the same time, fingers scrabbling around in the lining for the two gold pieces. He knew they were in this pocket. Or had they been in the other one? With a sinking feeling, he realized that he couldn't feel their weight in his cloak anywhere. It had been wet, heavier, and he hadn't noticed, but they must have fallen out when he picked up the cloak and tried to climb out the window. He might not have heard the thump of them on the carpet.

But he'd have seen them, wouldn't he? He gave up looking and met his father's gaze, his ears flat. "Sorry," he whispered.

His father frowned but didn't have time to say anything. The wolf had come out and was beckoning the bear and porcupine in. The porcupine said, "C'mon," and Coryn followed them inside. His father watched him go, making no move to follow.

The guard station was two rooms, each one half the floor space of the house. A small stair led up to a second story, but Coryn didn't spare the time to look at it. His attention was focused on the large desk where a uniformed wolf, slenderer than the one who'd led them in, stood attentively at the side of a small weasel, both looking across at a large bear in a rumpled velvet doublet. His fur was as mussed as if he'd just rolled out of bed, and his small eyes were further narrowed, staring at Coryn.

The worst part was his scent. Coryn could smell female skunk on him, and he was sure the wolf guards could too. It was so strong that probably the weasel could. But the main scent, the bear's scent, was awfully familiar, recalling dark rooms and the weight of silver to him. His heart sank. He could only hope the bear's sense of smell was worse than his.

"We came across this one sleeping in the Cathedral," the bear guard said, but before he could finish, the noble had risen to his feet. He jabbed his nose down at Coryn's chest and snuffled him, so close that had Coryn but opened his mouth, he could have bitten one of the jeweled earrings the bear wore. The smell of female skunk was overpowering enough to make him wrinkle his nose.

The bear's beady eyes fixed his, then the noble stood to his full height, with a look of disgust.

"It's him," he said. "He's been fornicating, but it's him."

The two wolf guards exchanged looks. Coryn suspected that they could smell where the bear had come from as well. The weasel got up from his chair, rubbed his eyes, and yawned. "You're sure?" he said.

"Positive." The bear folded his arms and glared at Coryn. "Go ahead, deny it."

"Can you read?" the weasel asked, more gently. When Coryn nodded, he picked up the parchment and showed the young wolf the list of items written on it. "Do these look familiar?"

Candelabras. Forks. Knives. Serving platter. Coryn shook his head.

The weasel shrugged. "Were you in this noble's house last night?"

"*Why* were you in my house?" The bear leaned forward, staring down at Coryn.

Coryn had concocted his story, but now it came time to tell it, he found the words difficult. "I—the window was open. I climbed in to see. I never saw any of that stuff. I never took anything!"

"Of course not," the bear said. "You *happened* to find the window open after a mysterious *odorless* thief somehow broke in and stole all my silver."

You're supposed to be gone, Coryn wanted to say. Out of town for the market. But the scent on the bear told him, perhaps, why the bear's family had left the city but he had not.

The weasel held up a paw. "Let's hold on, now. Was a rainy night, and if the thief was a rabbit or mouse, something with a weak scent, and he washed before, then this cub's scent might've overwhelmed it."

"I have an excellent nose." The bear folded his arms. Once again the wolves exchanged glances.

"Course you do, your lordship." The weasel nodded. "But without we got a confession, or he shows up with some of the stolen goods..."

"He's admitted to being in my house," the bear said. "That makes him guilty. If he didn't steal it, he knows who did."

"Your lordship, please consider—"

The bear interrupted the weasel. "I pay for your services, and I say he is the guilty one. Well?" he demanded of Coryn. "Where is my silver?"

"I don't know!" Coryn's heart beat faster. For a moment, he thought he might say he'd seen the Vergies on the river, but he couldn't come up with a way to make the story plausible. This was a test of his faith, of his courage and resolve. He met the bear's eyes and held fast.

"Very well." The bear turned away. "You may go to debtor's prison to work for the King, or you may enter my service. I have a small farm holding where you can pay off your debt. Ten years should do it."

"No." Coryn's father spoke from the doorway.

The bear turned to face him, as did the guards. He leaned against the door frame and did not make any move to enter. "What is the value of your silver? Ten years work, so...forty gold, am I correct, sir?"

"Hrmm." The bear lifted a massive paw to rub his muzzle. His eyes gleamed.

"I had been thinking fifty, rather."

"I can offer you ten, in coin, by the end of the year."

Coryn's ears stood straight up. Ten? They didn't have that kind of money. He turned to look back at his father, but the older wolf was only looking up at the noble, who frowned. "A quarter the value," he said.

"But in coin, within three months, sir." His father dipped his muzzle, a gesture Coryn had rarely seen him make. "Better to replace your silver quickly."

"Ten," the bear said, "and five each year thereafter for eight years."

Coryn's father shook his head. "We have but a poor farm. Two a year, for three years."

"Four a year for five."

Coryn watched the indifferent flick of his father's ears. "Three a year."

The bear folded his massive arms. "You are not in a strong position to bargain."

The older wolf spread his paws. "We have what we have. I

cannot promise more. I am but a simple farmer. Without my son to work the fields, I will not even have that much."

"Hrmm," the bear said again, shifting from one paw to the other. Coryn wrung his paws, looking back at the bear and the squinting of his tiny eyes.

"It sounds quite reasonable," the weasel said. "And there is no proof of guilt."

The bear turned on him. "You with your 'proof of guilt.' He admitted he was in my house!" He turned back to Coryn's father. "I will accept your payment. Ten gold within three months. The detective here can provide you with my address." He strode to the door, ignored Coryn's father's extended paw, and said, his muzzle close to the wolf's ear, "Or you could just give it to your son to deliver. He knows where I live."

The guard station was silent in his wake. The weasel sighed and sat back at the desk, picked up a quill, and began to write. The porcupine untied the rope from Coryn's paws. "S'pose you're free to go," he said.

Only then did Coryn's father step into the station. He dug into his pouch and handed a silver piece each to the bear and the porcupine. "My thanks for your courtesy in looking after my son, and for your hard work keeping the market safe."

Neither guard looked at Coryn. "Sorry for your trouble," the porcupine said, pocketing the coin. "Come on, we got to get back to our rounds." He tapped the bear's arm.

"Aye." The bear guard spent a moment longer looking at his silver, then slipped it into his pouch. He followed the porcupine out the door.

"You didn't have to give them money," Coryn said, stepping up to his father's side. "I didn't admit—I didn't do it."

"The *guards* work hard," his father said, glancing at the wolf guard before turning his attention to the weasel. "What was his name, and where does he live?"

"Marik Halinnen." The weasel looked up and recited an address. "Do you need that written?"

Coryn's father recited it back. "No," he said. "As he said, I can always send the cub."

Coryn's ears flattened. He'd proven himself true, and yet not only did his father not even meet his eye, he didn't say a word as they left the office, cutting off the weasel's apology. Coryn hurried after him, but his father seemed not to care whether or not he was following. They forged through the crowd, now full as the sun reached halfway into the sky, until they'd returned to the booth, and his father remained silent the whole way, which was worse than shouting. If he'd shouted, Coryn was getting ready to shout back, about how unfair it was that he'd been left to sit under a rainy stall all night, about how he never got to do anything. But he couldn't break down the barrier of his father's silence.

His father made all the sales that day, without another word to Coryn, and when they tore down the stall that night, he said barely more. Coryn was tasked with taking the spoiled barley and bread to the garbage piles on the outskirts of the city. The reek of it got in his nose all the way there and remained even after he'd thrown it past the scavengers who picked through the leavings.

On the way back, he paused at one of the cross-streets and looked down it. It nagged familiarly at him, and after a moment's staring through the people and trying to envision them gone, he realized that it was the street he and the rat had stopped at, for the rat to leave his gold. He could go back to the house, find the rat, or find someone who knew where he was.

Yes. Yes, if he pleaded his case, that they needed some of the rat's gold to pay the noble off, surely the rat would give him a couple more gold. And maybe he'd seen the two gold he'd given Coryn the previous night. Of course, Coryn entertained the possibility that the rat had taken them, but he was sure that in that case, it had been to keep them safe. And it had been well that he'd taken them, otherwise they might have been difficult to explain to the guards.

Though the rat couldn't have known he'd be caught...and if he had, if he had, then why had he not taken Coryn with him? Coryn knew he was sometimes difficult to wake, but surely the rat could have managed.

No. He couldn't doubt. He set off down the street, looking to his right for a familiar doorway. At first, he thought it looked too different in the fading evening light, that he would never find it. But then he saw the stonework, put his paw on the door and felt it give, and smelled his own scent, faintly, in the entrance where he'd waited. And there were the stairs, and the rat's scent on them. The top was shadowed, but Coryn climbed them anyway, nose lifted to test the air.

He did not catch the rat's scent, but smelled the sharp musk of a fox, and, as he reached closer to the top, the fresh scent of a different rat. At least it was a rat, and that might mean he knew the other.

Coryn didn't see anyone as he came up the landing, but when he turned, he found himself staring down the quarrel of a crossbow. "Evening," said the light voice of the vixen holding it, staring straight at him. "You've about thirty seconds to either explain yourself or be out the front door."

"I'm...I'm looking for Two-Claws," Coryn said, steeling himself. "I was here with him last night and I've lost him."

The vixen lowered the crossbow, showing rips in her tunic, and perked up her pewter-studded tall black ears. Her wary expression gave way to a grin, then a laugh. "Looking for Two-Claws, eh? You're not the first, nor will be the last. Eh?"

She'd glanced back at the other person in the large room, a black rat sitting in the back corner. He was looking curiously at

Coryn, running a claw absently down the white fur of his bare chest. "Aye," he said. "That's a slippery one, and no doubt. What business have you with him?"

"I just...things kind of went wrong, and I need to find him."

The vixen laughed sharply again, lowering the crossbow all the way and setting it on a table. "You won't find him here."

"Something went wrong," the rat said. "By Rodenta, what an astonishing surprise where that one's concerned."

"Now, now," the vixen said, "he came in here last night very happy, so something must have gone right."

"Oh, it often goes right for him. But I'll wager my take from last week that this poor cub was roped in somehow and took the punishment."

The vixen had merry golden eyes. "Is that it, pupling?"

"I'm of age," Coryn said hotly, "and no. He just left to get breakfast and then...then I was caught."

"Mm." The rat nodded sagely. "Funny how the guards show up right when he leaves for breakfast, aye?"

"He wouldn't call the guards," the vixen said. "My guess is it took him an awful long time to get breakfast. Likely he's still getting it. You might check in one of the bakeries, pupling. Mayhap he got his paws stuck in some dough."

Coryn flattened his ears. "It wasn't like that," he said.

The vixen reached up to touch his cheek ruff. "Oh, honey," she said. "Just go on home and thank Canis you've got your fur intact."

"But..." The urge to turn and run down the stairs was hard to fight. He lifted his chest. "The noble...the one he stole from... he's demanding gold from my family, and we don't have much."

The vixen's grin didn't waver. "We none of us have much," she said. "Times are rough."

"Go home," said the rat. "Wherever home is."

"My father..."

"...will be delighted to see you, pupling." The vixen stepped back. "There's nothing we can do here for you."

Coryn looked back from her to the rat, who shrugged and went back to oiling the tools on the stool in front of him. The vixen straightened her tunic, her tail swishing slowly behind her. The faint sunlight making its way through the dirty windows glimmered in the studs in her ears. Let me be a thief, Coryn wanted to say. I can do it. But he saw nothing forgiving in her eyes.

He could stay here anyway. But that would be running away. He owed it to his father to go back and work, to help pay off the debt to Halinnen. It had been a fun adventure, but the morning was what his life was going to be: responsibility and payment. He lifted his muzzle, said, "Thank you," and made his way stiffly down the stairs and back out into the street.

The shadows were long by the time he rejoined his father at the cart. They rode with two other farmers from Deverin in their own carts, staring off the side of the road while the other farmers, Lokyl and Aryss, counted money and told tales of the market. How exciting the big city was, Lokyl said: he'd seen a noble come by his stall in person, not sending her servant. Maybe he could sell his barley to her next market. They talked about her dress and how gracefully she walked, and then about two of the servants who'd been particularly curvaceous. How much more attractive the ladies in the city were, even those of low birth.

They didn't know the half of it, Coryn thought. He recalled his adventure, and perhaps his father saw the slight hint of a smile, because he coughed at that point and said, "The ten gold will come out of your bride price."

That jolted Coryn out of his reverie. "But...that was to buy our own land."

"Aye. But you'll be working my land to help pay off the debt anyway." His father never even looked at him.

He wanted to protest, but after all, he was the one who'd gone off at night, who'd stolen from the noble. He was the one who knew that stealing was fun as long as you didn't get caught, who had somehow allowed himself to get caught. This would be the beginning of a long, dreary life, but at least he would have a wife, and he would have his memory of Divalia.

He looked back over his shoulder at the moonlight striking the buildings, and the spires of the Great Cathedral. Up in one of those windows, he'd spent last night in the company of a mysterious, sexy rat, and he'd had an exotic drink, and he'd met a noble. He'd seen a master thief in action, even helped him. If he had nothing else, he thought as the cart rattled down the road, at least he had those memories. His father could never take those. He leaned back and closed his eyes. In his mind, it was dark and raining again, and a long whiplike tail beckoned for him to follow.

CHAPTER 1

This would be the last time Coryn would guide his mount Elly along the lesser-used path along the crest of the hills (looking down on the well-trodden path that followed the course of the river below), and it was not a bad day for a last memory. The sun had passed its zenith, and though a few clouds dotted the sky, none of them obscured the light. All around Coryn, trees glowed auburn and gold, with a few skeletal branches poking out as grim heralds of winter. The breeze had a distinct chill, but not enough to make the wolf draw his threadbare cloak around him. After months of summer heat, he was used to panting all day, and this welcome change brought a smile to his lips. He inhaled deeply and relished the refreshing coolness in his chest and on his tongue.

No stone marker showed the point where he left Lord Deverin's land, but an hour back he'd passed the house of the Fairchilds, a large bear family who farmed corn with a side business of apples and pigs, and he knew they were the farthest west of Lord Barclaw's people. The cider he'd bought from them still filled his canteen, weak because it was the newest harvest, but sweet and tart nonetheless. He took a drink and urged Elly up the dirt path to the top of the first hill, her gait slowing to a plod on the gentle slope.

A copse of aspen trees that now shone almost as bright a yellow as the sun crowned the third hill along this trail. From the top of the first and the second, the aspens blocked his view of a certain point on the horizon, but once he arrived at the copse and rode around it, a small point like the tip of a needle jutted up out of a dark patch amid the hazy line of green trees. There, two days' ride away (or one long day), stood the city of Divalia, the capital of Tephos. At its center, the small point that reached up to the sky was the central spire of the Great Cathedral.

Coryn sat while Elly grazed, staring at that spire and remembering, as he always did, his adventure in that wondrous building. The thief who'd shown him how to climb up the side, open a window, and sneak into that sacred space had made him feel special, a wolf plucked out of the market to partake in a grand adventure. And then that thief, a rat named Two-Claws, had vanished, and Coryn's adventure had turned for the worse.

He knew it was silly, but he'd always felt that if he could go back to the Cathedral, he could recapture that sense of wonder. At least he could appreciate the Cathedral properly, which he'd always wanted to do: as a grown wolf, not a young cub tripping over his own tail at the prospect of adventure, too blind to see what was happening around him.

Until two years ago, the journey to pay off his debt from that adventure had taken him all the way to the capital itself, albeit yearly rather than monthly. It was probably better this way, and not only because it was two fewer days of traveling. Being so close to the cathedral and never allowed to go inside had hurt more than looking at it from a distance (and he was convinced that his father had known that and deliberately taken Coryn as close as he could manage, every time they'd traveled together). Here, it appeared properly framed in his past.

Birds sang and insects buzzed in the stillness. To his right, in the shade of the aspens, a small clearing tempted him with shade and a soft carpet of grass. On the way back, he told himself, took one last look at the distant Cathedral, and rode on.

After rejoining the main road, another hour of riding brought him in view of a large estate house, four rows of windows tall, with a modest chapel spire at the eastern end. The light stone gleamed in the afternoon sun, mottled grey and green colors that rose to a fortified crenellation even though Coryn knew there hadn't been a war here in two generations. Half a dozen bears patrolled the roof nonetheless ("patrolled" here meant "leant on the stone and looked bored, probably asleep").

The gate house was another matter. A short ride brought him to a wooden gate where a bear trudged out to meet him. "Halt," he said in a bored tone, and then perked up. "Oh, aye, Coryn. Lovely day for a ride this time, eh? Won't need a change of clothes to go in."

"Not today." The wolf smiled. "Nice to see you, Podo. How's the cub?"

The bear raised his arm and slashed an imaginary sword back and forth. "Taking to his lessons. Going to be a soldier, that one."

"Ursus will he won't be needed."

"Ursus will it," Podo echoed. "Long as Ferrenis keeps to themselves. Licking their wounds still, I hear."

"Been thirty years," Coryn mused. "How much licking can one do? What about the north?"

"Trouble there, maybe, aye." Podo's smile wavered. "Nobody's being sent up that I've heard of. Anyway, won't be a concern of yours."

"No, I suppose not." Coryn looked up at the windows over the great doors that led into the estate, which Lord Barclaw insisted on calling a "castle." "How is his lordship's humor today?"

"I've heard nothing, but then, I never do, not except 'Podo, get down to the gate!'" The bear laughed. "And then, 'Podo, time for dinner.'" He patted his stomach. "Never miss a dinner call."

"See that you don't." Coryn smiled.

Podo moved to lift the gate. "Ah, on that subject, see that they give you some of Nan's coriander bread for your traveling supper. She's gotten a shipment of spices from Divalia and who knows how long they'll last?"

"Or how long they'll last for the like of you and me, eh?" Coryn rode past with a smile.

Podo saluted him. "Indeed."

It wasn't worth mentioning to the bear that this would be his last visit to Castle Barclaw. They shared these moments, Coryn's arrival and sometimes his departure, once a month, and beyond that they had little contact. Still, Podo was the friendliest of the people in Castle Barclaw, so Coryn did hesitate and ask, "Will you be here in an hour?"

"Unless there's an attack or the dinner bell rings early." The bear grinned widely.

"All right. I'll see you on the way out," Coryn promised, and rode forward into the courtyard in front of the house, not even enclosed by walls as a proper castle's courtyard should be, but with a wooden fence barely high enough to keep in the mounts.

The stable master, a portly skunk, eyed him as he came in and then called for a young bear cub to take Elly. Coryn dismounted and held out the reins for the young bear to take, with a smile and a "thank you" that went mostly unacknowledged as the cub's full attention went to guiding the mount toward the stables. Coryn made sure that Elly was behaving, then followed a uniformed weasel servant into the house proper.

When he was finally admitted to see the Exchequer after a quarter of an hour wait, she looked up from behind her great oak desk and gestured Coryn to a plain wooden chair. "A month goes by so quickly these days," the slender bear said, opening a small cabinet and sorting through pieces of paper with a paw. "Ah, here we are. Oh!" She examined the paper, scratching at the greying fur on the side of her muzzle. "This is your last payment, isn't it?"

"Yes, milady," Coryn said. He weighed the small pouch in his paw and then placed it on the desk in front of her.

She opened it and shook the three silver pieces onto the wood. After poking at each one with a claw, she nodded. "This is all in order." She looked over the top of her wire-framed spectacles. "I hope it has proven an instructive lesson."

Coryn restrained the flutter of anger. The eighteen-year-old cub who'd incurred this debt was long gone, the lesson learned from his foolishness imprinted long ago. These last three pieces of silver were far from the highest price paid for that adventure. "Yes, milady," he said.

"Five years of debt for one night of recklessness." She pulled a quill and ink from a drawer, dipped the quill, and made a mark on the paper. "Here, so you may see it." She pushed the paper across the desk.

Coryn knew the old paper well, from the title reading "Debt Owed By Coryn of Doubleford to Marik Halinnen" and the first three lines marking payments in gold once a year, down to the very last entry, "Payment Number 24, three silver," the one with a fresh X next to it. "It looks correct," he said.

"It is correct." The bear took the paper back. "We will keep it here for a time, not that I expect anyone will come around asking after it. Now go on with you. Best not to keep my brother waiting."

"Yes, milady. Thank you." Coryn stood and walked stiffly out of the room.

He knew that he should feel some relief at the repayment of his debt, but it had been part of his life for so long that he could not actually believe it was over. Perhaps when next month came around and he didn't have to ride to Castle Barclaw, the reality would sink in. Now, however, he had one more visit to make before he could return home.

* * *

He had been up this stair enough times that his paw rested in a familiar series of locations all the way up to the large parlor where Lord Barclaw received his guests. It smelled of wine and bears mostly, although if Coryn put his nose to the rugs or the couches, he would likely pick up odors of food and other species who'd come to visit. The old Lord didn't entertain as much as he used to, Coryn was told, so some of the scents would be a month old or more. But wine lingered, something in the sour fruit and sharp alcohol remaining potent for a good long while.

Sour smells tended to persist, Coryn had learned. Spill fresh milk and the smell would be gone in a week. But fail to clean it up properly so that the spilt milk went sour, and you'd be wrinkling your nose for months.

His meetings with Lord Barclaw made up the most intrusive but overall least onerous part of his punishment. There were days when he would have preferred to skip this part, but the monthly silver could have been spent hiring field hands or improving the blades of their plows. Had he been offered the choice to keep the money and double the frequency of these meetings, he would have accepted without hesitation.

An aspect of this was flattering, to be sure. That Lord Barclaw had purchased his debt and insisted upon a monthly visit made Coryn feel attractive in a way that very few other things did these days. The workers he'd dallied with in the past had been released; the boys and girls in the village had grown and married or moved away, and though the new crop of boys and girls were only a few years younger, Coryn didn't know them, hadn't grown up with them, and was generally now seen as a "sir" and not someone to disappear into the back of a barn with for a few pleasant minutes, even though he felt not much different than he had at sixteen or eighteen. He preferred to focus on feeling attractive rather than dwelling on the situation he'd been forced into that made him, in effect, a prostitute.

To Lord Barclaw, thirty years his senior (or more, perhaps), Coryn was no different than those boys and girls of eighteen. That was nice. The other side of that was that there was not the delicious little tension he'd had with all those others, that they might like each other enough to keep meeting behind barns and in grain storage sheds through marriages, cubs, and adulthood. It had taken Coryn most of his years to realize that Genora, the wife of Lightfoot the rancher, did not simply come over to bake pies for them because she felt sorry for motherless cubs and their widower father.

It had been a year or more since he'd had one of her pies. He should see if she could come over, or at least bring some of the berries she harvested from their land for Lucy to try her paw at baking.

The door at the far side of the room opened, and a slender wolf in a dark green jacket and trousers stepped through. He held the door and said very precisely, "Lord Barclaw is ready for you."

"Thank you, Dek," Coryn said. The wolf did not reply, and Coryn did not expect him to.

He walked through the door into a small anteroom with a cot on which Dek slept, through the open door on the other side and into the large bedroom of Lord Barclaw.

The curtains had been drawn so that the afternoon sun did not light up the room, but enough light squeezed past the thick velvet that Coryn had no trouble making out the bulk of Lord Barclaw. The bear sat on his couch rather than on the bed, back against one corner, one leg stretched out along the couch and the other bent so that his paw rested on the thick rug. He wore a doublet that shimmered in the dim light, but from the waist down he was naked, his brown pelt visible from the claws on his feet all the way up to the thick red shaft his paw was curled around.

"Ah, Coryn." The paw lifted and reached up to beckon the young wolf forward. His tone sounded surprised, as though he hadn't been expecting a visitor, or hadn't been expecting Coryn specifically. He often did that, acted as though he were in a brothel in Divalia and had unexpectedly seen someone he knew. It seemed to make him happy, and Coryn never challenged it. For him, it was a service he needed to perform.

"Hello, milord." Coryn stepped onto the other edge of the rug and walked slowly forward. "You look well."

"The leg has been bothering me again, I fear." The bear's rich, deep voice shook only a little. "But such small pains are forgotten. Let me see you properly."

Coryn nodded, stepping out of his trousers first and then pulling his tunic off. He stood naked in front of the bear, paws at his sides, and then reached down to cup his sac and sheath to show them off. His erection had already slid partway out of his sheath, which was a good thing, because otherwise the bear would ask in an aggrieved tone whether Coryn wasn't happy to see him, and worse than not being excited was desperately trying to make yourself excited when you weren't.

By now, though, he had learned some tricks, like thinking about the act itself and not any of the surrounding circumstances. He waited until Lord Barclaw said, "Come closer, come closer," and then obliged, standing a foot away. The bear's paw reached out and traced down his side and thigh, then teased claws up his sac and closed around his shaft. "So lovely," he murmured.

"Thank you, milord." Coryn wagged his tail.

When the bear withdrew his paw, that was the signal for Coryn to get to his knees. He placed one paw on Lord Barclaw's immense thigh and lowered himself to the floor. Coryn always remembered the bear's shaft being larger, but he circled it easily with his other paw. Slowly he drew his tongue up it.

"Aaaaah." The bear's entire chest rose and fell in a long pleasurable exhalation. His paw came to rest on Coryn's shoulder.

Coryn licked up, learning the taste of the bear over again. Pre already dripped from the tip, salty on his tongue. He cupped the large sac—this at least was as large as he remembered—and held the bear's quivering erection steady as he licked up it over and over, teasing the tip.

Lord Barclaw made low, breathy pants, and when Coryn's tongue hit a particular ridge, the bear's breath hitched. Coryn pursed his lips and slid them over the bear's tip, taking special care to rub along that ridge. He was rewarded with a shudder and a tight grip on his shoulder. Renewing his attentions, he squeezed the bear's thigh, feeling the tension there, and slid his muzzle down, letting the thick shaft fill his mouth.

The paw on his shoulder pushed gently. "Not—not too quickly, my boy."

"Mm," he said, without letting his muzzle free. Honestly, he didn't want to get this over with; he just got excited and eager for the bear to respond to his attentions. Going slow was nice, too, so he did as the bear wished for several more minutes, bobbing his muzzle up and down, letting his tongue work along the shaft, and trying to respond properly to the bear's signals.

In this pleasant rhythm, it was easy to lose himself in the physical intimacy, to forget that he was a farmer and the shaft in his mouth belonged to a lord. The other issues, the reasons for this meeting and the knowledge of what would and would not happen after Lord Barclaw's climax, receded into the background as Coryn focused on bringing that climax about in as pleasurable a way as possible.

After a good while, he speeded up his strokes again, and this time the bear did not object. With special attention paid to the spots he knew were sensitive and a paw cupping the large sac, Coryn pushed his muzzle down onto the very hard shaft over and over. Under his paw, the thigh quivered and jumped, and the paw on his shoulder moved to the back of his head, gripping him so tightly it was painful.

Twice he thought the bear's climax was coming, and twice the fast, deep moans got quicker and louder. Finally, Lord Barclaw let out a roar, pushed the wolf's head down, and a flood of warmth filled Coryn's mouth. He gulped, remembering the unfortunate time when he'd gagged and spattered the bear's fur, but this time his throat cooperated and he swallowed once, twice, and then the flood slowed and the bear relaxed with a long, loud, "Ahhhhhhhh ahh."

Coryn waited until the pressure on the back of his head eased and then carefully let the throbbing shaft slide from between his lips. He licked about the inside of his mouth. "Thank you, milord," he said.

"Ah ha. Ah. Well. That is one part that still works, thank Ursus. Very nice, Coryn, very nice."

The wolf rose and padded back to where his clothes rested. He pulled on his trousers and then his tunic. "Good day, milord," he said.

"Ah, Coryn. Wait."

This was unexpected. Coryn perked his ears toward the bear reclining on the couch. "Yes, milord?"

"This, ah, this is your last payment, if I am to understand my sister correctly?"

"Yes, milord."

"And I believe you celebrated a birthday not too long ago?"

It had been four months. "Yes, milord."

"Well, well." Lord Barclaw struggled to sit upright on the couch. "It's a memorable occasion, then, would you say?"

Coryn nodded. "I suppose so." His heart sped up. Here at the end of his punishment, would this be the day that the bear reciprocated his attentions? Or, better yet—no, he couldn't hope for that.

"I took the liberty of preparing a gift for you. For the occasion, you know."

Hope shifted into apprehension. Gifts from lords could be anything from useful money to an obligation like a prized horse that Coryn had no resources to care for and no way to sell. "It's too kind of you, milord." His hope surged, and words spilled out of him. "Are—are you taking me to Divalia?"

"To Divalia? My boy—well, I suppose sometime in the future, a state visit, that might be pleasant, to have you in my quarters when I return from a dull meeting—but no, my gift is much better than that."

It wouldn't be. But Coryn waited patiently, only a slight flagging in his tail the sign that hope had left him. "There's an old bear lived a couple miles south of here," Lord Barclaw said. "He had a small farm, grew wheat if I recall, and had bees for honey and mead as well. I don't know if the bees are still there, but I can have Dek look into that. I'd like to see Lord Deverin tell anyone what each farmer in his land grows, much less his name. Varchan."

"Milord?"

"Varchan was the name of this old bear. He had no cubs and no family, so when he died, his estate came to me. Well, I have petitioners, you know, people who have no land of their own. Sometimes these farms may go to them. There are three farms that border his, and two of them want to add his land to theirs. But." The bear tapped his head. "I have been thinking that I will be so sad when your time here is done, and how it would be nice to see you again, and then the perfect solution presented itself."

"It's very kind of you," Coryn murmured, but the bear spoke over him.

"I'm going to give you the farm. You will move there and live nearby and continue your visits. They needn't be more than once a month. I know that a farm is a lot of work. But you farm wheat already, so you know how to work the land."

"Barley," Coryn said.

"Yes, barley, well, it's a grain all the same, isn't it?" The bear frowned. "Did you understand what I said? I'm giving you a farm. Land."

"Yes, milord. Thank you so much. It's very generous."

"Then it's done. I'll have Dek bring in the papers. Dek!"

"Milord." Coryn spoke quickly. "I—it is very generous of you, but I can't sign papers now."

The frown deepened. "If you really must wash yourself, then you may avail yourself of my room, but do hurry. Ah, Dek." The prim wolf had entered the room and waited attentively at the doorway. "Please fetch those papers for Varchan's farm, would you?"

"Yes, sir." The wolf disappeared again.

"And my pants!" Lord Barclaw called after him.

"It's not the washing," Coryn said quickly. "I mean that my sister and I have been running our own farm, and if I leave, she wouldn't be able to manage by herself."

"What? She's not married? How old is she?"

"She's two years older than me," Coryn said. "We don't have a bride-price, and she has a cub, so it's been difficult."

"Cub." The bear blinked. "Ah, her husband died. That is difficult, but not a terrible problem. A cub proves she's of healthy stock—where there's one cub, more will follow, heh heh."

"She wants to stay on our farm, not follow a husband somewhere." Coryn didn't correct the bear; how his sister had come to be in her position was not important, and moreover, it was largely his fault. "There have been suitors, but they wanted to take her away."

"All right, all right," Lord Barclaw grumbled. Dek returned then with a folded pair of trousers in one paw and a sheaf of papers in the other. "No, no, Dek, take them away. Wait! Not the pants, I'll take them. No, on second thought, take them all away."

The wolf followed each of these instructions immediately and quickly, with the result that he walked two steps into the room, turned and walked two steps back, turned again and took one step and then turned one last time and left the room, all without a glance or a word to Coryn. Coryn watched him go and wondered—not for the first time—whether Dek would want to give him the release that he hadn't gotten from Lord Barclaw.

"Coryn!"

He turned back to the bear on the couch. "Sorry, milord."

"Come sit here." The bear gestured to the far side of the couch, just beyond where his foot rested.

Coryn took slow, small steps, very unlike Dek's, but Barclaw didn't waver nor speak again until the wolf had seated himself on the soft fabric of the couch. From here, the glistening trails on the bear's still-hard shaft showed much more clearly.

"Very good." Barclaw leaned back. "Now listen well, cub. I

am not in the habit of having my gifts refused. Perhaps you do not comprehend what this farm is worth. Two other farmers, very rich ones, want it very much! But I have kept it from them to give to you. Do you understand?"

"Yes, milord," Coryn said. "Thank you, milord."

"I am not a tyrant. I understand that family is important and that you may need to make arrangements for your sister. Therefore I will allow you one month to secure the ownership of your farm, after which time you will return here to me. Is that understood?"

"Yes, milord."

"I'll send word to Deverin's steward to look for a wolf to marry your sister, and I'll have him send any suitors directly to your farm. Once that's arranged, you'll return to sign the papers."

"Yes, milord."

"All right, then. Come here."

Coryn got up and stepped obediently into the bear's embrace. "Thank you again, milord. It's very generous of you. I'm sorry if I'm not as grateful as I should be."

"It was a surprise," Barclaw said into Coryn's ear. "I understand that. And I'm no tyrant. I thought you enjoyed our time together. Don't you?"

Coryn stepped back and nodded; what else could he do? "You may go," Barclaw told him. "I'll see you in a month."

The wolf bowed, turned, and left the bedroom.

Nobody stopped him in the hallways, on the stairs, or out the front door. He reclaimed Elly from the stables after a wait of several minutes. There was nobody else waiting, but the stable master wanted him to know how unimportant he was.

Podo stood at the gatehouse and didn't even spare him a glance as he approached; people leaving the castle didn't demand any attention unless the Lord himself was leaving, and in that case there would be a dozen mounts on the road at least. So Coryn stopped and called to the guard. "Podo!"

The bear turned. A wide grin split his features. "Ho, Coryn! Another visit done so soon. Will you be home before dark?"

Coryn squinted at the sun directly ahead of him. "It'll be a near thing this time of year, but if I hurry and don't stop too much along the way..."

"Get on with you then!" Podo laughed. "Don't risk bandits on my account. I'll see you in another month's time, aye?"

Coryn looked back at the large stone manor. "Aye," he said. "Say, Podo. You see farmers come and go here as well, do you not? Come to make a complaint or bring some of their harvest?"

The bear tilted his head. "I suppose. Sometimes, aye. None as often as you, though."

"Do they seem happy? Content?"

Podo laughed. "Farmers? I suppose. They mostly seem tired."

"But they like Lord Barclaw?"

The bear's smile wavered. "Course. We all love our Lord."

"Good..." Coryn looked around too, but there was nobody nearby. "I'll see you in a month, then. Best to your son."

"Best to your sister and niece." Podo's smile regained its ease. "Hurry home now."

The sun remained his guide for the first hour or so, dipping to the left or right as the path followed hills and gullies, but always shining directly into Coryn's eyes so that he kept his paw up to shade them.

Lord Barclaw's offer consumed his thoughts. The motivation behind the gift was clear: the bear wanted to keep getting his pole shined for the foreseeable future, even once a month. As expensive and desirable as the farm might be, it was nothing to a lord who oversaw many of them.

Whether Coryn could even work a wheat farm was likely

irrelevant to Lord Barclaw. Wheat and barley were both grains, but the methods of farming might be quite different. He didn't know any wheat farmers; he would have to find one and ask.

The gift of a farm, however simple it might be, would increase the prospects of his family. With him settled elsewhere, his sister could offer their family farm as her bride-price and perhaps attract a more desirable suitor, especially if Lord Deverin bestirred himself to take even a modicum of interest in the matter (no; Lord Barclaw had said it would be the lord's steward, not the lord himself, so perhaps that was more likely). Adding another family to their own would allow them to work the back fields without hiring extra workers—or would give them the means to hire extra workers—and would make Lucy's future even more secure. By all rights, he should take this gift, should have taken it the moment it was offered.

What had held him back? Maybe it had been that he'd been so looking forward to this being his last visit that the prospect of continuing his service to Lord Barclaw had automatically met with resistance. That was simply emotion, though. That shouldn't stop him from doing the best thing for his family. Emotion was how he'd gotten into this mess in the first place.

His attachment to the farm where he'd grown up was stronger, but that was also just emotion, when it came down to it. The farm had been important to his father; in all Coryn's memories, one strong moment was a morning when he'd been maybe six years old. His mother had still been alive then, but his father had left her and Ki after breakfast and taken Coryn to the road that ran past their farm. From that elevation, the two wolves could look out over nearly all of the land. The sky had been clear that day, the sun bright over the dirt-brown of the fields and the green tufts of grass in the space between the house and road, the wood of the house and barn glowing softly. "This is ours," his father had said, pointing out across all of it.

"People will try to take it from us, but whatever you do, Coryn, this land is yours. Don't be weak. If you're weak, people will take advantage of you, and you'll lose it."

That wasn't what was happening now, though. Was it? Ki would still have the land, so it would remain in the family. And Coryn wouldn't be weak if he accepted a gift, even if that gift took him away from the farm. Would he?

He approached the fork that led up to his copse. The sun hovered a paw's breadth above the horizon; the wiser course would be to take the direct route. But Coryn steered his mount to the right anyway and into the shadows cast by the trees atop the hill. His little tradition might get him home in the dark, but there wasn't much for bandits to raid around his farm. He would be safe.

The sun returned to his eyes as he crested the hill, shining through the leaves of the aspens and limning them in gold. This time he dismounted and tied Elly to one of the slender tree trunks. She had walked all day and probably the Barclaw stable hands had not given her any food, judging from the way she attacked the nearby grass. She deserved the rest, Coryn told himself as he walked to the flat rock and sat down there.

The spire of the Great Cathedral broke the horizon so many miles away. In the peace of the clearing, the whispering of the aspen leaves became the murmurs of a congregation around him, the leaves became stained glass breaking up the light of the afternoon sun, and the smell of grass and earth became old wood and stone. He sat high up in the private rooms of the Cathedral, the breeze from the open window ruffling his fur, and as he closed his eyes, he felt the grandeur of the building around him.

What if he wasn't alone up here in the Cathedral? What if, as he listened to the morning services, someone stole up behind him? His whiskers twitched and his paw traced down his other arm, mimicking the light touch of Two-Claws. What's this, he heard in his head, come out to look at the services happening?

He would turn and smile, his whiskers rising, and he'd put a paw on the rat's leg. I needed something to do while you were gone, he would say.

I brought breakfast, Two-Claws would tell him. Some rolls from the market. Come on, let's go back and eat.

And they would retreat back to the room with the open window, now letting sunlight in rather than night mist. The rolls lay in a cloth napkin on the floor of the little room, but as Coryn closed the door behind them, Two-Claws wouldn't go for the food. Rather, he'd reach out for Coryn's exposed sheath. Mayhap a touch of fun for other parts of us before we tend to our bellies? he'd say, trailing claws up and down.

Coryn's paw unfastened his trousers, finding his sheath already thick from the fantasy and his shaft two inches clear of it. His claws were the rat's delicate fingers, teasing him to full hardness. They would play along his exposed skin and then down to the sensitive fur of his sac, cupping it. His fingers would also find the rat's maleness, as excited and ready as his own.

They would sit down side by side, the morning air caressing them both, paws holding each other as their bodies leaned together, sharing warmth and something more important than warmth as their paws worked together. They would tease each other to the edge and then smile and say, "Not yet," and rub their muzzles together (this was not something Two-Claws had ever done, but here he was at Coryn's bidding) and then when their breathing had evened out, would resume their strokes.

Sometimes Coryn made this last for a good long time, but today in the background of his fantasy, his reasonable mind reminded him that the sun was sinking quickly toward the horizon and he couldn't sit here forever. So he leaned back and let Two-Claws's imaginary paws tighten around his shaft and pump harder.

The feeling grew in him, and up here he could let out his moans in a way he couldn't in his attic bedroom, with Ki and Lucy just downstairs. They echoed in the aspens and in the cathedral in his mind as his paw pulled him to the brink and over it. Moans became gasps became pants as he leaned back, finishing off his fantasy with a few last pumps.

The cathedral, the rolls, and finally Two-Claws all fell away, leaving him panting in the cool breeze. The smell of his seed rose to join that of the aspens and the earth around him, but he allowed himself a few moments to relax into the fading images of his fantasy.

When he looked back to the horizon, the Cathedral remained there, miles away, and Two-Claws likely just as far. He rubbed his paw on the ground and tore up some leaves to wipe off whatever mess remained on his midsection.

Elly waited patiently for him to untie her and lift himself up onto her back again. He took one more look at the horizon and then set out on the road home.

Ki had often told him to forget what had happened in Divalia, and though she meant he should forget the mistakes he'd made and his father's lingering resentment, he always heard that he should forget about Two-Claws and the Cathedral. He had tried to put that night out of his mind, but it always came back.

If he could just visit the Cathedral one more time, then maybe he could remember it differently. If he walked under its great stone arches and took in its stained glass, then maybe the memory of a rat's tongue in the dark upper rooms would lose some of its power over him.

(Or maybe the rat would find him again)

The fantasy that Two-Claws would be waiting for him by the

Cathedral belonged in the romantic books Ki had inherited from their mother, gifts from a more prosperous time ("trash," his father had called them). Ki didn't care for the stories, but they found that Lucy loved them, so Coryn read from the books while Ki and Lucy worked in the kitchen or mended clothes. The characters in those books valued love over all, taking stupid risks and giving up their livelihood for a chance at romance, and somehow in the stories everything worked out in the end.

This would never be him, but he could not let go of the desperate hope that one day, it might still be. This wasn't related to Lord Barclaw's offer—except in the faint hope that Lord Barclaw might bring him to Divalia one day—but it was an emotion that made it difficult for him to make other decisions.

So as he passed the Fairchilds' house and back into the lands of Lord Deverin, Coryn came up with a plan that would at least put off his decision. He would go back to Divalia one last time, for the marketplace in one week, and he would visit the Cathedral. There he would see that his romantic fantasies were childish foolishness and he would erase them from his life once and for all.

* * *

The sun had set well before he arrived home, leaving the evening cool enough that Coryn wrapped a cloak around himself. There were two places where he'd been attacked by bandits in the past, but he didn't carry much coin on him, and Elly was older and in worse shape than the mounts bandits tended to ride (if they rode). Only once had he actually been injured; the other time they took the meager coin he had and went on their way grumbling.

No bandits bothered him this night. When he spotted the thin trickle of wood smoke from his home, about ten minutes away, he stopped at the stream and removed his clothes to bathe in the icy water, washing off the remaining scent of his fantasy. When he'd done, he pulled his cloak around his wet fur for modesty, stuffed the rest of his clothes in the saddle bag, and mounted Elly again.

Through the chill breeze of night, he hurried the rest of the way to his house, casting an eye over the fields and the storage shed. In the moonlight, only mice stirred in the undergrowth as owls soared silently overhead trying to locate the source of the scurrying. Everything looked right.

The stable stood dark and empty, a small building optimistically large enough to house three mounts, with a loft above the stalls. Elly went obediently into the nearest stall and poked her long face into the bucket to see if any mealworms remained there. After rubbing her rough scaled rump affectionately, Coryn took the saddlebag and went around to his front door.

Two muzzles turned as he opened the door: Ki, his height and build but with browner fur and grey ears lacking the black tips his had; Lucy, whose black-tipped ears had only just reached her mother's waist in height. Both pairs of grey-green eyes brightened when they saw him, but only Lucy ran over to hug him.

"I'm wet," he told her as her little arms wrapped around his thigh.

She laughed. "I know. I don't care. I'm happy you're home." Her little tail wagged. "I made a pie!"

Ki, tending to the fire, poked at the logs and then stood. "I didn't know when you'd be back, so we only just started it. I'll pull out some dried beef and we'll boil it with cabbage." She gestured toward the fire. "Sit down and dry off."

He brushed muzzles with her on his way to the fire, Lucy clinging to his cloak. "Thanks," he said. "Where's this pie of Lucy's?"

"Wait until after dinner." Ki pointed to the back of the fire. "It's roasting there."

"I just wanted to smell it. What did you put in it?"

"I picked mouse-apples!"

"Aren't they sour?"

"A little." Ki walked back to the counter. "This late, they've sweetened some, and I added winterberries. Lucy says it will be fine to eat, so we'll trust her."

"I rolled the crust myself," Lucy said.

"That's very impressive." Coryn sat by the fire, opening his cloak a little to let his fur dry, trying to stay modest.

"Mommy held my paws," the cub confessed. "But next time she said I can do it myself."

"You can try," Ki said. "You're almost strong enough. How was your trip, Coryn? You made the last payment?"

"I did." The heat of the fire felt very nice on his wet fur. "I thought I might take the wagon to market next week."

Ki's ears went back. "Lucy, hon, would you take this pot up to the spring and get some water for dinner while I get the cabbage ready?"

"By myself?"

"I'll be watching you from the window."

Coryn spoke up. "You can take Elly if you want. She's having dinner in the stable."

"All right." This gave Lucy more confidence. She took the pot from Ki, walked to the door, and then looked back. "You'll be watching?"

Ki walked to the window. "From right here."

"All right." The cub pulled the door open and stepped out.

When the door shut, Ki said, "Why do you want to go back?"

Coryn stared into the fire. "I think it's time."

"You haven't gone since Father joined the Circle, and now you've paid off the debt you think things have changed?"

"Things have changed. I'm not a cub anymore." He brought his tail around so it could get some of the fire's heat as well. "The harvest is done, so you don't need me around every day."

"Does this mean you're not going to hire Ralli to sell our goods? Or are you going along with him? That means extra money for lodging." Ralli, a middle-aged widower wolf, had no family to speak of and made a living doing farm work around the area, like many others.

"I know." His own ears flattened. "I have a little money set aside, and I want to go back to Divalia."

Ki was silent for a moment and then said, "She's spilled the water and is going back. Poor Elly seems very confused."

Coryn smiled. "It's just that...I finally feel free of the guilt from what I did. I'd like to go back and see the city with fresh eyes. All the times I went back with Pa, I couldn't forget it. He wouldn't let me forget it. And after he joined the Circle..."

"Yes, I'm looking," his sister said, and it took him a half-second to realize that she was talking to Lucy, as she waved through the window. "Father's passing had nothing to do with you. Canis took him at his time, that's all."

He'd heard that many times and from many people, Ki most often of all. Deliberately, he pushed away the memory. "It's just one visit. I want to see how it's changed. I want to go see the Cathedral again."

"Alone this time?" she teased.

She meant it kindly, so he chuckled. "I won't turn down any offers I get."

"Keep that heart open, that's the spirit. Here comes Lucy."

The door opened and in came the cub with a pot of water and soaking wet arms. So while Ki boiled their supper, Lucy and Coryn sat by the fire and he told her about the aspens and the castle and the sunset, making some parts prettier and leaving out others.

And after dinner they all ate Lucy's pie, and though Coryn would never have taken it to market to sell, he thought it was delicious.

* * *

Twice more in the next week Ki asked if he was serious about going to Divalia, and both times he confirmed that he was serious without revealing anything about the underlying reasons why.

He did tell her that Lord Barclaw would be arranging for suitors to come calling, and this got her whiskers twitching. "What suitors?" she demanded quietly, up in his attic one night after Lucy had gone to sleep. "I don't want a husband."

"It would be a good thing for the farm," he said. "A bride-price and another wolf around, a father for Lucy."

"Lucy's father is ten miles away with his new wife and two cubs. If he wants to see her, he can get on his mount and come see her. You've seen how often he's done that. She seems to be doing quite well with just you around."

"But a husband for you..."

"To do what?" she snapped. "Order me around my own farm? Get another cub on me? I love Lucy, and she's going to inherit this farm when you and I are gone. It will stay in the family. With your debt paid, we'll be able to hire more field hands and maybe get something from that fallow field next year. We don't need anyone else."

To press the point further would be to admit that he was contemplating leaving, so he just said, "I know. But Lord Barclaw perceived a need and would not be dissuaded, so please just meet with them. Maybe you'll like one of them."

"Hmph. I've met most of the eligible wolves around here."

"They might not be from around here. Maybe someone will

arrive who also draws, or who likes your drawings, or who, I don't know, who writes poetry to go along with your drawings. I'm hopeless at any of that."

Her ears went from back to splayed, and she came over to put a paw on his shoulder. "You're a good farmer and a good uncle to Lucy, and that's the most important thing. No suitor is going to be better than that. If I want a quick turn in the shed, there's Essen, and if I want someone to appreciate my drawings —besides you and Lucy—there's Carilyn over at Radford. Truly," she said, "I have everything I want and need right now."

"All right," he said, and smiled so he wouldn't show how he envied her that peace.

The suitors were going to come whether Ki wanted them or not, so over the next week Coryn had many more conversations with her, eventually securing a promise that she would at least be polite to them. "After all," he reasoned, "if you haven't met them, you don't know them. One of them might be very nice."

"If he's very nice," Ki retorted, "what's he doing coming all the way down here? Fine, I'll give them a chance. But this goes in your ledger."

"I hope it'll balance when you meet a wolf who tumbles you head over tail."

She scoffed. "Those meetings only happen in stories. It might happen that one of these errant wolves so desperate for land that they travel all the way into our territory is someone who would also be a good friend to me and Lucy and you, and then maybe we can come to some arrangement. But put that tumbling out of your mind."

Already she said things like this anytime Coryn talked about "waiting for a special someone," especially since his adventure in Divalia. He'd told her and his father that Two-Claws was a thief who'd teased a young wolf cub with stories of the glamour and excitement of the world of thieves. Coryn had never told them that Two-Claws was also the one who'd broken into the Cathedral with him and slept with him there, nor that he'd gotten caught because he was waiting for the rat to return. He'd said that he ran into the Cathedral for shelter and had taken off his wet clothes to dry. His father never questioned that story; after all, the only seed the older wolf might have (probably had) smelled had been Coryn's own, while Two-Claws' had disappeared down his throat. Ki had never said anything directly, but the way she'd started disparaging romantic stories told him that she suspected what Coryn was hiding.

Gaiaday came around two days after Coryn's visit to Lord Barclaw, so the three of them put on their best clothes and took Elly on the hour-long ride past three other farms to the small town called Doubleford, with its feed merchant, market, ale-house and church.

Several of their friends, arriving around the same time for the same reason, greeted them on their way in. The main topic of conversation was the upcoming trip to Divalia for the autumn market, and when Coryn told his friends that he would be joining the caravan, their tails wagged and they clapped him on the back.

"Ferri gave up this spring," Lokyl, the big black wolf, said in his deep bass voice. "He decided it wasn't worth the expense to sell in the city even with the extra money."

"And Podia decided Sanwyn spent too much money on whores to be worth the extra they took in, so he hasn't gone since last year." Aryss, a wolf very light of fur but closer to Coryn's height and build than the massive Lokyl, laughed heartily.

Lokyl winked at him. "Serves him right for coming back with fleas. Told him not to go to that brothel by the river."

"He had to on account of she looked at the money and they were the cheapest."

Coryn smiled. "I'm glad to be going again."

"Hey, you'd best be careful too." Aryss nudged him with an elbow and nodded meaningfully toward Ki. "She keeps your money, doesn't she?"

"I won't be frequenting the brothels," Coryn said. "I'm going to behave myself."

"Anyway," Lokyl said, "the boy brothels are cleaner and more expensive."

"Not all of them." Aryss grimaced and scratched his side.

Coryn hadn't known that Aryss liked males, or maybe he had and it had been a long time ago, when he'd had many wolves closer to his age to play with? The knowledge felt more like a reminder than a revelation. "I only want to sell our barley and visit the Cathedral," Coryn said.

"Ay, well, keep your clothes on this time." Lokyl gave a hearty laugh. "Come on, services ready to start."

They all squeezed into the small church, thirty or so wolf families with two fox families, two bear families, and one family of mice. The cantor, an elderly wolf, led them in a song in praise of Canis but didn't forget to add Ursus and Rodenta to the prayers afterwards. Lucy had only just begun to understand what the services meant, and even less recently learned that the time to ask questions was not during the service itself. Coryn enjoyed watching her rapt expression, ears, eyes, and nose focused forward while they sang.

This church had memories of his family, memories of when he was Lucy's age sitting next to his father, who cuffed him if he made noise, Ki on his other side next to their mother. To avoid those memories, Coryn imagined the great arched ceiling of the Great Cathedral and the bright stained glass all around him, even though the smells and sounds crowded around him in the small church as they would not in the great expanse of the Cathedral. Someday he would like to take Ki and Lucy there, if only to marvel at the building itself. Maybe after this visit, when he had sorted out all his emotions about it.

After the services, he talked with Lokyl and Aryss to arrange when they would meet for the trip up. "Do you need space in our cart?" Aryss asked.

"We've got one," Coryn said. "We haven't used it in months, so I'll take a look at it before Musteliday and make sure it's in working order."

Lokyl's ears perked up. "Want me to come over tomorrow? I love woodworking and I'd be glad to help."

"Sure. Thank you." Coryn smiled.

"I'll bring Cabi. He and Lucy can play together."

"Tell him to be ready to pick mouse-apples. Lucy's been making pies."

Coryn relayed this news to Ki, and as soon as her ears flattened he said, "He's just coming to help me with the cart, that's all."

"Was it your idea for him to come over?"

"Well...no, but—"

She sighed. "It's fine. As long as it doesn't become a habit."

"We're not signing a marriage contract for Lucy. She's barely five."

Ki's ears came back up and she gave him a patient look, the kind his teacher had given him when he was having trouble with arithmetic. "I know we're not doing that now, but before you know it she'll be fourteen and Cabi will be fifteen and then Lokyl will be saying," and here she imitated his deep voice, "goodness, the cubs are such good friends, why not join our farms together?"

"If they do become friends," Coryn argued, "what's wrong with that?"

"I want Lucy to have a choice about marriage. I don't want her shackled to the first boy she meets."

"That shouldn't mean she's not allowed to have any friends."

"Friends are fine. Have Gersha come over."

"Hyren and Zola live an hour that way." Coryn pointed out of town, the opposite way from home.

Ki threw up her paws. "I said it was fine."

So they left it at that, and the following day Lokyl came over with his cub Cabi, who at one year older than Lucy already stood two paws above her. But the two cubs played together well, gathered a basket full of small, sour apples, and made multiple pies that Ki helped them bake.

Lokyl, meanwhile, helped Coryn inspect the cart and talked about what he could expect from the market. "Autumn's better than spring. You've got just barley or other things?"

"Ki's baking some barley loaves. We have a few bottles of barley wine from the last few years that I can bring, too. Maybe twenty."

"Wine is good. That'll go fast. Tell you what." The large wolf ran a paw over one of the cart wheels and then applied his planing tool to it. "There's this weasel, works for the Crowned Head, always wants barley to make their ale and I never have enough for him. I'll send him your way. Else you're likely to come back with half your barley."

"Thank you," Coryn said. "That would be a great relief."

"With Ferri not going, there'll be even less barley, so it's good you're bringing yours. Want to keep money coming into our little town, don't we?" He pulled the tool away and rubbed a leathery finger pad over the wood again. "There you are. Smooth as one of those expensive whores you won't be frequenting."

Coryn smiled. "Does it make such a difference?"

"Ah," Lokyl said, "it's not just that they're cleaner, but they've more experience too."

Coryn laughed. "I mean the wheels. We won't be on roads most of the way."

"I know. I think it does. Little bumps and cracks, they can pick up mud and stones and before you know it, you're bouncing along like..." Lokyl winked at him. "Like one of the cheaper whores."

The analogies seemed obviously pointed to get Coryn to ask a question, so he did. "You've been to the expensive brothels?"

"Oh, on occasion." Now Lokyl leaned against the cart, his chest puffed out a little. "Willa doesn't check the money we get back, and I keep my expenses reasonable so we always have enough. And I never fuck a wolf." He wagged a finger at Coryn. "If you go with boys, that's not so much a problem for you, but you shouldn't go with wolves anyway. Otters, rabbits, even a nice bear girl, they're all different."

"How many different species have you been with?"

Lokyl counted on his fingers. "Those three, Willa of course, fox, raccoon. Skunk, once, just to see how it was." He laughed and waved a paw in front of his nose. "Most of the Mustela and Rodenta crew are too small for me. Oh! I did do a rat once. But that was a long time ago and it wasn't in a brothel."

"A rat?" Coryn rubbed his paws together, reminding himself that Lokyl was definitely talking about a girl.

"I was...fifteen maybe? It was my second or third trip with my father, so I must have been fifteen. No, wait, sixteen. Anyway, it was the king before this one, but it was before my father paid for me to go to brothels. This rat came sniffing around the market and I told her to get lost, but she said she'd fuck me for a meal. So I fucked her and then I gave her two slices of bread." He laughed again. "It wasn't great but still the cheapest I've gotten, not counting playing around when we were growing up around here."

"Yeah," Coryn said.

"Not as long ago for you, is it? But it dries up quick. Everyone gets married and then they don't want to fuck around. You're lucky, though."

"Huh? How's that?"

"You like boys. Guys, sometimes they'll fuck around because that's not really cheating. You're not gonna get with cub or anything."

"Right," Coryn said. "I guess I am lucky."

CHAPTER 2

Ki and Coryn loaded up the cart for the trip with Lucy running around being "helpful," until Ki told her to go look after Elly, and then the loading went much more smoothly.

"Are you sure about this trip?" Ki asked, arranging the sacks in the back of the cart as Coryn hefted them up. "You'll be gone a week and you'll have to pay for meals and lodging. With as little as we have, it might make more sense to pay Doran to take it."

"I'll bring along feed for Elly, so I won't have to buy that along the way, and I'll bring a loaf for myself. Lokyl already offered me a line on selling most of our barley so hopefully I won't bring any back." He lifted two bottles of barley-wine up to her, then two more, and finally the box they'd been resting in.

"Leaving me to do all the baking and brewing by myself."

"Not all of it." Coryn grinned up at her. "Just a week's worth. And Lucy's old enough now to help with the husking."

"I'll save you the first mash." Ki grinned back and wagged her tail. "Since you're going to the city anyway, why don't you see if you can find some nice cloth so I can make clothes for us?

Something in a deep blue would go well with our fur. We haven't got anything like that."

"I'll look," Coryn promised. "And maybe a scented powder for you and Lucy."

"I won't put it on for the suitors," Ki said.

"I didn't say you should. I just want to get something nice for you."

Her ears came back up. "All right then." She surveyed the cart. "That's most of this sorted. Let's see if we can't bake another loaf of bread or three before you leave."

Coryn hitched up Elly to the cart in the darkness of early morning, dawn close enough for his sensitive eyes to see by. His and Elly's feet crunched the frost on the ground as they set out, moonlit puffs of their breath preceding them on the rough trail that led out to the road.

The sun hadn't risen by the time he met Lokyl and Aryss at the crossroads north of town. "Ready?" Lokyl called in his booming voice. He brandished an old sword that didn't gleam in the pre-dawn light. Aryss, in the cart beside him, had a crossbow next to him on the seat.

"I didn't bring any weapons," Coryn said. "Should I have? Will there be trouble?"

"Was a couple years ago," Aryss said. "Hasn't been in a while though. Still, Canis gave us noses to sniff the trail ahead, didn't he?"

"Too true, too true," cried Lokyl. "And now there's three of us again, we won't be as tempting a target for single bandits. Mayhap you can find yourself a weapon in Divalia, Coryn. What are you practiced with?"

"A scythe," Coryn said. "We're done the harvest; I could have brought ours."

Lokyl laughed, taking the lead of their little caravan. "You'll want a scimitar, then. It's much the same notion." He mimed sweeping back and forth. "Only you'll be harvesting the heads of your enemies rather than your crop."

"If we can find an inexpensive one. I'd rather spend my coin on clothes for Ki and Lucy."

"My goodness, mate, one would think you were married!" Lokyl guffawed.

Aryss fell in behind Coryn and called from his cart, "Don't mind him. He loves to swing that sword about, but he's only stabbed one person with it and that's himself."

"Careful!" Lokyl shouted from the front cart, waving his sword in the air. "I'll make it two!"

"Why don't you leave off the bragging and let's have a round of The Lusty Barmaid," Aryss yelled back.

So Lokyl started singing the tavern song that they'd all known since they were old enough to listen to their fathers outside the public-house doors.

There was a barmaid in Rideupon Lock
And for half a silver she'd ride on your cock
Come here, my lass, and settle your ass
I've ten silver bright, you'll be here all night
And a hey a ho, let's give her a go,
The barmaid of Rideupon Lock

There were countless verses, most of them with fictional towns that rhymed with some word for "cock," or "tits," or "muff," like the barmaid from Dive-Over-Lick who would dive on your dick, or the barmaid from Shinesbury Todd who would shine up your rod, and so on and so forth. Sometimes they were just lazy, like the barmaid from Showusser Fits who would, well, it wasn't hard to guess the rhyme. Coryn was pleased that he recalled one verse that neither of the others knew, and surprised to find how many they knew that he didn't. "You'll hear more of them at the market for sure," Aryss told him. "At least one of the nights."

"Do all the merchants go out drinking together?"

"Not all. Us Canids usually do, and sometimes the Ursids tag along with us. The others go off on their own."

The song and conversation carried them over rolling hills down to the river road they would follow up to Divalia. Here there was a crossroad that Coryn was accustomed to taking, the right turn leading him to Lord Barclaw's lands, and Elly did in fact start turning before he corrected her. Neither of the other two wolves noticed.

It felt strange but good to leave that turning behind. The river road ran too low to see the Great Cathedral from here over the trees and hills, but Coryn knew it was there, felt it pulling him toward the city.

Every two or three hours they passed an inn with a stable, and the closer they got to Divalia, the more crowded the road became, so they rode single file on the edge nearest the river bank. The river burbled along well below the high water mark, coursing around small dirt islands near the shore, and once or twice larger islands farther out, made more solid by stands of willow trees. Coryn wondered idly if anyone lived on them, especially the ones near an inn. Ki sometimes made willow tea, so he presumed you could live off willow bark and whatever other things lived on the island. There wouldn't be any Lord Barclaw to worry about, nor suitors for Ki that she wouldn't like.

But there'd also be no barley wine nor bread, and no other people to share your life, unless you rowed across to the inn and took your company there with travelers, listening to stories and passing them along. Sometimes, perhaps, one particular traveler would invite you up to his room for a night. He hummed to himself and sang words in his head:

There's a rat who lives in Rock-on-Pew

For a smile he'll put his cock in you

The verse and the thoughts that accompanied it had his sheath full and his shaft poking out of it. He grinned, rubbed his pants, and turned his thoughts to something else.

They didn't stay in an inn for the night but found a place just off the road where they could circle their carts and sleep in the back atop the stores. There would be two nights before they arrived in Divalia, and not only did this save the cost of an inn, it helped them protect their carts and stores.

On the second night, Coryn was jolted awake from his sleep by a touch on his shoulder. He scrambled about in the sacks of barley before he heard clearly Aryss's whisper.

"Shh, shh, it's only me. Don't make a ruckus."

He quieted, and Aryss did too, head up and ears perked. Lokyl's deep, even snoring came from his cart, and behind that the river burbled and no other noises disturbed the night.

"All right," Aryss whispered. "Lok sleeps like a log, but can't be too careful."

"What's the matter?" Coryn whispered back.

"I just thought you might like some company tonight." Aryss pushed his pants down in an easy motion, revealing his shaft half out of his sheath. "I'll suck you if you'll suck me."

"Oh." Coryn's sheath stirred.

"It's all right if you don't want to. I don't get to suck as much cock as I'd like so I thought I'd ask."

"Yeah, I don't either—I mean—okay. Yes."

Aryss smiled. "You want to go first?"

"Go first like suck first?" Coryn nodded. "I can. I'm not ready yet."

So he twisted around and rubbed his whiskers along Aryss's

sheath and cock, then licked up it while the older wolf leaned back and breathed his pleasure out into the cool night air.

This felt different, better than his night with Lord Barclaw. He took pride in being able to get Aryss to squirm, to arch his back, to pant as Coryn took the wolf's long shaft all the way into his muzzle, and finally to bury his muzzle in the barley sacks, moaning muffled by the cloth and grain as he spurted warmth onto Coryn's tongue.

Coryn licked him clean, to more squirming, then lay back and pushed his own pants down. The blow job had gotten his own cock out of his sheath, so he stroked it while he waited for Aryss to recover.

"By Canis," the wolf breathed finally. "You're good at that."

Coryn's tail thumped against the sacks of grain. "Thank you."

"I hope I'm not a disappointment. As I said...I haven't had as much practice as I would like."

"Well, the last one didn't do anything in return, so just offering is going to be an improvement."

Aryss rolled onto his side and reached out a paw to caress Coryn's fur, teasing close to his sheath and then cupping his sac. "You've got a nice piece."

"Thank you." That compliment was nice too, but Coryn felt he had little to do with it, other than keeping his fur trimmed.

The feel of Aryss's fingers as they slid up his shaft was very nice, and the feel of his tongue was even nicer. Despite his protestation, he was more than competent once he took Coryn's shaft into his muzzle. He slid up and down, used his tongue, and responded to Coryn's body language by speeding up and sucking harder the more Coryn tensed and huffed.

And when Coryn finally came, Aryss kept his lips closed and gulped, and then slowly slid off as Coryn collapsed back into the sacks of grain. "Thanks," the other wolf whispered, and clambered down out of the cart.

The next morning there was a delay because Elly must have felt she hadn't gotten enough to eat and kept veering off the trail to browse. Coryn tried to keep her in line with the others, but the independence he prized in her now worked against him, and finally they had to stop for a short time to let her have her fill.

"You may not have a wife, but you're beholden to a lady all the same," Lokyl laughed.

"Just means he'll make a good husband when the right one comes along." Aryss's mount also took advantage of the break to graze, though he preferred the short grasses and not the bushes that Elly liked.

Coryn wished that Lokyl would go on ahead so that he could suggest to Aryss that they take advantage of this short break, but Lokyl would never do that, and besides, Aryss leaned back in his seat and closed his eyes while his mount grazed, so he might not have been as ready as Coryn was.

The previous night had doubled the number of times Coryn usually had sex in a month, and now he found himself keyed up and hoping that he and Aryss could have some time alone in Divalia. Not that he thought anything romantic might blossom between them; it was cheaper than a brothel, that was all. And he could always go to a brothel.

Soon enough, they were back on the road, but it seemed the gods were conspiring to keep them from reaching Divalia that day. First a light rain started, and then it thickened. This wasn't a problem for their stores, safely wrapped in oilcloth, but it muddied the road and slowed their pace considerably.

Then Lokyl's mount, normally very steady of disposition, shied at a crack of thunder and pulled his cart half into a muddy ditch. It took them an hour to pull the cart back onto the road, by which time all three of them were soaked and spattered in mud.

"Not as bad as two years ago, remember that one?" Lokyl said cheerfully as they were on their way.

"You mean the spring market, the one where your cart overturned?" Aryss called past Coryn.

"Aye." Lokyl shook his head. "Our goods are all safe and dry, and the rain will wash this mud off us soon enough."

They'd all stripped down to underclothes to keep the mud from their regular clothes, which had caused Coryn some moments of worry, especially when he was behind Aryss staring at the wolf's rear under his sodden tail, wrapped in wet cloth that clung to the fur. His underthings clung tightly to his sheath and would reveal any arousal, so he kept his attention on the very unsexy smells and sights and tried not to look at the other two nearly-naked male wolves, including the one who'd blown him the previous night. Normally it wasn't a problem looking at his friends without getting aroused; normally, he hadn't had sex with one of them the night before.

Back on his cart, he was free to fantasize, although when his shaft poked out against his wet and muddy clothes, he didn't give in to the temptation to finish himself there in the cart. That, one of the others would certainly notice, if not during the act, then from the smell the rain would only accentuate before washing it away.

At sundown, they stopped and shared another meal and then each of them crept under an oilcloth in the back of their cart for some small measure of shelter. Coryn thought he would lie awake all night in case Aryss came by again, but the steady beat of rain on the cloth and the warmth in the small, enclosed space put him to sleep quickly, and then it was morning and Lokyl was shouting at them to wake up.

The rain had moved on overnight, leaving a fresh-smelling world and a clarity to the air that had Coryn taking deep breaths, his nose twitching to scents both familiar and new. The river beside them sparkled in the intermittent sunlight and kept his ears perked with splashes of fish and birds and the background rushing sound of the water against rocks and banks. Meanwhile, on the road, the scents of travelers and the contents of their carts kept him interested when his nose turned in that direction.

"There we go!" Lokyl called as his cart crested a small rise on the trail, leaving the river in a gully a ways below them. The large wolf pointed ahead, and as Coryn's cart reached the top of the hill, the buildings of Divalia came into view.

There was the wall and the cluster of buildings outside it, mostly low houses and a few temporary-looking structures of sticks and cloth. Behind the walls rose the cold grey stone of the Palace of Divalia, and next to that, the graceful dome and spire of the Great Cathedral.

They were close enough for Coryn to make out two of the six columns that surrounded the dome, but not close enough for him to see which gods stood atop them. "Three hours' ride?" he called ahead to Lokyl, now descending the hill.

"About that, if we don't run into another muddy patch."

"I love this hill," Aryss said behind Coryn. "From here the city is beautiful."

"Only from here?" Coryn called back as he descended the hill and the city disappeared below the horizon again.

"Moreso from here. Up close it's dirty and there are cutpurses and thieves. From here you can only see the Cathedral and the Palace, and it looks very grand."

"They're pretty grand up close."

"Smellier, too," Aryss said.

"Careful, Aryss," Lokyl called back with a booming laugh. "Coryn's got a mistress in Divalia all right, and she's twenty stories tall with a great dome and spire atop."

Coryn lay his ears back. "Is that so?" Aryss called forward. "I'd only heard that he explored it unofficially."

"He was moved to great pleasure by its beauty," Lokyl cackled. "Or at least moved to remove his clothing. Isn't that right, Coryn?"

Caught in the middle, Coryn could not race forward nor stop and let the others go on ahead, both of which he dearly wished to do at the moment. "I love the Cathedral," he said, sidestepping the actual question. "When I saw it up close I thought it was the most amazing building I'd ever seen. I want to go see it again."

"The question is," Aryss said, "whether you'll go by yourself or whether you'll be looking for someone to take with you."

"If there's someone wanting to go with me," Coryn said, "then I'll take them. And if not, I'll go by myself."

"Sounds like I'm right," Lokyl crowed.

"I'll go with you for services on Gaiaday," Aryss said.

"Careful he doesn't try to show you one of the back rooms," Lokyl called.

Coryn flattened his ears again, but Aryss retorted, "What makes you think I wouldn't go?"

Lokyl laughed heartily. "I'm sure you would! But don't get caught."

The joking put Coryn at ease enough to raise his ears again and say, "I won't get caught again, don't worry," and this brought laughs from both his companions and a merciful end to the conversation.

They arrived outside the walls of Divalia just after the sun hit its zenith, joining a long train of carts waiting to enter the city, which at least gave them time to pull their damp clothes back on. Elly grew bored with the waiting and tried to pull out of line several times, making Coryn dismount to give her some of the apples Ki had sent with him. The treats kept her calm, and he only had to give her two of them in the hour they stood in line.

The guards asked where they were from and what they carried and then called that information back into a small room where a fox wrote it down on a piece of paper. Once the three of them had been waved through, they rode forward into a wide street, and Coryn was back in Divalia for the first time in over two years.

There were smells; Aryss was right about that. Baked bread and roasted meats and laundry, and a whiff of the acrid stench of tanning solution when the wind shifted just the right way. There were rabbits and weasels and mice and foxes, bobcats and raccoons and wolves and bears. There was brick dust and fresh wood and earth, there was rotting wood, garbage and urine. Coryn felt the presence of thousands of people around him in the air even as they hurried past him, ran in front of his cart, called over him from one window to another. The last time he'd been here, it had been beside his father, and all these smells had been tempered by that presence. With his father beside him, the city was not open to explore, but a reminder of the "worst thing" he'd done. Now, though that memory wasn't gone, he felt lighter. His tail wagged against the seat.

Lokyl led them to the market street and found the Farmers' Guild Office at the end of it, where he pushed Coryn in front of the raccoon sitting at a wide wooden desk. "This is Coryn. His father was Porlin, and he's from the same farm, in Lord Deverin's land."

The raccoon pulled out a ledger, checked it, then asked Coryn for his payment. He produced the two silver coins and received in exchange a copper badge. "Wear this at all times," the raccoon said, "and bring it back when the market's over to get one of your silver back."

"Thanks." Coryn pinned the badge to his shirt.

Lokyl and Aryss paid and received their badges. "Now," Lokyl said, "let's see which spots have been left to us latecomers."

Guards stood at either end of the street but barely glanced at their badges and did not challenge them as they steered their carts through, looking from side to side at all the wooden stands already piled with cloth-covered goods. There were not three spots together, it turned out. One spot sat halfway down the street, a wooden stand with one broken board (explaining why it sat unclaimed), and then two almost across from each other down at the end of the street, near the cul-de-sac that ended the market. Some spots were available on the side street, the one where Coryn's father had set up his stall the night of Coryn's adventure, but Aryss and Lokyl did not even glance in that direction when there were still stalls on the main street.

"I'm new," Coryn said. "I'll take the broken one."

"You're new, so you should be where one of us can keep you company," Lokyl said. "My customers will find me no matter what. You and Aryss take the better stands."

"The better one is the one closer to the entrance," Aryss grumbled.

"I can't show as much with the broken board," Lokyl countered.

"You two take whichever ones you want and I'll pick from what's left." Coryn looked back down the side street. One of the cloth-covered bundles on a stall shifted, and Coryn realized that it was a person sleeping under a blanket.

Lokyl and Aryss bickered a little longer and eventually Lokyl took the stall with the broken board. "Come on," Aryss said to Coryn as they left the larger wolf behind.

For the next hour, they pulled bread and wine and sacks of milled barley off their carts and arranged them in the stalls. Coryn hadn't done this in years, and had never done it alone, but his paws and eyes remembered the arrangements his father had used. He barely looked over at Aryss's stall the whole time.

Still, it took him longer to finish, and the other wolf came over to stand in front of his stall. "You'll want to keep the wine back a little," Aryss said. "Thieves will run off with it otherwise."

"Are there more thieves than there were years ago?" Coryn shifted the bottles back so they weren't right at the front of the stall.

"Hard to say." Aryss gestured, "Market's bigger than it was. Crowds come in, thieves mingle with them and slip a bottle under their cloaks. Look for anyone in a cloak and don't trust them."

"My father said to watch their eyes," Coryn said. "Customers will look at the merchandise, but thieves will look at the merchants."

"Aye, but easier to look for cloaks." Aryss laughed. "Come on, let's stable our mounts and go find a pub. My bones could use a bit of relaxing after that journey."

"Aryss," Coryn said as the older wolf turned. "If there's a chance to...you know, as we did that night...I'd be glad of some company again."

Aryss turned at his words and nodded. "It was pleasant enough. Understand, I've no need to make a habit of it."

"No, no," Coryn said hastily. "But...would be cheaper than the brothels, ey?"

"Oh aye. But skilled though your tongue is, it's not as warm nor as soft as a lady's depths. I've a mind to seek out the latter, myself." He patted Coryn on the shoulder. "Perhaps the brothels will be full, or the market slow. And if not, there's the ride home."

"I just thought it would be nice to not be in a cart." Coryn left his stall to walk alongside Aryss down the street.

The other wolf was silent for a moment, his ears flicking

around as though listening for something in the bustle of the city around them. "Don't make this out to be more than it is," he said.

"No," Coryn protested, cursing his excitement. It was being here in the city that did it, rekindling that romanticism even when he hadn't meant it that way. Aryss saw through his words to those feelings. "It's only—" He restrained his excitement. "I haven't had much company of that kind, and I was pleased to share it. It will be at your convenience, of course. And not when we're back home."

"All right." Aryss got up onto his cart, and Coryn climbed aboard his as well. "Let's get that drink."

They rejoined Lokyl, who'd made a very good showing of his broken stall, and the three of them rode around to a nearby stable, where they left their carts and mounts for a silver each to cover the two days of the market. Coryn tallied his expenses so far and calculated in his head how much he would have to sell to make the amount they usually received from the market. "I hope there are a lot of customers," he said moodily as he trailed the other wolves down the street.

"We never have to bring much back from the Divalia market," Lokyl said.

"Even when we're set all the way in the back," Aryss grumbled.

"You'll do fine. And this way you can keep an eye on each other."

"You keep saying that," Aryss said, "but you didn't take one of those stalls."

Lokyl turned, paws on his hips. "Fine," he said, "I'll buy the first round. Will that stop your complaining?"

Aryss grinned widely, showing his fangs. "For the first round, at least."

"And you?" The big wolf turned to Coryn.

KYELL GOLD

"I've no complaints," Coryn said. "I'm grateful for your company and advice."

Lokyl shook his head. "You're far too good-natured. All right, come on then. If I'm buying, I'm picking the place, and I say we go to the Maudlin Marten."

He strode forward so quickly that Coryn and Aryss had to hurry to keep up, though there was no danger of losing sight of the ears that stuck up over most of the crowd. "Don't plan on drinking more than he pays for," Aryss told Coryn as they pushed their way past a pair of raccoons. "The Marten is on the expensive side, but Lokyl likes it because nobles go there, and four years ago he talked to one noble who bought some of his wine and now buys two bottles every year. He keeps hoping for another."

"Is it close to the palace?" Coryn asked.

"Not too far, and aye, not too far from the Cathedral, but I'd counsel you to stay with us tonight and save your adventures for tomorrow."

"Why's that?"

Aryss checked ahead to keep an eye on Lokyl. "Do as you like, of course. But if you get arrested, at least tomorrow night you'll have a purse full of tomorrow's earnings to help grease the ropes the police put on you."

Coryn folded his ears back. "I'm not going to get arrested," he said. "The day after tomorrow morning, I'm going to the Cathedral for services and that's all. You said you'd come with me."

"So I will. I'm just advising you in case one tankard fills your head with ideas."

"I'll drink with you and then go sleep—" Coryn paused. "Where do we sleep?" As a cub, he'd slept in the stall, but his father had often been out all night.

"In the stalls, or if you feel confident in your sales, you can take a room at the Wandering Star, right next to the market. It'll cost three coppers, five if you want a meal with it."

"Three copper for a room?" Coryn gaped.

"Welcome to the city," Aryss said, and held open the door of a raucous pub.

The three wolves had to press into a small area without chairs, holding their tankards amid a crowd of bears, raccoons, mice, foxes, weasels, mink, badgers, and probably a couple more species Coryn couldn't see. He had to keep rubbing his nose at the different scents, not to mention the thick scent of the ale and the smoke of the fire.

The other wolves' nostrils flared, but they didn't rub them, and whenever Coryn did, their smiles curved upward a little. Coryn didn't care; he wasn't rubbing his nose out of irritation, but because he wanted to keep inhaling his own scent as a break so that the new scents would be fresh anew and he might catch one he hadn't before. The ale had a strong wheat character, different from the barley wine he was used to, and Aryss and Lokyl pointed out nobles (suspected nobles, at any rate) around the pub, and Coryn took it all in.

He had never been to a pub in Divalia before. Lokyl had been when he was fifteen. Maybe if Coryn's father had taken him to a pub and not left him alone in the market in a rainstorm, the "worst thing" wouldn't have happened.

He stopped at that and stared down at his tankard. And maybe, free of the stress of paying off a debt, his father would still be alive. Ki had often told him not to blame himself for their father's death, but it had been hard for him to listen. Maybe she'd been right. Maybe their father's death had been his own fault, because he'd insisted on continuing to treat Coryn as a cub. Or because he'd insisted on indulging his own appetites while ignoring his cub's desires.

These thoughts emboldened him. Not enough to go up to

one of the nobles, as Lokyl did, and not enough to put his arm around a barmaid's waist, as Aryss did (even had the barmaid been a cute male rabbit—but maybe if she'd been a cute male rat, maybe then).

But emboldened enough that when Aryss and the barmaid went off together, and Lokyl looked to be deep in conversation with the noble, Coryn made his way back to the market himself. And emboldened enough that when he saw a figure in a cloak hurrying down a dark alley that reminded him of the alley Two-Claws had led him down, he hurried after it and called, "Ho! You there!"

The figure didn't stop, so Coryn called, "I'm looking for Two-Claws! Tell him to come to the market, if you know him!"

He stood and watched as the figure disappeared around a corner. His sense of adventure satisfied for the moment, he returned to the market, showed his token to the guards, and curled up under his cloth, dreaming happily of being shaken awake by a familiar paw.

* * *

"Coryn, get up."

He stirred. "Mwuh?"

"Sun'll be up in a few minutes. Get your stall ready."

Coryn rolled over and looked up into Aryss's muzzle. For a moment he'd had the wild thought that Two-Claws had found him, and the minor disappointment of seeing Aryss was followed quickly by crashing shame at his drunken, bold cry in the alley the night before. He'd called for Two-Claws? What did he think was going to happen? That the thief would remember a wolf cub from five years ago, magically be in earshot, and, least likely of all, want to respond? He flattened his ears.

Aryss mistook the reason for the gesture. "I let you sleep as long as I could," he said, sounding mildly annoyed. "That one ale hit you hard, eh?"

"The tankards were big." Coryn rubbed his eyes.

"Head hurt at all?" When Coryn shook his head, Aryss snorted. "Lucky. Oh to be young again. Where did you get off to last night?"

"Just came here." Coryn threw the cloth off and stood, stretching. "What about you? Did you get lost in that barmaid's depths?"

"Hardly." Aryss's tail wagged, though. "She wanted too much coin for that. I had enough to feel the fur of her paw, though. Very soft."

"Good." Coryn uncovered his merchandise and rearranged it where the cloth had disturbed it.

Aryss cleared his throat. "If you want, we can go back tonight and you can have a turn. A paw's a paw, isn't it, and it's interesting to feel someone else's."

"Maybe, thank you," Coryn said. "Did Lokyl secure the exclusive sale of barley to Lord Badger?"

Aryss stifled a laugh. "Not as far as I know. I returned and found him on his second tankard looking for another target. He didn't find one."

"Perhaps tonight, then. Good luck with the market today."

"Aye, you too." The other wolf clasped Coryn's paw and then hurried back to his own stall.

A moment later, the first customers came hurrying down the street. Coryn stayed attentive, and soon enough he was exchanging his wine and bread for coin.

Business stayed steady most of the day, with busy patches and lulls. Some of the customers talked to Coryn about his land or his grain, some asked what he thought of the King's new tax, and others spoke not at all as they held out their coin. At midday, a weasel pushed a small cart full of steaming nuts and sausages through the market, and Coryn gratefully bought some from her.

She came around again as the sun was setting, her stock much depleted, and this time she asked whether he would trade a loaf of his bread for a pair of sausages. He agreed happily; the bread would fetch him two-thirds of what he would have paid for the sausages.

When the sun set, the guards at the entrance to the market rang their bells, causing a flurry of activity as customers made their last purchases. Slowly they cleared out, and Coryn realized that his legs hurt. He sat on the floor of his stall and ate the sausages slowly, savoring them.

Aryss sauntered over, looking around the stall. "Seems you did well enough for yourself," he said.

"Aye," Coryn said around a mouthful. "That brewer Lokyl sent over helped a great deal. Still got a dozen bottles of wine and," he craned his neck to count, "twice that many loaves."

"You'll sell all that tomorrow, even with the short day." Aryss sat at the entrance to the stall and took a small cake out of his pocket. "What did that weasel want with you?"

Coryn perked his ears. "She was selling sausages. Didn't she come to your stall, too?"

"Not her. The one with the brooch." Aryss fluttered fingers at his throat. "Gold, something like a cluster of leaves. I didn't look too closely."

"I don't remember a weasel with a brooch."

"She came to the stall and said she was looking for Coryn from Deverin, and I pointed across the way. You were busy with that bear, but she definitely looked where I pointed and saw you."

Coryn shook his head. "She didn't come over. I don't think I saw a female weasel all afternoon except for the sausage one."

The older wolf frowned, and his ears went back. "Someone

knows your name and wanted to know where you were? That's not good."

There weren't many people in Divalia who knew his name and where he was from. Coryn felt a little thrill. Maybe his call from last night had actually reached Two-Claws' ears. "I'm sure it isn't anything to worry about."

"You don't know the city," Aryss said. "You think it's all grand cathedrals and palaces and such, but there are other elements here as well, dangerous ones. Did your father owe any debts here?"

"I don't think so. Not that I knew, I mean."

Aryss looked around at the stall. "Perhaps you'd best stay with your stall tonight."

"No." He spoke gently but firmly. "I'm not staying here. Even if it doesn't rain."

"Rain? Why would it rain?"

Why would he be thinking about that night and the rain? To remind himself of how disastrous it had been; to continue to excoriate himself for his stupid optimism the night before. "The last time I was here, my father left me at the stall overnight in the rain. I'm not going to sleep here again. I'm going to go out with you two and get another tankard—just one—and I'm going to sleep in a bed."

"If someone's looking for your stall—"

"There are guards. What do I have here that's worth stealing?" Coryn gestured around. "Even if all this was stolen, I've made enough for this trip to be worthwhile." For that to be completely true, he would have to not have a tankard and maybe not sleep in a private room, but it was close enough to true.

The other wolf didn't bring his ears up. "What else happened five years ago? Could someone from that time be looking to settle a debt?"

"The only debt from that adventure is settled." Bringing up

the debt made Coryn feel even more stubborn. He got to his feet as he saw Lokyl walking toward them. "And if someone comes around here looking for me...I'd rather be elsewhere."

"Elsewhere?" Lokyl boomed. "You're coming back to the Marten with us. It's been a good day and I've a mind to spend some of this coin. Nobles or whores, we'll see who's the most eager for my company."

"I can't wait," Coryn said. "Lead on."

Aryss gave him a long look but got to his feet and didn't say anything about the weasel to Lokyl.

The Maudlin Marten proved, if anything, busier than the night before, but Lokyl found them a little space to crowd around in near a group of other canid merchants from the market: two wolves, two foxes, one coyote. They'd barely exchanged three sentences before he said, "Ah, there's that badger again. Just a moment, I'm off to conclude last night's work."

"Chasing the nobles again," one of the foxes said with a laugh.

"He's persistent, I'll give him that," Aryss said. "For his efforts, he gets a bit more coin and a lot of worry, but I suppose it's worthwhile. Me, I'm happy enough to take what the market gives me and spend my leisure time in pursuit of leisure."

"How much more coin does he get from the nobles?" Coryn asked.

The coyote chimed in. "He won't say, but it isn't enough to stop him selling at the market with the rest of us, is it? He likes the prestige of selling to nobles, as though nobles weren't simply people like the rest of us who happened to be born to a better station."

"You talk like someone who has spent time with nobles," a fox scoffed. "As if any of us poor merchants would be given more than a moment or two."

"The king is chosen by the gods," Coryn blurted out, thinking about Lord Barclaw.

The other fox nodded, while the others exchanged looks. Aryss raised his eyebrows and then took a long drink of his ale. "Aye, I suppose he is at that."

Coryn turned to the other wolf to talk privately. "What time should we leave for the services tomorrow? At first bells?"

"If you wait for the first bells, you'll have a seat near the back. I don't mind that, but if you want to be near the front, take a copper to the innkeeper and ask him to come fetch us at Matins, then we'll take the walk over together."

"Which one is the innkeeper?" Coryn peered through the crowd to the bar, behind which a fox and raccoon poured and served drinks.

"Oh, we're not staying here." Aryss laughed. "I mean, you're welcome to if you want to spend another whole silver. No, I know a place near the Cathedral that won't charge but three coppers. We'll be sharing a room, maybe with some others, but I don't imagine you'll object to that."

"No, that's fine," Coryn said. He was going to add that he'd prefer if there weren't others, but then he remembered Aryss saying he didn't want to make their trysts a regular thing. Maybe he shouldn't seem too eager. If there were others, nothing would happen, and if there weren't, maybe still nothing would happen. While they were in the city, Aryss seemed more interested in sampling the variety of lovers available to him than going back to Coryn.

And that was fine. In Coryn's mind, the weasel with the brooch had been sent to find out if he were really who he said he was, and that had rekindled his dreams of being reunited with Two-Claws. Likely the rat would come find him in due course. He had to know how long the market lasted, and he'd come find

Coryn probably tonight or tomorrow night before he had to load up the cart to ride back.

He and Aryss finished their tankards at about the same time, and Lokyl still hadn't returned from his talk. "Come on," the older wolf said. "If we're getting up at Matins, I want to be asleep sooner rather than later."

Aryss led him to an inn called "The Wandering Priest," where indeed three coppers secured them a bed in a large room with two others. For another copper, the innkeeper agreed to wake them at Matins, or at least to have someone do it.

As it happened, the copper had perhaps been unnecessary; when they introduced themselves to the raccoons who occupied the other beds, a father and son, the father told them that they had also paid a copper to be awakened at Matins for the Cathedral's services. "We would've woken you for nothing," he said.

"It's no worry," Coryn said. "This way we're assured of all being awoken. I doubt they'll forget both of us."

"Most of their business relies on waking travelers to see the services." Aryss stretched out on his bed. "They wouldn't forget any of us."

Coryn, too, lay down, but was too excited about seeing the Cathedral to sleep. His mind raced, pulling every scrap of memory together to paint a picture of the building he'd walk into the next morning, anticipating what it would be like.

Divalia was never as quiet as his farm was, and even at night the streets bustled with moderate activity. But up on the second floor of the inn, Coryn felt isolated from the city, here with one snoring companion and the steady breathing of two others. So when a scraping came from outside the window, it stood out among the other noises and his ears perked up.

He lay perfectly still, holding his breath, waiting for the noise to come again so he could pick it out from the snores and breathing around him. But the night remained still and the noise did not come back. No rat appeared at the window.

* * *

In the morning, his first thought was that he'd missed Matins and the services. But then a bell tolled, and footsteps sounded on the stairs outside, and a moment later a plump weasel poked her head in the door. "Wakey wakey," she called. "Matins has rung."

She was gone before anyone could respond, but Coryn was up and pulling on his trousers and shirt while the rest rubbed sleep from their eyes. "All right, all right," Aryss grumbled as Coryn paced by the door. "We've plenty of time."

Their first view of the Cathedral was as a great dark shape looming forbidding in front of the palace. Not even the gold spire shone in the darkness. Coryn searched out the statue of Rodenta that should have stood on the side facing him, but he might as well have looked for her form in the clouds that covered the moon.

A crowd of people already waited at the front of the Cathedral, and those Coryn could smell before he could see them. "Are we too late?" he asked Aryss in a low voice.

"Let's see when we round the corner," the older wolf said.

So Coryn hurried to the corner—a gentle corner, not a sharp one, because the Cathedral had six sides—and poked his head around it. There before the immense double doors of the Cathedral stood a crowd of some fifty people of all species.

"There's so many of them," he complained when Aryss caught up to him.

"Not so many when you divide by six," Aryss pointed out.

Coryn looked more closely at the crowd and saw that indeed, they were divided into Houses as neatly as if someone had put up barriers. The raccoons and bears stood to the far right, mice and rabbits to the far left, and between them stood wolves and foxes, weasels and skunks, deer and elk, and a small cluster of bobcats and lynx. "There's only a dozen canids," Coryn said, and ran for that group, seeing a pair of coyotes also approaching them.

Aryss laughed, taking his time, and joined Coryn ahead of the two coyotes, who also seemed amused at Coryn's haste. They introduced themselves as Alyssa and Mariana. "First time?" Mariana asked.

"Essentially," Aryss replied. "He snuck into the Cathedral as a youth but hasn't been to a proper service yet."

"Ah," Alyssa replied, "it's a grand sight. We live not too far from here and whenever we have an excuse to come into the city, we make sure to spend a Gaiaday here."

"What do you do?" Coryn asked.

"We're weavers. We live in Lord Pancher's court and make all the clothes for their family, and sometimes we come down here to sell our wares. And you?"

"Barley farmers from Deverin," Aryss answered. "We only get to the city once or twice a year."

"So," Mariana said, "how did you come to sneak into the Cathedral? Wanted to be a thief in your youth?"

Alyssa slipped a paw around Mariana's waist. "Our son did," she said. "He was forever raiding the kitchen and showing us what he'd gotten away with."

"Only," Mariana continued with a smile, "the cook would come at the end of the week and present us with a full accounting of it."

"He was so embarrassed, years later, when we showed him."

Aryss gave a sideways look at Coryn. "Such seems to be the lot of many of those who want to be thieves."

"So what happened?" Mariana asked. "Go on, tell us?"

"Oh," Coryn said, "it was many years ago, but..." He looked up the walls of the Cathedral and felt a rush of pride. "I climbed up to the top and slipped in a window there."

Both coyotes gaped. "By yourself?"

It was a better story if he'd done it by himself, but less believable. Aryss didn't know there had been someone else, but then again, Coryn had never told his version of the story before. "No," he admitted. "I...followed someone. A thief."

Aryss's ears went up, while the coyotes' ears went back slightly. "Did you steal anything?" Mariana asked.

"No!" Coryn said quickly. "I wanted to go inside, but my father wasn't going to let me. This—thief—said he could show me. So we went inside and dried off. It was raining."

"And then he was caught, as naked as Canis made him." Aryss guffawed. "Can you imagine?"

"I took off my clothes because they were wet," Coryn said. "The thief's clothes dried faster and he left first."

"Poor boy!" Alyssa reached out to stroke his arm. "I suppose that's what you get for consorting with thieves. Think about how much worse it could have been, though."

"And," Mariana added, ears coming up now she'd learned that Coryn hadn't stolen anything, "you got a good story out of it. You climbed this wall? I couldn't imagine."

"The follies of youth," Alyssa agreed, looking up.

Following their gazes, Coryn could hardly believe he'd done it. At any point, he might have fallen and died. But he had, he really had.

Aryss, beside him, looked up as well. His laughter had died down, the smile replaced with a thoughtful look. "I don't think you get enough credit for that part of the story. I'd thought you went in through one of the side doors."

"And it was raining?" Mariana asked. "Canis must have been watching over you, surely."

"I will remember to thank him this morning," Coryn said, "as I do every week."

This was a little bit of a lie. In the first year after his misadventure, he had complained to Canis more than thanked him. But he had slowly come around to understanding that there had been good as well as bad, and that there continued to be good in his life.

They asked about the coyotes' weaving trade with an eye to perhaps exchanging goods, and Alyssa said that they didn't need very many things, but politely agreed to come by and look at their barley wine. They talked about the weather and the harvest; weather was much less important to the weavers, who bought wool and flax threads and spun them into garments, but they did use some plants to dye their fabric, and the important ones they grew themselves, so they had some experience in common. And Coryn enjoyed hearing how they would design and create their garments.

By this time, the sun had risen and the gold spire atop the Cathedral glowed brightly, as did the gold reliefs elsewhere. This side, facing the palace, shone more brightly than any of the others (Mariana told them) so that the nobles lucky enough to look out over the Cathedral could see its glory every morning.

As she was saying this, bells tolled loudly enough to make some of the cubs in the crowd cry. Everyone who had been sitting on the street got up, and a murmur of anticipation went through the crowd. Coryn bounced back and forth on the balls of his feet until Aryss laughed at him. "Steady on there," the older wolf said. "We'll all get in."

Behind them, the crowd almost filled the great open square, numbering in the hundreds by Coryn's count. His tail wagged and he turned back to look again at the front of the Cathedral: on the stone of the archway were carved likenesses of many of the great kings of Tephos, arms raised to hold up the church.

And inside the archway sat two great wooden doors, whose carved reliefs he could now make out clearly: all six of the gods, their First Children, and Gaia at the center blessing all.

He'd never seen the carvings up close before and now took a moment to marvel at them. The Cathedral had stood for hundreds of years, and the paws that had shaped these likenesses were long dead. But their creations remained to inspire him and everyone in the crowd, everyone who passed through these doors every day of every year.

Did Aryss feel the same about them? He didn't get a chance to ask, because at that moment the great wooden doors creaked open.

A cool rush of air swept out over them. Coryn and many others craned their necks to see through the doors into a space that looked dark at first, and then glowed with the daylight streaming through stained glass windows. The two people who pushed open the doors were a fox and a rabbit, both clad in white robes, and behind them stood a similarly white-clad bear, arms outstretched. "Welcome to the Great Cathedral of Divalia," she said. "Please enter respectfully and find your House. Services will begin when everyone is seated."

Though people all around Coryn had crowded impatiently to the opening of the doors, everyone walked through into the coolness of the Cathedral slowly and reverently. Coryn looked up and all over as he entered, ears and nose twitching to catch every scent and sound of the great building. Each of the six pillars of the Cathedral formed an arch with its opposite number, and all three arches met in the middle of the domed ceiling, covered with frescoes of the six gods surrounding Gaia, a beatific figure in robes with tan fur, a tail that could have belonged to any or none of them, and a bright golden sun for a face.

"Come on," Aryss said. "You want a close seat, right?"

"Yes." Coryn followed the other wolf and the two coyotes to the fourth row in front of a pulpit decorated with a relief of Canis showing his children the Path, pointing to his nose to tell them how to remember it. Once seated, Coryn's eyes kept flicking around to admire the stained glass windows, which showed stories from each of the six books. They reached from ten feet above the floor all the way to the walkways that ran around the upper reaches of the cathedral.

His ears folded back. Up there, on one of those walkways, he'd peered down at the congregation five years ago. How could he have thought he would be hidden? Any movement up there would draw the eye, any flicker of shadow even. So far up and yet so exposed. He would have been better off down here, among the crowd. Though that would have been more difficult without his clothes.

An old wolf climbed into the pulpit in front of them and opened a large book. The crowd quieted all around the Cathedral, not just in the Canis section. Some murmurs still reached Coryn's ears, which came back up as anticipation thrilled through him. He knew their cantor well back home, knew what to expect, but here he might get deeper wisdom, closer to Gaia. The wolf's outfit looked identical to the Doubleford cantor's, if perhaps the white robe was less thread-bare, the symbol of Canis on the front embroidered rather than sewn on.

"Welcome, all my children."

The female voice startled him. The wolf hadn't spoken, but stood with head bowed and paws together reverently. Coryn lifted his eyes and there, above the wolf and facing away from them, a bear stood with her paws raised. Her white robe bore gold trim that gleamed in the glass-colored light, and though she stood well above Coryn, he could make out the symbols of three of the Houses on the back of the robe; the others must be on the front. "May Gaia's blessing be upon you," she said.

"Thank you, Mother," the congregation murmured. The wolf in the pulpit joined them in this response.

"Remember that I love you all." Her voice rang throughout the large stone building, seeming to amplify and echo. "Today we remember the lesson Gaia spoke to her six children which She called 'The Care of Each Other.'"

They did not get this lesson often in Doubleford, being mostly wolves there, but Coryn knew it as well as any of Gaia's lessons. He listened raptly to the bear's melodic voice go through the text of the lesson, turning every so often so that she faced all six of the Houses in turn. When she had finished the text, she paused and then went on. "Just as six columns hold up this great building, so do all six houses work together to hold up the throne and the country. We must all help each other, regardless of species, for if even one of the columns of this cathedral were to crumble, all of it would come down."

As the echoes of the words died away, Coryn felt the weight of the stone over him. How did it all stay up? Only through the efforts of all of them working together.

"Now please attend to the words of your cantor and may you go forth from this place with Gaia's blessing."

All six of the cantors—at least, the three that Coryn could see, the wolf in front of him and the bear to his right and the lynx to his left—lifted their heads. Six voices sounded, but the cathedral's design elevated the wolf's words above the others. "Welcome, children of Canis," he said.

His voice didn't resonate through the cathedral the way the bear's had, but his quiet steadiness filled Coryn with peace. He did not tell a story from the book of Canis, but in the spirit of the lesson, a story from the book of Rodenta about the necessity of being thrifty. Coryn had never heard the story and listened, rapt, until the wolf closed the sermon with the instruction that all of them could learn from listening to their neighbors.

"Hmph," Mariana said in a low voice. Her words were directed at Alyssa, but Coryn, sitting just beyond them, heard well enough. "I'd rather hear from our book, not another."

"I know," Alyssa replied, and then turned to direct her answer more toward her partner, and he didn't hear the rest.

"I like it," he said in a low voice. "I never get to hear those other books, so it's nice to know."

"You can read them, but they're not for you," Mariana said.

"They're for everyone," Coryn insisted. "Or else we'd just get the Book of Canis and not the Book of Gaia." That had been what the bear's sermon was about, hadn't it? How they all had to learn from each other?

Mariana gave him an appraising look, but the cantor was asking them all to join him in song, so the argument died in the joyful notes of the Song of the Pack. The other Houses all sang their songs at the same time, and at the end the bear reappeared above the others and led them all in the First Song.

After that, the bear smiled out at the congregation. "Go forth, children of Gaia. But on your way out, if you would, greet someone from another House. Introduce yourself."

Mariana and Alyssa had no intention of doing so, it was clear. They stayed close to Aryss and Coryn as the four canids left the cathedral. Coryn, though, looked through the crowd of pointed ears and long muzzles for different species, and his heart jumped when he spotted a family of rats making their way out behind the canids. "Wait a moment," he said to Aryss. "I'm going to go introduce myself to those rats."

He left without waiting for an answer, pushing through the crowd. The rats weren't Two-Claws, none of them were, but that didn't matter. This might make up for his indiscretion and foolish action. Rodenta would look kindly on him and would no doubt forgive him. This encounter with rats in the Cathedral was how Canis and Rodenta wanted him to behave.

The tallest rat looked up in mild surprise as Coryn approached them. The wolf clasped his paws together and bowed. "I'm Coryn," he said.

"Hello." The rat bowed back. "I'm Oric, and this is my wife Pella." He didn't introduce the two kits, and the kits seemed thoroughly uninterested in Coryn.

"It's nice to meet you," Coryn said. "Gaia go with you."

"Gaia go with you," the adults replied.

Coryn made his way back in the direction of Aryss, although it took him twice as long to find his friend again. The coyotes had left them, gone to their business for the day, but Aryss said they had promised to visit the market and say hello.

"You're not hoping to bed them tonight," Coryn stated flatly. "Even I noticed—"

"That they're with each other, yes, pup, I know. They were good company, and it's always good to make friends, especially friends in service to a lord, you see?"

"Ah, yes." Coryn fell in step beside the older wolf. "I hope they do come visit."

Aryss waggled his paw. "I'd say it's a coin's flip chance. But we tried, didn't we?"

"Aye, that we did."

The older wolf gave him a long grin. "Did you find what you sought?"

"Yes," Coryn said. "Well, perhaps. I wanted to feel closer to Canis and I got that."

"I don't believe you sought only that." Aryss guided them down a less busy street. "Not that it's any business of mine, but if it were, I would counsel you to seek out new experiences rather than revisiting old. The old are never what you remember and will never change."

Coryn could have corrected the older wolf, could have told him that this new experience was about replacing the old so he could leave it behind, but he let Aryss think he was dispensing wisdom. The other wolf's comment had scratched at doubts Coryn had; could he really be leaving behind his past when only the night before last he'd called out to it?

It was all very well for Aryss to talk about not dwelling on the past. What had he done that would be worth dwelling on? He'd inherited a farm, worked on it his whole life, married a local wolf, and had a daughter. He'd never climbed the Great Cathedral at night in the rain, never sneaked into a noble's window to steal enough silver to feed the whole town of Doubleford for years, never had a secret tryst in a dusty store-room that smelled of ancient stone and reverence. He'd never been left behind with more questions than answers.

That train of thought led Coryn back down a road he didn't want to travel. Aryss might not have had the same experiences, but he was right: the past should be left in the past. No matter what Coryn felt, he knew that was right. So he kept his muzzle shut and followed Aryss back to the market. He had one more day here, and then he would go home to change his life.

CHAPTER 3

Aryss set a brisk pace through Divalia back to the market. Coryn lagged behind as he tried to fix in his memory the grandeur of the Great Cathedral and the service he'd just heard, the smells and sights of the statues and frescoes, the feel of the wooden bench, the warmth of the people around him.

They'd gotten about halfway back when Aryss said, "Lots of guards out today."

"Huh?" Coryn stopped and took stock of his surroundings. Past the crowd that surrounded them on the street, raised voices made their way to his ears. A cluster of uniformed guards stood in front of a large ornate building with a sign over the door proclaiming it the "Grain Merchant Exchange," and around the guards a looser crowd gawked.

Coryn's ears lay back, the shame and humiliation of his arrest flooding back into him as he saw the red uniforms. Not that the guards who'd arrested him had been anything but polite; in fact, if not for his father, they probably would have let him go. He curled his tail between his legs.

"Wonder what's going on." Aryss made for the crowd.

Coryn hunched his shoulders. "I'll see you back at the market,' he said. "I'll keep an eye on your booth."

The older wolf paused and then said, "You know your way?" When Coryn nodded, he said, "All right," and split off through the crowd.

The way wasn't hard to find: down this main street until he saw the blue coats of the guards—not the city guards, the ones hired by the Merchants' Guild—and the market was just beyond them. He showed his badge and they let him through with the warning that the market would be opening at the sounding of Terce from the Cathedral, which would happen "shortly."

"Thanks," Coryn said, and walked down to his stall. On the way he passed a merchant selling cloth who had a nice bolt of blue flax that he thought Ki might like, so he spent a few minutes haggling to trade some wine for it and returned to his stall feeling pleased with himself. The market hadn't opened by that time, so once he'd uncovered his goods, he went over to Aryss's stall and uncovered the other wolf's goods as well.

Aryss arrived with the first wave of customers filling the street with scent and sound and activity. Coryn wanted to ask what the guards had been investigating but had to hurry back to his own stall.

Gaiaday passed even more quickly than Herbiday had. The crowds were about the same, but on the second day, more of them wanted to haggle for bargains, so they took more time. In the middle of the day, a porcupine from the brewery that Lokyl knew came to Coryn's stall and spent several minutes with him working out a deal for the remaining sacks of barley.

That set Coryn at ease for the rest of the day, because it meant that he'd be coming home with a handsome profit, even after his nights at the inn. He set aside one bottle of barley wine to celebrate with that night and sold almost all the rest of his stock by the time the guards announced that the market would be ending with the sounding of Vespers at sunset.

Only after he'd counted everything and leaned over the front of his stall to see how Aryss was doing did he remember the weasel from the previous day. Nobody in a cloak had come by the stall, he was sure of it. When Aryss came over, Coryn asked, "Did you see that person in the cloak again?"

The older wolf shook his head. "Nay, not all day. Don't worry!" He clapped a paw on Coryn's shoulder. "If it was a thief, you've already sold everything. Precious little here to steal. Come, let's find Lokyl and celebrate."

"You did well too, then?"

Aryss laughed. "I did, and if we did, you can bet Lokyl did. Come on."

Coryn picked up the bottle of wine, but Aryss said, "Leave it. We'll get better at the public-house."

And indeed, when they came up to Lokyl's nearly-empty stall, the big wolf greeted them with slaps on the back. "Such a successful market! I did so well with my broken stall, you must have done better with yours."

They hadn't, but Aryss gave Coryn a knowing look and a smile, so the two of them nodded and let Lokyl sweep them along down the marketplace. "How was the service at the Cathedral?" he asked.

"Glorious," Coryn said promptly.

"Everything you imagined?"

"Oh, aye."

Lokyl turned to Aryss and winked broadly. "Did he keep his pants on this time?"

"It was a lovely service," Aryss said. "Bit dry, but we got to see the Gaiavox as well."

"Oh, aye, that's a true blessing." Lokyl made the sign of Canis with his paw over his chest. "And it seems her blessing made a difference today. The brewer's never needed so much barley. He says people are drinking more ale than ever."

"Then let's go add to that amount," Aryss said.

"You two are welcome to go," Lokyl said. "I've worked hard enough the last two nights and I've enough coin now that I'm going to go down to the Velvet Harbor."

"Say, that's not a bad idea." Aryss stroked his whiskers back. "They've good ale there as well. What say you, lad?"

"I'll go with you," Coryn said. "But I may sample only the ales."

Lokyl peered down at him. "They might have boys as well."

"Still," Coryn said.

"Don't pester the lad," Aryss said. "He knows his mind."

So they left the market, and the blue-coated guards reminded Coryn of that morning. "What were the guards about?" he asked Aryss.

"Something had been stolen," the other replied. "A fox next to me said it was a gold necklace, a beaver said it was gold coins. The guards were talking to a well-dressed bear about it."

A bear. Surely not the one Coryn had stolen from; that house was in the other direction. Still, his fur prickled, and he kept thinking about it all the way down the main street, the short winding street, and the long narrow street, all the way to the fragrant flower garden in front of the two-story wooden house with a painting of a large-breasted female cougar sitting naked in what appeared to be a sea as a ship sailed up between her legs.

"There are a lot of flowers," Coryn said.

Lokyl pointed up at the second-story windows. "Some brothels' rooms have no windows, or give out onto an alley, but these face the street, so the flowers mask whatever other smells might come from those rooms." He laughed. "Personally, I like being able to look over the lady's shoulder and see the people below going about their business."

"I like privacy, myself," Aryss said.

They passed through the thick smell of several different species of flowers, most of which Coryn did not know the name of, and entered a plushly appointed parlor, with velvet wallpaper and slightly worn couches upholstered in the same velvet fabric. A round porcupine stood over one of the couches, talking to a male mouse in a fancy blue and red waistcoat, but came over to the three of them as soon as they entered.

"Welcome, gents," she said, "and safe harbor to you. What's your pleasure tonight?"

"Two of us," Lokyl gestured to himself and Aryss, "would like something to wet our lips, and something else to wet our cocks. The third will have a drink and make up his mind about the other."

The porcupine let her eyes linger on Coryn, her smile remaining large. "I'm sure we can find something for all of you on both counts. Why don't you take a seat over here and Charika will bring your drinks. Ales all around?"

"Please," Lokyl said, and led the others over to the couch she'd indicated, at the far side of the room.

The ales were fine, though Coryn had enjoyed the ones at the public-house better. But Lokyl and Aryss drank them up and he didn't think they'd tasted them at all. "Do you know the girls here?" Aryss asked the big wolf.

"It's been six months," he said. "I don't know if Lila is still here, but if she is, she's fantastic."

"What is she?"

"Cougar."

"Mmm." Aryss leaned back. "I was hoping for a smaller species this time. Rabbit, maybe, or mouse."

"They have a good variety here. Clean, too."

The porcupine came back over right around the time their tankards were empty. "We have two ladies free for you gentlemen," she said. "I believe I heard one of you mention Lila the cougar. She'll be available later. Right now we have Adma, she's a mink, and Juna, she's a deer. Either of those appeal or would you like to wait?"

Lokyl laced his paws behind his head. "I believe I'll wait for Lila if that's all right."

"I'm happy to take the company of the mink." Aryss got to his feet. "What was her name, Adma?"

"That's right." The porcupine took his tankard and his paw. "Come on back now and we'll get you set up."

"Say, madam." Lokyl sat up, his eyes on Coryn. "Have you any boys here?"

She followed his look. "Oh, not tonight we don't. Lodi isn't working. Come back next week though."

"Ah, shame," Lokyl said as she led Aryss away. "If you want a girl, I'll put in for it. So you don't have to spend full coin. Maybe you'll like it."

Coryn splayed his ears. "I've been with girls," he said. "I liked it fine. You have fun with Lila. I'm going to take a walk."

He walked out through the flower garden with very little idea of where he was going to go. He liked the inn where they'd spent the previous night, but he didn't feel tired yet. Perhaps just a look at the Cathedral at night again. The flush of the morning's services had worn off to the point that he now wasn't sure he'd truly felt closer to Canis or Gaia. What was more, going back to the Cathedral and seeing it for what it was should have gotten rid of his childish fantasies about what it had meant to him, but they remained, lurking and occasionally surfacing in his thoughts. If he visited the Cathedral at night, maybe that would show him that there was nothing to his fantasies. There'd be no rat there, that was sure.

He walked in that direction, and then his ears perked to a low rushing noise, faint beneath the steps and murmurs of the people on the street. The river wasn't too far away. That was where Two-Claws had taken him to sell the things they'd stolen, to a boat under the Palace Bridge. Maybe the thieves who'd stolen something important this morning were down there. Maybe one of them was a rat he knew. No, that was ridiculous. But he didn't have any other destination in mind, and it was the sort of thing a responsible citizen might do. (Wasn't it?) If he could find out something useful about the theft, that was a good reason to go down to the river. (Wasn't it?)

The wind was blowing toward the river, so he couldn't smell it until right before he saw it opening up before him. He approached it along a street between a large bridge and a stair-case down to the river itself, and a number of people ambled back and forth along the street, some of them looking out over the dark expanse of the river to the glimmering lights on the other side.

Coryn walked to the stairs and hesitated before going down. A squirrel touched his arm, a merchant by the look of him, with a nicely woven tunic and voluminous trousers. He smelled of tea and perfume. "Excuse me," he said. "Only it's very dangerous down there. Cutthroats, you know?"

"Oh," Coryn said. "Thank you."

"I know you're a big wolf," the squirrel replied, "but they form gangs. Three or four of them would have your purse and maybe your life."

"I've been down there," he said. "I mean, I know some of the people—"

The squirrel drew back from him. Coryn finished lamely, "I mean, I can take care of myself."

"Your business is your own." The squirrel looked him up and

down, maybe reappraising his low-quality tunic, and then hurried on his way.

Nobody else tried to stop him. Coryn walked down the stairs slowly into the darkness, nose lifted. Down here, the miasma of the river overwhelmed everything. If he could stand to breathe it in, he could catch traces of other scents, but very few of those scents were helpful. Gold didn't have a scent, and he didn't know any of the thieves, especially the one who might have stolen something that morning.

He couldn't see very far down the river, but he remembered that the houseboat had been near the Palace Bridge. But which way was it? Under the bridge and onward, or the other way? He thought the Palace lay beyond the nearer bridge, so he padded along the bank.

His nose kept him alert. No other scents of people came to him as he walked under the bridge and out the other side. The footsteps of people above him pattered like rain, reminding him of the last time he'd been down here by the river. Now he was returning by himself, grown up now.

The next bridge he encountered, grand and ornate, had to be the Palace Bridge. He hurried his pace as he drew close to it, then slowed, worried about scaring away anyone who might be lurking there. As quietly as he could, he crept closer to the impenetrable darkness under the great stone structure.

A scrape from up ahead froze him in his tracks. The smells of the river washed over him, but no other smells penetrated the miasma. The light splashing of the water sounded to his right, but there was no creaking of wood or anything else that sounded like a houseboat. The feet above him weren't loud enough to mask another scrape like the one he was sure he'd heard.

What was he thinking, coming down here by himself? Coryn leaned against the rough stone wall, ears still perked. The scraping noise didn't come again, but it had made him realize what he'd walked into. He really was being a fool. Did he seriously think that a rat thief in Divalia would be waiting around for some wolf barely out of cubhood for five years?

Embarrassment lowered his tail and ears. His paw dropped to his side and brushed his purse, and that perked his ears up again. He was carrying most of the coin he'd earned over these two days. All it would take was one encounter with a cutpurse for him to lose everything he'd made.

He turned and made for the nearest stairs, heart hammering at his chest, ears swept back to listen for anyone pursuing him. Twice he stopped, sure that he'd heard that scrape again, but the night remained silent around him.

Finally he rejoined the crowds on the street, and with one paw on his purse, he made directly for the inn. They gave him a shared room and dinner, which he ate by himself before going up and lying down on one of the hay-stuffed beds. He felt young and foolish all over again. If his romantic fantasies escaped once in a while back home, that was perhaps a few minutes crying in the stable. But here, he'd walked into a dangerous area, fooling himself that it was for smart reasons when really he was still chasing adventure. No more. He was finished with that fantasy and with this city.

He'd made good coin this weekend, he'd gone to the Cathedral and seen a service. Perhaps in a few years, when his wheat farm produced enough, he would return to the market and visit the Cathedral again, if he missed its grandeur and the inspiration it had given him. Perhaps he would meet Lokyl and Aryss here and they would point him to a brothel where he could have a fun night with a boy he didn't know or even a girl, a fox or a deer or a badger or even a rat, just a nice night with no worry about other people finding out, or paying back a debt, or anything like that.

Because that was all he'd been to Two-Claws. He'd been a brothel boy that the rat hadn't had to pay for. He'd been wet and miserable in the market at night and the rat had rescued him from a night of boredom, taken him on adventures that had grown in his mind (though not climbing the Cathedral; if anything, he had forgotten how long that had taken and how scary it was because what had happened afterwards had been so special), and then had left him to his own devices in the upstairs room of the Great Cathedral. There had been no romance there.

* * *

Morning found his good humor somewhat returned. It didn't matter that a light rain slickened the streets and thickened the air; he was waking up in Divalia and yes, he had to return home today, but he felt Canis would bless their journey.

At the stable, his cart was the only one left, so he collected it, gave Elly some treats and saw that she'd been well cared for, and drove back to the market. At the entrance to the market, he showed his token to the goat guard and asked, "When do I collect back my silver piece?"

"On your way out," the guard told him. "You're with the other wolves, the big one and the old one? Best hurry; they came back half an hour ago."

"Oh! Thank you." Coryn hurried Elly down the crowded market street, dodging merchants who were already driving their carts out, past Lokyl's empty stall to the end where Aryss sat on a loaded cart.

"Ho there," Aryss said. "Lokyl's gone on ahead, but he'll wait for us outside the gates. He was impatient to be quit of the city."

"Dipped his cock in everything and now he's done with it?" Coryn grinned.

Aryss laughed. "Did you find a nice boy last night?"

"No, I—" Coryn hefted a sack of bread into the cart. "Went to the Five Coins, had dinner, fell asleep."

"We wondered, when you didn't arrive early."

"Next trip, perhaps."

"Aye, just tell us. We can point you to one or two likely places."

Coryn smiled and set to placing his last two bottles of wine in the back, but stopped partway through, lifting his nose. He thought he caught the smell of rat in the air, damp fur sharpening the scent even through the light rain. Nothing moved in any of the stalls around him, though, nothing but Aryss watching him and the merchants three stalls down finishing up their own loading. Perhaps it was just a residual scent thrown by the breeze, or it could be his imagination. No, he told himself. You've left Two-Claws behind; he's not going to appear here as you're loading the cart.

When everything was loaded, he threw the oilskin cloth over all of it, pleased at how little there was to cover, and then prepared to climb up to the driver's perch. He hadn't even lifted a foot when a noise like a clatter came from behind Aryss's cart. Both wolves perked their ears. "You heard that?" Aryss asked.

"Aye." Coryn walked around his cart and across the street to get a better look.

From the driver's perch, Aryss looked down. "Can't see anything here."

"Nor here." Coryn scanned the area and sniffed. "Maybe something the rain loosened."

"Or the wind blew in." Aryss settled back into his seat. "Come on, let's be on our way."

Coryn walked around the back of his cart, checking the oilcloth again. It looked slightly different, though he couldn't put his finger on how. The bulge of the sacks of barley was the same, though. He reached underneath it to feel the two bottles of wine, and there they were.

"Let's go!" Aryss called.

Coryn lifted the edge of the oilcloth enough to see Ki's blue fabric underneath the wine. If that was still there, he didn't care as much what someone else might have taken. He climbed up and urged Elly to follow the other cart out of the market.

They recovered their silver pieces at the market office and then made their way slowly to the city gates. The rain slowed all the traffic to a crawl, carts clogging the streets and inching along as though the thick smell of wet fur were dragging on their wheels. So when they passed a bakery, Aryss jumped down, trusting Coryn to mind his cart, and brought them back meat pies to eat while they waited, as well as another set for dinner that night.

The glimmer of the sun—as best they could see behind the scattered clouds—was halfway up the sky by the time Coryn and Aryss met the bear guards at the city gates, who gave their carts a cursory look and a sniff. One of them wrinkled his nose. "Smells like rat on your carts. You seen any this morning?"

"Many of them," Aryss said, waving back to the streets. "We noticed the smell too. Figured one was skulking around the carts. Nothing was missing, though."

"One behaving like a fugitive," the bear said. He lifted a corner of the oilcloth on Aryss's cart, barely looked under it, then moved to Coryn's. "There's a thief wanted by the guard, only he's given them the slip, see. You packed these up yourselves, did you?"

"Aye," Coryn said.

The other guard, on the other side, waved them to go on. The first guard lifted a corner of the oilcloth on Coryn's cart and let it fall again. "Right. Be on your way and good journey. Canis keep you."

"Ursus keep you as well," Coryn said, trying not to show too much interest at the mention of a rat thief. There had to be many; it couldn't be Two-Claws every time. Maybe he'd been lurking around the market earlier, looking for Coryn?

That had been earlier; now the market was gone, and the carts trundled down the muddy path through the shabby wooden houses outside the city walls. Coryn remembered his resolve to look toward his future and kept an eye on the road ahead as the noises of the city faded behind him.

Lokyl met them a little way down the road, sheltered beneath the boughs of a great pine tree. "Have you got enough to stay in an inn?" Lokyl called back as he drove his cart onto the road ahead of them.

Both Coryn and Aryss replied that they did, so the big wolf called, "Let's have the dinner at the Phoenix, then. They make a curry that's almost better than the lovelies who serve it to you."

"Sounds delightful," Aryss said, and Coryn agreed.

But when they reached the inn, they had to tie up their mounts and carts a good fifty yards away because there was no room anywhere closer. "This bodes ill," Lokyl said, but they trudged the distance to the inn anyway.

Sure enough, as they approached they saw two groups of wolves eating from steaming bowls outside under the meager shelter of the roof's overhang, obviously unable to find seating inside. And when they entered the sturdy two-story wood building beneath the red-and-gold painted sign, they found a room packed with wolves and scattered other species. "There's only one road to the Three Provinces," Lokyl said glumly.

"We could still get the curry and eat it outside," Coryn said. "And sleep on the road as we did before."

"Don't see as we have another choice," Lokyl said. "All right, well, we'll save some coin anyway."

The curry was as delicious as advertised, maybe more so in

the cool evening air with the rain pattering down just beyond the corner of the overhang the three wolves squeezed under. The spice burned Coryn's tongue but didn't linger, and the meat was tender and fatty. Big chunks of parsnip and turnip helped dull the fire of the spice and vary the texture of the meal.

When they'd finished, they returned the bowls and then walked back to their carts. At least the rain had let up by then, but the ground was still wet enough that Coryn's paws were heavy and caked with mud when he got back to the cart.

"We'll go a little down the road," Lokyl said. "Get away from the inn."

"Shouldn't we stay closer?" Coryn asked. "Nearer people?"

"Thieves look in carts parked near the inn. If we stay out in the middle of nowhere and keep our carts close together, it'll be harder for bandits or thieves to find us. And if they do, they might not bother with a group like us."

Coryn wasn't sure about the logic, but Lokyl was certain and Aryss wasn't arguing, and the two of them had more experience than he did. So he followed them down the road and off it far enough to be concealed behind a stand of trees. They pulled the carts around each other and tied up the mounts inside, and then each of them walked around to the backs of their carts to curl up and sleep.

Lokyl and Aryss went to sleep quickly, but Coryn wanted to get some of the mud off his feet and he could hear a stream nearby, so he took a short walk in that direction. The stream was cold, but he got most of the mud out from between his pads and toes.

Back at their camp, he walked by Aryss's cart to see if the older wolf were awake, but he was nothing but a shape under the oilcloth. So Coryn climbed into the back of his cart and lifted the cloth there.

The smell of rat emerged again. He registered it and then a

paw seized his muzzle and held it shut as a thin body pressed up against him out of the darkness under the cloth. "Don't yell," a voice hissed in his ear, breath stale. "You don't want to give away your old pal Two-Claws, do you?"

Coryn froze, his heart thudding against his ribs. The gaunt fingers held his muzzle tightly, and their claws pressed into the soft flesh around his lips. Slowly, he shook his head.

"Good," the voice said. "Now stay there and let me get a look at you."

Coryn sat very still as the rat pulled the cloth aside. The scant light from the cloud-covered sky was enough for Coryn to make out the rat's pointed muzzle and rounded ears, one of which bore a large tear in it. The tunic he wore was dirty and patched, and the small bag he held at his side was in no better shape. His dark eyes gleamed in the night, and so did his claws, but nothing else; he did not appear to be holding a weapon.

"Well," the rat said. "You do look a treat. It's been years, eh?"

"Five years." Coryn swallowed. "Is it really you?"

The rat spread his arms wide. "In the flesh."

"I called for you."

"I know. Word got back to me." Fangs showed with the rat's smile.

Coryn's eyes traveled over the thin body and restless tail. "I...I never thought I'd see you again."

"Ay, same. Coryn of..." He snapped his fingers. "My memory fails me, I'm afraid. Somewhere to the south, though."

"Doubleford, in Deverin." Coryn's throat was dry, though he'd drunk at the stream.

"Doubleford! That was it." The rat's smile was not exactly inspiring; it looked more as though he was eyeing a tasty meal than a former lover.

"But—" All around him were his bottles of wine, Ki's blue cloth, a few loaves of bread, his oilcloth, his cart. The figure of the rat thief in the middle of all this did not jibe. "I went to try to find you last night. By the river. The houseboat."

"Ah, of course, old Moneybags. He got fitted for a nice pair of iron bracelets couple years back and now we mostly go to a weasel in an attic of a building I won't say no more about." His whiskers rose with his smile. "But you remembered the boat. That's good."

"I remember more than that. I remember..." Coryn twisted his paws around each other.

"Heh heh." The rat reached down to the bottom of his tunic and rubbed there. "I remember that too."

Coryn had many questions, but one burst to the forefront. "Why did you wait until I was leaving to find me?"

Two-Claws sat back and curled his skinny tail around himself. "Ah, truth be told, I had some affairs to put in order. One can't just go on a journey at the drop of a hat, can one?"

"You mean to come all the way to Doubleford? You could've seen me in Divalia."

"I could have, but then you might not have wanted to bring me back to Doubleford. And I've, ah, I've had enough of the city, as it happens. Canis and Rodenta must ha' conspired to bring you back to Divalia just at the time I was thinking I'd be well quit of the place. I've a mind to spend some time on a farm, and I thought to meself, wouldn't it be grand if young Coryn came back and could bring me to such a place?"

"I—what? I can't bring you to town. Everyone knows everyone there. How will I explain it?"

"Say you hired me to help on the farm. I'll do it, too. Might be I don't know what to do, but I'm a quick study, and if you've clothes that need mending, my fingers are nimble enough for that."

"There's nothing to steal there. People aren't rich like in the city."

Two-Claws laughed. "I well know what I'm leaving behind and riding toward."

"I don't know..." Coryn sighed. "I wish you'd asked me in Divalia. I would've said to wait, and we could figure out a better way for you to come to Doubleford."

"Ay, well." The rat grinned. "That's why I dinna ask you in Divalia."

* * *

It could be terribly confusing getting what one wanted, Coryn reflected the following morning as they set off again. For two days he'd wandered Divalia remembering his adventure and trying—unsuccessfully—not to think about a rat thief, and now that thief was curled up in the back of his cart. His mind flew not to the chaste night they'd spent together in the cart, nor the steamier night they'd spent in the Great Cathedral, but rather to how he would explain Two-Claws to Ki, where the rat would stay, whether the skinny, light-fingered thief could actually do farm work to earn his keep, whether he would expect to do farm work, and even whether he would come to services with them on Gaiaday.

Above all, his mind kept returning to his doubts. He had tried to push all his romantic fantasies out of his mind, but here was the rat giving them life again. No; Two-Claws had taken advantage of him five years ago and no doubt was again. Coryn was a convenient escape at a time when the rat needed one. It had probably been him the guards were looking for. That's why he didn't want to wait.

Still, Coryn hadn't thrown the rat out of his cart—how could he, this far from the city? Even though he knew that was part of the calculation, why Two-Claws had hidden in his cart rather than approaching him directly. As a thief he was used to subterfuge and taking what he wanted rather than being up front about it. Coryn had to understand that. Canis said that if you despised people for treading off the path rather than showing them how to get back on it, you were liable to slip off the path yourself. Perhaps this was a test from Canis, a stray to bring back to the path.

He followed Aryss and Lokyl down the road, keeping his thoughts to himself even when they launched into the barmaid song again. "Ho," Aryss called back, "Coryn, going to give us some of your verses? I don't remember how they go."

"Oh, aye," he said, but it took him a moment to remember, and he sang them half-heartedly.

"Tired out from his adventures," Lokyl boomed back. "I wager he's done more than he's telling us."

"He can keep his adventures to himself," Aryss said. "But if he discovered a new inn or brothel, he'd tell us, I'm sure."

"I didn't," Coryn said, and now he was wondering what Aryss and Lokyl would say at the appearance of a new rat on his farm, especially one that spoke with a noticeable Divalia accent. At least they didn't know that the thief from five years ago had been a rat, though they were clever enough to put that together if they learned that Two-Claws had been a thief. The rat would be done with thieving now, though; Coryn would make him promise that.

That led him down a path: could he make the rat give up his old vocation? He could not. But, he reasoned, the rat wouldn't be coming to Doubleford if he wanted to continue thieving. There was nothing of value in that town, not more than you could find in any one block of Divalia. There was perhaps a silver chalice in the church, but nobody in the farming town was what you could call wealthy. Even Berkys, whose family owned two large farms, showed his wealth in his half-dozen mounts and his fancy Gaiaday clothes. What a rat would do with moderately nice clothes and a half-dozen mounts, even if Two-Claws were able to steal them, Coryn couldn't imagine.

So perhaps Two-Claws was ready to make a change. He held on to that hope through the day, and when they passed an inn and Lokyl asked if they wanted to try again, Coryn said, "Ah, let's just pull off the road. It was quieter and we've got enough food to get us through a night."

"He's worried about spending coin," Lokyl observed to Aryss as they rode on forward. "How expensive was this place you found, Coryn?"

"Perhaps one day I'll tell you," he said, heart thumping.

They found a small clearing near a stream and pulled the carts around in a circle as they had the previous night. They all went to wash and get water from the stream, where Coryn drank his fill and then filled the waterskin again.

As casually as he could, he lifted the edge of the oilcloth and slid the waterskin under it as he retrieved his dinner. The three of them sat around on their carts eating dried meat and barley bread while Coryn tried to pretend that the low sounds of drinking from his cart were nothing more than the burbling of the stream.

They hadn't told Lokyl about the services at the Cathedral, not in detail, so Aryss and Coryn took it in turn to tell him about the coyotes they'd met, the pastor, and the Gaiavox. Coryn enjoyed remembering the service and went on at length about the grandeur of the Cathedral, all the scents inside it and the history and the feeling of being close to Canis, enough so that when he ran out of breath, Lokyl laughed.

"You've convinced me," he said. "Next trip I'll attend the services with you both. Better to go in the front than in the side, eh?"

Coryn glanced down at the cloth in his cart, but it didn't

shift. If Two-Claws was listening, he didn't react at all. "It was much easier," he said, and that got a guffaw out of Lokyl.

As the sky darkened and the stars brightened, their conversation turned to the nobles of Divalia—mostly Lokyl telling them about the two he'd talked to and not secured any kind of deal with—and then to the brothel the previous night. Lokyl had enjoyed reacquainting himself with Lila, while Aryss praised the mink's talents but said that her scent distracted him.

"And tomorrow," Lokyl said, "it's back home to the wife and the fields."

"Aye." Aryss stretched. "The city's nice, but only for a short stay."

"Not much to be done until spring, though," Coryn said. "Mostly church and repairs, some hunting and baking."

"And teaching," Lokyl said. "Cubs are at that age."

"Oh aye. Lucy will be going to school for the first time this winter."

"Cabi can show her around."

"Mm." Coryn didn't want to rebuff Lokyl's offer, but couldn't accept it in light of Ki's objection, so he remained noncommittal.

Aryss stretched. "It's been a nice journey," he said, "so let's get our rest and be ready for tomorrow. Canis grant us the fine weather to make it quick."

"Canis grant it," Coryn and Lokyl murmured in response as all three wolves settled into the backs of their carts.

Coryn waited until he couldn't hear any movement from the other two carts and then lifted the cloth over his goods, breathing in the thick scent of rat. A skinny paw reached out to his arm. "Thanks for the water," Two-Claws whispered.

"Do you have food?" Coryn whispered back.

"Aye, brought some with me. Don't need much."

Coryn scooted under the cloth, closer to the rat. Scent and warmth enveloped him. "Hope the ride wasn't too bad."

"Heh. 'Twas no worse'n I expected. Poked me nose out for air now and again. Is it always so sweet out here?"

He couldn't see the rat's expression under the dark cloth. "Yes."

"Mmm. Nice. Could get used to this." As the rat said those words, his paw slid along Coryn's side to his stomach and rested there.

"So I thought," Coryn breathed, "that I'll go directly to the farm, and when those two are out of sight, you come ride with me up front and I'll introduce you to my sister. You're a—a Divalian who was asking for work around the market, and you said you'd work cheap, so I brought you back to the farm to work with us. You—do want to work, don't you?"

"I'm quit of the city," Two-Claws said. "I'll be happy to stay with you and if I have to work then I'll work. Just show me what to do."

The rat had changed a little in five years. Coryn remembered him being assertive—though he had snuck onto the cart, and there might well be more to his departure from the city than he was letting on. "There won't be a lot to do, but we can find work for you until the spring. You can stay in the stable with Elly. It's sheltered and warm there."

"Who's Elly?"

"My mount. The one pulling the cart."

"Ah," the rat breathed, and his paw inched lower. "I was rather hoping to share a warmer bed."

Coryn gulped, his sheath warming, and then he froze at the creak of another cart outside. "Shh, shh!"

Both of them kept very still as a wolf stepped to the ground and then padded over to Coryn's cart so quietly that if he weren't listening, he probably wouldn't have heard, and if he were asleep—like Lokyl audibly was—he wouldn't have been awakened.

He patted the rat and slid out from under the paw with some regret, sliding to the back of his cart right as Aryss's head poked over it. "Ah," the other wolf said softly, "you heard me. That mean you're..."

"Ah," Coryn breathed.

Aryss's nostrils flared, and he looked up. "Is that...a rat?"

"Oh," Coryn gulped and made a show of sniffing around. "It's still that scent from when we loaded. I think maybe there was a rat sleeping in the cart at the stable."

"Huh." The older wolf shook his head. "Those stables are usually better than that. Doesn't matter." He started climbing into Coryn's cart.

Coryn grabbed the older wolf's arm. "Wait," he said.

Aryss stopped with one leg over the back of the cart. "What?"

There was no way Coryn could tell him that he didn't want to have sex here because of the rat in his cart, and he was aroused enough from his contact with the rat that he'd already hesitated too long. The other wolf leaned in. "You worried about the noise? Lokyl didn't wake before, so why should he now?"

"I'm surprised you're interested, that's all," Coryn said. "I mean, you spent last night, er, the night before last, with—a mink, was it?"

Aryss climbed nimbly over the back and dropped to a soft landing, barely making the cart creak. "Aye, but I like the smell of a wolf and, truth be told, I enjoy a nice length in my muzzle as much as a muzzle on my length." He pushed his pants down. "And you didn't visit a brothel, so I suspect you're as eager as I am."

When Coryn didn't move, Aryss tilted his head. "If you're not in the right mood, I understand. I'd thought you were quite eager, though. Did I misread?"

If his goal was to keep Aryss from being suspicious, Coryn

realized he was not doing a very good job. And he did want to get off, more so now that he was staring at Aryss's sheath and the cock sliding out of it, and anyway, if he refused and went back under the tarp with Two-Claws, Aryss was awake now and would probably hear them.

He pushed his pants down as well. Aryss grinned at Coryn's erection. "Ah, I didn't think I had."

They sat down away from the oilcloth. Aryss pushed Coryn back first, bending his head down to take Coryn into his warm muzzle.

The older wolf had been right; this was welcome. It had been days since their tryst on the journey up to Divalia, and Coryn had been pent up remembering his adventure with Two-Claws anyway. Now, with the rat so close his scent lingered in Coryn's nose, it was easy to close his eyes and imagine the rat's muzzle was the one drawing his arousal up and up, the rat's tongue sliding along him, rubbing up around his tip. When the strokes pulled him over the top and his body shuddered, the mouth he emptied himself into was the rat's, at least until he opened his eyes and looked into Aryss's long satisfied smile.

"My turn," the older wolf said, and sat back, legs spread, his erection standing tall with the knot already swollen.

So Coryn, trying not to think about the rat lying just a few feet away and listening to everything, knelt and took Aryss's shaft into his muzzle. Here he couldn't imagine that he was with Two-Claws, at least not as easily, because the wolf's shaft was thick against his tongue and tasted strongly of wolf. He didn't need to be thinking of anyone in particular to do well at this task, though, so by the time Aryss gulped and bucked and coated Coryn's tongue with musk and warmth, Coryn was well pleased to be helping his friend reach release.

He swallowed, lifted his muzzle, and sat up. Aryss, leaning back on his elbows, panted and stared up at the night sky.

"Smells like we'll have nice weather for the ride back tomorrow," he said.

"Aye." Coryn pulled up his pants and sat with his back against the side of the cart, arms folded over his knees. "Would be nice."

"And then back to life." Aryss rubbed a paw down his thigh. "Coat's coming in already. Soon enough there will be snow."

"And the Winter Festival," Coryn said. But that was two months away, and he'd likely be on his new farm by then.

"Ah, I'm too old for that." Aryss laughed. "But you young pups enjoy it." He got to his feet and pulled his pants up, patting the bulge of his sheath. "Perhaps the evening of the carnival I'll see if you've a few minutes to spare."

Coryn nodded. "I'm certain I will," he said, and then cursed himself for being too eager. But Aryss smiled, and after all, Coryn had been eager in Divalia, too, and that hadn't stopped the older wolf from visiting him tonight.

He waited until Aryss had climbed over the cart and dropped to the ground, padded back to his own cart, and gotten in, and then Coryn waited another several minutes. From where he was, he couldn't hear Aryss's breathing, only Lokyl's snoring, so he didn't know for sure when Aryss had fallen asleep, but after he judged that enough time had passed, he crept back under the cloth.

Two-Claws lay there still, his breath silent. Coryn reached out a paw, but before he could touch the thin body, fingers seized his wrist and the rat's eyes flew open.

"Wasn't sure you'd be coming back," Two-Claws whispered. "Sounds like you had a good night's entertainment already."

Coryn's ears burned and flattened against his head. "Aryss— one of the other wolves—he likes to maybe take some time of an evening."

"Not my place to question," the rat said. "An' I can wait a day or two to reacquaint myself with that body."

"Okay." Coryn still wasn't sure how he was going to explain Two-Claws to Ki and Lucy, but he couldn't leave the rat on the side of the road, nor did he want to drop him in Doubleford and allow him to fend for himself.

"Heard you making up stories for the other," the rat said softly. "You've a thief's quickness in your mind, if not your paws."

That brought Coryn's ears up against the cloth and gave his tail a shiver of a wag. "Thank you. I don't have much opportunity to exercise it."

"Keep your tools sharp, that's what they say." The rat lay his head against Coryn's shoulder. "Couldn't sleep much in the cart, so I'm going to go now. You staying here?"

This time, the rat was sure to be there when he woke up. "I'm not going anywhere," Coryn said.

He drifted off to sleep, woke with a jerk that also awoke the rat, and then tried to settle back to sleep, but he kept thinking about what would happen if Aryss or Lokyl came to the cart to wake him in the morning. What if they threw the cloth off and found Two-Claws there pressed against him?

So Coryn kept checking the light outside the cloth, sleeping for short periods of time, and finally when he peeked out he saw what he thought was a glimmer of dawn. He slid out from under the cloth (Two-Claws stayed asleep this time) and stood in the back of his cart.

Dawn was likely another hour away, and both the other wolves remained asleep. Coryn hopped lightly out of his cart and risked a quick walk to the stream to get a drink and rub the cold water around his eyes and muzzle.

He hurried back, but he needn't have worried; Aryss and Lokyl remained asleep for another half hour. Coryn spent the time sorting out what food he had left and leaving half of it under the cloth for Two-Claws to find when he woke up. Then he went to sit against Elly and stroked her scales until the mount turned her great head to blink at him through sleepy slit-pupiled eyes.

As he had on the journey to the city, Aryss gave no indication that anything had passed between him and Coryn the previous night. He and Lokyl also went to the stream to drink and relieve themselves, so Coryn hitched up their mounts to the carts and took the opportunity to check on Two-Claws.

The rat woke quickly at Coryn's touch. "I left you food," the wolf said. "We should be on the road for half the day and then we'll get home. I was thinking that I'd let you out a little before the farm and you can walk up after, like you came from the town."

"Why?" Two-Claws fixed his eyes on Coryn. "You 'shamed of me?"

"I—no, it'll just be easier to explain. If you show up in the cart with me, how will I explain how Lokyl and Aryss didn't see you?"

"Why d'you have to? Just say you let me ride in your cart. Did they look in your cart?"

"Aryss did, last night."

"Didn't look under the cloth, did he?"

Coryn huffed. "No, but..."

"Listen." The rat grinned at him. "I know you think 'cause I'm a thief that I take to lies like an otter to water. But lies are like fleas. If you don't keep 'em under control they get all over you until you can't think of anything else. Best to stick as close to the truth as y'can, and also don't lie down with someone who's got lies all over him." The rat scratched at his hip. "Or fleas. But I'm clean, I promise."

The others were on their way back, rustling through the

undergrowth. Coryn sighed. "All right," he said, and let the cloth fall.

The last part of the journey passed with little event, unless you counted Lokyl spotting something shiny on the path and coming up with a leather strap with a brass buckle on the end. "I'll wager someone threw this out," he said, rubbing the torn end. "Thought it wouldn't be useful. But look at that leather. It's good quality!"

"A nice find." Aryss turned back to Coryn and met his smile. Neither of them would have stopped for a piece of garbage on the road, but Lokyl liked to turn refuse into crafts.

Coryn spent much of the time thinking about what he would do when he got home. Logically, he should take Two-Claws and go off to Lord Barclaw's place, accept his offer, and start a life on that farm with the rat. It made the most sense. But as that decision drew nearer, he found himself reluctant to make it. Part of him had been resigned to a life as Lord Barclaw's prostitute (more or less) as a punishment of sorts for his foolish belief in romance. This trip to Divalia was supposed to have quenched the last embers of that belief so that he could do what was best for his family. Instead, the object of his romance sat, improbably but undeniably, in the back of his cart returning home with him.

If he brought Two-Claws to Lord Barclaw's farm, how would the rat feel about Coryn's obligations to the lord? How would Coryn feel about them? With the rat as a companion, Coryn now saw a future where he could turn away Lord Barclaw's offer —while at the same time, a part of his mind that sounded awfully like his father warned him not to get too comfortable, that a thief was always a thief, that good things were not fated to happen to him.

His father had undoubtedly spoken more than a few words on the ride home five years ago, but the only ones Coryn remembered came when they had left the city gates behind. "I raised you to know better than to keep that kind of company," he'd said. And then he'd waited, as though Coryn could give him a reason for his behavior. But Coryn hadn't had any.

Nor did he have any now, except that Two-Claws needed him, and Canis taught that one should always offer help where needed. Unless, he remembered, that help would pull one off the path—there was the parable of the Stray Fox to remember. There wasn't any temptation in Doubleford, though, no chance for Two-Claws to pull Coryn off Canis's path. And anyway he would be alert for that. He wouldn't make the same mistakes he had five years ago.

At the crossroads where they'd met, Lokyl and Aryss were to continue on south while Coryn took the smaller road back to his farm. All three got down from their carts to embrace. "A good journey," Lokyl said. "I hope you'll join us in the spring as well."

"I'd like to," Coryn replied, turning to embrace Aryss even as he wondered where he would be come spring.

"You're welcome anytime," the older wolf said with a slight smile meant only for Coryn.

"See you on Gaiaday," Coryn said, waving as he hurried back to his cart.

"Aye, unless you'd like me to bring Cabi over to play with Lucy," Lokyl called.

"I'll ask Ki," Coryn promised.

Fifteen minutes down the road, he pulled Elly to a stop again at a patch of grass that she quite willingly bent to graze. Nobody else was on the road, and when Coryn perked his ears and turned his head, the only sound in any direction came from the leaves rustling and the birds in the wood. Finally he turned. "You can come out," he said to the cloth in the back of his cart.

For two seconds, nothing happened. Had Two-Claws run out on him again? But then the cloth rustled, and the rat's pointed muzzle appeared at the edge, followed soon by the rat himself.

He stood in the back of the cart and dusted himself off. In the sunlight he looked even scruffier than Coryn had remembered, his tunic torn and stained in several places. One ear had a sizable chunk missing from it, and a white-furred scar ran down over the eye on the same side. At least his fur, though dirty, looked healthy.

Two-Claws spread his arms out under Coryn's gaze. "Here I am," he said. "Like what you see?"

Coryn touched his ear. "Did you get that in a fight?"

"Oh, aye." The rat scrambled over the cloth to join Coryn up on the driving-board. "No end of fights among thieves, but they stop at scars and disfigurement." He settled himself and winked. "You should see the other fellow."

"So what do we tell my sister when we get to the farm?"

"Sister, eh?" The rat leaned back as Coryn urged Elly to finish her snack and get back on the road. "No wife? Woulda thought a strapping young wolf like you would be married off."

"Not yet," Coryn said. It didn't seem very polite to explain why right at this moment, so he added, "Ki—that's my sister—has a daughter, Lucy. The father isn't around anymore."

"Ah. Shame, that." Two-Claws closed his eyes and breathed in the sun. "Have you told her 'bout our little history?"

"She knows that I got in trouble in Divalia." Coryn chose his words carefully. "But I don't think I mentioned your name." He hadn't told the name to anyone. "I might have mentioned that you were a rat."

"All right." The rat scratched along his scar. "You mind her knowing?"

Coryn exhaled. "She won't be happy. But...probably better not to keep a secret. Like you said."

"Aye. Smallest o' lies then. I got into a spot o' trouble in the city and remembered that sweet young wolf from Doubleford. Got a ride from a wolf heading farther along, left me in

Doubleford. I asked about and found my way here, and you picked me up on the cart."

The wolf picked up a stray barley stem—the things found their way all over the cart—and chewed on it. "Who did you ask in Doubleford? Everyone knows everyone."

"Who might I have asked?"

"It doesn't matter; Ki might well ask them when we go in to church." He sighed. "Maybe it would be best if you actually went into town and asked and then came out to the farm on your own."

"Or," the rat said, "we might have met in the city and you kept me well hid all the way home so as not to have to explain to your friends."

"I suppose that might work," Coryn admitted.

Two-Claws laced his paws behind his head. "I like that one seeing as how it means I don't need to move."

Coryn turned it over in his head. "All right," he said. "I think it will work."

"Course it'll work. People don't wanna think. Give 'em something that hangs together an' they won't poke at it none."

"You don't know Ki," Coryn said.

"Ah. Snooping type, is she?"

"Not necessarily. Just smart. Lucy is the snooping type."

"Lucy's the daughter?"

"Aye."

Two-Claws nodded. "I like cubs. Lookin' forward to meeting her."

"Okay." He hoped Lucy would like the rat. "We farm barley, and we've already done the harvest, so there's not much to do over the winter months. We'll bake bread—Ki did a lot of that for the market already—and sort through the seeds for spring planting, and the storehouse needs some repairs. A storm damaged the roof this summer. Ki's been wanting to keep chickens, and Lucy's old enough now to help, so I was going to build a coop this winter." If, he reminded himself, he was still here in the winter.

"I'm good with my paws. Never built nothin' but I'm a quick study."

"And there's not much in the way of valuables. Most of the gold in town is in the church, and you wouldn't steal from the church."

"Not this one," Two-Claws said without opening his eyes. "You don't have to keep tellin' me there's no valuables here. I told you, Rodenta told me to find a new trail to follow and I'm done with thievery."

Privately, Coryn wondered at this. Two-Claws was older than he was and had been thieving longer. If someone had told Coryn to stop being a barley farmer and take up...a merchant trade on a ship, maybe, or even being a thief, would he be able to do it? Then again, if he felt it was Canis who'd told him, if he'd received the message in that Great Cathedral with the eyes of the Six on him and the Gaiavox herself speaking...as he was thinking about this charge to take on the rat...then aye, he could see it. "How old are you?"

The rat cracked open one eye to look at him. "Old enough to know better and young enough to earn my keep."

Coryn's ears folded back, embarrassed that he'd asked such a personal question. "There aren't many rats in Doubleford. I don't know of any others, in fact."

"Why would I need other rats?"

Having grown up around mostly wolves, Coryn didn't know how to answer this question. "For—for companionship?"

"Ay, well, assuming your friend from last night don't make a habit of visiting," the rat rested a paw high on Coryn's thigh, "I'll have all the companionship I'm likely to need."

That brought the wolf's ears up again. This wasn't an

obscure sign from Canis in need of interpretation; this was a clear signal. It didn't mean romance, he reminded himself, only sex, but that was enough for now. "I'd be, uh, glad to renew our acquaintance," he said.

Two-Claws closed his eyes and laughed, a clean sound with some sharpness in it. "That a fancy way of saying you're happy to rub sheaths with me? I'm hoping your taste hasn't changed much."

"Not much as far as I know."

"What," the rat said with a sly grin, "never felt the touch of your own muzzle?"

"Oh—not in years." Coryn flushed again, this time in plea-sure, as he took the rat's double meaning.

"S'pose you're not as limber as you used to be. I hear farm life is rough on a body."

"I haven't had any complaints," Coryn said.

"Ooh-ho." The rat's eyes opened again. "So you've kept your bed warm. Don't worry, I won't claim you nor get in your way."

"It's not like that." Coryn guided Elly around a curve, taking the fork that led to his farm. "There hasn't been anyone here in a couple years."

"I thought you hadn't been back to the city since our adventure."

"A few times, but with my father and he wouldn't let me out of his sight." The wolf breathed in. "Smell that?"

Two-Claws wrinkled his nose. "Smells like rot."

"Fermentation. Barley wine. We make it throughout the fall, until we run out."

"Smells like ale."

"It's more like ale than like wine from grapes, but we call it barley wine."

"I'm looking forward to sampling it."

"We've plenty."

They crested a hill, and up ahead of them rose the familiar frames of the storehouse, the stable, and the house. Behind them stretched the fields, both harvested and fallow. Coryn smiled and his tail wagged, and he stretched out his arm. "There it is," he said. "Home."

"Home," echoed Two-Claws, sitting up now with his eyes fully open.

CHAPTER 4

They'd barely gotten halfway to the stable when Lucy came running out of the house. "Uncle!" she called. "And Elly!"

The mount pulled up, huffing and arching her neck as the wolf cub ran up to her and ran paws over the scales of her head. "Did you have a good journey?"

The last part of that word trailed off as Lucy spotted Two-Claws sitting next to Coryn. Her paw stopped and her eyes grew huge. The rat stood and executed a bow, harder than it looked on the thin driving-board. "Good day, young lass. My name's Clement, and how might I have the honor of callin' you?"

The cub's eyes went to Coryn, who hid his surprise at the false name behind a smile. "It's all right. He's a friend of mine."

"I'm Lucy," the cub said.

"Lucy! What a delightful name. Am I right in thinkin' you're the one this mount..." The rat turned to Coryn. "Elly was her name, was it? You're the one Elly looks to for comfort?"

"I give her treats sometimes." At that moment, Elly pushed her great head against Lucy's paw and made the grunting noise that meant she was impatient. Lucy set to rubbing the scales again.

"I see she likes your attentions better than Coryn's here. He hasn't rubbed her face the whole time we've been traveling."

Lucy's ears came up and her tail wagged. "She likes this spot right here." Her claws worked behind the jaw.

"Did you bring a treat for her?" Two-Claws asked.

"No. I heard the cart and came running out." Back at the house, Ki appeared in the doorway, relaxed, but straightening as she spotted the rat.

"Run back to the house and get a treat and meet us in the stable," Coryn said. "We'll unhitch the cart, and you can take care of Elly while we unload."

"All right!" Lucy kissed the scaly nose and got a huff in return, and then she turned and ran back to the house.

Coryn urged Elly toward the stables. "'Clement'?" he asked softly.

"Occurred to me that should anyone from the city come askin' after Two-Claws, might be best if fewer people know that name. Don't fret, I won't forget it."

"All right." They pulled up outside the storehouse. "Get down now and go around to that other side." Two-Claws obeyed him, and Coryn jumped down as well. "You'll find a knot where the leather fastens to her harness, and then goes and loops through the cart. Don't unfasten the knot, but follow that leather strap to the harness." As he spoke, his fingers traced the motions. "And there you'll find four buckles that cinch the harness. We only want to undo the topmost and bottommost one." He unfastened them quickly, and Two-Claws, to his credit, was not too far behind. "Now I'll lead Elly to the stables. You start bringing whatever's in the cart to the storehouse." He paused and then added, "If you please."

The rat peered at him over Elly's back. "If I'm to work for

you, prob'ly best you don't ask me 'if you please,'" he said. "I know my place here, at least while the sun's up."

Coryn nodded and led Elly toward the small stable while Two-Claws—or maybe he should start thinking of him as Clement?—pulled the oilcloth from the back of the cart and took a bottle of barley wine into the storehouse.

He got Elly into her stall and gave her a pile of grass to eat. As he was opening the satchel hanging to one side to see if any mealworms were left, footsteps sounded behind him, but Ki's scent rather than Lucy's came to him on the breeze. "Hired some help in the city, did you? Or is this one of my suitors?"

"His name's Clement," Coryn said. He wanted to go on with the story they'd planned, but the truth of his adventure weighed on him. How would Ki react if she knew that this was the rat who'd cost them so much?

"And?" She came to stand near him. "There's no mealworms. I thought we'd run to get some from Molyna when you got back."

He let the flap of the satchel drop closed. "He's—he's the rat I met five years ago."

Ki's ears went up and her eyes widened. "Him?"

Coryn nodded. "But it wasn't his fault, what happened. I was young, I didn't understand really—anyway, he found me at the market and remembered me and said he got in some trouble in the city and wanted to get away for a bit. Asked if he could come stay here through the winter."

"No." His sister folded her arms as her ears went back.

"I told you, it's not his fault. And you even said that what happened—"

"I don't care about what happened five years ago. The debt is paid, it's done, we have our lives the way they are. What kind of trouble did he get into in the city?"

Coryn blinked. "Oh. I—he didn't say. But he's a thief, so I assume—"

"What if it's something really valuable, something that they'll send guards after? Who saw him talking to you in Divalia?"

"Nobody." That, he was confident about. "I didn't even know he was in my cart until we were outside the city. I mean—he approached me outside the city."

Ki shook her head. "He hid himself in your cart?"

"Curse it," Coryn swore. "Yes, but—I said he could."

"So you did talk to him in the city."

"No, I—" He leaned against the wall. "I went looking for him," he admitted. "But I didn't find him. He heard about it and hid in my cart so I wouldn't be lying if the guards asked about him."

"And did they?" Ki asked.

Coryn flattened his ears. "They asked about a rat thief. I assume there's more than one in the city."

"Oh, Coryn." Ki looked out of the stable. "You understand why he can't stay, right?"

"I've already told him he can," he said.

"You're not the only one on this farm. There's Lucy to think about."

"I know," Coryn said. "But—"

"No buts. I won't put my daughter in danger."

When she got that tone, it was very difficult to argue with Ki. "Can he at least stay the night and we can talk about it in the morning?"

She looked steadily at him. "Fine. He is helping to unload, after all."

"All right." Coryn tapped the satchel. "Maybe I'll take him over to Molyna's to bring some wine for another bag of meal-worms. Have we the bag of bran to take?"

"It's there beside the satchel, and yes, that would probably be for the best." Ki's ears came up and her tone softened. "I'm sorry, Coryn. You seem excited about seeing him again. Maybe he can find a place on another farm."

"Nobody's going to be hiring now the harvest is over."

"So why should we be?"

"I thought he could help with some of the work I'd planned to do over the winter." He pointed up to where light shone through cracks in the roof of the stable. "See, even this roof was damaged. I was going to fix the storehouse roof and I don't know if I'll get to this one. He could help build a chicken coop, or...or..."

Ki shook her head. "We can hire people to do those things."

"He'd work for less money. Maybe no money, just a roof and meals."

"And what does a *thief* from Divalia know about carpentry? Don't you think it more likely that we wake up one morning and he's gone along with all our money?"

"He wouldn't do that," Coryn said, suppressing the 'again' in his mind.

"How do you know? You knew him for one night five years ago. Even if he were completely trustworthy then, does a trustworthy person hide in a cart rather than ask directly? You've no idea how he could have changed from the rat you met."

"For the better, I hope," Coryn said. "I'm older and wiser—I know, maybe not wise, but wis*er*. And I think he is too. Wiser, I mean. He's definitely older."

"If he stays around here, you can still see him," Ki said.

Coryn folded his arms. "What if I don't stay around here?"

His sister lay her ears back. "What does that mean? Where would you go?"

The words had just come out, and now Coryn had to

backpedal. "I—If you find a suitor," he said, "and get married, and he comes to live here—he wouldn't want me around."

She glared at him. "And so you'd leave and go where? Go be a thief in Divalia? You can't leave," she said before he could answer. "Lucy looks up to you."

He waited for her to say that she'd miss him as well, and her ears did splay out and her eyes softened. She opened her mouth and then her ears perked up. "Where is Lucy? She was going to come back and see Elly."

They looked at each other and then both hurried for the door, Coryn a step behind Ki. The cart sat empty in front of the storehouse, the whole farm quiet. Both wolves perked their ears and lifted their noses to the wind, but it was blowing in from the fields and brought no trace of either rat or wolf cub.

"There, you've got it," a soft voice said from the storehouse, and Lucy gave a small yip in response. Before either Coryn or Ki could move, Lucy burst out from the storehouse.

"Mommy!" she called, and when she spotted Ki, ran directly to her holding out a short piece of rope. "Look! Clement taught me to tie a hitch! Now I can take Elly for walks and tie her up!"

Ki took the rope as the rat strolled out of the storehouse, gave Coryn a smile, and leaned against the door frame. "That's a sturdy knot," Ki said, and turned to the rat. "I don't know this one."

"Ah, we teach it to our young'uns in the city. It's not a simple knot but 'tis easier if you have a sharp mind and your fingers haven't yet caught up." He bowed. "My name's Clement, ma'am, and I'm very grateful to be made welcome to your farm."

"Mommy!" Lucy tugged at Ki's skirt. "Clement says he can fix our clock and he can show me how to fix clocks too!"

Ki lowered the rope and laughed, bringing Lucy to her side. "You're a farmer, not a clockmaker."

"Simple repairs, ma'am." Clement bowed again. "Handy if

someone's thrown out a clock because they don't know how to fix it. Works with other mechanisms as well."

"That is interesting." Ki gave the rope back to Lucy. "I think Coryn has an errand to run with you. We will see you back here for dinner."

Clement watched Ki herd Lucy back to the house. "Do we ride to this place or walk?"

"We could ride, but Elly's had a hard couple days and besides, the longer we're away from Ki the better." Coryn walked into the stable to get the satchel and the large sack of bran. "Can you fetch two bottles of barley wine?"

"Oh aye." Clement disappeared and then emerged from the storehouse as Coryn slung the satchel over his shoulder. The rat held out both bottles, no doubt intending to put them into the dirty mealworm satchel, but Coryn took one and left him the other. The rat didn't ask, just tucked the bottle into the crook of one arm and hustled along at the wolf's side down the road. "She didn't seem to take a shine to me, that's for sure."

"She says you can stay the night, but then you have to leave tomorrow."

"Hang on." The skinny rat placed a paw on Coryn's arm. "My memory might be playin' tricks on me but I do remember a pair of balls between your legs. Ain't you the head of household here?"

"Technically I guess our father left the farm to me, but—Ki's worried about Lucy."

"What," Clement scoffed, "like I'll teach her to take to thievin'? Don't worry, I ain't here for that nohow."

"No. She's worried that someone will come from Divalia looking for you."

The rat fell silent, and by the time he spoke again, the farm was well out of sight behind them. "Few years back I woulda said there's no chance of that. Lost a couple friends since then, realized there's always a chance of things you wouldn'ta predicted. I'd say I gave the guards no shadow to chase, but... there's a chance, sure."

"What did you steal?" Coryn asked, eyeing the rat's skinny frame and threadbare clothes. "It can't be very big."

"Who says I brought it with me?" Clement grinned at him.

"Fine," Coryn said. "Keep your secrets."

"Oh, Cor." The rat's grin widened. "The less you know, the less you can tell anyone who might come 'round. I'll tell you this: I didn't bring it with me. It's hid safe in the city, and there's no-one likely to find it without me telling them where to look."

"Why steal it if you didn't want to keep it or sell it?" Coryn asked, trying not to wag his tail at the short familiar name the rat had called him and the friendship it implied.

The rat laughed. "Why did you climb up the side of the Cathedral? Had you always a yearning to risk your life? Or was there a burning desire to see the inside and not wait for daybreak?"

"You told me to."

"Aye, there you go. Sometimes you do things an' it's not about the thing itself."

Coryn nodded. "I suppose it doesn't matter as long as the guards don't follow you to Doubleford."

"Don't see how they could, but maybe once they've failed to find me in the city, they'll send people out to all the surrounding towns. Don't see why they'd waste their time doing that, but even so, that should be weeks if not months."

Coryn trudged over the ground and kicked a small cluster of fallen leaves. "Don't worry, though. If she won't let you stay, I'll go with you."

"Won't come to that," the rat said cheerfully. "Won't have you kicked out of yer own home."

"I might have—" Coryn stopped. "There might be—I mean, we can find another place to go."

Clement looked sharply at him. "What other place?"

"Oh, I just, I have some relatives over in Oncit," Coryn grasped at the name of the province on the other side of Deverin from Barclaw, "and they have a farm, and we might be able to work there."

"Still," Clement said. "Not your direct family. Your sister and niece seem to like you, leastways far as I could tell from a few minutes."

"They do, but." Coryn shrugged. "If I have to leave, I have to leave."

"Your sister can manage the farm?"

"She'll find someone to marry." Coryn tucked his tail between his legs.

Clement thought about that for several steps and then said, "Let's see it don't come to that, ey? How can I set her mind at ease?"

Coryn had been projecting fantasies of running off with the rat, fantasies that were satisfying in one respect, but he felt a wash of relief at the prospect that he might not have to leave Ki and Lucy yet. "You could just tell her what you told me."

The rat stroked his whiskers. "Aye, perhaps in part, but I feel it's better not to lean so hard on the thievery angle of it all, not with your sister, eh?"

"Maybe that's true." Coryn sighed. "What else can you do? Around a farm, I mean. Can you really repair clocks?"

"Aye, I'm good with mechanisms. I wasn't lying about that." The rat grinned. "It's a bad lie that's easily found out."

They walked on through low brush and trees bare of most of their leaves and came to a crossroads. "That way," Coryn pointed to the left, "goes to the main town. It's another half hour walk perhaps."

"What lies in the fair town of Doubleford?" Clement asked.

"The church, of course. A general store, a public-house and public stable, and an office for Lord Deverin's tax collector and other officials."

"Tax collector? When do you pay your taxes?"

"Around midwinter, once the harvest is all in and we've sold what we're going to sell. Then again in midsummer when we know what the spring planting will yield. Speaking of that, I should do all our accounts in the next two weeks to see what we owe. Sometimes we can pay in goods, but we haven't much left this year."

"Surely that's a good thing?"

"Oh aye," Coryn said. "The market did quite well for us this year, and in the spring as well."

"And now you've a willing soul to work your farm for free rather than pay, you can keep more of that coin." The rat perked his ears. "Perhaps this is the angle to take with your sister."

"I presume we're going to feed you as well," Coryn said with a grin.

"A scrap of food, a roof to sleep under, I can make do with very little." The rat put his free paw to his slender waist. "Been practicing my whole life."

"We'll give you more than scraps."

"Have to prove myself useful first." They walked on a little, and then Clement said, "What if I could help Lucy with somethin'? She took a likin' to me."

"She knows her way around the farm well enough. She'll be taking schooling from the teacher in town—oh, the school is in town as well—anyway, she'll be learning her letters and such there."

Clement tapped the wine bottle thoughtfully. "I won't say as I know much about schools, but is anyone teaching her such things as bargaining to get the best price?"

"Mostly around here we deal with people we know, so we don't do a lot of that," Coryn said.

"Ah, so neither you nor your sister would be any good at it, I presume." The rat smiled. "Not casting shadows! If you've no call for it, there's no reason to be good at it. I'd have no idea how to make this." He held up the bottle.

"But when would we have call to bargain?" Coryn asked.

"Ah, you'd be surprised. Even with friends, there's often a little chance here and there." He pointed on ahead. "I'll tell you what, I'll show you up here."

"Oh, you don't have to. Not with Molyna."

"Close friend, is that?"

"No, but—she grows mealworms for everyone in the town."

"And the price is a bag of grain—"

"Bran. It's the coating on the grain. When we grind barley to make flour, we sift out the bran. Her mealworms eat it."

"Ah." Clement nodded. "So you give her bran and she gives you mealworms."

"And we take some wine along as well."

"Always? Is that the price?"

"Well..." Coryn looked at the brown bottle and the liquid sloshing inside it. "We bring wine because it's a courtesy and we have a lot of it, and we want to give her something for the trouble of growing the mealworms."

"All right. Well, I'll keep my nose up and eyes open and we'll see what we see."

"Don't offend Molyna. Nobody else in town grows mealworms. If we can't buy from her we'll have to ride out to Caverns or Plainfield and find someone there who sells them."

"Tch," Clement said. "People who don't know how to bargain always worry about offendin'. I can tell when someone's willin' to bargain and when they're not. Didn't I just finish tellin' you I know about this kinda thing? Give me a little credit."

It felt strange to be bringing this person from his past into his normal everyday life, but he'd already brought Clement to the farm. It wouldn't be any stranger bringing him to Molyna, would it? And if he could prove some kind of skill that would be useful for Lucy, some reason to stick around for a month, then it would be worth it for sure.

Why, a voice asked in his head, *are you trying to make him part of your family if you're only going to leave again?*

Because, he told it, because...maybe Ki won't find a suitor. Maybe she'll ask me to stay and run the farm, and maybe Clement can stay with us.

Fool, said the voice. *Take Lord Barclaw's farm, exile yourself. It's what you deserve.*

But the rat beside him was trying to change his life. There was a flicker of hope that maybe Coryn could, too. Not yet, Coryn said. Not yet.

Molyna's farm lay at the edge of a small forest and consisted of a house and two large barns where she raised mealworms. The land here was rocky; little grew except for berry bushes, which Molyna harvested and tended as best she could.

The harvest would be long over by now, but when they approached, Coryn spotted the slender grey wolf outside among the bushes, bending over now and again to pull something from the ground. Coryn moved around to approach from upwind so that she caught his scent even before he raised an arm and said, "Ho! Molyna!"

She waved back to them and then pointed toward the closer of the two barns. Coryn and Clement walked up a slight rise in that direction, and after pulling a few more things from the ground (weeds, Coryn saw as they got closer), Molyna came to meet them.

"Good day, Coryn," she said, leaning forward. "Canis guide you."

"Canis guide you," he repeated, bringing his muzzle close to hers to exchange scents.

She turned her gaze to Clement. "I was going to say that Lucy's grown up quickly, but then I smelled rat. Who's your companion here?"

"I'm Clement, ma'am." The rat bowed and leaned forward, presenting his snout. "Canis guide you."

She tilted her head and then sniffed him, though from farther away than she'd sniffed Coryn. "Rodenta keep you," she said. "Are you new to Doubleford?"

"I am." Clement straightened and smiled. "Late of Divalia where I plied my trade as an apprentice clockmaker, seeking a healthier life in the country with my friend Coryn here whom I met at the market. He sang the praises of the land and people of Doubleford, and I had to come see for myself."

Molyna folded her arms, a smile tugging at her lips. "And?"

Clement bowed. "He didn't do the people justice, from what little I've seen."

"Hah. Younger folk than you, and of my own species, have attempted to win me over with flattery." But she looked pleased as she turned back to Coryn. "You intend to begin repairing clocks?"

"He's skilled with all kinds of mechanical contraptions," Coryn said. "But to start out he might help us with some repairs around the farm this winter, until he sees what else he can do." The half-truth came more easily to him than he would have thought possible.

Molyna nodded, then dropped her gaze to the bottles they each held. "Is that barley wine?"

"It is." Coryn held out his bottle, and Clement did the same.

The wolf took both bottles, cradling them in the crook of her arm, then gestured to the storehouse. "Come on. You can leave the bran here and take your mealworms."

The storehouse, a stone-walled building, stood about as large as the house but with only one floor and no windows—rather, the windows had been boarded up and only cracks of light showed through. This was enough for both Coryn and Molyna to see well, and Clement didn't seem to have any problems navigating the rough floor either. A bit less than half of the floor had been walled off from the rest, and Molyna led them through another door into this space, where a wave of heat assaulted them.

"Hot in 'ere," Clement said.

"Aye, the worms die in the cold." Molyna pointed to five large stone troughs with stoves between them. "Come winter, I only run one of the barns because I have to burn so much wood to keep them warm."

"Next time we come we'll bring some wood," Coryn said.

Clement studied the troughs, walking around them while Molyna and Coryn went over to one and used Molyna's large sifter to pull a writhing mass of mealworms from the tub, shaking them until most of the large bits of bran had fallen out. Coryn held his satchel out and the other wolf tipped the worms into it. After one more scoop, the satchel was full.

"This 'ere's interesting," Clement said. "Burns lots of wood in the winter, you said, ey?"

"Yes." Molyna turned to the rat. "Two stoves and all this space to heat."

"Mm." Clement scratched at the floor. "Just dirt floor?"

"Yes." The wolf tilted her head again. "Why?"

"Mechanism's not just clocks, you see?" Clement gestured to the room. "Don't make sense you should heat up all this space. I wager if you could just heat the worms, you could make do with one stove easy."

"Probably," Molyna agreed. "Have you a mechanism that can do that?"

"Ay, maybe." Clement rubbed his whiskers. "Only an idea, you see. Might take a bit o' work."

"What's the idea?"

"Oh," Clement said, "Strickly speakin' I'm meant to be workin' with Coryn this winter."

Coryn started to say, "It's okay," but Clement cut him off. "However," he said, "I'm certain he wouldn't mind me helpin' out a bit here and there, and maybe you could thank him with some gift, same as he thanks you with some barley wine."

There was a tense moment when Coryn thought Molyna would snap at the rat, then turn to him and tell him that wasn't how friends acted, but then she laughed and clapped the rat on the shoulder. "Tell me your idea, and if I like it, I'll send you home with a jar of preserves."

Clement's smile widened. "Coryn did bring two bottles of wine."

"All right, all right." Molyna didn't lose her good humor. "If it's a good idea, it's worth two jars."

"Aye, fair enough." The rat pointed to the floor. "There's houses in the city with two floors or three floors and always they have the fire on the bottom." He gestured up with his paws. "The fire burns upward, you see."

"We know that." But Molyna's smile had turned thoughtful.

"So it don't work so well having the stove next to the worms. What you do is you dig out a hole in the floor, leave yourself room to feed the stove, put the worms around the hole, and cover the whole thing. Build a little room inside this one, maybe."

"Or," Molyna said, "put the troughs across the hole, directly above the stove."

"Aye, if you dig the hole properly." Clement looked pleased. "You might also build a platform to raise the worms up, but in my judgment that seems t'be more work, an' also if you put the stove in the ground, the fire got nowhere else to go."

Molyna examined the ground, digging at it with the claws of her feet. "That's not a bad idea," she said. "Save me a good deal of firewood."

"Worth two jars of preserves?" Clement asked.

The wolf rubbed her muzzle and then nodded. "Aye, and more, if it works. I'll need to hire people to help with the digging."

"Coryn hasn't told me," the rat said, "but is it only you here?"

Molyna left off scraping at the floor to look Clement square in the eye. "Aye, it is, and has been for a decade. I've no trouble managing on my own."

"Speakin' as one who's been on me own since I was ten, I got nothing but respect." Clement half-bowed.

"Maybe," Coryn said, "Clement and I could come help you with the digging. Before it gets too cold, or the ground might freeze."

"Not in here," Molyna said, "but aye, the offer is appreciated. I'd pay."

"We wouldn't charge as much as others might," Coryn said.

"True enough. I'm pleased just to be of help." Clement stood straight, and though he was not as tall as either wolf, Coryn felt him equal in stature.

Molyna fetched the two jars of preserves and sent them on their way with a promise from Coryn to return within the week and discuss the work that needed to be done. Clement carried the preserves while Coryn carried the satchel, and with the sun halfway down the sky, they set back out for home.

"That was well done," Coryn said, "but I don't see that it was bargaining."

"What?" cried Clement. He held up both jars. "Did you not see how I got an extra jar of preserves just for giving advice?"

"Oh, I suppose so." Coryn grinned. "I meant that you didn't ask for more in exchange for the mealworms."

"No," Clement said. "How would that look? You and she been trading this way a long time an' here I comes tellin' her she must pay you more? She'd look askance at it. But my information, that was a new thing, an' I'm a new person, an' sure enough, she tried to give me less than what that was worth. I showed her I won't be an easy mark, and she respected that."

"And," Coryn reflected, "perhaps there's an excuse for you to stay around a little while longer."

"Aye." The rat looked smug. "I was rather thinking that myself." His thin tail whipped back and forth.

"And if not, I'm sure Molyna will let you sleep in the barn with the worms."

"Hold up." Clement stopped and tilted his muzzle up to look the wolf right in the eyes.

"What?" Coryn stumbled a bit but met the searching gaze.

"That was a joke."

"Sort of?" Coryn splayed his ears and curled his tail against his leg. "Sorry, I thought—"

"No, it was good. I was wondering if you knew how to do that." Clement lifted his muzzle and brushed it against Coryn's, and then set off back down the path.

CHAPTER 5

By the time they returned to the farm, the sun had settled almost all the way to the horizon. "Say," Clement said, "how do those worms taste? Ever tried one?"

Coryn laughed. "Are you that hungry? We're home and dinner will be ready soon."

"Just curious. Ain't you curious?"

"Well...when I was a cub I did try one. Ki dared me." He shrugged. "It tasted weird, not bad. Earthy, kind of."

"All right. So Elly's not gettin' some delicacy here."

"No." Coryn lowered the satchel from his shoulder as they approached the stable. "She needs more than just hay and grass, and we don't want to give her meat. Some folks give their mounts mice and rats, but we don't have traps for them. In winter we don't see a lot of them anyway."

"I've caught a few rats in my day, both the upright kind and the non." Clement grinned. "If someone'll eat them—the four-footers, I mean, here—I don't mind putting my mind to it again."

"Maybe." Coryn's ears perked. "That's another thing to mention to Ki."

They opened the stable door and were greeted with loud snorting honks. "Hey," Clement said, "settle down, girl, it's just us."

"That's not Elly." Coryn dropped the satchel and took a few steps forward. Elly stood quietly in her stall, and across from her the stall appeared empty until he got up to it and saw the mount shying toward the back, snorting. When it saw him it gave another loud honk.

"Shy fella, huh?" Clement asked.

"Some are." Coryn approached the stall and shook some mealworms into the bin at the front.

"I been around mounts," Clement said. "I know there's some don't like people so much."

"Right, sorry." The wolf stepped back and spoke softly to the mount. "There you go. Eat as much as you want."

It eyed him but clearly had seen the mealworms. One hesitant step, then another, and then it dove its head into the bin and ate, pulling up again to make sure he hadn't moved. Coryn took a step closer, and the great scaly head came up in alarm. The mount took a step back, snorting.

"Wouldn't get much closer if I were you," Clement advised.

"I've been around mounts too," Coryn said mildly, and took some mealworms from the satchel in one paw, which he held out. "Come on, there, want a few more? It's okay, I won't hurt you, you can have them. These are for you."

The mount snorted but eyed the wolf's paw. Coryn moved half a step closer, so his paw was just outside the stable door. He didn't say anything, and after a moment the mount stopped snorting. Its eyes flicked from his paw to his muzzle and back down, but it didn't move.

After a moment, Clement said, "Best give it up. Like as not he'll only go for his owner."

"Can you feed Elly while I'm waiting?" Coryn replied softly.

"Why you bothering with this? What's it prove if some stranger's mount likes you or not?"

"Nothing, really." Coryn kept his eyes on the mount's, his paw out even as the mealworms wriggled around in it. "I just like to know I can do it."

"Aren't you bothered by who might be riding it?" Clement fingered the saddle bags hanging next to the stall: clean, unscuffed leather dyed black with red and gold trim.

Coryn looked out the stable door and toward the house. "It's put away well, so whoever came is a welcome guest, and we'll see them in a moment. It's nobody I know or I'd recognize the mount."

"And you're not worried about a stranger here with your sister and niece?"

Coryn laughed. "No more than Ki was worried about me going off to Molyna's with a stranger. Travelers stop here on occasion when they don't want to pay for a public-house. Farms are open to wanderers if they have something to trade."

The rat shook his head with a grin. "Fair enough. So how long do we wait here before...ah."

At that moment, the mount came up and licked at Coryn's paw with its long bluish tongue, scooping up the mealworms. Slowly, Coryn brought his other paw around and brushed its cheek. It flinched but didn't pull back until there were no more worms in his paw.

"Well done," Clement said softly.

Coryn smiled and wiped his paws on his tunic. "Let's go in and see who our guest is, shall we?"

When they approached the house, the smell of roasted fowl seeped out, and Coryn raised his eyebrows, his whiskers fluffing out. "Ki's making roast. Must be someone she wants to impress —ah."

"Ah?"

"We were going to be getting suitors for Ki. This must be the first of them."

"To marry her?"

Coryn nodded. "Aye."

The rat held him back as he reached for the door. "Hold up," he said. "When you talked about leaving…sounded like you thought she could find a husband after you left. But you knew this was happening."

"I didn't know it was going to happen today." Coryn flattened his ears.

Clement folded his arms. "You been thinkin' about leaving."

"Not—" Coryn looked at the stable, at the forest beyond it. "Not necessarily."

"Rubbish," Clement said. "Why?"

"I've brought a lot of trouble to this family." Coryn sighed. "The way we live now, it's…my fault." Only it was partly the rat's fault too, wasn't it? No; Coryn had made the decision to go with him, to steal, to climb the Cathedral. And from that, everything else: the debt, the breaking off of his engagement when the news spread, taking Ki's bride-price to pay his debt, the breaking off of her engagement, his father's death.

"Don't seem too bad to me."

"No, but—" Now Coryn took the rat's paw. "Please don't say anything to Ki or Lucy. If it happens, it happens, but I promise I'll take you with me if I do go."

Clement nodded. "An' when do you decide that? What makes you decide?"

"I have a month."

The rat frowned. "Someone puttin' screws to you?"

"No, I mean—I gave myself a month—" Coryn took a breath. "Please, just, just don't tell anyone."

Clement sized him up and then said, "A'right, well, wasn't my business yesterday and en't my business today. You just tell me where I'm to bunk."

"Thank you," Coryn said.

"All right." The rat gripped his arm. "Let's go see this fellow, then."

His first impression of the suitor was bright, almost blinding gold catching the light of the fire and lanterns and collecting it, reflecting it in shimmering patterns draped over the fellow's shoulders and flowing down his back to where his grey-brown tail curled. The second was of his warm smile and butter-smooth voice as he spoke to Lucy, both of them sitting around the square wooden table while Ki prepared greens at the stove.

"And so Wolf turned back, but Coyote went ever on, though the stones of the path slipped beneath his paws and the thorns caught at his fur. After another day, Coyote came to a place where even the Sun and Moon would no longer venture, and the path became shrouded in mist so that he could barely see where to place one foot in front of the other. So determined was he to learn the secrets of the End of the World that he went on even through this, even as his fur was torn out in clumps and his feet ached from the stones and his stomach cried out from hunger. 'Surely,' he thought, 'the secrets that lay over the edge of the world must be great if the path is so difficult!'"

The wolf's ears had flicked back at the opening of the door, and now he turned. Coryn gestured for him to finish the story. Lucy, rapt, barely noticed the hesitation as the stranger returned his attention to her. "He traveled until Time no longer meant anything to him, until there was nothing but the path, now walled in with thorn bushes as hard as stone and black as night. When he rested, he made sure to lie with his head pointing forward so that when he woke he would not turn around. He walked and he walked and he walked."

Here he paused long enough that Lucy cried out, "Did he reach the End of the World?"

"He did," the wolf said with a smile. "He walked and walked and then his feet found an edge. The thorns and the path stopped, but the mist went on. Coyote had reached the place he sought, and all the secrets lay beyond. But he hesitated, as you might if you faced a step into an unknown space."

"I wouldn't hesitate," Lucy said.

"Wolf would be proud of you." The wolf gave her a serious nod. "Coyote did step forward and off the edge, and he fell through the mist."

Lucy's eyes widened and she leaned forward. "What did he find?"

"He fell for a long time, so long that he fell...asleep."

"He fell *asleep*?" She sat straight up, indignant. "He did not."

"He did. When you first step off a precipice, it is very exciting, and for most of us, it stops being exciting very shortly after. But imagine if you simply fell and fell and fell, for hours. There was nothing to see and nothing to do and he was very tired. So he fell asleep."

Lucy folded her arms and said nothing. The wolf smiled. "He woke up...in his own bed, in his own house."

"What?" The cub yelped. "So he didn't learn any secrets at all?"

"That all depends on how you look at it," the wolf said. "And that is the story of Coyote at the End of the World. And now I hope you will excuse me so I may make introductions." He rose and walked toward Coryn. "You are Lucy's uncle, I take it?"

"Yes. I'm Coryn." Coryn extended an arm and his muzzle.

The other wolf grasped his arm and brought his muzzle close enough for them to smell each other. "I am Galan, from Radbridge."

"The city?" Clement asked.

Galan turned and released Coryn's arm. "Aye, the city, where Lord Deverin resides. And whom have I the pleasure of addressing?" He did not extend his arm or his muzzle.

"Clement," the rat said. "Late of Divalia, which is also a city. Mayhap you've heard of it."

"I know Divalia well. We do trade there, but we prefer our land of Deverin's sweet smells to the thick air of the capital."

"Clement is only passing through," Ki said from the stove. "On his way south. He'll be leaving come morning."

"I'll be here for dinner, though." The rat peered around Galan to the square table. "S'pose I can sit at a corner if need be."

"I rather thought," Ki said, "that you could take your dinner in your room above the stable."

"Ah," Galan said, "then we'll be sharing quarters for a night. I too planned to rest here and return to Radbridge in the morning."

"Lovely," Clement said. "Do you snore?"

The roast fowl was just about done, so Coryn went over to the stove where Ki was cooking the greens in a large saucepan. "I can carve it when it's done," he said, and then, as Galan engaged Lucy in another story, lowered his voice. "It would be unkind to banish Clement to the stables if you mean for him to only stay the one night."

"You'd rather invite him to your room, I'm sure," Ki replied, "but you know that can't happen."

"I know—" Coryn stopped, confused. "No, I'm talking about dinner. He can sleep in the stables. I know our agreement about others sleeping in the house."

"Oh." Ki stopped stirring the dark green leaves for a moment and stared down at them. "We have another guest now, one you arranged for, and what would it look like if we have him eating at the table with a vagrant?"

Coryn lay his ears back. "First of all, he's not a vagrant. He's offered to stay here and work on the farm, and you turned him down."

"That doesn't mean he has a home to go back to. Working vagrants are still vagrants."

"Second of all, if you don't care about suitors, why do you care what Galan thinks of us? Won't it reflect well on us that we treat strangers with hospitality, as Canis instructs?" When she remained impassive, he said, "Ki. It means a lot to me."

Ki exhaled and stopped stirring the greens to face him. "I'm trying to protect you as well as Lucy, Cor," she said in a low voice.

"I know," he said softly, and smiled to underscore his words. He didn't feel that he needed protecting, but it was nice that Ki was looking out for him. "But...I have a good feeling."

She studied his muzzle and then returned his smile. "Yes, fine. He can eat here."

Coryn didn't let his tail wag, but he smiled. "Also, you should hear what he did at Molyna's farm."

"What?"

He sniffed and checked through the grate of the stove. "Oh, I think the chicken's done. You must care what he thinks at least a little."

"It's the one I got from the Whitefoots while you were gone. We were going to eat it as a celebration when you came back anyway. The meat will keep, and I'll make a wine stew tomorrow."

"Using a chicken on the first suitor, eh?" Coryn peered over Ki's shoulder as he opened the door to the stove. "He is a good-looking one, I'll admit that."

"He's nothing special." Ki returned her attention to the greens. "Take the fowl out and carve it, then."

Grinning, Coryn took the steaming fowl to the table and set

it out, to Lucy's excited squeals and appreciative smiles from both Clement and Galan. "Lucy," he said as he whetted his carving knife, "could you run to the barn and fetch the short stool for Clement? We'll fit everyone around this table."

"Of course!" The cub beamed up at Clement, and Coryn was glad to see she hadn't lost her affection for him in the wave of stories from Galan.

"I'll just go along with her," Clement said.

Ki lifted the pot of greens from the stove and said, "Lucy can carry the stool by herself," but by the time she'd turned, both the rat and cub were gone. She sighed and brought the pot to the table.

By the time Lucy and Clement returned carrying the stool between them, Coryn had almost finished carving the bird. Ki had brought out their three tin plates and two of the fancier pottery plates for the guests, though Coryn saw the hesitation as she set one in front of Clement and knew she would've given him a tin one if she could've figured out how to do it without seeming inhospitable.

She did serve Galan first and then Coryn and Lucy before Clement, and then took food for herself and sat down. If Clement felt slighted, he didn't give any sign; he ate with gusto and complimented Ki several times on the meal. Galan, though less enthusiastic, also praised Ki's cooking.

"So," Coryn asked after they'd all been seated, "tell me a little about yourself, Galan."

The other wolf rubbed his paws on the cloth napkins Ki had laid out and then straightened the gold-threaded vest he wore over his light blue tunic. "I'm the third son of a merchant who has no hope of inheriting his father's business and so I'm looking for a place I can make my own. I've always loved farms. When I was young, I was sent to work on my cousin's farm come harvest time."

"Oh, what did you do for him?" Ki asked.

"Whatever he needed." Galan smiled. "I helped bind hay bales, I picked fruit, I dug up a fallow field. I was not much older than Lucy the first time I went, and I was sent there for three years."

Coryn and Ki exchanged amused looks—someone who had spent three harvests on a farm and then wanted to run one could wind up as had Toler, the wolf who had come down from Divalia and bought a farm because he thought it would be fun. Two scant harvests later, despite all the help from his neighbors, he'd sold the farm for less than he'd paid and returned to the city. But here, Ki would be around to help run the farm and teach Galan what he hadn't learned as a cub.

"My cousin still has a farm," he went on, "and I could see about contacting him to arrange for trade."

At that, Ki's ears perked a little more, and Coryn's did too. "We get along well with our neighbors," Ki said, "and we don't want for much," although he had mentioned fruit, and the prospect of having a reliable trading partner for fruit was very tempting.

"Of course, of course." Galan picked up another piece of the chicken and gathered some greens with it. "It's clear that your farm is quite successful. My father will be able to pay a handsome bride-price for it, should your fancy turn my way."

"Well, I don't know," Ki said. "I'm told there will be other suitors, you know."

"Say," Clement said, "what does your father sell, exactly?"

Galan blinked and looked at Clement as though he hadn't realized the rat was there. "Oh, er, he deals in—he owns a shop in Radbridge where he sells food from farms in that area."

"Oh, that's quite nice," Coryn said. "Perhaps if you do marry Ki, we can send some of our barley wine to him."

"He doesn't deal in drink," Galan said. "Only fruits and

meats, and he buys mostly from local farms along the Rad. Otherwise there's the expense of bringing them, you know."

"I know," Coryn said. "I sold much of our barley up in Divalia."

"Why not come to Radbridge?" Galan asked.

"We make so little, we can really only go to one market, and the buyers in Divalia can pay more than the buyers in Radbridge, enough to make it worth the extra trip," Ki told him.

"An' besides," Clement said, "Divalia's much more interesting."

"Oh?" Galan asked. "You've been to Radbridge, then?"

"I haven't," the rat replied, "but I'm just going to guess you haven't a Great Cathedral or royal palace there."

The wolf set his jaw, then smiled and turned to Ki. "There are other pleasures in Radbridge, of course, but I've had enough time to sample them and I'm ready to build a life elsewhere."

"Can't argue with that." Clement picked up another piece of chicken. "Takes a mite longer to get tired of Divalia, but that's what I'm doing as well."

"Oh," Galan said politely. "And where are you bound in the morning?"

"Ah, I'll see where the wind takes me." The rat smiled. "I've had an offer of work that I might explore. Doubleford's got a lovely quiet feel to it that's very restful after the bustle of the city."

"It does at that. I'm not used to being able to hear silence in Radbridge. Seems there's always someone moving about or owls hooting or carriage wheels rattling. This is a nice change. And of course the company is better than most of what I'm used to in Radbridge."

"Oh, surely not," Ki said, and Coryn was surprised at her mellow tone and the slight splay of her ears.

"You might be surprised," Galan said. "Many of the people in

Radbridge are quite uninterested in talking about anything outside their particular world. My brothers who are going to take over our father's business talk about nothing but the business, the people they meet, the deals they make, and so on."

"The people they buy the fruits and meats from," Clement said.

"Aye, of course." Galan turned. "Whereas here I find an intelligent, curious cub, a capable mother, and a well-traveled brother."

Coryn exchanged a glance with Clement, who did not seem perturbed at being left out, but more intrigued by Galan the way he'd been intrigued by Molyna's barn. Coryn didn't see what was so interesting about Galan, though if he thought about it, it was perhaps a little strange that someone who seemed so accustomed to city life was eager to move to a farm. But Coryn himself was thinking about leaving one farm for another; maybe Galan had reasons that were more private than he was willing to talk about in the first meeting with a family.

"Coryn's not that well-traveled," Ki said with a short laugh. "He's been to Barclaw and Divalia."

"And Radbridge, once, with Father," Coryn reminded her.

"That was years ago."

"Still."

Galan smiled, and Clement spoke up. "Still, I wager that's more of the world than many in Doubleford have seen."

"It's more than I've seen," Lucy said. "I keep asking him to take me but he never does."

Coryn looked at her and couldn't help his grin. "You haven't asked me in a year or so."

Lucy looked down. "Mommy said not to bother you."

"It's all right," Coryn said. "Maybe in a couple years you can come on a trip."

"You're not much younger than I was on my first trip to a

farm." Galan made a show of measuring her. "I'd wager you could be helpful in a year, even."

Lucy brightened and wagged her tail, and Ki said, "Well, we'll see."

When dinner was over, they sat around the stove, and Coryn added some wood to it, as a chill had crept into the air. Galan asked Coryn about the farm, but he let Ki talk while he sat beside Clement. With the sun down and only the smell remaining of the meal, Coryn had turned his mind to the problem of allowing Clement to stay, and the more immediate problem of how to get some time alone with the rat before morning, in case he couldn't.

Clement seemed unburdened by either of those worries, keeping his attention on Ki as she talked about planting barley and the future raising of chickens. And when Lucy yawned, Clement was the one who stood and said, "Aye, the cub got the right of it, I'd say. If we're to be off in the morning, best turn in now and catch all forty of our winks, eh?"

Galan rose more slowly but did nod. "It's only a few hours back," he said. "I needn't leave at sunup."

"We'll be getting up to do the chores then, so there's not much point to you staying any later." Ki stood and smoothed down her dress. "But it's been a great pleasure to meet you."

"I presume we will at least have a chance to say our good-byes come morning," Galan said, and bent to Lucy. "I'd hate to leave without a good-bye."

"I'll say good-bye!" Lucy promised, and extended her paw up for him to grasp. "It's been very nice meeting you, sir."

Galan shook it solemnly. "It has been my distinct pleasure to meet you as well, young Lucy."

Ki offered him an old blanket, which he refused, saying he'd brought his own, while Lucy turned to Clement and wrapped the skinny rat in a hug. "Thanks for teaching me a knot," she said. "I hope you stay close."

"Ah, I plan to," he said, wrapping an arm around her shoulders. "If we've time in the morning, p'raps I can show you a little trick with grass blades."

Her ears perked up. "Oh, I hope so!"

"In the meantime," the rat said to Ki, "if that blanket's not being put to other use, I'd welcome it."

Ki hesitated only a second, then gave a quick nod and held out the blanket to Clement, who took it and tucked it under one arm.

"I'll walk you to the stables while Ki puts Lucy to bed," Coryn said, an idea forming in his head.

So he led Galan and Clement out to the stable and showed them the ladder up to the loft. "There's hay up there and it should be comfortable. I've slept up there on warm nights sometimes."

"Excellent," Galan said. "Reminds me of my nights on the farm. I'll get my things from my saddlebags."

Coryn had hoped Galan would go up first, leaving him to have a word with Clement, so now he had to change his plan. "I'll make sure there's enough," he told the rat, gesturing toward the ladder. "I haven't been up there in a week or two."

Clement grinned at him and hustled up the ladder quicker than Coryn could follow. When the wolf got to the top, the rat had already moved to the corner of the loft farthest from the ladder, reclining on a pile of hay. "Seems like there's plenty here," he said. "I can sleep here and Galan over yonder." He gestured along the other wall, where another stack of hay stood piled.

"That pile's older," Coryn said, walking over to him. "You've got a good nose."

"For more than just hay." Clement stood and brought his

nose up to Coryn's, lowering his voice. "Say, if I was to feel restless tonight and take a little walk around the farm, maybe to that storeroom, what time do you think I might be most likely to encounter some pleasant company?"

Coryn was going to ask questions, but Galan moved below, and he knew his time was limited. "An hour," he said quickly. "I'll have a candle in my window, up on the top floor. If it's lit, I'm there. If it's out, I'm out."

"I'll look for it." The rat smiled and licked his nose and then settled back onto the hay just as Galan's head emerged in the loft. Louder, Clement went on, "This'll do nicely. Softer'n many a bed I've slept in, that's for certain."

"Larger than many I've passed a night in." Galan paused and then walked over to the older hay, against the wall, where he threw down a blanket. A moment later the scent reached Coryn of some perfume from the blanket, but an old scent, one absorbed into the cloth by years of proximity rather than by deliberate application. The scent tickled at his memory, but he couldn't quite place it, and it wouldn't be very polite for him to go over and smell his guest's blanket.

"I hope you'll both be comfortable here," Coryn said. "You know where the outhouse is; I'm afraid we haven't a pot here, but the night's not too cold now."

"We'll be well sheltered here," Clement said. "Thank you kindly for your hospitality."

"My thanks as well," Galan echoed.

"Rest well," Coryn said, and made his way back down the ladder.

* * *

Halfway back to the house, he wondered whether Clement could reckon an hour of time the way he could, and reassured himself that the rat would certainly have told him if "an hour" wasn't sufficient to specify a meeting time. Even if it weren't, the night was chilly and there was no real reason for him to return to the loft that wouldn't make Galan suspicious, so he hurried back to the house.

Ki was nowhere in evidence, probably asleep or nearly so in the room she and Lucy shared, the one that had belonged to their parents. Coryn spent a little time cleaning up as much as he could, setting the few uneaten greens aside and stacking the plates for Ki or Lucy to wash at the stream in the morning.

When that was done, he lit a candle and climbed the ladder to the attic room. The space above the main room was where Coryn slept; the space above Ki and Lucy's bedroom was set aside for storage. Even that smaller space was barely a quarter full with keepsakes from their parents and other odds and ends that weren't worth selling or were only useful once or twice a year—a bolt of cloth left over from Lucy's clothes, some barley wine that they wanted to age to see how it tasted, some fancy clothes for the Day of the Pack services.

Coryn's bedroom held not even that many things: a pallet stuffed with feathers that he'd inherited from his father, an old plain chest that held most of his clothing and other belongings, and a shelf where three books rested: a reading primer, the Book of Canis, and an almanac his parents had bought some ten years prior.

He set the candle in the window facing the stables and went to his chest, rummaging below the clothes for the small jar there. There wasn't much oil left, hadn't been since the last time he'd been with Erren, a year or more ago—no, less than a year, because it had been before the first snow. He thought there was some, though, and upon opening it he found that he was right. In the light of the candle, the oil glistened as it slid around the bottom of the jar. Enough for at least one night, he thought, and he could get more in Doubleford this week.

Barely half the hour had passed, so he sat down on the bed, tail flicking, and waited. Already as he thought about meeting the rat, his sheath warmed and grew hard, drawing his paw to it. Funny, he thought, he'd had more sex in the past two weeks than in the previous three months, and yet he still felt anxious and excited.

He'd imagined this night so many times, and yet the reality differed from any of his imaginings. For one thing, he'd always pictured their reunion in Divalia, not in the Great Cathedral itself, but at least within walking distance of it. For another, they'd always had a private room in his fantasies, where the self-assured thief had taken the lead, guiding Coryn through all the things Coryn secretly wanted to do. And for a third—Clement was real, more complicated and independent than Coryn's fantasy rat. They'd spent the entire day together—only one day, granted, but with the weight of their history behind them, that day had been as memorable as their first meeting.

And now Clement had shown interest in meeting him, and had to know what was intended. So Coryn was going to relive the final part of his adventure five years ago, only this time Coryn was older and more experienced, this time the night wouldn't recede so quickly into a dreamlike fantasy, and this time if the rat was gone in the morning he wouldn't be subject to a debt that crippled his family.

After another half hour, roughly, Coryn listened for any movement from Ki or Lucy, but the house was silent. He extinguished the candle and made his way down the ladder as quietly as he could, skipping the creaky rung and landing softly on the floor. There he listened again, but neither his sister nor niece stirred, so he made for the door and left the house.

The storeroom door stood ajar. Coryn slipped inside and

stopped, letting his eyes adjust to the darkness of the window-less building. It wasn't very large; maybe half the size of his house without a second story. He breathed in but couldn't catch any scent of rat; the air smelled of him and Ki, of the acrid tang of metal from the plough and the canvas of seed bags and, as most of the farm did, of barley.

"Hsst."

The noise came from his right, behind the plough and seed bags. He made his way carefully around the large metal shape and only then caught the barest scent of rat.

Clement was an outline in the darkness, lying almost against the wall on a bed of three canvas bags. He patted the space next to him and Coryn lay down there. "Glad you're here," he said in a low voice. "Did you come as soon as the candle went out?"

"Nah," Clement whispered. "Came as soon as Galan went to sleep. Didn't wanna go to sleep and I dunno how to judge an hour really without a cathedral remindin' me."

"Oh. Sorry. I could've come earlier."

"No worries." The rat put a paw on his side. "We're here now an' that's what matters."

"Yeah." Coryn reached over to the rat's side and found fur there. He traced lower, past the ribs, and met nothing but fur all the way down to the rat's muscled thigh. "You're—you're naked."

"Aye, well." The rat's fingers pushed their way under Coryn's tunic to tug at his underthings. "I didn't misread the invitation, did I?"

"No, no." Coryn helped push his underthings off, and when they were halfway down, he struggled out of his tunic.

Clement tossed the underclothes onto the tunic and dragged his claws through Coryn's belly fur. "There, that's much better," he said, and his fingers brushed Coryn's erect shaft. "Ah, much better indeed."

Coryn squirmed and panted, his hips jerking forward at the touch. He gripped Clement's side. "Ah," he gasped.

The rat's fingers closed around his warmth. "Someone was lookin' forward to this." His other paw took Coryn's fingers and guided them to a similarly erect cock just below the rat's stomach. "Someone else was, too." His eyes, gleaming in the dim light, gave a slow wink.

The touch drew a soft moan from Coryn. He couldn't concentrate on the feel of the warm skin under his fingers while his own warm skin was being stroked so sensually. He'd thought he was as hard as he could get, but under Clement's fingers his shaft filled and throbbed, his knot already growing. Though he'd had more experience than the young wolf he'd been five years ago, he felt his movements jerky and unpracticed compared to Clement's smooth strokes.

The world narrowed down to the two shafts and the warmth and smell of the rat. Here up close, with his clothing nearby but not on him, Coryn breathed in the rat himself. His scent carried some of the complexity of Divalia, the people and the buildings there, the air he breathed that infused him with the city's scent like a signature. Alongside that, his scent combined a tangy sharpness and dry dustiness, like an old stone building with metal fixtures, maybe bronze or tarnished silver. He pulled the rat to him and breathed heavily into the fur between his ears.

"A' right, a' right." Clement withdrew his paw and nuzzled Coryn's chest. "I've a feeling you wanted to do more than just dampen paws, eh?"

"Ah...huh...yeah." Coryn felt around the floor around him. "Got a jar...some oils..."

"That's the stuff. You, ah, you the givin' type or the takin' type?"

It took Coryn a moment to sort out what the rat meant. "Oh, I, uh, I can take. If that's okay."

"More'n okay." The rat's smile glimmered under his eyes. "I can go either way m'self. It's all enjoyable."

"Yeah." Coryn's mouth was dry.

Stillness surrounded them. "So," the rat said after a moment. "Where's these oils, then?"

Oh, Canis, it was really going to happen. Coryn's desperate fingers found the jar, gripped it, brought it to the space between them with a muffled thump against the canvas bags.

Clement took the jar and opened it. He sniffed and then ran his finger around inside. "Not much left."

"It's enough," Coryn panted.

"Lucky I'm not a bear."

Coryn froze. "What?"

The rat applied his slick fingers to his shaft. "I said, lucky I'm not a bear. You seen the size on one o' them? No, probably not. Anyway, it'd take all this oil just to cover his cock and then what would be left for you?"

"I've…" Coryn licked his lips, trying to get more moisture to his mouth. "I've seen a bear."

Clement stopped and his eyes shifted up to meet Coryn's. "Oh aye?" he said with interest. "Seen a bit more of the world than you let on, then."

"A bit."

"So, this bear." The rat finished and rubbed his fingers around the jar again. "He take or give?"

"Um. Neither. Just my muzzle." Coryn stared at the fingers.

Clement nodded. "You've taken before, though?"

"Uh huh." Coryn swallowed. "That jar was full when I bought it."

"Ha." The rat smiled. "Roll on over then, there's a good lad."

Coryn rolled away from the rat and lifted his tail away from his rear. Clement's fingers ruffled through the fur at his tail's base, then probed and found their way inside him, slick with oil. He draw in a sharp gasp as the rat slickened him and then forced himself to breathe evenly. This was no different than the time with Erren.

Except that it was, this was Two-Claws, this was their adventure in the Cathedral continued. He would not let the rat disappear again in the morning, no matter what it took to convince Ki.

"Ready?" Clement whispered softly.

"Uh huh," Coryn managed back.

"Mmm." The rat pressed up behind him, the tip of his cock pressing at and then entering Coryn, gliding slowly in. Once he was situated, he draped an arm over Coryn's side, and Coryn reached for it, finding the slick fingers and gripping them. "Ahh," Clement breathed, "that's nice."

He started to thrust in and out, and Coryn closed his eyes. This was—

A scrape outside, soft, but maybe sounding like a footstep. He squeezed Clement's paw. "Stop stop stop," he hissed.

"Sorry. Too fast?" The rat stilled. "Want me to—"

"Shh!"

They lay together, Coryn's heart pounding. Maybe he'd imagined it? No, there it was again, definitely a footstep this time, multiple footsteps, and the murmur of low voices. Clement stiffened and now he knew the rat had heard too.

"Galan?" Clement breathed in his ear.

"Not alone," Coryn breathed back.

The rat didn't answer, but slowly pulled all the way out. Coryn's own cock was flagging as his mind raced, distracted. He and Ki had an agreement that if they wanted to have play time with someone, the first one to the storeroom or stables got to use it, but that was usually if they planned it out ahead of time. He hadn't told her and she hadn't told him of her plans, and if

Galan hadn't noticed that Clement was missing, they wouldn't know to stay in the stable loft.

The door creaked. Ki would know that it shouldn't be open.

Sure enough, a moment later, her voice, unsure, came into the darkness. "Coryn?"

He didn't want to answer her, but a moment later the vision flashed into his head of her bringing Galan in and discovering them or, worse, not discovering them. "Aye," he said, and then, because his throat was dry. "I'm here."

"Oh." Ki chuckled. "Sorry." The door creaked again as it closed.

Coryn and Clement lay there for a moment and then Clement said, "Simple as that?"

"Simple as that."

Another pause, and the rat's arm withdrew from Coryn's side. "Might take me a moment to get back into the spirit, here."

"Me too." Coryn reached down to his cock, which had retreated into his sheath. He rubbed, trying to banish thoughts of his sister, of the reality of his circumstances here, but when Clement asked if he was ready, he said he was, more out of hope than truthfulness.

Once the rat was inside him again and the rat's fingers returned to his sheath, though, Coryn found it easier to focus on the physical. Clement came with a soft gasp and a hard press of his hips against Coryn's rear; a minute or two later, Coryn gave in to the quick strokes and shuddered as well, splattering the canvas bags with his seed.

They lay there for several minutes as the smell of Coryn's seed grew stronger and the rat's shaft eventually slid out of him. Presently Clement spoke. "I could go back to the loft," he said softly. "But I 'spect it's being used much the same way."

"It's all right," Coryn said. "We can stay here a bit if it's not too cold for you."

"Slept on worse, that's for sure." The rat drew his fingers lazily through Coryn's chest fur. "And mostly with much worse company."

Coryn's tail wagged back against Clement's stomach. Now that the urgency of sex was over, one thought remained nagging at his mind, keeping him from the sleep he would usually fall into. He didn't want to say anything about it, but if he didn't he felt that eventually he would be shouting it at himself in his head, so he reached back and touched Clement's hip.

"Mm," the rat said.

"You, ah." Coryn closed his eyes. "You won't leave without saying good-bye, will you?"

Clement nosed between his shoulder blades. "I ain't that kind of rat," he murmured sleepily.

But you are, Coryn wanted to say. You did. The words caught in his throat, kept there by the silence and contentment in the storeroom, the comfort he felt in this moment. He didn't want to ruin it.

His mind wouldn't stay quiet, though. *What if he does leave again?* Then he's gone, he told himself. He'll probably go to Molyna's, and I'll be able to see him anyway. *If he wants, now that he's gotten what he wanted from you.* What he wanted was sanctuary, and he got that, and he's still lying here beside me. *For now.*

All right then, he demanded of himself. What do *I* want? In a month—maybe sooner—I'm going to maybe leave this farm forever. Do I think he'll come with me? Do I think Ki will let him stay here if I decide to stay?

If you're going to trust him—trust him. Take him at his word.

Look where that got you last time. But that voice was faint now, or perhaps sleep had caught up with him. He put his paw over the rat's, held it against his chest, and drifted off to sleep.

* * *

He woke with a familiar chill in his nose and the tips of his ears, and an unfamiliar warmth against his back. Dim light filtered into the storeroom, enough for him to tell that dawn was imminent and he should be up to help with the chores.

Clement woke as soon as he rolled away, eyes shining up in the dim light. "Don't tell me you're leaving."

"Got to do chores," Coryn said. "I was going to wake you up."

The rat stretched out. His body, which could pass for lean when hidden by clothes, looked positively unhealthy when stretching pulled his skin and fur taut over the very obvious bones beneath. Coryn felt immediately guilty; had Clement eaten enough for dinner? But the rat seemed very satisfied with the state of the morning, flashing a smile up. "Hard not to wake me. Been up twice already this night what with noises and such."

"Noises?" Coryn reached for his clothes.

"Aye. Once I suspect was your sister returning to the house. Another I couldn't tell. Something prowling around, an animal of some sort."

Coryn pulled up his underthings. "Maybe a forest cat. We have them around here. They take chickens if we don't keep them locked up."

"Aye, that was it, I reckon. Sounded small and light on its feet."

"And that woke you up?"

The rat flicked his own ear and glanced up toward it. "Not as big as yours but when I sleep, they're on guard."

"Well...that's good, I guess."

"Mixed bag. Saved my life once or twice, but it's been years since I slept through the night."

"Years?" Coryn slid his tunic over his head. "I can't imagine that."

"You get used to it." Clement sniffed and picked up the

canvas bag that Coryn had come on. "I s'pose you won't want to be using this."

"I can wash it off."

The rat didn't put the bag down. "If your sister won't let me stay, you think I could keep it?"

"Probably." Coryn tilted his head. "Wait, what do you mean 'if'? You think you can change her mind? I thought you were going to go to Molyna's."

"Ah well, I've a last play to make." The rat scratched his nose. "Especially considering the events of last night."

"What—us?" Coryn shook his head. "I don't think she'll care. I mean, I'd really like for you to stay, but she knew that already."

"Put your heart back in its case, dear," the rat said with a smile. "I don't mean us, lovely though that was. If anything, it's added to my resolve to stay here past sunrise. No, I mean your sister's dalliance."

"Oh, that. There was nothing amiss about it."

"Except that it means your sister might think favorably of our friend Galan," Clement said quietly.

"He did come here to woo her," Coryn said.

"And a good job of it he did. But—well, let me have a few words with your sister before I leave and we'll see if she might find me useful around here."

"Because of what you might offer Molyna? I think she'll just ask you to go stay there."

Clement grinned a toothy grin. "Let me have a few words, ay?"

Trust him, Coryn reminded himself. "All right. Let's go; maybe you can catch her before she starts on her chores."

But as he dressed, his resolve to trust the rat wavered. It wasn't only that the rat, in an unguarded moment, had said he wasn't the kind of rat to leave Coryn when he had done exactly that, though that was part of it. He could think his way around the statement: maybe Clement wasn't that kind of rat *anymore*. The problem was that his scent was different. Not so different, not so's Coryn would notice next to a clothed rat. But naked, in an intimate embrace, though the notes of the rat's scent were the same as he remembered, the relative strength of those notes had been different—he thought. And Two-Claws had smelled of the river; Clement did not.

Scents could change, and maybe after Two-Claws had stopped working with the houseboat fox, the river had similarly left his scent. Maybe he'd lived in different quarters, maybe he'd eaten different foods; there were a lot of things that could affect a person's scent. And Coryn's memory might be wrong, too. But the little doubts nibbled away at his trust until he quieted them. If he was going to trust Clement, he would do it.

Both dressed, they left the storeroom for the chill of morning. Outside, the wet grass chilled their paws, and with each step they disturbed tendrils of fog that lay about. Past the soft sounds of the wild birds starting their days, Coryn heard movement in the house. "They're up but haven't started the chores yet," he told Clement.

"Aye, and to my ear, sounds as though Galan is still abed." The rat stroked his whiskers back. "Most excellent." He slid one paw into the pocket of the threadbare pants he wore.

As Coryn opened the door, the smell of porridge floated to his nose along with the warmth of the stove-heated house. "Uncle!" Lucy cried from the table, which made Ki turn from the stove and perk her ears.

"Good morning, you two. I trust you passed a pleasant night?"

"Quite pleasant, thank you," Clement said. "I've no cause to complain."

"My brother's hospitality is exceptional when he puts his mind to it." Ki winked at Coryn. "So I'm told."

"Uncle, why didn't you get Galan as well when you went to fetch Clement for breakfast?" Lucy wanted to know.

"He was still asleep," Coryn said. "But you know, it smells like the porridge is almost ready, so why don't you go fetch him?"

"May I?" Lucy turned toward the stove.

"Go ahead," Ki told her. "But don't go farther than the top of the ladder. And if he doesn't answer after two tries, come right back."

"Yes, Mommy." Lucy jumped down from the chair and hurried to the door.

Clement made his way up to the stove, leaning against the wall behind it so he could face Ki. "Smells lovely," he said.

"I thought I'd give you some breakfast before you take to the road." Ki kept stirring the pot.

"Much appreciated." Clement dug in his pocket. "I suppose you were rather taken with Galan?"

"Not that it's any of your affair," Ki said, "but we also passed a pleasant night. It's nice to spend time with someone who doesn't smell of the country."

"Meaning he's cleaned his fur in the last month," Coryn put in.

"Aye, that he has," Clement said. "One can smell it on him even with his clothes on."

Ki's ears splayed. "Coryn, would you fetch some bowls?"

"The thing is," Clement went on as Coryn walked to the cupboard to get bowls, "that perfume is nice. It's nicer than a merchant's third son would have, at least if that merchant sells 'fruits and meats.' Maybe a precious gem seller or a silversmith, but—"

"I suppose you have a great experience of gem sellers and silversmiths," Ki interrupted coolly.

Clement paused long enough that Coryn turned to look at

him. The rat was staring down at his paws and then his lips curved into a smile. "If we're being honest, then no, not the folk themselves. But I've been in their houses and smelled their scents often enough to know." He glanced up, and Ki must have looked dubious, because he went on. "Folk will try all manner of deception to hide their wealth, but their scent is the one thing they rarely disguise because that's how their friends and colleagues notice their standing. Better perfumes means better class of people, and there's no noble in the world will buy a cheap lavender scent when they can afford an expensive Northern musk oil."

Ki removed the pot from the stove and took it to the table with a look out the window to see if Lucy and Galan were coming back; they were not yet visible. "And I suppose you, a thief, know all the scents there are."

"*Former* thief," Clement corrected, unfazed by the directness with which she addressed his vocation, "and aye, we learn them well. One sniff at a door can tell you more about what's inside than a week of watching the door."

Coryn set the bowls on the table and took up a station at the window to watch for Galan's return. "So," Ki said, ladling out porridge into the bowls with perhaps a little too much energy, "you think he smells too nice to be what he says he is."

"He does." Clement produced a folded paper from his pocket. "And indeed, he en't." He held the paper out to Ki.

She looked at it but finished serving the porridge, returned the pot to the stove, and wiped her paws before approaching Clement. "I thought you said you were a former thief."

"So I am. I didn't steal this, merely borrowed it so you might have a chance to see it."

"Borrowed." Ki snorted but took the paper from him and unfolded it. She scanned it, and her ears flattened as she did. When she'd finished, she folded it and gave it back to him. "I suggest you return this while he's eating his breakfast," she said in a decidedly neutral tone.

"He's coming," Coryn said softly.

When Lucy led Galan into the house, he beamed around at all of them. "I could smell the porridge from outside. I can't wait to try it."

Ki had ladled out two bowls. "Coryn, take one to Galan, if you please."

"Of course." He eyed the paper in Clement's paw, still curious to know what it said, and set the bowl in front of Galan with a spoon. "Here you are."

"It's been an age since I had porridge that smelled like this," the other wolf said as he picked up the spoon.

"Oh, has it?" Clement slid the paper across the table to Galan. "By the by, I found this on the floor of the stable this morning near your bag. Reckon it belongs to you."

The wolf froze, staring at the paper, his spoon halfway down to the bowl. Ki turned at the stove, watching.

In the silence, Lucy looked around at the grownups. Her tail wagged, then slowed. "Isn't it good to give something back?" she asked.

Galan looked from the note up to the rat's neutral expression. "You had no right to go through my bag."

"Told you, I found it," Clement said, his tone bland.

"We both know..." Galan slapped his paw down on the note and pulled it toward him, then shoved it into his pants pocket.

Ki cleared her throat. "I don't know as you have the standing to accuse anyone of lying."

Galan looked at her and then stood up, leaving his spoon in the porridge. "I'm not terribly hungry, I find," he said. "I think I should get started on my journey home."

Lucy climbed up onto his chair once he'd stepped away from it. "Is the porridge not good? It smells lovely."

"I thank you for your hospitality," Galan said stiffly to Ki, and then walked to the door without saying anything to Lucy. He opened the door and walked out into the quietly brightening morning.

"I don't understand why he left," Lucy complained when the door had closed behind him.

"I'm not sure I do either," Coryn said, coming to stand beside her.

Ki brought two more bowls to the table. "Well, Lucy, he told a lie. You can go ahead and have his porridge."

The cub's eyes grew round as she sat down. "That's bad. What did he say?"

Ki sat, and Coryn sat with her. "Remember how he said he was the son of a merchant and he was here because he used to farm?" Lucy nodded, and Ki gestured to her bowl. "Eat your porridge. It turns out that that wasn't true, and he was here because someone else told him to come here."

Lucy swallowed a mouthful of porridge. "Is that what the paper said?" she asked, spraying flecks of porridge across the table.

"Something like that," Ki said.

"It's a good thing Clement found it then." The cub turned her gaze on the rat.

"Yes, it is." Ki met Coryn's eyes, then bent to her own bowl.

"Lovely morning," the rat said, and they talked about the weather for the rest of their breakfast.

When they'd all finished, Lucy said, "May I feed Ella this morning?"

"Of course," Ki said. "Thank you."

Unexpectedly, Lucy walked up to Clement. "Are you leaving soon as well?"

"Aye, I suppose I am, but don't worry, li'l one, I shan't be too far."

Ki perked her ears at that. "What do you mean?"

"Oh," Coryn said when Clement didn't answer, "only that Molyna was quite impressed with him and might offer him a place to stay."

"I like Molyna," Lucy said, "but Mama doesn't let me go there often."

"Maybe if I'm there, you'll have more reason, ay?" Clement crouched down so he was her height and held his arms out. "Now come here and promise me you'll visit."

"I promise!" Lucy hugged him and wagged her tail, then bounced out the door toward the stable.

"You never did tell me what he did at Molyna's." Ki didn't turn around from the wash basin, but she swiveled her ears back.

"And I want to know what was in that letter," Coryn said. "It seems important. Maybe it would be nice to have him stay here?"

Now Ki half-turned, enough to meet Coryn's eye. "Tell me about Molyna's now, and he can tell you about the letter on your way to fetch water from the spring."

That was a nice reprieve; he wouldn't have to say good-bye to Clement right away. So between the two of them they talked about the rat's idea at Molyna's barn and how pleased Molyna had been. "I haven't actually asked her if I can stay, but I feel my prospects are good," Clement concluded.

"I see." Ki nodded. "That's interesting indeed. Coryn, the water, please?"

So Coryn and Clement rode Elly the mile to the spring, empty water skins flapping on either side of her flanks. "So, the letter?" Coryn asked once they were out of earshot of the farm, walking slowly up the trail.

Clement laughed. "Was from Lord Deverin's steward to young Galan's father telling him that it would be a great favor if one of his sons'd go pay court to this farmer widow, and mentioning that it might be good for Galan. 'Calm him down,' I think was the Lord's words. Anyway, was quite clear the lad's father was no merchant but a noble friend of the Lord, and also I believe made some mention of farm life being a punishment."

Coryn shook his head. "Why would he keep that letter with him?"

"It had the directions to the farm on it," Clement said. "Likely couldn't be bothered to copy them out onto another page."

They rode in silence for a moment and then laughter bubbled up out of Coryn's throat. It burst out in one, "Ha ha!" and then he tried to restrain himself.

"What's funny?" Clement asked.

Coryn shook his head. He held in the laughs for another few steps of Elly's plodding walk and then tried to explain. "He was walking around with that...hee hee hee!" The laughs took over again. Behind him, Clement gave a little chuckle, waiting for Coryn to gain possession of himself.

Coryn gasped and wiped his eyes, and tried to explain again. "He was sent here...because he's a failure...and he couldn't even do this right. He thought so..." The giggles bubbled up again. "So, so much of himself...and he was walking around with that letter in his pack."

Now Clement chuckled along with him. "Not surprising when you think of it. Rarely seen someone fail over an' over an' then succeed. Actually, never seen a body fail over an' over unless they're a noble, 'cause anyone else fails once and that's it."

That quelled Coryn's giggles for a little bit. "Sometimes you get second chances," he said. "But then you should be even more careful with them."

"Aye," Clement said.

They plodded along in silence, and then Clement said. "Just as well. Not the sort your sister would want to marry anyway."

"Definitely not."

"Oh, I don't just mean the lyin' and the failin'. But kind of, because that kind of thing happens in certain families, you see what I mean?"

"No, not really."

"Ay, well..." Clement clicked his teeth, thinking. "How to put this delicate-like? I'll just say in families like that, t'isn't so uncommon that husband and wife are bonded by more'n just marriage."

"More than..."

"I mean, like, Galan might only have one set of grandparents, is what I'm sayin'."

"Only...oh!" Coryn understood then. "Really? I mean, here, I know someone who married her cousin..."

"You know one. In noble families, happens all the time. They're funny about 'blood,' you know, wanting to keep ever'thing in the family, and sometimes they keep a li'l too much in the family, and then you wind up with fools like Galan who think their blood entitles 'em to whatever they want and don't got the smarts to figure anything out and don't got the industr'us nature to make up for lack of smarts."

That made Coryn think of Lord Barclaw, who certainly wasn't the brightest person Coryn knew, although the bear did have a wide array of knowledge. He also had that tendency of thinking he was entitled to everything. "Probably best they didn't marry, aye," the wolf said. "Although if they did have a cub, maybe he could at least stand upright without help."

Clement snorted. "I think that's askin' a lot of our friend Galan. Lots of times those nobles can't have cubs 'tall."

"He was certainly giving it a try last night, but joke's on him." Coryn started to giggle again. "Ki's not even in season."

"Don't know as he could even tell." That set Coryn off again, and Clement joined him this time, the two of them laughing heartily the rest of the way to the spring.

Water bubbled out from a cluster of rocks and trickled down to a pool that fed a small stream. Coryn showed Clement how they filled the water skins from the pool while Elly drank, and then loaded them onto her back. The rat took the lesson seriously and helped with the heavy skins, then offered to walk alongside Elly when Coryn did the same. "Must be heavy for the poor thing," he said.

"It's downhill, somewhat," Coryn said, "but aye, why burden her with more than needed?"

The rat nodded and walked on the other side of the great reptilian head as Coryn led her down the trail. Once or twice, they caught each other's eye and started to laugh, and the pleasant feeling stayed with Coryn all the way back to the house.

There, as they unloaded the water bags at the door, he remembered that Clement would be leaving momentarily. The thought slowed him, a bag of water over his shoulder, until Ki barked at him. "Coryn! Are you going to carry that around all day or bring it in?"

"Sorry," he mumbled, and brought the bag in to sit next to the wash basin.

When all the bags were inside, Ki touched his arm. "Before you take her to the stables, I've been having a thought. Since it seems your friend," she said, even though Clement stood right in the doorway and could hear them, "will just be down the road at Molyna's anyway, and since you and Lucy have taken a shine to him...and since he spotted a fraud before any of us did...I suppose he may stay in the loft for a few days longer. As long as there's work to do around the farm, and," here she wagged a finger at Clement. "As long as there are no incidents. You understand me?"

The rat beamed and bowed. "Yes'm," he said. "Thank you kindly."

"We'll house and feed you, and in return you'll make yourself useful here. If Molyna wants your services, she can make her own arrangement with you. Is that agreeable?"

"Very much so."

"All right." Ki released Coryn's arm with a smile. "Go put Elly away. I'll wash and then I've some clothes to mend."

Coryn couldn't keep his tail from wagging as he and Clement walked the mount to the stable. "You did it," he said. "You convinced her."

"Told you I was a practiced haggler." The rat grinned.

"The thing is..." Coryn pitched his voice low. "I'm almost sure I saw you take that note from Galan's pack before you'd ever met him."

The rat raised his eyebrows. "Not sayin' I did, but if I did, why, it's always best to know more about someone than they know about you."

"But how did you know the paper would be important?"

"Didn't." The rat shrugged. "But there's places people keep important things, and there's a feel they have. You get to know it if you've been in the business this long." He rested thin fingers on Coryn's wrist.

The wolf smiled and his tail wagged, any lingering doubts about Clement receding before the warmth of that touch. The next few days were secure, and the future lay too far away to think about right now.

CHAPTER 6

Lucy came running around the storeroom corner and called up to where Coryn knelt on the roof. "Uncle!"

He'd already set down the shingles and looked over the side at the sound of her footsteps. "What is it? No, stay down there."

She climbed up three rungs of the ladder before she stopped, her ears splaying out. "There's another wolf who wants to marry Mommy, and this one's in a big wagon!"

"A wagon?" Coryn stood so that he could see over the angle of the roof. Sure enough, a small carriage, light wood with brass trim pulled by two mounts, stood politely on the road beyond their property as though waiting to be invited in. The driver, a wolf, sat stiffly on the driving board but did not appear to be looking toward the house.

"Mommy said that she shouldn't go meet them herself because it would look bad and because Clement isn't here you should go meet them and bring them to the stable if they want but she doesn't know if there's room for the wagon and if there isn't then they can keep it in town." Lucy announced all of this in one breath, her tail back to wagging.

"All right." Coryn made his way down the roof toward the ladder. "Go on down."

Lucy dropped to the ground and waited there for him. "Can I come over with you?"

"Better not," he said. "Doesn't Mommy need help in the kitchen?"

The cub kicked at the dirt. "She always needs help."

"Then you'd better go." Coryn got down to the ground and propelled Lucy toward the house. "I'll take care of this."

"Are you going to figure out something about him like Clement does?"

"I'll try my best."

"Will you tell me what it is?"

He smiled down at her earnest expression. "Does Clement tell you what he finds, or does he wait for Mommy to tell you?"

Her ears went from perked to splayed out again. "He waits."

"Then Mommy will decide when to tell you." They'd reached the front door, and he patted her back. "Go on, and I'll be back in a moment."

"Tell them they better not be lying!" she called, and disappeared into the house.

Coryn smiled and then put on a serious expression as he climbed the short rise up to the road. This was the first suitor to come in a carriage, which he felt was an indication that Lord Deverin's steward had grown more serious. The two who'd arrived after Galan had been alone on mounts and, like him, had not been entirely truthful about their positions and motivations. Neither of them had been of Galan's station, and neither had been as attractive, at least not enough to entice Ki out of the house at night. "If Galan was the best Lord Deverin has to offer," she'd said tartly, "we might as well tell him to stop sending them."

Now it appeared he might have received that message

anyway. Coryn wished that Clement weren't over at Molyna's today; he trusted the rat's perceptions better than his own. He would have to do his best, and Clement would be back tonight.

He wanted Ki to be happy, but as the days had stretched into two weeks, he'd become more and more convinced that she would be happiest if everything stayed as it was now. If this suitor really were worthy of Ki and Lucy, perhaps they would ask Coryn and Clement to leave. Or else the suitor would take Ki to his farm and leave Coryn and Clement here. He'd been resigned to this fate just a few weeks ago, but Clement had provided a spark to the family: Lucy adored him and even Ki had thawed toward the rat. More importantly, Clement reminded Coryn every day that his past didn't have to define his future.

The coat of arms on the carriage had faded, but as Coryn got closer he could make out more details, and they rang somewhat familiar. Maybe they were from the same house as one of the other suitors? No; that didn't seem right. He studied them and tried to remember where he'd seen them.

"Ahem."

Coryn's head snapped up to see the wolf looking down at him. "Sorry," he said. "It's only that your crest looks familiar. Welcome to our farm."

"Are you Coryn?" the driver asked.

"Aye, that's me."

"Please enter the carriage."

Coryn tilted his head. "Me? Aren't you here for my sister?"

The wolf straightened the clean tunic he wore under his vest. "My orders are to find Coryn at this farm and tell him to get into the carriage."

"Oh. All right." Coryn stepped down to the carriage and reached for the door. As he did, the odor of bear reached him and he knew where he'd seen that crest: it was Lord Barclaw's.

His paw froze on the door. Had Lord Barclaw come all this way to see him? Had something gone wrong?

The door opened without his help, and a stronger odor of bear wafted out. Not Lord Barclaw; someone younger, someone Coryn didn't know. A deep voice rumbled, "Are you going to get in? If I'm to get back tonight I can't wait on your pleasure forever."

It had barely been a minute, but Coryn hurried up into the carriage anyway. There was not much room in it for him; the light brown bear's legs came all the way to the seat across, leaving Coryn a corner to squeeze himself into. He did his best, catching the familiar scent of Lord Barclaw's laundry soap on the bear's light blue vest, coat, and trousers and feeling very conscious of his stained tunic and panting tongue.

The bear pulled the door closed, making the carriage feel even smaller, and looked Coryn up and down with an appraising eye. "So you're the wolf."

"I...I'm *a* wolf."

"You're the wolf the lord wants to deed the farm to. I'm Cantril." He extended a paw, but not to grasp; the large fingers held a paper.

"I'm Coryn." Coryn glanced at the paper and then took it hesitantly.

"Obviously," Cantril said. "Can you read?"

"Yes." Coryn held the paper in front of him. His eyes had adjusted to the light in the carriage by now and he could make out the word "DEED," and below it the name of a farm and a location.

Cantril fussed with a pouch on the seat next to him and pulled out an inkpot and pen. "Lord Barclaw wants you to sign the deed now to make the transfer easier in two weeks."

"Oh. Now?" Coryn stared at the paper and then held it back out to the bear. "I was told I would have a month to decide."

"I don't know whether you've noticed the change of seasons," Cantril said without taking the paper, "but winter is fast approaching. Lord Barclaw is anxious that you should be able to take up residence in the farm as soon as possible, and the later in the season, the more risk of a winter storm."

Coryn suspected that was not the only reason Lord Barclaw was anxious to have him closer as soon as possible. "I know about the seasons," he said, and looked pointedly out the window. "I live on a farm now. Lord Barclaw told me I had a month to decide, not that I had to move in a month."

The bear stared at him, dark eyes under thick brow ridges. "You can decide later, I suppose, but sign the deed now so you can act on your decision at the time."

He had the distinct feeling that the bear wasn't understanding what he was trying to say. He dropped the deed on the bear's large thigh. "What if I decide I don't want the farm?"

Cantril didn't pick up the paper. He continued to stare at Coryn, long enough that the wolf made a small motion toward the door. Only then did the bear speak. "You're being gifted a parcel of land." He spoke slowly, the way Coryn might have explained something to Lucy two years ago. "This land is yours. It's fertile, or at least it has been recently."

Coryn resisted the temptation to speak equally slowly in return. "What if I don't want to leave my family to go live on this farm? He said he would arrange for suitors for my sister, and none of them have been satisfactory so far."

The bear shook his head. "I was told that you should sign the deed. I was not told anything about a decision or about suitors."

"I don't know why not," Coryn said. "Lord Barclaw definitely told me to come back in a month with my decision."

"Perhaps he couldn't conceive that you would turn down a

gift of free land." The bear punctuated these last four words with stabs of his finger onto his thigh next to the deed.

"Or maybe he wants to pressure me into making the decision he wants me to make." Coryn pushed the door open.

Cantril gripped his wrist. "I was told to return with a signed deed."

The great paw around his slender arm might have intimidated him a month ago (or it might not have, he liked to think), but even as Coryn started to sit back down, he thought about what it would mean to sign the deed. It would mean leaving Ki and Lucy; it would mean perhaps leaving Clement as well, although perhaps the rat might come with him. Most of all, though, it would mean allowing his mistake of five years ago to continue to dictate the terms of his life.

It's what you deserve.

But the voice in his head was fainter, more easily set aside now. He remained off the seat and moved one foot deliberately out of the carriage. "I'm sorry to disappoint you and Lord Barclaw," he said, "but I haven't made my decision yet." When the bear didn't release him, Coryn said, "You'd best be on your way if you want to return home before sunset. The hills are harder on the return journey."

Cantril stared darkly for another moment and then released Coryn so abruptly that the wolf almost fell out of the carriage. "I hope for your sake that you make the correct decision," he said. "My impression is that the lord is most desirous of that outcome."

Coryn jumped down and reached for the door to close it, but it swung closed before he could touch it. Two sharp raps came a moment later, and the carriage set off down the road.

Lucy ran out of the house as he approached. "Are they going to come back tonight?" she asked. "Did you find out anything about them?"

"They weren't here for your mommy," Coryn said. "They just wanted directions."

Her ears splayed to either side. "Oh."

"Go help Mommy," Coryn said. "Clement will be back soon and then we'll have dinner."

That got her ears up and her tail wagging. "Okay!" She ran back into the house calling out, "Mommy! It wasn't a wolf for you!"

Coryn smiled after her and then stood for a moment in the early afternoon light and listened. No noise of carriage came to him, nothing but Ki and Lucy from the house and the sounds of birds and animals around him. He rubbed his ears and walked back to the storeroom, where there was still a roof that needed repair.

CHAPTER 7

The rain had come in the night and had not let up at dawn, a steady downpour that dripped down into the stable in at least three places that Coryn could count. None of them, fortunately, onto the wood over Elly's stall, nor onto the comfortable nest of hay and blankets where Clement slept and where, more often than not over the last few weeks, Coryn had also spent the night.

The rat's arm lay draped over Coryn's stomach, but his ears told him that the rat was awake. "I guess we need to fix this roof next," he said. "Mind if we check the storeroom roof first?"

"Maybe I should go sleep there." The rat squeezed him and shifted, rolling onto his back. "Couldn't sleep more'n a wink this whole night."

"We've been lucky with the rain." Coryn rolled onto his back as well, his paw reaching over to the rat's naked stomach to rest there. "But once it starts like this, it's likely to go on." He sniffed the air. "As wet as our fur's going to be, I'm glad we have a good store of wood laid in. It'll be a night for the stove for sure."

"Sounds lovely." Clement stretched. "Another day of work before we get there though."

Below them, Elly grunted and shifted, a low sound under the drumming of rain on the roof and the high-pitched drips coming into the stable. The blanket was warm under Coryn's bare dry fur, and he shifted, knowing he needed to get up. "Do you mind the work?" he said.

"Heh." Clement lifted his paws in the air and wiggled his fingers. "Less'n my fingers do, but they're healing and I'm still willin'."

"I mean...do you miss Divalia?"

"Ah, yeah." The rat laced fingers behind his head. "Course I do. If I said nay, you'd know I was lyin'. I miss the food, I miss the people, and aye, I miss the little challenges of goin' out and takin' what I need to survive. But tell you what I don't miss, that's the guard around every corner always lookin' at every rat like we just come from murderin' someone. I don't miss the pinch in my stomach those nights when all the locks are too strong. An' I don't miss walkin' up to a friend's shelter not knowin' if I'm gonna find 'em alive or dead or maybe just never see 'em again."

Coryn didn't say anything. After a moment Clement reached over to curl fingers around his bare wrist. "What I'm sayin' is, this is a change, and there's good an' bad in it. Been on the street my whole life an' I never had someone to lie in bed with an' listen to the rain, an' that's a plus as well. I'd dig a dozen meal-worm trenches if I get to have this after."

The wolf brought his paw over to rest on Clement's. "I'm glad to hear that," he said. "I like having you here. I'm glad we keep talking Ki into another week and another week."

"Gets easier each time. Helps that Lucy's such a bright li'l thing," Clement said. "If we was in Divalia I'd steal her some books. She'll be reading sooner than that school is likely to teach her."

"We can get books if we go back in the spring." Coryn's

thoughts went to the market. "You don't have to come back with me, though."

"Can test the waters when it comes to that point." Clement leaned back and smiled.

Another thought occurred to Coryn. "Won't you have to go back to Divalia sometime to get the thing...?"

The rat turned his head very slightly. "Wot thing? Oh, the *thing*. Aye, mayhap. Down the road it might be useful, for sure and certain."

"You're just going to leave it?"

Clement laughed. "Aye, m'dear, it's in one of the safest places I know of. So safe only one other person knows about the place, and I feel sure he won't go lookin' for it."

Coryn met the rat's amused stare. "Me? I might find it?"

Clement reached over to scratch behind Coryn's ear affectionately. "You might, if you put your mind to't."

This felt at that moment like the rat had far more confidence in him than Coryn had in himself. In all of the huge city of Divalia, where would he look for something an expert thief had hidden? What places did he even know about where a thief might hide something? "Oh," he said. "Is it—"

"Shh." The rat laid a finger across his lips and then brought his muzzle over to kiss the wolf. "Let's leave it unsaid and we'll hope you never need to find it. What would you do with it anyway?"

"I wouldn't even know what I was looking for," Coryn grumbled around the kiss, his tail wagging.

"Best that way." The rat pulled back and winked at him. "All right, all right, let's go fix this roof."

The rain was useful in that it showed exactly where the leaks were, so someone could go up and place the patches while the person below, in the loft, called out when the patches were situated correctly to stop the leaks. Coryn was all set to go out in the rain, but Clement stopped him. "I'll go get wet. I'm lighter and," he flexed his paws, "got better hold in the rain."

"I climbed the Great Cathedral in the rain," Coryn reminded him.

"Aye, five years ago." The rat grinned and squeezed Coryn's midriff. "You're a touch thicker than then, I'd wager."

"I fixed the storeroom roof," Coryn pointed out. "I know the stable roof."

"You've got thicker fur an' it'll take longer to dry."

Coryn laughed. "I'll stay warmer longer." He licked the rat's nose. "I'm going."

"A'right, but if you get cold, yell." The rat eyed the ceiling. "So I call out when the drips stop?"

"That'll help." Coryn put his pants on but left his shirt off. The air and rain would be chilly, but he didn't have many tunics and he preferred to keep them dry.

The stable had been built by his grandfather, unlike the storeroom, which Coryn remembered helping his father build. Toward the back of the loft, makeshift rungs had been nailed to the wall, leading up to a small, sheltered window from which one could climb out onto a ledge and make one's way easily to the roof. As cubs, Coryn and Ki had often climbed the rungs to jump into the soft piles of hay despite the threat of punishment if their parents caught them. They were not allowed onto the roof, but sometimes they snuck out there anyway, once they had grown enough to be able to pull themselves up from the ledge.

After a quick run through the rain to retrieve the roof patches from their storeroom, Coryn swarmed up the rungs and took one more look to judge around where the three leaks were. "I'll start there," he said, pointing, "and then that one and then that one."

"Aye," Clement said, positioning himself below the first.

They worked through the morning and managed to put

temporary patches on all three of the leaks, enough that Coryn would be able to come back when the weather was clear and finish the job.

Once he'd told Coryn where to put the patches, Clement fed Elly and cleaned out her stall. By the time Coryn slid back in through the window and descended the rungs, the rat had returned to the loft and was waiting with a blanket to wrap around the wet wolf. "Don't want to get the hay wet, as I recall," Clement said with a grin.

"True enough." Coryn hurried through the stacks of hay to descend the short ladder to the stable floor, and then shed the blanket to run with Clement to the house for breakfast.

* * *

The smell of porridge and the warmth of the stove gave the room a comfortable feel despite the thick smell of wet fur; Lucy and Ki had also been doing chores outside. "The nice thing," Ki said, "is that the rain barrels will be full. Save you a trip to the spring for the next few days."

"It's a good thing," Coryn said, "because I'll need to take Elly the day after tomorrow."

Ki perked her ears. "For what?"

Coryn looked very fixedly down at his porridge bowl. "Oh, just an errand I have to run." It had been a mistake to put off telling Ki and Clement about Lord Barclaw's offer, but at the beginning when he'd thought he would take it, he had found the moments with them too lovely to ruin with his imminent departure, and as Clement stayed another week, and another, Coryn had begun to hope that Lord Barclaw would forget. Then he could stay here on his farm where he'd rediscovered a life he was looking forward to.

Lord Barclaw hadn't forgotten. So Coryn would have to go

and face him, turn down his offer in person, and only now as he considered it did he wonder whether Lord Barclaw would accept his refusal. Giving Coryn a gift was not the only way to keep him around; Coryn could just as easily live in a cell in his castle. But if Coryn didn't go, Lord Barclaw would send someone else, maybe multiple someones, to drag Coryn back to his castle by force.

Now his sister stood with paws on her hips and even Clement had left off eating to give him a quizzical look. "To where, and for how long?" Ki asked.

"I'll be gone most of the day," Coryn said. "It's just a thing I have to do."

"Then why don't you want to tell me about it?" When he didn't answer, Ki said, "Come now. I don't need Clement to tell me that you're worried about something."

Coryn sighed. "I'm going back to see Lord Barclaw."

There was a short pause before Ki and Clement both said, "What?" but with very different tones.

"Why Lord Barclaw?" Clement asked.

"I thought you were done with him," Ki said. "The debt's paid, isn't it?"

"What debt?" Clement turned between the two wolves.

Ki patted Lucy on the shoulder. "Why don't you go have your porridge in the bedroom, dear?"

The cub flattened her ears. "Do I have to?"

"Yes." Ki picked up the bowl and put it in her paws. "Go."

Tail between her legs, Lucy took the bowl and sulked off to the bedroom. She left the door open, but Ki walked over to close it, shutting off the cub's "Awwww" from inside.

When she returned to the wooden table and sat across from Coryn and Clement, both she and the rat looked at Coryn expectantly. He ate one more bite of porridge, thinking about how he was going to explain it all, and then put down his spoon.

Briefly he told Clement about the debt he'd incurred for that theft five years ago, but he didn't take any pleasure in watching the rat's ears twitch. "But the reason I have to go back is because he offered me a farm. On his land."

Both sets of eyes watching him widened. "He offered you *land*?" Ki asked.

"He wants somethin' else from you," Clement guessed.

"Yes." Coryn inclined his head. "In addition to the money I've been paying him each month, the reason he bought the debt was that...he heard I was caught with a male thief."

"Oh."

"Ohhhhh."

"Well," Clement said after a moment. "Whatever you been givin' him must be top quality."

Ki shot him a look and raised an eyebrow. The rat grinned. "I got no complaints, but I dunno what a Lord might have at his disposal, ey?"

Coryn flattened his warm ears. "It doesn't matter."

"Take it as a compliment, lad," Clement said, patting his paw. "From the Lord, anyway. Was no secret what he liked in his bedchamber; his Lady was a male until a few years back."

"Did she—he—pass?" Ki asked.

Clement nodded. "Mate of mine went to the funeral."

"You knew a noble?" Her eyebrows rose even higher.

"Nah, nah." Clement chuckled. "Only there's sometimes crowds there an' people are often less careful about keepin' track of their valuables."

The eyebrows shot down into a glower. "That's terrible."

"I never went." Clement put a paw to his chest. "Mourning ought not to be disturbed. Weddings, now, big showy displays of wealth? That's fair game. Was fair game," he added hastily, "back when I did such things."

"Hmph."

"Let's drop a li'l wolf cub into the streets of Divalia with barely enough food to keep alive and see what honest, upright way she manages to survive," Clement said amiably. "Not sayin' what I done was right, but if you'd seen nobles wearing enough gold to feed yer family for a year, you'd feel like the scales could use a mite o' rebalancing, I promise."

Coryn cleared his throat. "So I have to go back and tell Lord Barclaw that I don't want to take the farm, that's all."

"Why couldn't you tell him when he offered?" Ki asked. Coryn licked his lips, and Ki's ears stood straight up. "The suitors," she said. "That's what you were waiting for. You thought if I married someone, then you could leave us."

"I—"

"If you want to leave, then do it," Ki said. "Lucy and I will be fine here by ourselves."

"Wait!" Coryn said as she half-rose from the table. "A whole farm, doubling our family's holdings? That's hard to turn down. I—I had to think about it."

Ki sat, looking warily at him. "That's true. It would be good for our wealth, if perhaps not for the family."

"I know. That was my thought, too."

"Then why are you turning it down now?" Her gaze traveled to Clement, who was staying very quiet. "Because of him?"

"In a way." Coryn took a breath and glanced at Lucy's bedroom. "Even when I didn't have to go to Lord Barclaw anymore, I still felt—I felt like I'd ruined so many things and I wasn't done paying for it yet."

Ki's ears splayed and she folded her arms. When she spoke again, her voice had softened. "So why shouldn't you and Clement go farm this other farm?"

Coryn turned to the rat, who looked to be struggling with a smile. "I'll go where you go," Clement said. "I'd miss little Lucy, though. And her mother, truth be told."

"Coryn is a terrible mess in the kitchen," Ki said with a smile.

"Not only for yer cooking, but I thank you for th'warning." The rat gave an answering grin.

"I can cook meat and vegetables," Coryn protested.

"You say 'cook,' I say 'burn,'" Ki said, "but I suppose it's all of a one."

Coryn shook his head and smiled. "The last few weeks since I came back from Divalia have been...very nice. I feel like a family. I don't want to leave that."

His sister tilted her head. "We didn't feel like a family before?"

"Did we? It isn't just since Father died, nor even since my mistake. If Lucy weren't here..."

Ki flattened her ears. "I've been very busy raising Lucy, I know."

"We both have," Coryn said. "That's not what I meant. I meant, would you and I still be living here? Lucy's a joy, and I love her. I love you both. But she's yours—as she should be. I'm not her father. Having Clement here feels like we both have someone now, and Lucy loves him, too."

"I do love you, Cor," Ki said softly. "I know we don't talk as we used to, but you could..."

"Ah, the lad's trying to say he's happy now," Clement said. "Leave him be."

"You keep saying 'lad,'" Coryn said. "I'm not that much younger than you. Am I?"

"Perhaps not in seasons, but in experience."

"That's for sure," Ki said.

"Hey." Coryn pointed a finger at her. "You're only two summers older than me and you've barely been out of Doubleford."

"There's wisdom you don't need to travel to get," Ki said with her muzzle pointed up.

"Like the wisdom to see through Galan's lies?" Coryn asked.

Ki opened her mouth, shut it, and then said, "You think I haven't noticed how much happier you are now? Why do you think I stopped objecting to Clement staying?"

"Because Lucy likes him?" Coryn said, half-jokingly to cover the smile Ki's question brought to his lips.

"What I'm angry about—not angry, really, but—it's that you didn't tell me about this Lord Barclaw farm when it happened."

"What I'm more worried about," Clement said with a claw-tap on the table, "is this Lord Barclaw and Coryn going to turn 'im down. In my experience, if a Lord wants somethin' bad enough to give you a piece o' land for it, he won't take 'no' for an answer."

Both wolves splayed their ears at that. "Well," Coryn said, "I know there's a risk—"

"He can accuse you of stealin' while you're there visitin' him and delivering your rejection. When you visit, are there ever valuables in the room?"

"I know," Coryn said. "I've thought about it. But I think—I think that he wants me to want to be there, if that makes sense? I don't think he would hold me against my will."

"To keep you in his company? Aye, he would. Mind, I'm only sayin' what I might do if I had his desires and all that wealth and power. There's other things too. Could take this farm."

"We're on Lord Deverin's land," Ki said faintly.

"He knows Deverin well enough to get him to send suitors here," Coryn reminded her, his hackles rising. "Or at least his steward. I'm sure Lord Deverin doesn't care about our farm."

"Likely not." Clement drummed his fingers on the table. "I suppose you could just not go back. See how much he really wants it. Might be too much trouble to come look for it."

"Ah," Coryn said. "About that."

Both of them gave him quizzical looks, and he cleared his throat. "He did send someone about a week or two ago. Wanted me to sign the deed right then."

"Guessing you didn't do that," Clement said, and when Coryn shook his head, the rat asked, "How'd he take it?"

"Ah...not well," Coryn said. "But it was—I mean, Lord Barclaw had told him to get a signature and he didn't, so maybe he was just unhappy that he wouldn't be able to do what his Lord asked?"

"Or," Ki said, her voice low, "he was unhappy because he knew how unhappy Lord Barclaw would be." She sighed. "Coryn, why...?"

"It's all my fault to begin with," he said.

"Not that thing." Ki glanced at Clement. "I mean, getting entangled with a Lord?"

"I'm sorry," he said, "but I don't see how I could have avoided it. He told me he'd bought my debt and then said he'd heard I was amenable to providing comfort to fellows like him, and what was I to say? 'Of course, my Lord, but I prefer them younger and more attractive'? Or should I just have been terrible at it and risk him selling the debt to someone else?"

"I know." Ki reached across the table. "I'm sorry. It was a bad situation all around."

"That bein' the case," Clement said, "and seein' as how I feel somewhat responsible for the start of all this, which you've all very kindly decided not to mention, what say I go with you to the Lord's? I might at least be able to see what he's about an' head off a scheme before it comes to pass?"

"Oh," Coryn said, "I don't know—"

"That's not a bad idea." Ki steepled her fingers and regarded Clement. "If you can get Coryn out of this arrangement, then as far as I'm concerned, you have a bed here for as long as you want it."

The rat's face broke into a broad smile. "Aye, that sounds like fair trade t'me."

"Yay!" came a cry from the bedroom, and all three of them, looking in that direction, saw the door cracked and the gleam of a small eye peering through.

They talked throughout the chores that day of how they might approach Lord Barclaw. Coryn recounted the talks he'd had with the old bear, which weren't frequent. The birthday present had been one of the longest they'd had. Still, the more he told Clement, the more (unsurprisingly) they decided that the old Lord was mostly lonely, not malicious. "He might also be a touch heartstruck by you," Clement said with a grin as they swept debris out of the storeroom.

"Oh, I don't think so," Coryn protested automatically, but he wasn't as sure as his words.

"If he's lonely we can suggest some other remedy, but if it's you he wants, that makes it trickier." The rat set down the broom and gave Coryn a steady look. "Tell me true: would you go visit him monthly if that's his price for not taking his gift?"

"If it meant I got to stay here and—" He'd been about to say, "and you could stay as well," but realized that was putting a lot on Clement, which the rat hadn't necessarily agreed to. "And be with Ki and Lucy, then yes, I suppose."

The rat nodded, with a little grin that told Coryn that maybe he'd heard the unspoken part of that sentence. "Right, we'll keep that one in our sleeve then. Never haggled with a Lord before but I reckon I can make it work."

"Maybe we could get advice from Lokyl," Coryn said. "He's dealt with some lords, I think."

"The trick to hagglin' is to know the least yer willing to give and then stay firm on it." Clement grinned. "But aye, worth gettin' all the advice we can."

"Stay firm" was easy advice to give, but Coryn wasn't sure

how easy it was going to be next to the powerful and forceful bear. Still, knowing that Clement would be there with him heartened him and made him believe it really would be possible, even when he remembered Cantril's intensity. The stable roof had been mended, and Molyna was well on her way to having a new way to keep her mealworms, and they'd be fixing the storeroom and building the chicken coop soon enough. Clement had made many things possible and had eased Coryn's life in general, so he was inclined to believe that the rat could do nearly anything.

As the sun sank lower in the sky, they prepared for their journey. They had decided that since Clement was so slight, they could both ride Elly there and back, with maybe an extra stop to rest her. Clement was looking forward to the ride after Coryn told him how pretty it was, "since all the way here I was buried in a wagon, heh."

Coryn was about to respond to that when his ears perked up. "Mounts," he said. "A lot of them."

The rat cocked his head. "I don't—ah, there they are. Right, this is me makin' myself scarce then. If it's bandits, give a yell." Before he'd even finished saying the words, he ran off to the stable.

Coryn walked to the house to warn Ki that there were riders. "What is it now?" she asked at the door. "Not another suitor?"

"No, it's a lot of them. You and Lucy stay here. I'll go out and meet them."

"If it's Lord Barclaw come to kidnap you," Ki said, "I'm coming out to fight."

"Don't worry." Coryn smiled. "He'd have sent a wagon."

She came closer. "Is it for Clement, you think?"

A month ago she would have been angry; now she was worried. "He thinks so." Coryn nodded his head slightly toward the stable. "So if they ask, you don't know anything about him."

"I'll tell Lucy too." Ki disappeared back into the house.

The riders had come into view by the time Coryn made his way out to the road. There were four mounts, each bearing a large rider: two cougars in front, a wolf and muscular skunk behind them. Each of them wore the same livery, a bright red tabard (though spattered with mud) with the royal crest on them over a dark blue tunic.

Coryn braced himself against a five-year-old memory, but the effect was fainter than it had been a month before. "Good evening," he said as casually as he could. "How can I help you?"

The cougar on the left, the taller of the two, spoke first. "Is this the farm of Coryn?"

"It is."

"And you are...?" The cougar leveled a look at him.

"I'm Coryn. What is this about?"

"We've had a report that you're harboring a rat we've been looking for." The cougar sounded bored. "Have you?"

"I don't know," Coryn parried. "What are you looking for him for?"

The cougar lowered his brow. "Is there a rat on this farm or not?"

"There was." Coryn forced himself not to look at the stable. "He moved on. He's been doing odd jobs around the town, I think."

"You won't mind if we look around, then, will you?" The cougar gestured to the two behind him without waiting for an answer from Coryn. "Check the house and the grounds. Lox and I will go with Coryn here over to those buildings." He nodded to the stable and the storeroom.

Coryn followed his gaze. "Of course," he said, hoping they would make enough noise that Clement would have time to hide, hoping the rat had been smart enough to gather his things.

He paid little attention as the wolf and skunk made their way to the house; Ki would be fine.

The two cougars dismounted and walked their mounts over to the stable. "Will you be staying here for the evening?" Coryn asked.

"We have to take the rat back to Divalia," the cougar replied.

The other one, Lox, said, "We'll probably stop at the inn a ways up the road and then get back to Divalia tomorrow."

If you find the rat, Coryn said quietly to himself. "We'd make do if you had to stay," he said. "Four extra plates is a lot, but my sister is equal to it."

"Five," said the lead cougar absently, and pointed at the two buildings. "Which one was the rat staying in while he was here?"

Coryn led him to the stable, making enough noise to let Clement know they were there as he guided the cougars and their mounts in. "You can tie up the mounts there if you like," he said, offering them space across from Elly, who regarded the newcomers placidly.

"Lox, check the loft," the lead cougar said, beginning by inspecting Elly's stall.

The other cougar climbed the ladder to the loft. Coryn tried not to watch him, tried not to be obviously listening for a shout, a scramble. He imagined Clement jumping from the loft and running past him out the door and planned in his head how he would swipe, seeming to try to catch him while letting the rat escape.

But seconds stretched into minutes, and Lox did not shout, nor did any rat leap from the loft in a terrified run. While the lead cougar poked his nose into all the stalls, Lox moved hay around and reappeared on the ladder several minutes later.

"Smells like rat," he reported with a long look at Coryn, "but no sign of him."

"Right." The lead guard turned to Coryn. "Take us to the other building."

They investigated the storeroom, which took longer because there were more places to hide. Coryn watched, his fur itching with the intrusion of the guard and his fear for Clement. He knew that the guard were working under orders of the king, to whom he owed allegiance, but he still had not forgotten how, five years ago, the guards hadn't even seemed interested in helping him but had stood by while his father and the noble bear had sentenced him.

The wolf appeared at the door of the storeroom. "Sir," he said. "The rat isn't in the house."

"All right. Lox, keep looking around here in case we missed something. Coryn, come with me." The cougar beckoned him with a paw and then addressed the wolf guard. "What does the informant say? Is this the right place?"

"He thinks so, sir, but he'll have to meet the farmer directly."

"Take him to the stables and ask him if the scent matches."

They were walking toward the house. Coryn's fur prickled. "What informant?" he asked.

The guards ignored him. "You checked the attic?" the cougar asked. "And all the closets?"

"Of course, sir," the wolf replied.

"Excuse me," Coryn said. "What informant?"

The cougar spared him a look, then turned back to the wolf. "Who else is in the house?"

"The farmer's sister and her daughter. We sent the daughter back to the bedroom. She was getting upset."

"What did you do to Lucy?" Coryn burst out, but by that time they were at the door of the house, where the other two mounts were tied, and the wolf opened it for the cougar to walk in and Coryn to follow him.

Ki stood by the stove, her ears splayed and flat. Seated at their table were the muscular skunk and...

Coryn stared at the rat, thin and scruffy, ears ragged, like a sharper-edged version of Clement. Where had he come from? He must have been trailing behind the others or seated on one of the mounts behind a bigger rider.

The rat smiled nastily and got up, walking over to him, and then pressed his nose into Coryn's fur. "Oh aye," he said, all teeth and rasping. "He's the one."

Coryn couldn't help but get the rat's scent, and it stirred a memory deep inside him. The rat met his eyes and his unfriendly smile widened. "See, he remembers me too," he said. "He knows his old pal Two-Claws."

"No," Coryn said automatically, though his nose was telling him the truth. That sharpness, the dustiness of Divalia, but in different proportions, a little of the river mixed in—this scent hadn't changed in five years. "You're not—"

"Not what?" The rat drew a claw down Coryn's cheek to his collarbone. "The same as I was five years ago? We all change. You grew up too."

"Wait," Ki said. "*He's* the one from five years ago?"

Two-Claws perked his ears back to her, keeping his eyes on Coryn all the while. His smile never wavered. "What, has ol' Clem passed himself off as me? That's a laugh. I thought he just traded on your fondness," here he pushed his thigh up into Coryn's sheath not too subtly, "for rats."

"I don't know what you're talking about," Coryn said bravely.

Two-Claws stepped back. "Ah, cub, don't feel bad for bein' deceived. I told that story plenty of times, that young wolf cub that helped me out one night and how I left him in the attic of the Cathedral. Nobody else climbs the Cathedral so they put it down to fancy, but Clem, he knows I can do it. He knew the truth of it. Like as not he found Divalia a bit too active for him and when this piece of driftwood floated by him he leapt for it, knowin' you'd be easy to fool."

"I'm not—" But he had been. He'd had suspicions and he'd kept quiet about them because he wanted Clement here, wanted the companionship, wanted to feel like the last five years had meant something. He'd been just as foolish a month ago as five years ago. *And again, your family is paying for it*, a resurgent voice in his head said scornfully.

And here was the rat, the real rat, and all that night had meant to him was an amusing story to tell about a foolish wolf cub. He hadn't had to pay for the crimes at all. "Hey," Coryn said to the cougar standing a little way off, "he robbed a bear noble. I was there. I already was punished for being part of it, but he hasn't been. I'll swear that he was the one with me. He already confessed to that!"

He turned to Two-Claws with a triumphant smile that faded as he saw the amusement on the rat's muzzle. "Ah, bless the simple country folk," Two-Claws said. "These fine gents have no interest in my past as long as I help them bring Clem back. Which I plan to do."

"We searched the whole farm and he's not here," the lead guard said.

"He's not where you could see him, which I'd expect. Possible that they sent him away, possible that they knew we were coming, but..." Two-Claws came up to Coryn again and ran his muzzle along Coryn's tunic. "I think he's still around here. Whyn't you let a thief catch a thief, eh?"

The lead guard gestured to the skunk. "You two ride a few minutes down the road in both directions, see if you come across him. Lox and I will stay here with the informant and see if the rat's hiding."

The wolf and skunk chorused, "Aye, sir," and hurried out the front door of the house. The cougars waited while Two-Claws, after a long look at Coryn, turned his attention to the rest of the room. "Don't 'spect he's in the house, but maybe, maybe." He walked around tapping the floor with a foot, looking as though he were thinking over a problem, and then opened the door to the bedroom.

"Lucy!" Ki called, running toward him. Lox, close to her, seized her arm to restrain her, and the leader, next to Coryn, put a paw on his arm as a warning. A moment later Lucy ran out of the bedroom and into Ki's arms, clinging to her waist.

"Are you all right?" Ki asked, but Lucy just pressed her muzzle into her mother's tunic and stayed quiet, her tail flat against her legs.

Two-Claws strolled out of the bedroom after a few minutes. "No hidey-holes that I could find. I'll try upstairs."

The feeling of intrusion doubled as the rat disappeared up the ladder and Coryn imagined those sharp fingers rifling through his things, amused at the "simple farmboy" and his meager possessions. To distract himself, he asked the leader, "What did this thief steal that's so important?"

The cougar didn't say anything, but after a moment the other one, Lox, spoke up. "Sir, if we tell them...they might understand the importance."

The leader gazed at Coryn with bored eyes. "He stole the Seal of Lord Fardew."

Coryn and Ki looked at each other, and he saw no more understanding in her eyes than he had. She said, "That sounds important."

"It's the signifier of the title," Lox said. "It's ceremonial but also it's important because it's what the king gives to the next person to hold the title."

"Isn't that Lord Fardew's son?" Coryn asked.

"Fardew is a landless peerage," the leader said.

Lox added, "That means that it's awarded by the King. The lord himself can't designate a successor."

"So," Ki said, "if someone had this seal, they could claim that the king gave it to them? They could make themselves a lord?"

"No," Lox said.

"Not someone like him." The leader nodded up at Coryn's room, from where Two-Claws hadn't yet emerged. "But if he sold it to someone, who kept it until the king dies and then appeared with it...it could be difficult."

"Is the king going to die?" Coryn couldn't help asking.

"No," Lox scoffed. "He's just saying, someone might hold onto this for years."

"It would be much harder to find in years. So we've been instructed to return it as soon as possible," the leader said.

Two-Claws came down the ladder. "Not up there," he said.

"Why are you trusting him?" Coryn asked the leader.

"He knows what will happen if he fails," the cougar said.

Two-Claws laughed, heading for the door. "Also, I told him certain things. See, there was a certain servant got a bit too in his cups at the tavern one night and let slip one or two details that led a few of us to think it might be possible to take it. Clem was one of us there, an' I admit I never thought he'd be the one to do it. But 'ere we are. Let's go out to t'other buildings, aye?"

They followed him out, the cougars pulling Coryn and Ki with them, Lucy clinging to Ki's tunic, still sniffling and scared. Coryn wanted to go comfort her, but didn't dare pull away from the guard holding his arm.

Two-Claws went first to the storeroom, where he tapped the floor again and pulled up burlap cloths and canvas, looking in places where Clement couldn't possibly have hidden. Coryn was going to laugh at him until he realized that Two-Claws wasn't looking just for Clement; he was also making sure that the seal wasn't hidden on Coryn's farm.

But it wasn't; Clement had said that he'd hidden it back in Divalia. Of course, the rat had lied about who he was, so why should Coryn believe anything he'd said?

While they were waiting, the wolf and skunk returned and reported that they hadn't found Clement anywhere on the road. The skunk had ridden all the way to Doubleford and had asked people there, but nobody had seen a rat.

Finally, Two-Claws signaled that there was nothing of interest in the storeroom, and the whole group marched to the stables. Coryn found himself hoping that Clement had gotten away, escaped through the woods, and then scoffed at himself. *Why do you want to protect someone who took advantage of you? Who's put your whole family in danger?* he asked himself.

If they didn't catch him, did Coryn really think they would walk away and leave him alone? He'd helped a thief commit a crime before; he'd seen the justice that followed. If they didn't catch the thief, they'd catch the people who'd helped him, and they already knew that Clement had stayed here, could probably tell from the scent that he'd stayed here for weeks.

Coryn looked up as he entered the stables and thought he saw the barest flicker of movement on the roof. Was it a bird? Or was he imagining things? The sun had almost set and the shadows were tricky, but the more he thought about it, the more sure he was that there'd been someone there.

If he'd been able to lead them to Two-Claws five years ago, they wouldn't have punished him as harshly, would they? He and his sister might be married. His father might still be alive.

Whoever this Lord Fardew was, it sounded like he was a favorite of the King, which meant that he was as powerful as Lord Barclaw, if not more so. He'd have Coryn paying him silver every month for the rest of his life, if he was even allowed to keep the farm. He'd barely been free of debt for a month and now its shadow loomed over him again. What would happen to Ki and Lucy if Two-Claws found Clement?

And what did he owe Clement, really? The rat had insinuated his way into Coryn's life on false pretenses. The real Two-Claws, now, that superior attitude leavened with just a little hint that he might care about Coryn, that was familiar. It had only been Coryn's hopeful nature that led him to believe that the rat who'd abandoned him five years ago might have had second thoughts. Clement was as much a deceiver as Two-Claws, only he hadn't had a chance to abandon Coryn yet.

Anger and hurt buzzing through him as he entered the stable, he turned to the lead cougar. His only chance to save his farm and Ki and Lucy was to cooperate fully, he felt. "I didn't know anything about the theft," he said. "He told me he was this rat, from years ago, and that he wanted to make up for what he'd done. Said he was tired of life in Divalia."

The cat studied him but didn't say anything. Two-Claws, though, jumped in. "Sounds right to me. Farmboy wouldn't suspect nothin'."

"I just want to make sure," Coryn said, "that you'll leave us alone when this is done. That you don't think I had anything to do with the theft."

"All right," the guard said.

Coryn took a breath. "He's on the roof. I saw him as we came in."

"Coryn!" Ki said.

He didn't look at her or at Lucy. "I thought he'd gone, but he hasn't. You can get up on the roof by a ladder in the loft that leads to a window."

"Lox," the lead guard said. "Go check it out."

As the other cougar climbed up to the loft, Ki said, "Come on, Lucy, let's go back to the house. If we're allowed."

"Wait until we've confirmed that the rat is on the roof," the cougar said, watching the loft.

From here, they couldn't see the ladder at the back wall, so they all waited in cold silence, all except for Two-Claws, who hummed happily to himself and tapped his claws against each other. Neither Ki nor Lucy looked at Coryn.

Lox's voice called down a few minutes later. "He's up here, sir. Or at least there's a rat here."

Without waiting for further permission, Ki took Lucy by the paw and led her out of the stable. The lead cougar turned to Coryn. "You can leave too, sir," he said. "We'll deal with getting the rat down."

He wanted to say good-bye to Clement, but if he did, the rat would find out that Coryn had betrayed him. Even though he was convinced he'd done the right thing, he didn't want to have to face the rat again. Memories of their nights together, of laughing with each other, of the hard work Clement had done pushed their way to the forefront of his thoughts so that his ears burned. No, he told himself, he'd done the right thing. All those memories were built on lies, a foundation of sand. And besides, if they hadn't found Clement but knew he'd been here, they would've been back for Coryn. The guards needed someone to blame.

He was glad to turn his back to the stable and walk across the yard in the dimming light. He paused partway to the house and then, rather than confront Ki, went to see to the space where the chicken coop would go. It would take longer to build now without Clement's help, but...

There should be something after the "but," something about being free of lies, but all Coryn could think was how lonely it would be. That was what life was; it was lonely. He'd forgotten that for a few weeks, and the reminder had come like a cuff across the muzzle.

Footsteps pattered behind him, and a sharp voice called out, "Ho! Farmer cub!"

Coryn kept walking, but Two-Claws caught up to him and grasped his arm. Coryn pulled it away, and the rat laughed. "There there," he said, "be mad at me if you like, but none o' this was my doin', you know. You brought it on y'self."

That stopped Coryn. "How did I bring it on myself?"

Two-Claws regarded him with amusement and then mimicked his voice. "'I'm looking for Two-Claws! Tell him to come to the market!'"

Coryn flattened his ears. "Aye," the rat said, "that call made its way back to me, and Clem as well. And Clem knew my story, for I told it enough times. Oh, don't look like that. Wasn't all about how easy a dupe you were. Was the sweetest score I'd had in quite a while." The rat winked languidly at him. "And your muzzle was a fair second. Maybe third. That honey wine was excellent."

How could he have thought that Clement had been this rat? Because he'd wanted to. He'd hoped that Two-Claws cared for him, would come back to him one day, when the reality was this hard-edged thief. "I've got chores to do," he said.

"Course you do. I just wanted to say that you've grown up. Not the easy dupe I remember. The way you gave Clem up to save yer family, that was smart." Two-Claws met Coryn's eyes and put a paw on his arm again. "It's just what I woulda done. What I did, come to think on't."

"You?" Coryn shook off the touch and glared at the rat. "What did you have to do with it?"

"Oh, when Clem stole that seal an' then disappeared, an' I heard he'd asked a weasel friend to look for you at the market, I figured it was a good chance t'get m'self clear of a few things the guard been after me for." Two-Claws placed his claws on Coryn's chest. "They'll get the seal back if they have to pull out all his claws an' teeth t'do it."

The rat's touch prickled and almost burned, but Coryn couldn't bring himself to remove it this time. Why should he feel bad that Clement was going to be tortured? Why should he feel so bad that he couldn't move, that his blood roared in his ears and the sight of Two-Claws in front of him wavered, blurry?

"Unless you know where it is," the rat said casually. "Less he told you."

Coryn didn't answer. "No," Two-Claws said, "he said you know nothin' about it. I don' see why you would. For him to tell you anythin', that'd be...that'd be careless and cruel. It'd make you part of the theft."

Coryn's tongue felt thick in his muzzle. "I don't know anything."

"Course you don't." The rat removed his paw and grinned. "Without they found Clem, the guard would've taken you, y'know. They talked about it. If I found his scent here, which I did."

This was a distraction, was easier to respond to. "Why should I believe you?"

"Believe me or don't, it don't bruise my tail. I just came over here to tell you that, and to say it's sweet you been carrying me in your heart all these years. Maybe one day when I retire, I'll come back."

"Don't bother." Coryn turned and marched toward the house, and this time only the rat's laughter followed.

But Two-Claws' words stuck with him. He walked outside still troubled and stood for a short time as the wolf and skunk retrieved their mounts from the stable. A shadowy group of people clustered by the road, but in the dim light at this distance he couldn't make out details. For a short time he watched, and then he didn't want to watch anymore, and he returned slowly to the house.

When he walked in, the house wasn't as warm as he'd expected. Ki stood leaning against the cold stove, and on the table sat a single plate with two pieces of bread and some of the cured salt pork they'd gotten in trade from last year's market.

Coryn sat down and picked up the bread, but he didn't feel like eating. He turned it over in his paws and sniffed it, and finally forced himself to take a bite. "Lucy's in bed?" he asked, just for something to say.

Ki looked away from him and didn't respond right away. When she did, her voice felt hollow. Not cold, but...numb. "When you go to Lord Barclaw tomorrow, you should take his farm."

Coryn looked up. His sister's ears were back and her arms folded. "What—I should?"

She looked at him with the same determination that she'd avoided his gaze with earlier. "Yes. You said we felt like a family, and you just betrayed one of us, so I don't know that we're a family anymore. So you might as well take the land and go farm it."

"Ki—"

"I want Lucy to grow up understanding the value of family." Her voice stayed low, but tears glistened in her eyes.

Coryn rose from the table. "We knew him barely a month. He was a thief who you didn't even want to stay here in the first place."

"He made you happy. He made us all happy."

"I'm the one who fought for him."

"And you think that gives you the right to give him away?"

"I—I did this for us! You know, if they couldn't find him, they would've taken us prisoner. Someone has to pay for this crime."

She was quiet for a moment. "They said if they didn't find

him here, they'd have gone on to Doubleford. If they didn't find him there, maybe they would've kept on looking."

"They identified his scent. They knew he was here. That makes us part of it."

"Maybe they would've found him on the roof. That other rat seemed cunning enough to puzzle it out. But it wouldn't have come from your betrayal."

"Betrayal?" His own ears flattened. "Who's the betrayer? Me, or the, the," he waved an arm toward the outside. "The rat who lied when he came here, brought the royal guard to our town, and put us all in danger of having to be in debt to another lord just when we've gotten out of debt of one?"

"The rat you insisted we give a chance to, who proved over and over that we can trust him."

He got control of his voice and pointed outside. "This is what you were afraid of when he came here," he said. "Exactly this."

Her ears came partway back up. "You think you've done what Father would have done," she said.

He breathed heavily for a moment, annoyed that she had seen through him so easily—but then, she knew the story and she knew their father too. "He was protecting our family. If I hadn't sheltered that rat back then, if I'd just taken the guards to him—"

Ki sighed and slumped back against the stove. "He was trying to teach you a lesson."

"I know. That I have to be responsible for my actions."

She shook her head. "He was trying to teach you to obey him."

They'd never talked about the incident while their father was alive. After he'd died, there'd never been a time nor a reason to. "He—he was—"

"If he had vouched for you, told the guard there was no chance you were a thief, do you think the debt would have been as large as it was? If he'd asked you to explain yourself, allowed you to tell the story properly, would you have resented him all these years?"

Coryn swallowed. "I'm the one who made the mistake."

"Aye, and he's your father. He's supposed to support you, but he demanded obedience even at the cost of your freedom. How did that make you feel?" She didn't wait for an answer. "Because that's what you just did to that poor rat. And you did it behind his back, without even a word of explanation or the courage to betray him to his face."

He felt this was monstrously unfair, but none of it was untrue. "They're the king's guard. We have to obey them."

"But we don't have to do their job for them," she said, and wiped her eyes. "I want Lucy to grow up learning that family is important. I spent a lot of time teaching her not to listen to certain things our father said, and it exhausted me. I don't want to have to do that for another ten years. So." She pushed herself upright. "Take the farm. Go be Lord Barclaw's companion. I'll raise my daughter. Come say goodbye to her in the morning."

And Ki went into the bedroom and closed the door.

Coryn walked upstairs in a daze. Just a few hours ago, he'd been preparing to set out for Lord Barclaw's with the idea that he and Clement would come up with a plan to save the little family he'd built up around him. Now he was going to his bedroom alone, setting out tomorrow alone, and he'd lost not only a rat

(no, he hadn't "lost" Clement; Clement had never been what he'd said he was)

but also his sister and niece. Oh, he'd come see them; Ki wouldn't stay as mad as she was right now, and he'd come back for festival. They'd come out to see his farm.

He didn't want to leave them, but Ki had been very clear, and also clear that it was his fault. Which was unfair. He'd betrayed

Clement, sure, but the rat had lied to them first. He'd brought the guards here and endangered Coryn's family.

(Had he? He'd been honest about the danger. Two-Claws was the one who had led the guards here.)

Coryn rolled over on his bed. If Clement hadn't claimed to be Two-Claws, Coryn wouldn't have brought him here. He'd let that rat touch him, fuck him, all because of that lie. He pressed himself down into his bed and squirmed, feeling the rat's touch in his memory, all those pleasant memories now sullied and poisoned.

A sharp rap came from downstairs. "Farmer!" called one of the guards, and then, "Coryn," as though he'd only just remembered Coryn's name.

The wolf pushed himself out of bed, more because he was worried they'd wake Lucy than because he felt obliged to see what they wanted. He stumbled down the stairs and came to the door.

Outside stood Lox, looking bored. "Prisoner wants to talk to you before we leave," he said, and turned on his heel without waiting for an answer.

Wants to speak to me? What if I don't want to speak to him? Coryn wanted to ask, but the cougar was already halfway to the road by the time his half-asleep brain had formed the thought. He heaved a sigh and followed, trudging across the grass, his tail limp against his legs.

They had set up near the road, the other three guards and the two rats. Clement stood leaning against one of the mounts, his paws tied up in front of him, nobody else near him. Two-Claws stood closest, but he was talking to the skunk, who appeared to be doing his best not to listen to anything the rat was saying.

Lox led Coryn over to Clement. When the rat saw them, he smiled, though the smile was sad. "I'm going to stay here and listen," Lox said, and then gestured to Clement. "Say what you want and let the farmer get back to sleep."

Clement's smile made Coryn feel even worse. "Looks like I wasn't quite right about the danger," the rat said.

"They had help," Coryn replied.

Clement slid his eyes over to Two-Claws. "Aye, should've had my ear up for that one. Been jealous of me for a while. No love lost between thieves, and when I made that score..."

"I mean—"

"Makes me wish maybe I'd told you more about the score, you know. Won't be much use to me now, but you could've maybe used it. Would've made a nice negotiating piece for your journey, if you take my meaning."

It took him a moment to figure out that the rat meant he could've used the seal to offer in exchange to Lord Barclaw, or maybe to gain favor with the other lord, Fardew. Very aware of Lox's presence, Coryn said, "I wasn't counting on it, and now it doesn't seem like I'll have any need of it anyway."

"Why's that?"

"Oh," Coryn said, ears splaying out, "I'm going to take the farm."

"Not stay here with Ki and Lucy?"

"I turned you in," Coryn said.

Clement turned toward Two-Claws and then back to the wolf. "*You* did?"

"Not—I didn't call the guard. But when we were going into the stable, I saw you on the roof. You lied to me," Coryn said defensively. "If you ran away the guards might have arrested me or even my whole family."

The rat ducked his head. "Aye," he said softly. "They might at that."

Lox said no word to affirm or deny this. "I had to protect my family," Coryn said. "I had loyalty to a thief five years ago and it nearly ruined us."

"I understand," Clement said, looking truly miserable. "Believe me, had I known the guard were close I'da left days ago, not told you where I was going. The last thing I wanted was to harm you or Ki or Lucy."

"She's going to be heartbroken."

"That's kind of you to say. Been less'n a month and already she holds me to her heart."

"Yes, well," Coryn said. "You made an impression here."

"I'm sorry," Clement said. "I truly am. Been a thief all my life and thought I'd try something different. They tol' me I couldn't never have a family, but—well, they were right, turns out. But all the same, enjoyed life here more'n I thought I would. Even the work."

"Well, you stole that month just like you stole everything else," Coryn said. Why was Clement making this harder? Why couldn't he be the reprehensible thief Coryn knew he was?

"Maybe." Clement took a breath. "All I want is for you to know that I'm sorry and that I didn't lie. After that first one, I mean. I know that was a big 'un and you won't forgive it and I don't blame you. But all the rest of it was truly me. If that means anything to you."

Coryn wanted to say that it didn't, but he didn't want to lie, and in the end he settled for saying, "I hope they don't hang you."

"Ah," Clement said with a dry chuckle, "never fear for ol' Clem. They won't hang me 'less I tell them where the little bauble is, and I won't be doin' that until they promise not to hang me, so likely I'll be in that great jail in Divalia for a good while."

At this, Lox did give a short, "Hah." Coryn, who'd forgotten his presence, stepped back.

Clement raised his bound paws. "Tell Ki and Lucy I'm sorry, will you?"

"I'll tell them," Coryn said, and walked quickly back to the house.

If they were awake, neither Ki nor Lucy made a sound when he returned. He trudged up the stairs to his bed and fell down in it again, but sleep came no more easily to him than it had earlier. Clement had been trying to help him, clearly, telling him in the vicinity of the guard that he hadn't told Coryn anything about the stolen seal when in fact he had. "A place only two people would know," he'd said, and the more Coryn thought about it, the more he was sure that there was only one place that could be.

But what was he going to do with that knowledge? If they found it, Clement said, they'd hang him. Use it to barter with Lord Barclaw? Coryn didn't have anything more to barter for. Ki'd told him to leave and accept the farm, which was what Lord Barclaw wanted.

He tossed and turned, thinking about Clement's lie, about how the real Two-Claws didn't care about what had happened five years ago, about how Clement had tried to protect him after the guard had arrived, and about Clement hinting that Coryn could find the seal and use it to better his position with Lord Barclaw.

All the while, he felt acutely the chill, the lack of another warm body next to him. All the rest of it was truly me, Clement had said. Unsubtle manipulation, that, trying to make Coryn feel worse about what he'd done. Nothing a thief said could be trusted.

But...to what end? Lying about being Two-Claws, that had gotten Clement out of Divalia and a place on the farm and in Coryn's bed. Lying about his relationship with Coryn would get the wolf to what, go look for the seal he'd stolen? If Coryn found it, that would only be proof that Clement had stolen it.

No matter how he tried and tried to find a sinister meaning in those words, he felt in his heart that they had been a gift, a simple sentence that had decoupled the month from the lie that preceded it so that Coryn didn't have to feel that everything was tainted. As well as that, perhaps they signaled Clement also trying to convince himself that that month had been real and worthwhile.

Foolish cub. Foolish lovestruck romantic idiot.

Lying flat on his back with his tail pressed under him, he stared into the darkness of the room and tried to sort out his thoughts and feelings. There wasn't much choice left for him. Tomorrow he'd ride to Castle Barclaw and see the old bear, tell him he accepted his offer, and then probably ride out maybe with that other bear Cantril and see the farm, start to think about what it would take to make it livable for him. He'd move in as soon as possible, though he'd have to come back here and get some supplies—no, maybe he could insist that Lord Barclaw give him a mount and a wagon and a plow and enough to survive the winter. He might be able to get those concessions; if he played at still feeling the uncertainty he'd signaled by not signing the paper two weeks ago, the bear might be willing to offer him more to gain his acceptance. Coryn would have to judge how far he could push it before the lord's patience gave out and he threw Coryn in jail.

He wasn't particularly looking forward to any of this. It was just something he had to do, and that was better than nothing.

CHAPTER 8

I n the morning, clouds covered the sky. Coryn regarded the window from his bed; it was already late enough that light filled his room. Half-awake, he had the fleeting feeling that Clement was over in the stable, but the urge to go see the rat had barely made itself known before the memory of the previous night drowned it.

He tried to stifle his regrets. Just because you were sleeping with him doesn't mean he did nothing wrong, he told himself. Just because he helped you with the roof and helped Molyna with her mealworms and did chores without question and Ki and Lucy liked him doesn't mean that it wasn't right to turn him in to the guards.

But it was hard to continue to justify that thought when Ki had been so vocal in her criticism. Telling him to leave, to abandon her and Lucy? Saying they'd be better off without him? Surely that was anger of the moment, surely she didn't mean it. What had happened with Clement was unfortunate, but the rat had brought it on himself, and there were still three of them left here to live together on the farm.

With a night to think about it, surely Ki would take back her words. Coryn swung his legs out of bed. Yes, she'd tell him she was sorry, and he'd ride off to Lord Barclaw and try to get out of taking the farm, whatever he had to do. If it meant going back every month for visits, so be it. Lord Barclaw wanted Coryn to visit him, and he'd recognize that a visit a month was better than nothing at all, so he'd compromise. That was how things worked with lords and farmers, wasn't it?

With thoughts of Castle Barclaw's dungeons circling in his head, he descended the stairs. Lucy sat at the table staring at a bowl of porridge and didn't look up, but cupped her ears back.

"Good morning," Coryn said.

"Mommy says I'm to tell you good-bye," Lucy said. "You're going away."

"I am," he said. "Just for a little bit."

"She says you're going away because you were mean to Clement."

He came around the table and sat down across from her. "Your mommy and I had an argument about what to do," he said. "Clement did something wrong and I thought he should be punished for it. Your mommy didn't think so."

"She said he was trying to be good and we should have given him a chance. Don't you think we should have given him a chance?"

Her wide eyes stared up at him, and he couldn't look away. "Maybe," he said. "But the guards were here and if they didn't find him, they might have taken me instead."

"Oh." Lucy reflected on that. "But now you're leaving too."

"I'm sorry," was all Coryn could say to that.

Lucy got up from the table and walked over to him, and he pulled her up into his lap. "I'll see you again," he said. "I'll come visit, and maybe I can come help with the planting and harvest. This isn't good-bye forever, I promise."

She wrapped her arms around him. "I love you," she said.

"I love you too." He hugged her back.

When she got down, he said, "Tell Mommy I'm not taking Elly. I'll walk over to Aryss's farm and borrow one of his mounts. I don't know how long I'll be gone, and you'll need Elly around here."

"I'll tell her," Lucy promised. "And I'll feed Elly and take care of her every day."

"I know you will." He ruffled between her ears. "I wouldn't leave her with anyone else."

It tore at his heart to draw out the good-bye, so he picked up the bag in which he'd put his clothes and a few keepsakes, gave Lucy a kiss between the ears, and walked out.

Ki was working in the storeroom, no doubt there to avoid having to see him, so he walked quickly past the two buildings and out onto the road. It would be about an hour and a half to Aryss's farm, so likely he would have to spend the night at Castle Barclaw before riding out to see his new farm, but that was fine. Time was the one thing he had plenty of, now.

Since he'd been born he'd had chores to do, someone to answer to. When his father had died, he'd had to keep the farm going, keep making the payments to Lord Barclaw, make sure Ki and Lucy were taken care of. Now, for at least the rest of the day, he had nobody to answer to but himself. If he decided to keep walking past Aryss's farm, past Doubleford, and seek his fortune somewhere south of here, maybe in Oncit or Villutin or all the way south to Tistunish, nobody would miss him. Nobody except Lord Barclaw, and he would send an emissary to the farm, where Ki would say, I don't know, he left here a week ago, and they would assume he'd been killed by bandits or had suffered an accident along the way. And that would be the end of his story, as far as they knew.

The idea of complete freedom cheered him only slightly, because he knew he would not go even as far as Oncit, let alone

Tistunish. He was going to Castle Barclaw, he was going to take a farm, and he was going to live there, because that was what he had to do, the last legacy of his ill-fated adventure.

Besides, he was borrowing a mount from Aryss, and it would be quite rude to simply run off with it.

With the clouds filling the sky, there was no sun to relieve the chill in the air. Coryn walked briskly and mostly stayed warm, but the cold had settled well into his ears and nose by the time he got to Aryss's farm.

Aryss had a larger house than Coryn's: enough for him, his wife, and their two cubs, with room for more cubs should Canis send any along. His stables were a little way from the house, and instead of a small storeroom, Aryss had a series of small sheds. He believed that separating out his batches of grain was best; if mice got into one batch, the others might be spared. And behind the house lay the fields, twice the size of Coryn's but just as bare now, weeks after the harvest.

He spotted the old wolf right away, by one of the windows of his house hammering at something. "Ho," Coryn called as he got closer.

Aryss's ears swung back. He finished hammering whatever it was—it looked like he was fixing a shutter, Coryn could see now —and then turned and squinted. "Coryn?"

"Aye." Coryn raised a paw. "Good morning to you. I've a favor to ask."

"Of course." Aryss leaned back against the wall as Coryn approached, and lowered his voice. "I hope it's the kind of favor I can accommodate with my wife inside." He winked.

"As long as she hasn't too much attachment to one of your mounts," Coryn said.

"Ah, you want to borrow Dandi? Good, he's been itching to run. Come on." Aryss set off for the stables. "What's wrong with Elly?"

"Nothing. This is a long trip, a few days, and I didn't want to leave Ki and Lucy without her for that long. You can spare Dandi for a few days?"

"Aye, of course we can. I love having my small herd, but we've only work for one, and as I said, Dandi's hardly happy with a walk to the well. You'll be saving me the effort of running him."

"All right. I can give you a few coppers—"

"No, no." Aryss waved it aside. "We do favors for each other. No need to pay me."

Coryn didn't think it necessary to tell Aryss now that he'd be leaving the area. When he returned Dandi, he would tell him. "Before I go...did you think my father was a good wolf?"

Aryss half-turned, ears perked. "What brings this up?"

"You knew him longer than I did."

The other wolf stopped some twenty feet from the stable. "He did the best he could."

Coryn met Aryss's eyes. "That isn't what I asked you."

"Listen," Aryss said. "He's dead. Why not let him lie?"

Because it might be my fault that he's dead, at least partly, Coryn thought. Because he isn't dead, not really; he came between me and Ki last night. "I want to understand him better is all. I've never asked you about him. I never asked anyone else about him. I only knew him as my father, but now I want to know how other people saw him."

"All right. He's dead, I suppose, so it can't do any harm." Aryss took a breath. "He was a good farmer. He was honest and always dealt fairly with us. But, you know, he was a hard fellow. Losing your mother weighed hard on him and I think he always blamed himself. He was worried you and Ki would grow up and fail because you didn't understand how the world worked. So he laid down rules. Gorrisc—you remember him? Lokyl's father? Gorrisc told him once he was going to raise you cubs so straight you'd never bend. I remember the way he said that. And your father said, 'if they bend, they break,' and that was the end of it."

Coryn nodded. "That sounds like him."

Aryss tilted his head. "So I don't know. What makes someone 'good'? He was the best wolf he knew how to be, and he wanted the best for you. He might not have gone about that the best way, but he did *his* best. Does that answer your question?"

"Yes," Coryn said. "Thank you."

Dandi took more effort to control than Elly; he did want to run, as Aryss had said. Coryn gave him some rein once they got out onto the road, but then he had to pay attention because rocks and turns and other travelers came up faster than he was used to with Elly. So it wasn't until they had left behind the tame farmland and village for wilder woods, when Dandi had tired himself out and settled into an easier canter, that Coryn was able to settle his thoughts.

In his first wave of being angry at Ki, he'd thought that she was being as inflexible as their father had been. One little mistake and she was done with him? But maybe it wasn't all that little, and maybe it wasn't just one. When he'd turned in Clement, he'd been thinking about what his father had done, but he hadn't been thinking about it from his point of view; he'd been thinking about it as his father. He'd wanted to protect his family, but hadn't Clem also become part of his family, especially if everything since that first lie had been truth?

Looking back, he'd been doing what his father and others had told him to for most of his life. For years he'd paid the debt from his adventure, he'd stayed away from Divalia. When he'd dared to go back to Divalia, he'd called for Two-Claws and gone to the Cathedral, and those were the only things he'd done on his own. He'd set up his market stall where the others told him and how they'd told him; when he'd discovered Clement, he'd believed the rat and had done exactly what the rat had asked.

When the guard had come, he'd obeyed them and then had acted the way his father would have told him to.

And now, now he had nobody to tell him what to do. Only Lord Barclaw, who had ordered him to return to claim a farm, to live nearby and be his unofficial companion (*prostitute*, his mind whispered) for the rest of the old bear's life. A farm wasn't a bad payment for that, and it meant much more to Coryn than it did to the lord, for sure. It was a flattering valuation of his company, if you looked at it that way.

But if you looked at it another way, Coryn thought, he was freer than he'd ever been in his life. Ki had relieved him of obligation to his family (at least from her side). Clement was on his way to jail. Two-Claws had effectively disposed of any dream Coryn had of carrying his adventure forward. There was nothing tying him to anything except for a thread tugging him toward Castle Barclaw, and if Coryn thought about it that way, his shoulders lifted from the relief of obligations he'd spent a lifetime under.

With that relief, though, with that freedom, came uncertainty. If he could do anything he wanted, what should he do? The easy course was to follow the one remaining thread in his life, go to Castle Barclaw, accept the farm, and live for the next few years, or however long the lord lived, working the land and visiting the castle every couple weeks to take the bear into his muzzle. Not a bad life, and there were many who would take that over what they had now.

He came to the crossroads outside Doubleford and pulled Dandi to a halt. A right turn, along the east-west road, would take him to Castle Barclaw by sundown. Ahead, continuing north would bring him to Divalia in about two days' ride, maybe by sundown tomorrow if Dandi really wanted to run.

The idea that had been simmering in the back of his head came to the fore. What if he went to Divalia? He knew about where Clement had hidden the seal—it had to be in the Great Cathedral, in that upper room on the Rodenta side. When he'd visited the Cathedral with Aryss, he'd looked at the wall he'd climbed and it had seemed intimidating, but he'd done it once, so he could do it again.

And then what? After this romantic fantasy in which he re-created the most thrilling moment of his life, what would he do when he was standing in the room above the Cathedral with the seal in his paw? Sneak out of the Cathedral, possibly. Find Lord Fardew, perhaps. Negotiate for Clement's release? Unlikely.

Unlikely, but not impossible, was it?

He was already thinking about negotiating with Lord Barclaw; why not negotiate with this other lord? It would be easier, even. Coryn imagined himself offering the lord (a wolf, in his mind) his seal back, the lord's gratitude, Coryn saying modestly that all he wanted was the release of the prisoner supposed to have stolen it, since he obviously hadn't. Questions like "how did you come by it?" could be answered by coincidence. He happened to be in a part of town he'd been told to avoid and he'd noticed a loose stone in a building, in a bridge piling, in the street. Curious, he'd picked it up, and underneath it had been this gleam of gold.

Then why do you want the thief released? the lord would ask. All right, perhaps not the "found it somewhere" story. Someone, definitely not a rat, had started a fight, and in the midst of the fight he'd dropped the seal and then run away. Coryn had made inquiries and learned that someone was in jail for the theft, so in the spirit of Canis's commitment to just treatment for all, he wanted only for the innocent person to be released. That was how the plot would have gone in one of those romantic novels, but...

Dandi shook his head restlessly. Coryn broke out of his reverie and laughed. Juvenile fantasies, and why was he going through all of that trouble in his head to rescue Clement, who'd lied to him?

(*I didn't lie. After that first one, I mean.*)

Was this another pathetic attempt to infuse his life with adventure? The last time he'd followed a rat, he'd ended up in debt for five years.

But that rat he hadn't known, hadn't slept with (yet), hadn't worked beside for nearly a month.

(*All the rest of it was truly me.*)

Clement had put his family in danger, but so had Coryn, five years ago, and wouldn't he have wanted to be given a little more mercy? If Two-Claws had really valued him, had come to a daring rescue somehow, wouldn't he have felt grateful? Wouldn't that have acknowledged that something lay between them?

That wasn't the case with Two-Claws, but it was with Clement, and the fact that it had begun with a lie mattered less the more he thought about it. Coryn missed the rat already, his genial good humor and his industry, his cleverness and his warmth.

But Clement hadn't blamed him, wouldn't blame him, for whatever path he chose. Going to Castle Barclaw would be the sensible thing to do.

And it would be, as with most other things in his life, the path of least resistance. It would confirm that he was only what everyone expected of him, not even a little bit more.

After the disastrous night, his father's attitude toward him had changed. Coryn had been tasked with fixing the roof of the porch over the front door, and he'd misjudged and split one of the boards as he was trying to replace the part of the roof that had rotted. He'd had to go to his father to get another board, and he'd expected a remonstration about wasting wood and perhaps a lesson in where to hit a board so it wouldn't split. But his father had taken the split board without a word and given Coryn another. When Coryn, puzzled, said he was sorry for splitting the board, his father said, "I expected you might." That had been worse than a scolding.

He stared at the crossroads for another full minute. Dandi snorted and pawed at the ground, and Coryn leaned forward to pat the scaly head. "All right, boy," he said. "You want to run?" He turned Dandi's head northward toward Divalia. "Let's run."

CHAPTER 9

Dandi had rested enough that they sped along the road for the first hour, passing an inn and then another. Coryn judged that he could make it to the fourth one along the road, if his recollection of its location was correct.

With the wind in his fur, excitement rose in him. He was going on another adventure now, and as stupid and ill-conceived as it might be, he felt its rightness in his heart. He didn't want to go back to Lord Barclaw, and if he had to, he wanted to have accomplished something useful, or at least tried to. And maybe, if he did this, he could tell Ki about it, and she would see that his one mistake had been no more than that. After all, the one thing their father had never done was say he was sorry, in word or action.

Dandi's pace slowed as the sun sank in the sky, but they still reached the fourth inn a little after sundown, while twilight lingered around the shadows of the trees and only the brightest stars were visible in the sky. Coryn guided Dandi to the stable—there was plenty of room—and then took a room at the inn. After a pleasant meal, he lay down in the coarse bed, and though it was only wide enough for one, he imagined that there was a rat by his side.

Light rain continued in the morning, making the road sloppy, muddier, and slower. Dandi did not like the mud, and even when Coryn guided him to the firmer edges of the road, he seemed put off by the rain and had to be pressed to move at a canter.

And Dandi didn't even have fur to trap and hold the water, to weigh him down, unlike the wolf on his back. At any point, Coryn knew, he could turn around and go back toward Castle Barclaw, but he had made the decision and he would stick to it. Besides, he found himself unexpectedly eager to immerse himself in the busy streets of Divalia, eager to see the Cathedral again, and eager to go back to the room where he'd first bedded Two-Claws to look for the Seal of Lord Fardew.

There was nowhere else it could be. The story of that night was the only bit of Divalia that Clement and Coryn shared, and the only other places involved were the bear noble's quarters and the houseboat. The first wasn't secure enough, what with being visited by the bear and his family, and the other was gone. So it had to be in that upper room of the Cathedral.

That didn't necessarily mean that he would have to climb the walls of the Cathedral again. He could attend a service, hide himself inside, and sneak up when everyone had gone, perhaps. Or he could invent a reason to be in the building and then slip away. Something would happen, he was confident. Canis would not have shown him this path without there being a reward at the end of it.

Through the rain he rode all that day, keeping Dandi out of the mud as best he could, which was difficult when the mount got it into his head that he wanted to be in the middle of the road even if there was a huge puddle there. By the time they came to the next inn, Coryn was exhausted, so even though he'd planned on riding a little longer, he decided to stop for the night.

The stable was surprisingly full, but a young wolf pointed him to an empty stall, where Coryn spent more time cleaning Dandi off than he would have with Elly. Not that he didn't love his own mount, but Dandi was Aryss's mount, and any little thing that might go wrong—mud lodged in behind one of his talons, or a cut from a branch or stone—would be something that in Elly could be taken care of over time, but in Dandi would make Coryn feel guilty that he'd not taken care of him properly.

When he'd finished, he looked around the stable at the other mounts and noticed what he hadn't when he'd come in: the crest of the Divalia guard on the gear hung up outside two of the stalls. Even wet as it was, his fur prickled. It couldn't be—could it? They'd left the night before he had; they should be well ahead of him.

But no, they had said they were going to spend the night, and he'd walked to Aryss's, so that would make up for him having the faster mount. They could easily have gotten here a little before he did, with the rain equalizing the difference between their steadier and slower mounts and his faster one. He went over to the gear and sniffed: cougar and skunk, the same as two of the guards who'd taken Clement. And there was a faint smell of rat there as well.

What should he do? He'd already cleaned up Dandi, and the sun was well down by now. With Elly, maybe, *maybe* he would risk a muddy road on a night when clouds diluted the moonlight, half an hour or an hour down the road to the next inn. But something could happen to Dandi, and for that matter, something could happen to Coryn if Dandi fell, or if he met up with the kinds of people who rode the roads at night looking for single riders.

Maybe they'd already gone to their rooms. He would just have to be discreet when he went inside.

The young wolf in charge of the stables took his coin and pointed to the main building. "There'll be a fire in there, probably some mutton left as well." An empty greasy plate next to a candle showed that he'd partaken of the latter.

"What if all the rooms are full?" Coryn asked.

The wolf stared at him and then squinted at the horses in the stable. "Got more rooms than stalls, so can't see how all the rooms would be full."

"Could I sleep here in the stable?"

Now the wolf frowned. "Micha'll charge you same for a bale of hay as for a room. Take a room."

Coryn hesitated. If he insisted, the wolf would wonder why he was so reluctant to sleep in a warm inn with a fire, especially as soaked through as he was. The guards' crest hung prominently behind him, and it wouldn't be long before the connection became apparent. "All right," he said. "A fire does sound nice."

The wolf's ears flattened. "Aye, it does." He glared down at his candle as though scolding it for not being warmer. "Go, an' I'll look after yer mount."

"Thanks," Coryn said, and slipped the wolf another copper, which brightened his expression.

The inn, a large two-story building that stood a ten-second run from the stable, glowed with life through the windows. Coryn drew his dripping cloak up around his head and slipped through the door with as little fuss as he could.

At first glance, he didn't see any of the guards, and that relaxed him as he made his way through the crowded tables to the bar. Most of the patrons were well into either their meal or a large tankard of ale, and the smells of food made his stomach growl, reminding him of the meager lunch he'd stopped for in the shelter of a tree many hours ago.

The broad, laughing wolf behind the bar took a moment to get to Coryn, but when he did, he took in the wet cloak and fur and smiled sympathetically. "Four copper for a room with a hot meal by the fire, and we've got the back fire going too, if you can't find space to hang up that cloak here. Two beds free upstairs, one with those wolves," he pointed to a brown wolf and a grey wolf at a table halfway to the door, "and the other with some mice, but..." He searched the floor. "I think they've gone up already. I'll put you in with the wolves, shall I?"

"That's fine." The wolves had plates in front of them with plenty left to go and they seemed engaged in jovial conversation; Coryn would introduce himself once he'd made sure the guard were up in their rooms. "You're Micha?"

"That's me." The wolf's smile didn't waver. "You've stayed here before?"

"No, no. The stable wolf told me."

"Ah, Sylich. My sister's cub. Good lad. Your mount will be well tended."

Coryn slid coppers across the bar. "I don't doubt it."

"Go sit with those wolves and I'll bring your meal out."

Coryn glanced toward the fire, but all the space in front of it looked full of wet cloaks and people. "Where's the back fire?"

"Around those stairs, small room next to the kitchen. There were royal guards there but I think they've gone up." He leaned in close to Coryn. "They had a prisoner with them, can you imagine?"

"A prisoner?"

"Aye! They wouldn't say what, but they're taking him back to Divalia, I heard. I'd no idea the King's reach came down to these parts."

"His claws are long," Coryn said. "Did you see the prisoner?"

"Some mangy rat. I can well believe he's a thief."

Coryn nodded, his throat tight. "If they're still there, I won't disturb them," he said.

Micha acknowledged that with a nod and then went into the kitchen. For a moment, Coryn stood at the bar, and then walked over to the brown and grey wolf. "Evening," he said. "I'm Coryn and I'll be taking the spare bed in your room, according to our host."

The wolves introduced themselves as Raich (brown) and Perent (grey), and made room for him. He told them he'd be back in a moment as he peeled his cloak away from his fur and clothes. "Going to try to find a place to hang this to dry," he said.

"Good luck," Raich chuckled. "You're a little late for that."

"Going to try the back fire." Coryn pointed to the stairs. "Back in a moment."

He cast a sharper eye around the tables as he made his way to the foot of the stairs, and from there he could see the small doorway, about half the size of a normal door, and the dancing glow of the fire beyond it. Another step and two people came into view, two people Coryn knew: one cougar in a guard's uniform, and a scruffy rat, picking his teeth with a bone and smiling a nasty smile.

He ducked back out of sight so quickly that he almost bumped into a table. The rats at the table looked up at him curiously, and he realized how strange his behavior must seem, so he said, "Sorry," and moved back toward the main fire, where he found space for his cloak when a bobcat removed his to go upstairs.

Raich and Perent welcomed him back, and he'd barely sat down before Micha appeared with a bowl. "Not to make you talk during your supper," Raich said with cheerily perked ears, "but where are you bound and what drives you there?"

"Mmf." The meal was cubes of chewy mutton and a large

hunk of bread that had probably been baked that morning, but it was still excellent to Coryn's famished palate. He chewed several times and swallowed. "I'm going to, Di, er." It occurred to him that he shouldn't tell people he was going to Divalia, but he couldn't think of a convincing lie and he'd already started saying it, so he finished the word. "Divalia. I farm barley and I'm going to talk to a merchant we sell to. What he wants to buy will determine how we farm in the spring and what seed we buy this winter, if we need to buy any." He picked up another chunk of mutton. "And you two?"

Raich, the talkative one, told him they'd just come from Divalia and were headed to Deverin. They were merchants and, like him (they thought), were taking advantage of a slower time to go around and talk to their suppliers while their wives minded the store back in Radbridge. "We got agreements for them to send down some of the wood they're getting from the expeditions to the northern lands. Some of it's rare indeed, a thick dark wood that has a lovely sheen when polished. Perent here is the crafter and I'm the seller."

"What do you make?" Coryn asked between mouthfuls.

They made all kinds of things but mostly chairs and beds, sometimes larger pieces of furniture, sometimes smaller. It depended on what Perent saw in the wood. While Coryn finished his dinner, he kept his ears focused on his companions, but his eyes trained on the door by the stairs, to see when Two-Claws might come out.

As he ate, the thought occurred to him that if he could find which room Clement was in, he could help the rat escape. *No, idiot*, he told himself. Several people had seen him here, he'd given his real name, and if Clement did escape and somehow nobody noticed that he'd been at the inn where it happened, the guards would come right back to his farm first thing. And if he took Clement to Lord Barclaw's, well, it wouldn't take the royal guard long to catch up with him there.

No, he needed to stick to his original plan and keep his head down—literally, whenever Two-Claws and the cougar came out of that room. In the meantime, he made pleasant conversation with the two merchant wolves and filled his stomach with mutton and bread and ale.

It wasn't until he'd finished his dinner that he caught movement out of the corner of his eye and looked up to see the rat and cougar closing the door behind them. He ducked his head, licking some of the meat juices off his plate while trying to focus his ears to hear when they'd mounted the stairs.

It seemed to take a long time for their footsteps to hit the wooden boards, but eventually Coryn picked out the click of claws (that would be the rat) and the soft shush of clawless pads (the cougar) making their way up the stairs, getting fainter, and gone.

Then he dared to look up again, and sure enough, the stairs were empty. Raich, who'd been talking, didn't seem to notice Coryn's distraction. "Licking the bowl," he said, elbowing Perent. "You know, maybe these high society manners are overrated. Seems to me like Coryn's got the right idea. I only wish we'd thought of that."

Perent looked a little askance. "I suppose," he said.

"I, uh, ran out of bread," Coryn said, trying to cover. He licked his fingers clean.

"No, no," Raich cried. "Why rub your fingers around the bowl and then lick them clean the way we're told to do? I say lick the bowl and keep your fingers cleaner! What else do you farmers do that we ought to know about?"

Take in thieves and get confused about them, Coryn thought. "We're mostly the same as anyone else," he said. "Do you not know many farmers?"

That sent Raich off about how not many farmers bought their furniture, a discussion that continued even after they suggested retiring to the room. Coryn said that their furniture sounded very nice and if he lived in Radbridge or even nearer to it, he would probably buy some. "Very kind of you," Raich said as they walked up the stairs. "If you ever do come through the city, you know, we're on the market square. Well, a block off of it. If you go to the carpet merchant's place on the corner and then follow that road down, you'll find us."

"I'll look the next time I'm there," Coryn promised, following the two wolves to their room, where he took the empty bed and lay down with his bag at his side.

It took him a little while to sleep, because he was imagining Clement in one of the nearby rooms—maybe even just on the other side of the wall. He put his paw to the wall, but resisted the urge to press his ear to the wood; Raich or Perent might see him and wonder what he was doing.

Clement was probably asleep. This would be the most comfortably he would sleep for a long time, unless Coryn could help him. And now that he'd decided to help Clement and forgive the rat his lies (the one big lie), or at least to weigh the good against the bad (or to make up for what he'd done in turning the rat over), he found himself so anxious to help that he tossed and turned and at least once thought that he might as well go to the stables and take Dandi out, since he wasn't going to sleep. And then he rolled over and opened his eyes, and Raich and Perent were moving about the room in the early morning light.

Now he was faced with a dilemma: Get out early, get on the road, and hope to stay ahead of the guards, or wait, trail behind them all the way to Divalia, and make sure they didn't notice him. If he left early, Dandi would probably keep him ahead, but there was always the chance that they'd end up at the same inn again, or that something would slow the mount and they'd come up behind him.

But if he trailed behind them, and they stopped on the road and he came up, they might also spot him.

"Join us for a quick piece of bread before we get on our way?" Raich asked. "If you want a chance of making Divalia by sunset, you'd best be on the road now."

With some effort, Coryn shut down that voice that told him that meeting the guards here was a sign. He could do this. "Is there another road to the city?" He pulled himself up to a sitting position.

Perent and Raich looked at each other. "If it's just you," Raich said, "there's no need to follow the road. Keep the sun at your back and on the right until noon, then keep it on your left, and you'll come in sight of the city soon enough. But you won't make it by sunset and then where would you sleep?"

Perent spoke. "What's wrong with the road?"

"Nothing," Coryn said. "Only I worry about bandits, especially being alone."

"Don't know as you'd be safer off the road," Raich said.

"We never got attacked on the road," Perent added. "Did you?"

"No," Coryn admitted.

"The King's men patrol the road. Maybe not as much this time of year, but...best to stick to it."

"All right." Coryn stood. "I'll come down and share your company a little longer."

They picked up some bread and tea from the bar and ate by the fire, where Coryn's cloak had almost completely dried. Perent ate the (much fresher) bread while Raich sipped tea and shared more of what he and Perent had to look forward to on the road back. They knew it well enough that he could talk about the river crossing and the fish you could buy there, and the inn two hours outside of Radbridge—"We could make it home if we hurried, but we like Rinalda and her bread, and she bought some furniture from us."

"And why hurry?" Perent asked.

"True enough." Coryn had situated himself so that he could see the stairs, and he'd decided that when he was finished with his bread and tea, he'd leave. If the guards had come down by then, he'd follow them cautiously; if they hadn't, he'd give Dandi his head, weather permitting, and race for the city.

He'd just gotten halfway through his chunk of bread when a large group of feet descended the stairs. With ample warning, Coryn pulled his cloak up and leaned back against the wall where Perent's large form mostly hid him from sight.

There were the four guards and two rats he knew. Clement kept his head down, paws tied behind his back. Seeing him sent an impulse tugging at Coryn's heart to run over and apologize, tell him he was going to try to make it right, but he couldn't do that, not without giving away that he knew where the seal was.

The guards paid little attention to the rest of the bar, and Clement even less than that, but Two-Claws looked around, his sharp eyes scanning and probing, and Coryn had to hope that his half-hidden muzzle sitting with two other wolves looked inconspicuous enough that the rat wouldn't peer closer.

The guards marched Clement out the door, with Two-Claws trailing behind. Coryn couldn't help one look at the door as they left, and found Two-Claws staring straight back at him. He froze, but the rat didn't say anything, only paused for a moment, smiled slightly, and walked on out of the inn.

Coryn took his time after that, making his tea last until Raich and Perent had finished. They bid him good-bye and safe journey, which sentiment he returned earnestly, and then they made for the stables to prepare their mounts.

Most of the people at the inn left quickly after rising, so by this time, Coryn was one of the few left in the large downstairs room. Micha came over to ask him if everything was all right, and he said he was giving the road a little more time to dry out in the sun.

They talked about the unpredictability of weather in the winter and the smaller number of travelers on the road, and then Micha asked where Coryn was bound, and Coryn said Divalia, and Micha said, "I suppose you've resigned yourself to stopping one more night before reaching the city. If you'd left earlier you might have made it in a day, but I believe in winter they close the gates around sunset."

"Aye," Coryn nodded, making up more reasons on the spur of the moment. "I've borrowed a friend's mount and I'd as soon not ride him too hard."

"Good fellow." Micha clapped him on the shoulder. "Many I know would treat a borrowed mount worse than their own."

"This friend I want to keep," Coryn said, and Micha laughed.

When Coryn finally went out to the stables, to his surprise he found a red-uniformed cougar standing there making conversation with the stable hand—Sylich, if he recalled correctly. The cougar's ears perked; there was no question that he recognized Coryn. "Lox, is it?" Coryn asked.

"Aye." The cougar nodded at him. "Making for Divalia?"

Coryn told the story about the barley supplier, and the guard nodded throughout, though his long, ropy tail flicked from side to side. "Well," he said when Coryn had finished, "this is a happy coincidence. My mount pulled up a little lame this morning, and I've been asking this fine young wolf about treatments for it. Isn't that right?"

Sylich's splayed ears belied his, "Yes, sir."

"And as it happens, I was about to be on my way as well. If you don't mind being slowed, I'd greatly appreciate the company."

There was no doubt in Coryn's mind that the offer was not one he could refuse. He'd been spotted by the rat, if nobody else, and the guards had decided to escort him to Divalia to make sure he didn't try to carry out any mischief. After all, if he wanted to help Clement escape, it would be much easier on the road than from whatever prison they were taking him to.

"I would much appreciate an escort," Coryn said. "I was just telling my roommates how nervous I am as a lone rider approaching Divalia."

"Then it's settled." Lox smiled without humor and extended his paw to clasp the wolf's.

And so a few minutes later, Coryn rode out beside Lox. The day was pleasant, the sky clear and the sun warm despite a brisk breeze that carried the smell of trees and the nearby river with it. If not for his apprehension over the company, Coryn would have quite enjoyed the ride.

They moved at a quick walk, which frustrated Dandi enough that the mount kept breaking into a trot, making Coryn rein him in and apologize. Lox said he understood, and indeed, he seemed to be having similar troubles with his own mount, who did not show any signs of lameness. There was not much room for conversation as the two riders did their best to control the mounts, but they did talk about the weather, and Lox asked Coryn some questions about managing a farm.

When they stopped for lunch and tied the mounts up near each other, Dandi snorted, eyed the other mount, and went right to nibbling at the bark of the tree for insects. By the time Coryn and Lox had finished their small portions of dried meat, however, the other mount had come over to Dandi's side and shown enough interest that the mount gave up his disdain and grew playful, as much as he could manage when tied to a tree. And after that, they had less trouble keeping the two to a slower speed, because they wanted to stay together on the road.

This gave Coryn more of a chance to talk to Lox, after thinking during the morning and lunch about what he might even say. The company had been pleasant so far, so he felt comfortable broaching the risky topic of Clement. "I hope you don't mind," he started out, "if I talk about the thief you caught at my farm."

The cougar nodded. "I would be surprised if you didn't want to talk about him. What can I tell you?"

"You know that I had no idea he was a thief."

"Of course." Lox accepted this as easily as Coryn had accepted his mount's lameness.

"I was, er, involved in a theft many years ago. The rat might have told you." Lox did not comment on this, so Coryn went on. "My punishment was to replace the value of the stolen items even though I didn't have them and there wasn't much proof that I'd been there when they were taken."

"But there was some?" Lox asked.

"Er—yes. As I said, I was in the company of a thief..." Coryn massaged the facts of the night not only to make them more palatable to Lox, but to himself as well. "But I didn't really understand what we were doing. I was young, so I was there, but the thief—Two-Claws, the rat who was helping you..." There was no reason to hide that, and in fact Two-Claws had probably told them himself. "He took all the stolen goods. I didn't know where to find him. The guard only found me."

Lox gave one curt nod, staring ahead. Maybe confessing to being part of a theft had been the wrong tactic. Coryn said, "But I made restitution. My father and I paid back the value of the stolen goods over five years, and I haven't been involved in anything like that since then. And I won't. I learned my lesson."

"That's good to hear." Lox did turn to Coryn, though he didn't smile.

"But my question is...why wasn't Clement given the same chance? To make restitution?"

Lox didn't answer right away. "He may have been," he said. "Our captain would know if that offer was made, and he would communicate it in that case. I didn't hear anything about it. But I can guess.

"The Lord's Seal is an item of inestimable value. I would not imagine that anyone of his station—or yours or mine, come to that—would be able to repay its value over a single lifetime. So I would be surprised if any such offer were made. In your case, I presume the item was significantly less valuable, and the owner would be satisfied with money in place of its return. In this case that won't be an option."

"That makes sense." Coryn had guessed that, and it wasn't what he was really interested in anyway. "Then what will you do with him if you can't find the Seal?"

"All I know is we bring him back to the city and take him to the dungeon, and after that it's not my problem anymore."

"Have you ever known someone to steal something this valuable?"

"No."

"What's the biggest theft—the biggest crime, I suppose—you ever caught someone for?"

"Oh, hum." Lox's demeanor changed again, from cautious to thoughtful. "There was a skunk that killed three people in an inn."

"Canis's teeth!" Coryn swore. "All at once?"

"Over the course of two weeks. He'd sneak into rooms where people were sleeping alone and cut their throats, take their valuables. Once was dismissed as a personal quarrel, but he kept going back to the same inn. After the second time, we had a guard there every night out of uniform, and I happened to be the one there when he cut a beaver's throat and made a bit too much noise climbing out the window. I ran around and caught him with blood on his paws."

"And what happened to him?"

"Few months in the Royal Prison and then," Lox mimed a noose and jerked it up over his head. "Good riddance to 'im, too."

"Were you very scared when you went to catch him?" Coryn drew out the story even though he'd already gotten the information he wanted: the murderer had gone to the Royal Prison, and therefore Clement was likely also bound for a cell there.

"Not much," Lox said. "Murderers are cowards. If they could fight properly, they wouldn't sneak around in the night and cut sleeping throats. He didn't put up much of a fight, although he did nick me with his knife."

"I don't know that I could hold my own in a fight," Coryn said.

"I can teach you a few things if you like," Lox said. "When we stop for the night. There's an inn another few hours on that I think will work well."

Undoubtedly this would not be the inn that the rest of the guards would be stopping at. "That would be fine," Coryn said. "I'd like that, thank you."

By the end of the day, Lox's mount and Dandi had cemented their friendship, making low grunts back and forth as they trotted along the road. At the inn Lox guided them to as the light faded, sure enough, Coryn saw no sign of the other guards in the stables or in the main room.

This inn, closer to Divalia, had a greater variety of meat and also threw some parsnips in the bowl with the pork Coryn asked for. He enjoyed the meal, and Lox was a good enough conversationalist that he remained mostly distracted from thinking about his mission.

Afterwards, they retired to their room, which they did not

have to share with anyone else, and Coryn sat on his bedroll, ready to lie back and try to sleep, though he wasn't really tired. But Lox turned with two knives in his paw. "Did you want me to teach you some basics of fighting?"

Coryn got up, but eyed the points on the blades. "Do we have to do it with knives? I thought you were going to teach me grappling."

"I can do that too, but you'd best learn to defend yourself with a knife. Have you ever fought with one?" Coryn shook his head. "By Felis, do you even own one?" Again the headshake, Coryn feeling like a cub who'd forgotten to do one of his chores. "Well. Here." Lox flipped one of the knives around to catch it by the blade and held the handle out to Coryn.

The wolf took it gingerly. "All right," Lox said, "we can start with grappling, but before that I'm going to show you how to hold that knife, okay?" He reached out and rearranged Coryn's fingers, then held out his own knife. "Like this, you see? You secure it with these fingers, and the thumb goes along here. That lets you use the thumb to guide it and add pressure when you need to."

Coryn tried the grip and felt the increased control. "Thank you," he said. "This feels better."

"It's basic training," Lox said modestly. "Remember to keep the knife between you and the other fellow. Lots of people like to swing their arms out and make big swipes or stabs from the side." He held the knife in front of himself, pointed at Coryn. "When you're starting out, keep it like this, point toward the other fellow. Jab forward. Keep your grip on the knife."

Coryn held his knife the same way. "I understand."

Lox nodded approvingly and then put his knife down on the bedroll. "Now, grappling?"

They squared off on the floor of the small room. Lox showed Coryn where to put his feet, how to crouch slightly to make himself harder to push over, and how to use an opponent's strength against him. Coryn ended up on the floor several times, but he thought he was getting some good lessons out of it, and after about half an hour, he succeeded in pushing Lox over onto his bedroll.

Being close and physical with the cougar was bringing other thoughts to Coryn's head as well, even though Lox showed no interest in grappling in that way. He kept his arousal under control, focusing on the moves Lox showed him and on balancing his weight the way he was being taught.

After an hour, Lox said, "All right, I thought I was going to wear you out, but you've got a cub's bounce to your tail still. I'm ready to sleep, but good work. I'd wager you can hold your own with an inexperienced fighter now."

"I hope I don't have to," Coryn said.

"Being in a fight is different too. You can practice all of this, but when you have to decide to do it in a second, it's harder. If you haven't had practice in that, then good for you, but the first few times you'll probably make a mistake of some kind. We all do. I did." He held out his arm to Coryn and pointed out a fine line of white in the tan fur. "Rabbit with a knife. I didn't get my off-arm out of the way in time."

"I've got scars too," Coryn said. He lifted his tunic to show his stomach. "You can't see it, but..." He knew where the ridge of scar tissue was under his white fur. "I got kicked by a mount— not the one we have now, but the one before that. Gashed my stomach open and my mother thought I was going to die. I remember the surgeon from Doubleford, a wolf who smelled sharp like barley wine gone bad, but he had gentle paws and said it wasn't as bad as it looked. I got to stay in bed for a week and my sister had to do all my chores." He laughed. "She hated me. She said she was going to go stand behind a mount if it meant she got to lie about for a week."

His father had said little, only, "I told you not to stand there. You got what you deserved." And it had been that following winter that his mother had gotten sick and died.

"I've never been kicked." Lox did not take Coryn's implicit invitation to feel the scar on his stomach. "But it doesn't sound like fun."

"It isn't. And I was...six maybe? It was a long time ago." He let his tunic drop.

"Survivors, both of us," Lox said, and grinned. "Let's get our rest and take to the road fresh in the morning. If my mount permits, we might reach the city walls by sunset."

They might, but somehow Coryn doubted it. He believed Lox's mission was to make sure Coryn did not reach Divalia until Clement was securely in prison.

So he lay back in his bedroll, and as he had the night before, he imagined Clement lying next to him. His paw traced the fur on his stomach as the rat would do, and he remembered one night the rat asking about the scar when his fingers found it. Coryn had told him the story, and Clement had said, "I'd like to have met your mother." Coryn had asked the rat about his family and Clement had said, "They look after themselves and I look after myself and that's the end of our story." Then Coryn had remembered Clement saying he'd been on his own since he was ten, and he wondered.

After that, Clement had moved his fingers lower and teased Coryn's sheath, and they'd stopped talking about parents.

Now Coryn's fingers, substituting for the absent rat's, found his sheath already warm and full and aching for a touch. He stroked himself gently, then more firmly, and then stopped, aware of Lox's steady breathing in the other bed. His body wanted release, but he'd already basically invited the cougar to sleep with him when he'd pulled his tunic up, and the cougar had declined.

So he rolled over onto his stomach, pressing his sheath uncomfortably into the bed and hoping that would keep him from putting his paws on it. It did, but it also kept pressure on his sheath and that didn't make it any easier to go to sleep. Finally he slept, but fitfully, and he woke in the morning at first light before Lox was awake.

He could get up quietly, go get Dandi, and be on the road probably before the cougar woke. But that would seem suspicious; they had agreed to travel together and they'd gotten along well, so why would Coryn flee unless he had some reason not to want a guard around? No, he was going to have to stay in Lox's company all the way to Divalia, and hope that the guard left him in the city.

Which likely meant another night remembering Clement, pressing his erection into his bed. That was fine. He would spend his time thinking about the task ahead.

So he got up and pulled his tunic on. "Lox," he said, and then again, until the cougar stirred. "Ready for breakfast?"

The day passed much as the last one had, although the rain returned, so the two riders spent much of the day with their cloaks over their heads, riding single file along the road. Dandi did not like the mud and did not like being behind another mount, even one he was friendly with, so Coryn took the lead and checked back frequently under his dripping cloak to make sure Lox was keeping up. He always was.

Inns came more frequently the closer they got to Divalia. If not for the rain, Coryn would be able to see the Great Cathedral's spire by now. "Say," Lox called from behind him as they approached another inn, the grey of the sky a little darker than it had been half an hour before. "I know it's still light, but

I'm tired of being wet. What say we stop in here? Divalia's an easy ride from here and maybe it won't be raining tomorrow."

The way the clouds looked, Coryn rather thought it was going to rain for at least two more days, but he was also tired of being wet. "All right," he called back. "It looks crowded, though." Three carts stood outside the stables already.

"Happen I might get us a room anyway," Lox said. "I know this inn."

They had to share a stall in the stable, which Dandi did not like until he was given mealworms and then he didn't care. After they'd attended to their mounts, Lox led Coryn into the inn proper, where he greeted the owner, another cougar, with a hearty, "Golan, you old swindler!"

"Lox!" The cougar wiped his paws on his filthy apron. "Come to harass decent law-abiding folk again?"

Lox looked around. "Why, are there any here?"

Both of them laughed, and Lox pulled Coryn up to the bar. "Golan, this is Coryn, a farmer on his way to Divalia, and I'm escorting him along the way."

"Ah-ho." Golan eyed Coryn. "Doesn't look like the sort to afford a personal escort, but I suppose whatever the King's guard can do to line their pockets..."

"No, no." Lox waved that aside, though not without a flick of his tail. "Our paths coincided, and we thought two safer than one. So have you a space where two might spend a dry night?"

"For an honored servant of the King, of course we can make space. Only the very best accommodations."

Lox twisted up his muzzle and said to Coryn, "That means we'll be in the attic."

Golan smiled broadly. "It is the very finest attic."

The attic was as luxurious as Lox had sarcastically claimed it to be: a plain room with slanted ceilings and two bedrolls and enough dust to suggest that the servant responsible for sweeping rarely climbed the ladder to get to this room. Coryn had sneezed upon entering the room and Lox had sniffed several times. "Once the dust settles it won't be that bad," he said, unconvincingly. "But with all the dust, and—" He gestured from the center of the room, the only place either of them could stand fully upright, "the cramped quarters, I don't think we should practice fighting tonight."

"I agree," Coryn said. "I would hate to impose any further on your generosity anyway."

"It's no imposition." Lox laughed. "The way I see it, if I've helped you survive some moment in the future, it was a small price that I'm happy to pay."

"I appreciate that." Coryn crouched down to his bedroll, and for a few minutes as they settled in, they didn't talk.

When both were stretched out, though, Lox began to talk rather than going to sleep. "I'll be glad to get back to the city. We don't usually leave it in the guard, and my wife and cub will be missing me. And I them."

"How old is your cub?"

"Five. She's just starting to help her mother at the stove, and we're going to teach her her letters soon. I know, most people say girls don't need to learn them, but she's smart, and my captain said that more and more of the nobles looking to marry are interested in mates with education, so here's hoping a few letters help her marry above her station."

"I'm sure she'll make someone a wonderful wife," Coryn said, thinking of Lucy, "and I hope he can well take care of her."

"Thank you. What about you? That cub at the farm, was she yours?"

"My sister's. I'm not married."

"So your sister's cub will get the farm? Or are you still looking for a wife?" He hurried on to say, "There's no shame in being a confirmed bachelor. One of my friends swears he won't marry and he'll give all his property to the Church when he's gone."

"I imagine Lucy will inherit the farm," Coryn said, which was easier than explaining that he held out a fantasy of returning with Clement. It did remind him that Ki had told him not to come back.

"So you're still hoping to find a mate, but sounds like you don't think it'll happen?"

"Something like that. It would be a long shot."

"You know," Lox said, "Gaia and her children work in their own time. Is there someone you've got your eye on?"

"After a fashion."

"I courted my wife for over a year," Lox said. "When I started, there were two other fellows courting her, and they were both wealthier than I am. But I believed in myself, and we bonded over that year, and she convinced her parents that I was an acceptable match. So what I'm saying is, don't give up hope."

"I haven't," Coryn said. "Not quite yet."

"Good." And then Lox talked about his family for a little while as Coryn thought about how he would bring Clement back to Ki and she would forgive him and welcome him back to the farm. The fantasy felt so much more attractive than settling on Lord Barclaw's farm that he had half-convinced himself of its reality as he drifted off to sleep.

In the morning, clouds blanketed the sky, but at least the rain had stopped for the moment, as Lox had hoped. The ground remained soft, and the road was more crowded, so they set out at a leisurely pace again, Dandi picking his feet up whenever he hit a particularly muddy patch. In short order they could see the buildings of Divalia, and then Lox started talking again. "Where did you say your business in Divalia is?"

"It's near the Great Cathedral," Coryn said.

"Oh! Fancy part of town." Lox chuckled. "Well, if you want a recommendation for a place to stay, you should try the Four Quarters. It's a good place for a reasonable price because they don't serve food, only ale and lodging, but you can get the food a few blocks away at the permanent market."

"Thanks," Coryn said.

"And make time to visit the Cathedral too."

"I have." Coryn had an idea. "Do they allow people inside when there aren't services? To admire the sculpture and windows?"

"From sunup to sundown," Lox told him. "But you should go for the services if you're going to be there then. The Gaiavox is a wonder."

"I'll do my best," Coryn said. "I mean, I think I'll be around for Caniday services."

"Good, good. Do you visit Divalia often?"

"Not as much as I would like," Coryn said.

* * *

They arrived in late morning behind a long line of people waiting to be admitted to the city and chatted as they ambled forward. After fifteen minutes or so, the rider behind them, a tall fox, called, "Ho, guard, what did you do that they make you wait in line with the rest of us?"

Lox turned and smiled. "I'm escorting a friend."

The fox snorted and turned to the people behind him, talking loudly enough that they could hear him. "If there's a merchant they want to bother, of course they're there, but when they want to spend time with a friend, they take their time."

The cougar shook his head and turned back to Coryn. "It's funny how people are so brave to say things when they don't think we'll remember who they are or what they smell like."

The fox went very quiet after that. Coryn returned Lox's

smile, but the exchange reminded him that Lox was a royal guard. Whatever friendship they had formed on the trip would not stop Lox from arresting him, especially if he caught Coryn breaking into the Cathedral or trying to break Clement out of prison. The cougar wasn't staying in line because he liked Coryn's company; he was keeping an eye on him for as long as he could. He'd probably suggested the inn so that he could check and see how long Coryn was there.

When they finally got through the gate and into the main road, Lox waved Coryn off to the side. "As much as I would love to accompany you to the Cathedral—I don't manage to go nearly often enough—I do have to go find my captain and report back."

"Yes," Coryn said. "I'm glad your mount is feeling better."

Lox's ears twitched, but an expression of confusion only crossed his muzzle for a moment before he smiled and patted the scaly neck in front of him. "I am as well. I'm fond of the girl and wouldn't care to break in another."

"Thank you for the recommendations," Coryn said. "And thank you for the company."

"My pleasure." Lox leaned toward him. "I hope your business is concluded quickly so that you may return home before the weather gets worse."

Coryn looked up. "I think it'll hold for a few days. We usually don't get a real chill in the air until Leventh."

"Oh, the weather can change very quickly," Lox said. "If I were you, I would stay in Divalia as little time as possible."

The warning was quite clear. "I understand. Thank you."

"Safe travels," the cougar said, and urged his mount off down the road.

The spire of the Great Cathedral guided Coryn along the roads, and even though he had to keep firm control of Dandi, who was unused to the crowds, he had plenty of time to think about Lox's recommendations and Lox's warning.

If Coryn went to the Four Quarters, as Lox had advised, he could be walking into a place where he'd be observed and followed. But if he didn't go, would Lox think it suspicious? Would he think that Coryn had avoided the Four Quarters because he was trying to hide?

There didn't seem to be any solution. Either he went to the Four Quarters and voluntarily let himself be observed, or he avoided it and let Lox question his motives.

Or maybe Lox was going to forget about him, and it didn't matter at all.

He turned Dandi toward the Cathedral, his thoughts still whirling around and around. After ten minutes of riding, the Cathedral looming taller over him with each step, Dandi brought him down the curve of a street and in sight of an inn with a sign hanging out front: a wooden circle with each quarter painted a different color.

He was here, and it was a convenient place to rest. If he stayed or left, it shouldn't be because of Lox, but because of what was best for Coryn. A minute, then two, and he couldn't come up with a convincing reason to go anywhere else. So he guided Dandi around the back to the stables, turned him over to the skunk working there, and walked into the inn.

CHAPTER 10

The next morning, which was Ursiday, Coryn bought a small meat pie and sat under the yellowing leaves of an ancient oak tree in a small, crowded park across from the Cathedral. Ahead of him, a quarter mile away, the great stone palace rose forbidding and stern, so Coryn turned to his left and faced the elegance of the Great Cathedral instead.

Where the palace was several hundred feet of brownish-grey sandstone, murky and dark in parts and light in other patches, the Cathedral's pure grey basalt felt clean and elegant. The light and dark patches on the walls felt sharper and more well-ordered. Except for the entrances, the palace was largely undecorated, but everywhere Coryn looked on the Cathedral, carvings of different species played across the walls, all raising their heads to the sunburst atop the golden spire so that it seemed each tier of reliefs was holding up the one above it. Every species he knew figured into the walls around the entrance, and then each of the six towers was crowded with reliefs of that god's children. Canis's tower was on the far side of the entrance from where he was, but where the tower rose above the body of the great building he could still make out the foxes, wolves, and coyotes looking adoringly up.

The palace sprawled, it seemed to Coryn, but the Cathedral stood. It rose above the other buildings, narrowing and climbing to Gaia's sunburst at the top, yet still solid and unyielding. From the sunburst, his eye traveled down to Rodenta's tower, topped with a grey stone sculpture of Rodenta herself. Up there somewhere was a Lord's seal—whatever that looked like—that could unlock Coryn's future.

The sun had barely climbed a quarter of the way to its zenith, still well below the golden sun atop the Cathedral, when the great bells tolled, and the doors swung open to allow a crowd of bears, raccoons, and badgers to emerge into the plaza.

They dispersed from the Cathedral out into the city, going to jobs all over Divalia, some of them walking toward the palace (it was easy to pick out the nobles from the others simply by the bright, clean clothes they wore). As a carriage pulled away, it revealed the coat of arms on the one waiting behind it, and Coryn jumped up, startled. He ran behind the trunk of the great oak tree and watched from concealment as Lord Barclaw tottered out of the church, supported by another bear, and climbed clumsily into the carriage. The companion followed him, and a moment later the carriage creaked its way along the streets toward the palace.

Lord Barclaw was here and not at his castle? It couldn't have anything to do with Coryn. Perhaps he had obligations in Divalia, and if Coryn were at Castle Barclaw now, he would be meeting with that bear who'd come to the farm.

As the carriage clattered on down the street, Coryn felt silly for hiding behind the tree. As if Lord Barclaw would have recognized him at this distance. He was a nondescript wolf in a city full of them. So he stood, and when the crowd had thinned enough, he walked over to the Cathedral entrance.

A tall bear in white robes with the design of Ursus on the front greeted him and the others coming into the Cathedral to look around. "Be welcome in your house, my Brother's son," the bear said.

"Thank you, my Father's brother," Coryn replied.

Farther inside, a bear, two badgers, and a raccoon in light yellow robes gave visitors a little more guidance. The raccoon smiled and touched Coryn's arm to slow him down. "You are welcome to admire any of the artwork inside here," he told Coryn, and pointed out the murals over the entrances to the six towers. This main chamber, broken up with a few pillars, made up most of the space of the Cathedral, with the pulpits in the center and six groups of wooden pews radiating outward from them. Behind each group of pews stood a tower, and here was where the great murals were painted, each one depicting Gaia, a figure with a glowing sun for a head and equally bright paws and feet protruding from her white robe, creating one of her six children. Around the creation scenes stood the species belonging to that god, tiny compared to Gaia and the god she was birthing. "These murals," the raccoon said, "were painted by the great painter Calmosi over a hundred years ago. Some of the art is older than that." He pointed over Coryn's head. "The stained glass sunburst over the door was designed and installed over two hundred years ago."

Coryn found the mural of Rodenta and looked above it. There, near the ceiling, was the balcony he'd looked over five years ago. "What's in the towers?" he asked.

"The Cantors live there and keep their books and vestments. Other items are stored there as well. I'm afraid it is not permitted to enter the towers." The raccoon bowed. "Thank you and enjoy your visit." He released Coryn and stepped forward to intercept another visitor.

Coryn wandered around the Cathedral and made his way to

the Rodenta tower. While admiring the mural, he stole covert glances at the door, which was firmly closed. An old mink stood next to him for a time, during which Coryn glanced around the Cathedral to see who might be watching. The greeters stayed near the front, and nobody else seemed to be watching the tourists around the Cathedral.

When the mink moved away, Coryn ambled casually up to the door and tried it. At first it gave, and then it stopped after a fraction of an inch with a solid thunk. He stepped back and regarded the door, and a moment later the white-robed bear was at his side. "That tower is reserved for my brother," he said. "He's not to be disturbed now, and these residences are private."

"I'm sorry," Coryn said. "I—I didn't know."

It was stupid, an easily disproven lie, but the bear smiled and rested a heavy paw on his shoulder. "It is admirable that you seek to learn about the other children of Gaia. I confess, though, that the mural of Herbivora is my favorite." The paw turned Coryn around and pointed him at the mural.

It was lovely, and Coryn said so, but he did not stay much longer in the Cathedral to admire it. He would not be able to get up to the room from the inside; that was what he'd wanted to find out.

He could not climb up the side of the Cathedral during the day, so that left him several hours to spend in Divalia. He walked over to the permanent market to get some bread and cheese for lunch—though Lox had said it was cheap, it still cost twice as much as Coryn was used to paying in Doubleford.

Here he watched every guard's uniform he saw, but he didn't recognize any of them. If Lox intended to watch Coryn, he had either delegated it to another guard or would remain around the Four Quarters.

Feeling safer, Coryn thought ahead to that night and realized that he didn't know what he was looking for, other than it being a seal and small enough for Clement to hold while climbing the outside of the Cathedral. Perhaps someone could tell him. Maybe Clement himself? He badly wanted to see the rat again, to make sure he was safe, and he actually asked directions to the jail and set out that way before talking himself out of that plan. It was foolish, it was unlikely to work; why would the guard, who had not let Clement talk to Coryn unsupervised at the farm, do so now? Why would they let him see the rat at all?

He stopped and turned back, annoyed at himself and at the guard, and the great sprawling stone of the palace caught his eye. His feet took him back along the road toward it. There would be people there who knew what a royal seal looked like, for sure.

Past the Four Quarters, past the Cathedral, over to the palace gate. Below him the river eased along in its path, and here the crowd thinned. Only people with business in the palace belonged here.

This had stymied Coryn at first, until he'd realized that fate had put into his path the only possible way he could gain entry to the palace.

He walked up to the metal fence that surrounded the palace, to the gates flanked by guard houses and the bears who stood there. Behind the gates, some fifty feet away, the majestic front door of the palace loomed.

"Ay," the nearest bear guard said as Coryn walked up. "State yer business."

He composed himself, looked down respectfully, and said, "My name is Coryn, and I have business with Lord Barclaw."

The guard looked him up and down. Coryn tried his best to stand up straight and keep his tail firm. "Business, hah? What business you got?"

His rough city accent made Coryn more aware of his own speech, but he tried to put that aside. "He sent for me," Coryn said. "I mean, not here. I was supposed to meet him at Castle Barclaw." This was the clearest look he'd gotten at the front gate of the palace, past the two bears and through the gardens to the palace proper. The arch's keystone, three times Coryn's height over his head, looked to be the size of his chest. A crown carved into it in relief was the only decoration on the plain grey stone, but on the closed wooden doors, the royal crest had been painted. Another guard stood within reach of those doors and opened one of them for the others who walked up and whom, presumably, they knew.

"Then you'd best be off to Castle Barclaw," the guard rumbled. "Hear you can get there in a week if you walk fast."

He laughed, and the other guard joined in the laughter. Coryn stood his ground. "I saw him at services this morning. I know he's in the palace."

"Whether he is or not ain't no business of yours. You think anyone's allowed to walk into the palace?"

A few people had collected behind Coryn by this point, though none of them pushed to get past him. "I think if a Lord has business with someone then that person should be allowed to."

"Listen," the other guard said. "If you want an audience with a Lord, you have to see the Junior Steward. He'll put you on a list and then when you're on the list, we get told about it and you don't have to have Bonto there make fun of you."

"Still might," Bonto grunted.

"The Junior Steward receives requests in the afternoon at the side entrance, around that way. See, there's already people waiting."

Down the river a few hundred feet along the palace, perhaps a dozen people had gathered. "But Lord Barclaw knows me," Coryn protested.

"Then you should get an audience easily," the other guard

said. "Off with you now." He looked behind Coryn. "Afternoon, Solly."

A porcupine ambled past Coryn. "Afternoon, fellows." Coryn gauged for a moment the chance that he could get past the two bears at the moment they opened the gate for the porcupine, but even if Solly had been a sleeker, less pokey species, Bonto remained alert even as his companion opened the door. So the wolf sighed and turned around and walked along the fence.

* * *

The Junior Steward, a wolf a little shorter than Coryn, and a fox who seemed to be his assistant met each of the people waiting individually. From what Coryn could hear, most of those meetings consisted of explaining why the person wasn't allowed into the palace.

Maybe he should give up. There wasn't any assurance that he'd be able to see what a seal looked like, and part of him didn't want to see Lord Barclaw again. But if he walked away now and never went to Castle Barclaw, Lord Barclaw would come to him. It wasn't a question of whether the confrontation would happen, but when, and here he'd been given the chance to control it. Besides, he thought, his decision already made, when else would he have a chance to see the inside of the palace?

When Coryn's turn finally came, he met the Junior Steward's assistant first, a short fellow in a jaunty red tunic and cap. "What business do you have in the palace?" the fox asked tiredly.

Made somewhat desperate by hearing all the people turned away, Coryn said, "I'm Lord Barclaw's paramour."

That snapped the fox's ears and attention up. "What?"

"I'm used to meeting him at Castle Barclaw, but I'm in

Divalia on business and he was at services this morning, and I would like to see him."

"I, ah..." The fox stared at Coryn for another moment and then turned. "Master Horiz. Master Horiz!"

The wolf turned from the rabbit he was speaking to. "In a moment, Vik."

Vik swallowed and turned back to Coryn. "It'll be just a moment," he said.

They waited until the rabbit's business was done, and then the wolf, Master Horiz, turned to them. "What have we here?"

The fox gulped. "He, er, claims to be Lord Barclaw's paramour?"

"Oh, does he?" Master Horiz examined Coryn up and down. "He's the type, I suppose."

"Lord Barclaw likes wolves?" Vik asked.

"Young males." The wolf smiled. "What's your name, paramour?"

"Coryn. I'm a farmer."

Master Horiz cut him off with a gesture. "I don't care. If we go to Master Barclaw and tell him Coryn is here, he'll know who you are?"

"Yes," Coryn said confidently.

"All right. Vik, go to Lord Barclaw's quarters and tell his personal servant that Coryn is here to see him. Come back as quickly as you can. Coryn here will wait for an answer."

It wasn't a question. "Yes, sir," Vik said, and ran back through the gate, to the palace, and inside.

Master Horiz indicated that Coryn should stand to one side, and then he spoke to the next supplicant. And the next, and the one after that. As he was talking to the fourth, the fox reappeared and whispered into Master Horiz's ear.

The Junior Steward's ears stood up. He turned to Coryn with

a grin. "It seems you're telling the truth. Vik, take our paramour to his Lord."

The fox opened the gate and gestured for Coryn to follow, while the others stared enviously after him.

* * *

The interior of the palace was everything Coryn could have hoped for: marble-floored hallways, elegant sculptures every few paces, tapestries, paintings of elegantly dressed kings and queens, velvet wallpaper patterned with the symbols of the six Houses and Gaia's sunburst, nobles walking in brightly colored and beautifully patterned clothing, smells of delectable food and exotic scents that Coryn didn't have a name for. His feet trod on images of feral deer, cougars, mounts, woven in fabric softer than his softest clothes.

He wanted to spend more time gawking, looking at all the beautiful decorations and people, but Vik moved quickly, and Coryn had to hurry to keep up.

They strode quickly down one hallway and then up a white marble stair with statues of bears at the base. Upstairs, Vik hurried Coryn through quieter but just as lavishly decorated halls. The portraits up here seemed to be of lesser lords, to judge from the less showy clothes and jewelry they wore.

The fox stopped at a door next to a portrait of a younger Lord Barclaw with another bear, the two of them smiling at each other. He rapped sharply on the door while Coryn admired the painting.

The door opened to reveal a skunk in a neat, trim uniform. He nodded to Vik and then looked past the fox to the wolf. "This is him?"

"So he claims."

"Coryn, was it?" The skunk appraised him in a way that was

becoming very familiar.

"Yes."

"Hm. I see. Well, I suppose you'd better come in, then."

Coryn turned to thank Vik, but the fox was already hasty footsteps and a white-tipped red tail vanishing down the corridor. So he followed the skunk into the chambers, whereupon his nose was assaulted with the smells of bear, lavender, chamomile, and other flowers. He knew Lord Barclaw liked floral scents from the castle, but here they bloomed in such profusion that he kept turning to the bright red and yellow stitching on the chairs and expecting them to be a real flower garden. Portraits of bears crowded the walls here, as well as a large tapestry showing a castle that was perhaps meant to be Castle Barclaw; it was hard to tell from the blocky woven rendition.

From the first room, curtained doorways led away. One smelled strongly of bear, but the skunk didn't lead Coryn to that one; instead he led him through the other door into a short hallway and to a small, tile-floored room where the smell of flowers went from strong to overwhelming.

"Clothes off," the skunk said.

Coryn blinked. "What?"

"Lord Barclaw orders that you be perfumed before coming into his presence." The skunk gestured to a small wooden cabinet. "You may place your clothes atop that."

"Um...can I ask you a question?"

The skunk tapped his foot. "If you can do it while disrobing, certainly."

There didn't seem to be any way Coryn wasn't going to get scent powder rubbed into his fur, which probably meant he was going to end up with Lord Barclaw's cock in his mouth before too long. So he pulled his tunic off. "I heard that a Lord's seal was stolen."

"Aye. Lord Fardew." The skunk took his tunic and folded it deftly.

"I've never seen a Lord's seal. Does Lord Barclaw have one?"

"Lord Barclaw's title comes from his land." The skunk held out a paw for Coryn's pants. The wolf pulled them off and gave them to the servant. "There is no need for him to have a seal from the king. His land holdings are recorded."

Coryn hesitated over his underthings. "What is a seal exactly? It must be small to be stolen."

"All the clothes, please." The skunk didn't show any excitement or anticipation at seeing Coryn's privates.

So Coryn dropped his underthings, and the skunk took them and placed them atop the others. "I have not been privileged to see Lord Fardew's seal, but Lord Fardew's servant has told me that it is a gold coin the size of a paw, with the seal of the kingdom on one side and the symbol of Lord Fardew on the other." The skunk took one of the small wooden canisters of powder and shook some into his paw, then applied it to Coryn's chest.

The wolf closed his eyes and tried not to enjoy the skunk's gentle paws too much, but by the time they moved down his stomach to his sheath, his cock was already half out. He thought about apologizing, but the skunk powdered the fur with delicate fingers and then moved on. Coryn's fantasies about having a more intimate, emotional connection with the servant receded.

When all of Coryn's fur had been touched and he smelled as though he'd rolled in a garden of sweet violets, the skunk stepped back and brushed his paws clean. "I will take you to his Lordship," he said, and then as Coryn reached for his underthings, "No; you will retrieve your clothes later."

He led Coryn back out to the hallway. Coryn kept his tail curled between his legs and one paw hovering near his sheath even after he checked that the front door was closed. No other movement sounded in the suite of rooms, but the relative silence didn't offset the discomfort he felt at walking naked through even this small section of the palace.

At the back of the suite, the smell of bear grew stronger. The skunk opened a door to reveal an elegant bedroom, dimly lit by the light that strained through closed shutters. The carpet of the hall, which had felt luxurious, gave up half an inch to the thick wool in the bedroom, dyed a bright blue with yellow whorls and flourishes in it. A large vanity stood against the right wall, flanked by an ancient wooden chest; to the left, two identical wardrobes in dark mahogany wood crouched side by side, one of them hanging open while the other remained tightly closed.

But dominating the room directly in front of Coryn was the great four-poster bed with a velvet canopy and a tangled mound of cerulean blue sheets strewn around the great form of Lord Barclaw, who seemed partially sunken into the mattress.

The skunk coughed as they entered the room. "Coryn is here, your Lordship."

The bear raised his head. Coryn made out the small shine of his eyes in a shadowed muzzle. "It is Coryn, isn't it? Come over here where I can see you properly."

With the bedroom door behind him and Lord Barclaw's familiar voice in his ears, Coryn felt less self-conscious about his nakedness. He let his paw curl around his sheath rather than hiding it as he walked over to the side of the bed.

The bear tracked his movements, and when Coryn came within two feet of the side of the bed, said, "That will be all, Perroh. I will ring for you when I'm done."

"Yes, sir." The skunk bowed and retreated out the door, closing it behind him.

Some of what Coryn had thought were sheets were clothes, he now saw, which Lord Barclaw must have shed and simply tossed on the bed. The bear lay completely naked before him, one paw working at his sheath and half-erect cock. "It is delightful to see you," he said while stroking himself. "I had expected you two days ago at Castle Barclaw, and when you did not appear, I was rather cross. But here you are! I should have known."

His stroking was not getting him past half-erect. Coryn sighed. "Milord, would you like me to—"

"Yes, yes, come closer." The bear beckoned him with a paw. "No, over here," he insisted, patting the side of the bed when Coryn made to get up on the foot of it.

Coryn came up to the side of the bed, and Lord Barclaw reached over with his free paw to close his fingers around Coryn's sheath. "Ah, yes. You feel lovely even if you are not as excited to see me."

"I didn't know if I would be able to get in—" The large fingers gripped him uncomfortably tightly and then moved down to enfold his sac as well.

"Well, here you are. Mmmm. It is a lovely treat."

Coryn didn't know what to say to that, so he stood still while the bear squeezed and massaged his sheath and sac, none of which aroused him much at all. Finally the paw dropped away, and Lord Barclaw seemed no more erect than before. "Milord?" Coryn said.

The bear's paw patted the bed. "Come up and use your muzzle," he ordered.

"Milord, I wanted to talk to you—" He stopped. If he waited until after Lord Barclaw had finished, the bear would be in a better mood, possibly sleepy, and would take the rejection of the farm better.

Coryn also considered that he didn't have to reject the farm now. But if he didn't, Barclaw would look for him everywhere until Coryn told him in person.

"I don't want to hear talking," the bear said peevishly. "Use that muzzle the way I ordered you to, and afterwards perhaps you may speak."

The bear hadn't been quite this short with Coryn in the past; maybe he was still upset that Coryn hadn't come to his castle. Whatever the reason, Coryn's best course was to mollify him now.

So he climbed up onto the great soft bed and positioned himself between the bear's legs. At least the lord smelled good, which hadn't always been the case back at his own castle. Coryn slid a paw under the grey-streaked fur of the bear's sac and bent to take what protruded from the large sheath into his muzzle.

"Ahhhh." Lord Barclaw lay back, paws resting at his sides. "Ah yes. Oh, Coryn, I have missed you."

The bear's shaft fit easily into Coryn's mouth at first, but as he licked and sucked, it engorged and pushed farther out until it stretched his jaw in the way he remembered. He slipped into familiar rhythms up and down, holding the base of the bear's sheath with one paw while his muzzle worked along the thick shaft.

As Lord Barclaw grew more excited, his body shivered and his paw traveled up to Coryn's shoulder. A few minutes later, the paw settled between Coryn's ears, then pushed down as Coryn dove onto the bear's cock, releasing as he pulled up. The bear pushed his head down again, then again, faster, taking over Coryn's rhythm.

The wolf tried his best to go along with it, gagging once when the bear pushed down hard and forced the tip of his cock almost to Coryn's throat. This was new, but it wasn't hard to navigate, and it seemed to bring Lord Barclaw's arousal along faster than normal.

The bear shuddered and bucked, shaking the whole bed. Coryn thought he was close, especially when he cried out, "Ahh! Ah!" but it was a full fifteen more seconds of thrashing and squirming, gripping Coryn between the ears and holding the wolf down on the hard cock as Coryn licked the best he could, before the bear's warmth burst onto Coryn's tongue and ran down his throat as he tried to swallow.

"Aaaaahh. Aaaah." Two more waves of seed coated Coryn's tongue; he gulped and sputtered, letting some seed and saliva drip past his lips. Quickly he caught it in his paw, because Lord Barclaw didn't like being left messy.

"I would say that was worth waiting for, but it would have been just as welcome two days ago," Lord Barclaw panted. "You could have at least sent word."

"I'm sorry, milord." Coryn sat back on his knees, holding his sticky paw away from his body, and glanced down. He hoped the fur was as clean as it looked; between the thick musk and the flower scent, he couldn't tell. He made his way carefully off the bed.

"I'm glad you've come to see me. At least you did that."

"Yes, milord."

Lord Barclaw raised a paw and waved. "I return to Castle Barclaw in two days. You will come attend to me tomorrow, and then the day after you will ride back with me and we can conclude our business then."

"Ah," Coryn said. "Milord, I was hoping to talk about that with you."

"Yes, yes." The bear waved lazily. "We may speak at the castle."

"I have other obligations, milord." Coryn's heart pounded. "I won't be able to return to the castle with you."

"What? Nonsense. Of course you may."

"Milord, I have...I have business in the city that I cannot cut short."

The bear squinted at him. "Cannot? Or would prefer not to?"

"I cannot. It is important to my farm."

"Yes, well, you won't have to worry about that farm anymore soon enough."

Here was the moment, the time to say, "Milord, I cannot accept your gift." Coryn tried to pronounce the words, but they stuck in his throat. Lord Barclaw had been so peeved when Coryn had missed an appointment; how would he react to an outright refusal? He might call the skunk back and have him lock up Coryn's clothes to keep him here. Or lock up Coryn himself. And then the seal would never be found, and Clement would sit and rot in jail forever.

So he swallowed and said, "Yes, milord. But I would prefer not to leave my sister and her cub with unfinished business. Family is important to me."

"Ahh." Lord Barclaw lay back in his bed. "Ring that bell for me, will you?" He gestured with one large paw to the nightstand.

Coryn stepped over to the small bell, picked it up, and shook it. "Not like that," Lord Barclaw said irritably. "Loudly. Or he'll pretend not to hear it."

"Yes, milord." Coryn shook the bell loudly enough that he had to flatten his ears.

A moment later, the door opened, and the skunk stood there. "Yes, your Lordship?"

"I'm done with Coryn. But you may expect him tomorrow afternoon as well. See to it that the guards allow him in."

The skunk—Coryn had heard his name but couldn't remember it—bowed. "Yes, your Lordship." He gestured to Coryn. "This way, please."

Coryn followed him back to the tiled room. "I have taken the liberty of perfuming your clothes," the skunk said.

"Uh...thank you," Coryn said. The scent of violets wasn't objectionable, but the action felt intrusive.

As he dressed, the skunk watched him and, after a moment, spoke. "You asked about the theft of Lord Fardew's seal."

"Oh. Yes," Coryn said, pulling his trousers up. With clothes on, he felt more secure.

"I know Lord Fardew's personal servant. He is an excellent weasel."

"Oh?" He held his tunic to his muzzle. The smell of violets did not assault his nose too strongly, which spoke to the skunk's judgment.

"He was dismissed after the theft."

Coryn pulled the tunic over his head. "Did he steal it?"

"Of course not!" That was the most animated the skunk had gotten in Coryn's presence. "But he was responsible for its safe-keeping, so Lord Fardew assumed he had given away its location."

"That doesn't seem fair."

"No indeed." The skunk reached out to straighten Coryn's tunic. "Personal servants have been dismissed for less. So I hope you do not intend to disappoint his Lordship."

Coryn flattened his ears. "He wouldn't dismiss you for me not showing up."

"I pray not, but his Lordship asked me to be responsible for your return, and he has not grown more generous in his old age."

"He's giving me a farm," Coryn said before he could help himself.

The skunk eyed him. "I presume it is a farm close to his castle from which he may solicit frequent visits like today's?"

"Well...yes."

"If that is a pleasing arrangement to you then I wish you all the best." The skunk opened the door for him.

"I'm sorry," Coryn said, stepping toward the door. "I can't recall your name."

"My name is Perroh." The skunk gave him the slightest of smiles. "I look forward to seeing you tomorrow, Coryn."

CHAPTER 11

Somewhat to his surprise, the sun still hung red in the afternoon sky. His experience at the palace felt like it had lasted for hours, but it had been one and a half at the most. He walked back toward the Cathedral, and only then realized that he was hungry. So he stopped at a small shop and bought a dried sausage and a piece of bread.

From a plaza on the other side of the Cathedral he ate his lunch and stared at the Rodenta tower. As it had a month ago, it looked forbidding and absolutely impossible to climb. But the longer he examined it, the more he noticed the little reliefs here and there. He remembered gripping the head of a stone squirrel and then bracing his feet on it; he remembered the wide tail of a carved beaver below a ledge where he'd rested.

By the time he'd finished his meal, he had convinced himself that he could make the climb. He would have to wait until the middle of the night, but he could do it, could get up there and find the seal where it had been concealed. He had to. Clement was counting on him.

He spent the rest of the daylight hours at the market, where he found a silver Canis pendant for Ki and a little wooden puzzle for Lucy. He hoped that once he'd rescued Clement—or even if he failed—that they would take him back, and he wanted to show them that he'd been thinking about them in Divalia.

With the lengthening shadows fading into dusk, Coryn found a public house near the Four Quarters and paid for a dinner. He wanted to be well fed and rested before going out on his mission.

As he sat and ate the warm bread and roast fowl, two other wolves asked to join his otherwise empty table. "Of course," he said, and so they joined him. They were a married couple from Tistunish making their first visit to Divalia, so excited at the prospect of attending Caniday services that their tails didn't stop wagging the whole dinner.

Coryn told them that he was in Divalia on business but that he was also excited to visit the Cathedral. "We would be happy to join you in the morning," the husband gushed. "Now that we know another wolf in the city, we should all go together."

Both of them smiled warmly at him and so he said, "Yes, of course."

"Lovely! We'll meet you down here," the wife said. "Just after Prime? We want to be sure to get in."

"You won't have any trouble, if I recall from a month ago," Coryn said. "But I'll meet you here then."

He took his leave of them and returned to the Four Quarters in good spirits. After a nap of a few hours, he would be in good shape to attempt the climb of the Cathedral to save his friend, and then tomorrow would sort itself out after that.

A few people waved to him from one room with the door open, and he waved back. Other open doors let onto empty rooms or rooms with only one guest, and he wondered whether the others who'd shared his room had moved on.

The other three beds in his room were empty, but a shape

was sitting on the one he'd slept in last night. So everyone hadn't gone, or else someone new had arrived. Coryn closed the door behind him. "That's—" He was going to tell the person that that was the bed he'd claimed, with all his things near it, but then he realized that the person on the bed was not any of the room's previous occupants but was, in fact, someone he knew.

In a panic, he reached for the door, but his paw had barely closed over the handle when the figure leapt from the bed. Its paw gripped his wrist before he could pull the door open, and the smell of rat overcame him. "Now now, cub, let's not run away. I haven't said my piece yet."

Coryn tugged, but then the point of a knife pressed against his stomach, and Two-Claws said, "I'd much rather you go sit on the bed, what d'you say?"

Would Lox's fighting lessons would be enough for him to overpower the rat? The grip on his wrist didn't let up, and he knew that the slightest movement would be the excuse the rat needed to plunge the knife into him. So he let go of the door handle and walked stiffly over to the bed, the rat at his side.

"That's a good lad." Two-Claws released him and took a step back, standing between him and the door with the blade exposed, point toward Coryn. That reminded him of Lox's teachings as well, and the knife in his pack that might as well be back on the farm for all the good it would do him now. "Let's have a polite conversation, an' then if you don't wish to see me again, you needn't."

Coryn's throat felt tight. "I don't know what you want to talk to me about."

"Ha ha!" Two-Claws laughed without humor, his dark glittering eyes never leaving Coryn's. "Haven't started yet, have I? Give me time." He waved the knife in a slow circle. "You comin' back to Divalia, it's a little dodgy, wouldn't you say?"

"I—I don't know what you mean. I have business here—"

"Aye, you told that guard as much. So he told you where to stay, an' told me what he told you. He believed you, mind. Leastways, he thought there was a chance you's telling the truth. Me, I don't think so." The rat's smile stretched. "Turns out I was right, seems like. Didn't visit a merchant today, did you? Went to the Cathedral, very virtuous, went to the palace, had to go around a couple times to get in, had lunch, watched the Cathedral again, came back here."

"I, uh," Coryn's mind raced back over his day, "I met him inside the palace. He was there talking to a Lord."

Two-Claws' eyes narrowed. "I don't believe that."

"You weren't inside the palace, were you?"

For the first time, the rat's confidence flickered. "Maybe true. Don't mean that's what you were doing."

"I guess it comes down to whether you trust me." Coryn tried to get his racing heart under control.

"Course I don't trust you," Two-Claws said. "What were you doing in the palace?"

Coryn sat up straighter. "Meeting with the merchant."

"Liar."

"That's what you say."

"Aye, with a score of years experience in telling liars. Anyway, even if it's true, it don't mean that's the only thing you're doin' here. Plannin' to go out to the jail tonight?"

"I don't even know where the jail is." He gambled that the rat hadn't been close enough to hear when he'd asked directions to it from the merchant.

"Pff." The rat almost spit. "Asked the guard about it, that's what he said."

Coryn didn't think he'd asked Lox directly, but Lox had talked about the jail. Maybe that's how he'd interpreted Coryn's interest. "I didn't, and I don't know where it is. I don't know how to prove that to you."

"Don't matter." Two-Claws waved the knife. "Way I figure, you got two reasons for coming here. Either you want to break Clem outta jail, which is noble and stupid and fits a charming wolf cub, or..." He paused and studied Coryn. "Or Clem did tell you where he hid the score an' you're here to get it."

Coryn kept himself very still. "He didn't tell me," he said.

The rat nodded and then walked over to him slowly, keeping the knife out. Coryn's heartbeat, which he'd managed to calm a little, sped up again. "Don't know as I believe that. You wouldn't lie to yer ol' pal Two-Claws, would you?"

"N-no," Coryn said, trying to keep his eyes on the rat's eyes, but finding it difficult to resist the hypnotic sway of the knife point. He tried to remember all the things Lox had taught him and wished again that his knife were in his paw and not in his pack.

The rat stopped and weighed the knife in his paw, then sheathed it in a quick, fluid motion. "Don't blame you," he said. "I wouldn't tell me neither. But let me tell you a proposition right quick."

Coryn didn't say anything even when given room to do so. Two-Claws went on. "If Clem did tell you where the li'l thing is, no doubt it's in a hidey-hole easy for a rat to get to. Maybe not so much a strapping wolf cub." He leaned closer. "Besides which, how you figure t'sell it? Houseboat's long gone and you don't know where to go. So here's my bargain. You tell me where it is and I'll go get it, sell it, an' we'll split the take." He reached down and Coryn flinched, thinking he was going for the knife again, but instead the rat's paw cupped his own groin. "Then after, we can celebrate like we did years ago, eh? Haven't forgotten that night, I promise ya."

Having already given one blow job he wasn't excited about, the prospect of another did very little for Coryn. "Even if Clem had told me, why would I trust you?" He tried to keep his voice steady and was mostly successful. "You'd go get it and then I'd never see you again."

"Fair." Two-Claws stepped back. "What's your idea, then?"

"I told you, he didn't tell me."

"Stickin' to your story." The rat nodded. "Don't mind if I search your tunic and bag here, then?"

"Go ahead."

Two-Claws patted down Coryn's trousers, taking the chance to grope him, and then searched the bag. He found the necklace and wooden puzzle and replaced them without saying anything. The knife earned Coryn a grin, but Two-Claws didn't take that either. The rat let the pack drop to the ground, then walked over and then sat with his back to the closed door. "Right, then. I'll kip here 'til morning, then go back to followin' you all over the city. Mind, if you retrieve it an' we got no deal, I'll just take it." The rat wiggled his paws. "You might not even notice."

Coryn settled back into his bed and tried not to watch the rat at the door, though he couldn't help hearing the raspy breathing, in and out. What was he going to do? He couldn't go get the seal during the day, but now he couldn't leave his room as he'd planned.

If he called the innkeeper and told him there was a thief in his room—but no, Two-Claws would slip away and then Coryn would be back to square one. He could overpower the rat, tie him up maybe? But no, he wouldn't put his fledgling fighting skills up against those of a rat who'd spent all of his years on the streets.

The scent of flowers tickled his nose, and a breath of cool air led him to look over at the window. That was how Two-Claws had gotten in, and it remained open. There was enough of a gap for a rat to clamber through, and maybe a wolf.

Coryn checked on the rat, but no eyeshine showed on his

face and his breathing remained steady and even. A few more seconds, and then Coryn shifted on his bed, keeping his eyes on the rat. No movement, and Two-Claws' eyes remained closed. Slowly the wolf stepped out of bed, keeping his claws clear of the wood as best he could. He pulled the knife from his bag with only a hiss of cloth. Still Two-Claws remained asleep, breathing in and out, paws folded over his stomach.

The gap in the window looked smaller the closer he got to it, but he fit his feet and hips through, and then his chest and shoulders, as quietly as he could. Every scrape, every noise, made him freeze, as though if Two-Claws woke, he wouldn't notice the wolf half out of the window. This happened four times before he worked his shoulders through, and finally pulled his head out.

It was quite a drop to the ground, but the wall of the inn was studded with half-finished beams. Coryn scrabbled against the wall with both feet until one of them found a beam he could rest on. With one last look at the sleeping rat, he ducked below the window and clambered down to the ground.

He landed with a thump and froze again, looked up. Nothing stirred, no pointy muzzle poked out, so Coryn steadied his breathing. He slid the knife into his belt and got his bearings.

Behind the inn there was only a dirty alley and a building three feet away, but at the end of the alley the main street shone with lamplight. To make it harder for Two-Claws to track him, if he awoke and found Coryn gone, the wolf searched out piles of refuse to step in that would mask his scent. This made his feet sticky by the time he reached the main street. He didn't like the unclean feeling, nor the smell, but he told himself that the stickiness might be an advantage in climbing the cathedral wall.

In a sense, he was glad Two-Claws had come to his room. He'd been bothered by the nagging suspicion that someone was watching him at the Four Quarters, and now he knew for sure. Still, he glanced at each of the few people he saw on the street to make sure none of them was a cougar or a guard. On the latter count he needn't have worried; guards were plentiful in the city during the day, but even though it was not yet fully dark and the streets were nowhere near empty, not a single red uniform met his eye.

There would be hours before the streets were deserted enough for him to risk climbing the Cathedral wall, but he headed in that direction anyway. The Rodenta tower, he recalled, faced away from the palace and the plaza, and that was likely why Two-Claws (and Clement) had chosen it to climb.

That area of town might be less crowded, but it wasn't deserted, not yet. A pair of raccoons stood in conversation right across from the base of the tower, and a weasel sat on the street fiddling with a woven basket in his lap. Others hurried along the street or strolled around beneath the moon and stars.

Last time he'd climbed the Cathedral, it had been raining, but that meant there had been cloud cover and less light. He would've been harder to spot amid the dark and shadowy reliefs on the wall, except when he was moving. Tonight, silvery light bathed the building, throwing every stone face into sharp contrasts of light and shadow. A wolf would stand out, and anyone below might call the guard.

He had hours to wait, though, and the ragged edges of clouds were visible around the sky. They might well gather and provide cover for him, if Canis (and Rodenta) approved of his effort. In the meantime, he strolled along the Cathedral's face, turned left down a cross street, then turned left again along a street parallel to the Cathedral.

After a short time, he found a narrow space between buildings that could not even properly be called an alley. It did take

him all the way back to the Cathedral and afforded him a
concealed (albeit dirty) place to wait for the traffic in the street to
die down. He sniffed around for a spot that was slightly less
dirty and sat there cross-legged, curling his tail around him and
leaning back against the chilly brick wall.

While he waited, he examined the Cathedral and tried to
remember how he'd scaled it five years ago. He'd started there,
he was pretty sure, at the large porcupine, then climbed up the
mouse and the other mouse, and then there was a ledge where
he'd gotten his bearings. Mainly he'd been following Two-
Claws' lead, not picking out the path for himself. But now he
could remember it, couldn't he? There, and there, and...

He snapped his head up. His neck ached, the light had
dimmed and shifted, and the sounds of the street outside had
died down. How long had he been asleep? He jumped to his
feet, panicked that he'd slept through the night and dawn was
on the way.

A moment to come to his senses showed him that was not
the case. The horizon showed no trace of light; in fact, patchy
clouds had rolled in to obscure the moon and some of the stars.
All along the street that circled the Cathedral, Coryn only saw
one other person, a fox hurrying away who disappeared from
view in another moment.

Thank Canis, he'd woken at the right time to start his climb.
He hesitated and then reminded himself that time was of the
essence: he'd need to not only climb up, but possibly down as
well if he couldn't find a way down from the inside or if the
doors were locked.

So he hurried across the street, and before he could think
too much, he leapt up the statue of the porcupine and climbed it
quickly, getting up to the first ledge in short order. There he
risked a look around the street and froze at a flicker out of the

corner of his eye. But no; when he turned, it proved to be merely a flutter of cloth at the front of a shop.

Don't look down again, he told himself sternly, and gripped the head of a stone squirrel. The stickiness on his feet did help him keep his grip, and though he was older, the climb felt easier than he remembered it being.

What was more difficult was that this wasn't a daring adventure with a new friend who was climbing confidently ahead of him, a point Coryn could train his eyes on. He scanned up for places to set his paws and feet, but every so often he felt the urge to see how high up he'd climbed and had to set his head resolutely facing upward.

His ears, though, remained cupped back to face the ground, alert for any noise of someone below him. Not that he could do anything but keep climbing at this point, but he would certainly prefer to know than not.

One leg up, one paw up, the other leg up, the other paw up. Over and over he repeated this, and now another difference from five years ago made itself known: Coryn was getting tired. He could complete the climb—he had to now—but he doubted whether he would trust himself to climb back down. Twice he stopped, when no obvious hold presented itself, and then he remembered the cunning way Two-Claws had navigated these places. His memory proved accurate; his climb continued.

He had no concept of how long it took him to reach the statue of Rodenta, climb up onto her back, and sidle over to the narrow ledge nearby, but reach it he did finally, settling down with a sigh of relief. Now he could look across the roofs of the city, and over to the palace, and marvel at how far above it all he was. Down there, people went about their lives, ran errands, ate, drank, and slept, and nobody had any idea that a wolf had climbed to the roof of the Cathedral to save his friend. The thought brought a smile to his lips.

Then the thought occurred to him that the window might not be open, in which case he would have to break the glass, which he did not want to do. But when he pressed his fingers to the edge, the window swung inward with only a small creak. Coryn breathed a prayer of thanks to Canis— and Rodenta too, for good measure—and slid through the window.

The room filled his nose with a stale old scent that brought memories crowding into his head. The smell of wet fur was absent, but otherwise the musty smell of old carpet and old leather, the wood of the furniture, the trace smell of four-legged mice, and the stone of the Cathedral, all combined to remind him of that shivering wet wolf from five years ago who'd followed a rat into this room. It hardly looked large enough for two people to lie on the floor together and do the things they'd done, but that was probably the fault of the shadows.

Indistinct skeletons of chairs and the looming dark shapes of wardrobes, too, were familiar. Two-Claws had gone out through the only door and come back with a candle, but Coryn wasn't sure he wanted to risk leaving this room, even though the Cathedral was silent.

After working open one of the wardrobes and spending several fruitless minutes staring into its dark interior, it became clear that he would need a candle, or else he was going to have to feel around and leave his scent more strongly on everything. The room didn't feel as though people visited often enough that anyone would notice, but he preferred to remain as stealthy as possible. Given the choice between sneaking out to get a candle and pawing through a lot of old clothes and Canis knew what else, he opted for the candle.

The hallway outside the room stretched to either side (he remembered this too), with another door that led out to a balcony overlooking the main space of the Cathedral. Even without people, even without the sun to shine through the stained-glass windows, the building held a regal majesty that slowed Coryn's steps as he sniffed for wax.

He found it in a small cupboard, which turned out to hold four candles of various sizes. Coryn selected the largest and then was faced with the problem of how to light it. Thin smoke smells reached his nose, so there was a fire burning somewhere if only he could find it. Two-Claws had found a fire somewhere nearby five years ago, but wherever that had been wasn't evident to Coryn, or else it was no longer kept burning at night.

In an enclosed space, scents were hard to track, and a strong acrid smell like smoke harder than most, but Coryn went, on his instinct, to the winding spiral stair that led from the hallway down to the main chambers of the Rodenta cantor and their assistants, walking on his heels so his toe claws wouldn't click on the stone. He kept his ears perked, but no other sounds disturbed the silence.

The stair wound down through darkness and cold for a long, long time—partly, Coryn thought, explaining why the upstairs rooms were so deserted—but finally he came to a door at the base, closed but with flickers of light playing around the edges. The smell of smoke covered any other odors that might filter through the cracks, so Coryn pressed his ear to the door but still heard nothing. Cautiously, he eased the door open.

The air on the other side felt warmer and a good deal smokier, a small hallway barely wide enough for Coryn to fit through. Most importantly, in one of the sconces on the wall opposite the two doors, a torch burned smokily.

Coryn hurried over to it and lit the candle, and then footsteps scraped along the floor behind one of the doors. He ran to the stair, not even caring if his claws hit the stone, and pushed the stairway door closed behind him with a squeak. He pressed against it, his heart pounding.

On the other side of the door, a latch clicked and hinges

creaked. "Is someone there?" an old voice called. Footsteps slowed and then approached Coryn.

As fast as he could, Coryn fled up the stair on his heels, protecting the candle's flame and hoping that as many turns of the stair as he could put between himself and the door would be enough to hide the flame and that the smoke would cover his scent. It seemed like a lot to hope for, so as he ran up the stairs he said a quick prayer to Rodenta. *I'm on a mission to save one of yours, please hide me!*

He made it up four, perhaps five circuits of the narrow spiral before the door creaked open below him. He stopped, shielding the candle, and held his breath.

"Is someone there?" the voice repeated, louder.

Coryn's heart thudded in his ears. He stayed frozen on the cold stair, the flame of the candle flickering in front of his paw, rendering the rest of the world around him dark so that the voice seemed to float up from a bottomless void. "Hello?" it called.

After what seemed an eternity, the door creaked shut again. Coryn exhaled and resumed the long climb back up the tower.

His legs protested before he'd gone very far, so he slowed his pace even more. There were no markers, no way to know how far he was up the stair. All he could do was take one step after another, guarding the precious candle flame with his paw.

There seemed to be twice as many stairs going up as there'd been on the way down. After a time, the air on his whiskers moved more quickly, and Coryn became convinced that around the next turn he would find the hallway. When the hallway did not appear, he decided it would be the next turn, and found more stairs. It wasn't until he'd settled into a dull acceptance of the eternal staircase that he took one more step up and found himself on a landing facing the hallway.

With an involuntary cry of relief, he stumbled forward, his

legs almost giving out before he regained his balance. From the open space, he looked through the door that led into the Cathedral before remembering that his candle made him extremely visible to anyone who might be wandering around below, and he hurried into the closed hallway, and from there into the little storage room.

The walk up the stairs had already taken half an inch from his candle, but he should have enough light to search the room, and there were more candles if this one got low. He started with the wardrobe, pushing aside the old, yellowed robes and coughing at the dust, looking in all the corners and in any pockets that might hold a gold seal.

When he found nothing except clothing, he moved on to the old chests, digging through their contents, where he found many beetles among the papers and faded sashes with the sign of Rodenta on them, but nothing of gold or even metal.

Coryn sat down in one of the chairs, resting his legs, and looked around the room. Was it possible that the seal wasn't here? Had he misinterpreted Clement's words somehow? The rat had said, "A place only you and I would know." No, it hadn't been about Coryn; Coryn had maybe taken it that way, though. The rat's words had been... "only two people in the world might find it."

So it had to be this room, somewhere in here, something he hadn't seen. He searched behind the chests, under the wardrobes, on top of the wardrobes, and found nothing but dust, mouse droppings, and more beetles. He went back out into the hallway and searched the cupboard where the candles were, taking another in the process. Still nothing.

There had to be something he was missing. He didn't want to leave this room without exhausting all the possibilities, because it wasn't likely he would have a chance to get back. He returned to the room and went back through the wardrobes and the chests, with as little luck as before.

There was no golden seal here. He must have misinterpreted Clement's words. With a sinking heart, he realized that when Clement had said that about "only two people," he'd thought Clement *was* Two-Claws. But what if Clement meant himself and Two-Claws? After all, Clement and Coryn didn't share any history. Clement and Two-Claws, though, they did. Had Coryn done all this work for nothing?

He stared into the flickering candle. No. If Two-Claws knew of a place that only he and Clement knew about, he would've gone there right away. He wouldn't have followed Coryn around hoping the wolf knew where the seal was. Besides, when Coryn had asked if he could find it, Clement had said he might.

The only other possibility finally made its way into his mind: Clement had been lying to him. The rat had been trying to make Coryn feel special, trying to ingratiate himself by bringing the wolf in on a secret when there wasn't one.

(But then why bring it up again when the guards were going to take him away?)

No, it must have been another lie, a harmless one (so Clem thought), one to make someone he cared about feel better. That wasn't so bad. That, Coryn could forgive.

His second candle was close to guttering. He blew it out, replaced both stubs in the hallway, and eyed the door and the stairs. He did not feel up to climbing down the Cathedral again, so he would take the stairs and make whatever excuse he needed to when he reached the bottom.

A creak came from the room behind him. He turned, fur bristling in alarm.

The hallway and the room, the whole Cathedral, lay still around Coryn. He stared at the darkness of the storage room.

Should he investigate the noise, or should he hurry down the stairs?

In the moment of indecision, a shadow flitted through the doorway. Before Coryn could do more than squint at it, it had covered the ground between them. The point of a knife pressed into Coryn's stomach. "Ho there," Two-Claws said. "What say we discuss proper shares?"

The rat guided him back to the room, where the window stood fully open. "Now," he said, "off with them pretty clothes, every stitch."

"What?" Coryn stood, feeling stupid. "But I..."

The rat grinned with narrowed eyes. "Ah, precious wolfling," he said, "I'm not after that sheath of yours, nor what's under your tail, though perhaps if you're nice you might get a little rat in your muzzle." With his free paw, he squeezed his own groin. "I mean to search you, and it's much easier if the clothes I'm searching ain't near you when I search 'em. So come on." He gestured with the knife.

"I don't have it." Coryn spread his paws. "It's not here."

"Ay, you'll forgive me if I don't take your word." Two-Claws took a step closer. "I can cut the clothes off you if you like."

Coryn stepped back, his tail hitting one of the wardrobes. He pulled his tunic off, then his trousers and underthings, leaving only the knife Lox had given him and the slim belt around his waist. "Toss 'em over there. The knife too." Two-Claws gestured, and Coryn obediently threw his clothes over near the large chest, then removed the knife and did the same with it.

"How did you find me?" he asked, one paw shielding his sheath as the rat went around to the far side of the clothes.

"Find you?" Two-Claws knelt, keeping his eyes and knife on Coryn as his other paw picked up, felt through, and discarded each of Coryn's garments in turn. "I followed you."

"Followed—but I disguised my scent."

Two-Claws finished and tossed the clothes away in annoyance. "Course you did. But I had eyes on you from the moment you left the room. Thought y'self quite clever, going out the window. I knew you'd go the moment you thought you could get past me, once I made it clear you wouldn't have another chance. So I pretended to sleep, eyes closed, nappy nappy, and sure as scents, there you went out the window."

Coryn let out an exasperated sigh at himself, and Two-Claws grinned. "Ah, cub, I know bein' a thief sits in your heart, but that's th'only place it is. I had to wake you up so you didn't sleep the night in the alley."

"*You* woke me up?"

"Aye. Couple small pebbles dropped on yer from the roof where I was watchin'. Will say, you climbed the Cathedral right nice. Found all those same footholds. Took my lessons well to heart."

"It was hard," Coryn said sullenly.

"Aye, well, wouldn't be a good hidin' place if anyone could get to it, would it?" Two-Claws poked at Coryn's clothes again with the knife. "Tell me what Clem said to you. No use pretendin' he said nothin'. I don't believe you came up here just to reflect on our night of passion an' plunder."

"Can I put my clothes back on?" Coryn asked, to stall.

"No. I'm enjoyin' the view. An' no need to hide your privates; nothin' I've not seen." The knife waved. "Tell me what he said. Word for word, best you can remember."

Coryn closed his eyes and cast his mind back. "He said...it was hidden in a safe place. He said only two people would know where to look for it and he wasn't worried the other would look, and he was looking at me when he said that."

Two-Claws nodded thoughtfully. "An' you figured it'd be here, 'cause you thought he was me, and this is the place known to both of us." He looked around the room. "Not a bad idea.

Don't think it's quite right, though. This room don't get used often but it isn't quite as safe as you might think. Anyone might come up from the Church and look through anything, and then where'd you be?"

"I climbed those stairs," Coryn said. "They were dusty. I don't think they come up here much at all."

"'Not much' is a sight different from 'not at all,' especially if you don't know when you might get back to retrieve it." Two-Claws sat with his back to the chest, still keeping his eyes fixed on Coryn. "What'd you plan to do with it anyway? Got someone interested in buying?" His eyes narrowed. "That's what you were doing in the palace, ay?"

"No." Coryn debated whether or not to be honest, and decided he was tired of lying and pretending. Two-Claws might laugh at him and call him a naïve farmboy, and maybe that's what he was. "I want to give it back to Lord Fardew and have him set Clement free."

Two-Claws stared at him and then let out a sharp laugh. "Ah ha ha! Here I thought you meant to save your farm or buy a new one or buy yourself some new clothes." He poked at Coryn's clothes with one foot. "Clem's attached himself to you, eh? Had a rat-shaped hole in that heart of yours all these years?" The rat clucked. "Ah, cub, I only thought to take yer innocence."

"And the gold pieces you promised me."

"Aye, those too." Two-Claws played with his knife. "It's sweet you've been taken in by Clem, and in only a few weeks, too, but he'll have to stay in prison. Y'unnerstand, it's him or me."

"I'd choose him."

"I know you would, an' that's why t'isn't up to you." Two-Claws grinned. "I'll put my head t'work on't and let's say once I sell the seal, I'll give you back those two gold pieces for your trouble. A climb up here shouldn't go unrewarded, after all."

"Not twice, anyway," Coryn said.

"What, you don't think you got a reward last time? I don't flatter myself I was your first, but the experience must've left some impression." Coryn didn't say anything, and Two-Claws went on. "P'raps it was the excitement of thievery. You said you enjoyed the adventure, as I recall. An' here you are, seeking out adventure again."

"I didn't seek it," Coryn said. "Clement came and found me."

"An' you came here to rescue him. Climb the Cathedral again, find the seal, an' then go to Lord Fardew and beg forgiveness. How you expect that'll go? Suppose the Lord will take the seal and declare all forgiven? Or d'you think he might put you in jail as well for bein' an accomplice? You'd be reunited with Clem all right. Ha ha!"

"I know people in the palace," Coryn said through gritted teeth.

"Aye, so do I. When it comes to how the nobility treats us commoners, I know that too. They use us until we got no use left an' then they don't care what happens. Unless we offend them; then they kill us."

"If you spend your life stealing from them, of course they do." Coryn spoke bravely, but the memory of Lord Barclaw weighed down his words and kept his tone flatter than he meant it to be.

"If you don't spend your life stealin' from them, you get only what they see fit to give you, an' who wants to live on dust and rainwater?" Two-Claws shook his head. "You play at bein' a thief, cub, but you've not got what takes here." He tapped his heart.

"What's that?" Coryn asked. "A cold stone?"

The rat raised his eyebrows. "Aye, more or less. Thief has to look out for himself first an' the job second, an' after that, whatever may come over 'is mood."

"Clement was a good thief," Coryn said, "and he has a heart.

He wanted me to find the seal to help myself, not to rescue him. That was my idea."

"If he wanted you to find the seal, sure as scents it was for his own ends."

"I really don't think it was."

"Ay, we can argue all night. I knew him years, you knew him weeks."

Coryn folded his arms. "You knew him so well, you figure out why he gave me a clue. How did it help him if I found it?"

The rat spread his paws. "P'raps he knew yer tender heart and thought you'd come find it for him if he got himself nicked. Or he thought you'd never make use of his secret and thought himself clever."

"He had to have known that it would bring me up here one day. If the seal isn't up here, then why?"

Two-Claws nodded. "Aye, that's the question, isn't it?" He scratched behind one ear. "I reckon you misread what he said, is all. 'Only two people know where it is.' S'pose t'other person wasn't you. S'pose he wasn't tellin' you where it was, but just braggin'? Who'd be the other person?"

Who indeed? Coryn cast his mind back to when Clement had said those words to him, lying in the loft amid the blankets and the hay. He didn't think Clement had been bragging; the rat had been earnest, telling Coryn a secret. And he'd definitely said that Coryn might find it if he put his mind to it. He could see Clement lying there with that smile, looking not too different from the rat sitting across the room from him, but different in so many important ways...

Coryn's ears went up. There was one place he hadn't looked yet, one place where a small golden seal might be hidden, one clue in what Clement had said that he'd overlooked. But he would have to get rid of Two-Claws to find it, and he had no idea how he was going to do that. He'd already failed at it once.

I expected you might.

No. He had gotten this far, come this close. This was his redemption for what had happened in this very room five years ago, proof that when he followed his own heart, he could—ah. Maybe there was an idea.

"Don't suppose there's much use in working at the puzzle here," Two-Claws said. "And if this was yer best guess, not much use in you either."

For a moment, Coryn's heart jumped. Was the rat going to leave him up here? But then Two-Claws went on. "So we'll climb down together an' then you can go take your rest. I'll likely join you, seein' as how your room's more cozy than the little hole I got, an' then I'll see you to the gates tomorrow."

"I, ah, I have business in the palace again." Coryn stalled for time, trying to figure out how he could remain behind here.

"Course you do." Two-Claws' eyes narrowed. "Maybe I'll go in with you this time."

Now was the time for Coryn to try his last gambit. If this failed, he would have to look for an opportunity while climbing down, which he did not relish. "All right," he said. "But my legs are tired. I went all the way downstairs to light a candle and back up. Why don't we..." He tried to lick his lips in an alluring way, but his mouth was dry, and the lick didn't feel very alluring. He had to smack his lips afterwards. "Relive some other memories?"

He watched the rat's smile, his heart still pounding. If he could get Two-Claws off his guard, maybe he could overpower him and tie him up. Leave him here while Coryn escaped with the treasure (if he was right), a neat reversal.

"Ay, why not, if you're beggin' to get that mouth around it again?" Keeping the knife steady, the rat pushed his pants down and gripped his sheath, pumping it rapidly. "I'll get it ready for you. You don't need to do nothin' 'cept get on your knees."

He'd have to put his clothes on eventually, but he could do that after. Coryn knelt in front of the rat, whose seat on the big wooden chest let him look down on the wolf. If he sat back on his heels, the rat's sheath and emerging shaft were right at his eye level.

"That's a good lad," the rat cooed. "Helpin' me along, you are."

Indeed, the pink shaft was halfway out and pushing farther, enough that the rat took his paw away from it and leaned back. The rat's musk and the sight of his sheath stirred memories in Coryn, enough to arouse him even though his mind was more on how he was going to tie up Two-Claws than on whether the rat might suck him off in return.

When Coryn didn't lean forward immediately, Two-Claws spread his legs and said, "All right, get to it."

Two cocks he didn't really want to put in his mouth in the same day. Well, he'd finished Lord Barclaw; he could finish this rat. It wasn't that he didn't enjoy having someone's cock in his mouth. It was that he would rather it happen under circumstances of his choice.

He had offered, this time. And if he closed his eyes and forgot about all of the last five years, he might be up here with Two-Claws again five years ago, but this time he knew what he was doing and he didn't expect that he and the rat would live a happily ever after life of adventure. He wished he could let eighteen-year-old him see the future in this room so that he wouldn't be so crushed the next morning, or perhaps he could make better decisions in the moment. But that cub had grown into this wolf, and all those experiences were part of him. He leaned forward and took the hard pink shaft into his muzzle.

"Ahh, yeah." Two-Claws kept the knife very near Coryn's ear; the wolf's whiskers told him that. He tried to ignore it, sliding his lips up and down and pressing his tongue against the rat's shaft. "Ah, learned a few tricks, have you?"

"Mm," Coryn said, and sucked harder, bracing his paws on the rat's thighs. He'd have to pin the knife arm first, then—how had Lox shown him? Keep his weight lower than the other one and throw him over. If he could get the rat onto his stomach, he could pin him there, he was pretty sure, and then he'd just have to tie up his arms.

And if he couldn't get the knife away?

He had to get the knife away.

The rat let out another moan, but he wasn't shuddering yet. Coryn would have to wait until right after he'd finished, when he'd be least on his guard. He gripped the rat's thin, muscled legs more tightly and bobbed his muzzle up and down, searching with his tongue for those spots that got a reaction out of the rat.

He was rewarded with a few shudders and a moan, and as he kept going, he focused on those spots. Two-Claws squirmed more, moaned more, and his leg started kicking under Coryn's paw. Coryn pressed his lips up and down faster, losing himself in the excitement of bringing someone else to climax before he remembered that he would have to act quickly in that moment.

And then that moment was there, the rat's body jerking as his seed splashed onto Coryn's tongue. If Coryn had acted with that first spasm, things might have gone differently, but out of habit he waited a few more seconds for the rat's climax to run its course, and then he grabbed for the knife arm.

He still caught Two-Claws by surprise, enough that when he twisted the arm, the rat dropped the knife. But as Coryn swung his weight to one side and tried to pull the rat face down to the floor, Two-Claws brought his other arm around to cuff Coryn hard on his ear.

The wolf's head rang, but he kept hold of the arm and some of his leverage, forcing the lighter rat to the floor. Two-Claws talked the whole time. "Oh, you would, would you? I thought you had somethin' planned. Think you c'n get the best of me? Ha!" Coryn kept his muzzle grimly shut, trying to pin down the writhing form under him and fend off the lightning-fast arm that scratched at his nose, punched him in the stomach, and grabbed at his sheath —he was able to keep those tender parts out of reach, thankfully.

But after several seconds of flailing, Two-Claws landed a blow to the side of Coryn's muzzle that staggered him back. He kept his grip on the rat's arm, but lost his leverage and allowed Two-Claws to get to his feet.

"Ha! You're no fighter neither." The rat struggled to free his arm, aiming a kick at Coryn's groin which the wolf, out of instinct as much as anything, managed to deflect. "I'm gonna knock you out and drag your body through that window and throw you off!"

Coryn could only remember what Lox had told him about weight, get his weight low, so he dropped to the ground and tried to throw the rat across his body. But Two-Claws resisted, and he wasn't light enough for Coryn to throw him bodily, so he went staggering and tripped on Coryn's side.

"Then I'm gonna go to the jail and—"

There was a heavy thud. Two-Claws' head connected with the heavy wooden chest, and the rat dropped, dazed.

Coryn scrambled to his knees. Two-Claws was holding his head, still moving, but wobbly. Coryn tried to pull both arms behind the rat's back so he could tie them together, but Two-Claws squirmed again and got one paw free. Desperate, Coryn swung the rat against the wooden chest again, and again the rat's head struck it. This time Two-Claws fell to the ground and lay still, and Coryn smelled blood. He checked, but the rat was still breathing, his eyelids fluttering.

He pulled on his underthings and tunic while looking around the room for something to tie up Two-Claws with. Nothing seemed right, unless he was going to take one of the ancient robes hanging in the wardrobe and bind the rat in that, and that seemed rather sacrilegious. He settled for dragging the rat into one of the wardrobes and closing the door.

If he hurried, he could check his theory and run back through the room and down the stairs. So he walked to the window and crawled out onto the ledge.

Two-Claws had scratched behind his ear, and Coryn remembered Clement doing that often as well. He thought that his friend might've done it while he was talking about where the seal was hidden. And then he thought, Two-Claws was right, you wouldn't want to hide something valuable in a room that anyone might visit, not if you were going to leave the thing there for a while.

But there was a place near here that Clement might have hidden a small gold treasure, a place that nobody would think to visit unless they reached this room the way only a few people knew how.

Coryn straightened and looked along the ledge at the statue of Rodenta, standing tall with her flowing robes and the simple crown set above her large, hollow ears.

The problem that presented itself immediately (there would be many other problems soon enough) was that the statue of Rodenta stood nearly three times taller than Coryn himself. She wore a flowing robe that offered few of the obvious climbing holds that the reliefs and building structures had on his way up, and even the arms that extended forward, which might be strong enough for Coryn to sit on, looked well out of reach even if he jumped for them.

Not that jumping was an attractive option, since the statue's shoulders weren't above the narrow ledge Coryn stood on.

There was only an inch or two of room around the statue's base where it extended out from the wall, meaning that to reach the arms, Coryn would have to jump out over the street and hope that he caught them.

Climbing up the front of the statue might be easier if Rodenta had clothing under the robe whose folds would provide places for Coryn's paws to grip, but he couldn't see that and wouldn't know until he was already dangling over a hundred-foot drop.

He edged closer to the statue. Nothing gleamed inside the ear to this side, so he stepped over the ropelike tail (as thick around as his thigh) and found his way along the train of her robe to the ledge on the other side. Here there was only one window and then four feet of the ledge had crumbled away before the rest stretched along to the statue of Mustela.

There was room enough for Coryn to stand, back to the wall, and look up at the right ear of the statue. And here on this side, just visible over a sculpted tuft of fur in the ear, was a small arc of gold, like the top edge of a large golden coin.

He shivered with excitement. Now all he had to do was traverse the fifteen feet between here and there. Clement had done it, so there had to be a way, even if it wasn't obvious to Coryn's inexperienced eye.

Perhaps he could climb up the wall behind him and then drop down, or jump over? There were a few spots where the wall seemed climbable before it reached the spire. But Rodenta leaned away from the wall, and the wall angled back toward the spire, so it would be about a ten-foot jump between the wall and her head, and Coryn did not want to risk that.

He crept closer to the statue and examined the robe, and there he found the answer, or at least what he thought was the answer. Weather had pitted the stone, leaving small indentations here and there and roughness on the surface; the statue was exposed to the elements and would feel every rainfall, every gust of wind like the ones ruffling Coryn's fur now. He traced his fingers over the stone and looked up the smooth curve of the carved robe that covered Rodenta's back. It would be twelve feet until he got to her shoulder, where it looked like he could hold on to the collar of the robe and then pull himself up to the ear.

It would be a difficult climb. Her back wasn't vertical, but it wasn't far off, and the way the robe draped around her meant that if he slid to either side, he would be very likely to miss the ledge and keep going all the way down to the street.

Stalling, he looked around again to see if there were any other way he could possibly reach the statue's ear, but no other solution came to him. He sighed and turned back to the statue. At least it wasn't raining tonight. If this were the night he'd first come up here with Two-Claws, in even that drizzling wet, the stone would be that much slicker, and he wouldn't dare attempt it.

He found a little spot to place his right foot, and then reached up and hooked his claws into a shallow depression in the stone. His grip felt tenuous at best, and when he put his weight on the right foot, it skidded down the stone. Panic flashed through him for a half-second before he landed back on the ledge, heart pounding.

All right, he was fine. He would have to make more sure of his footholds. To help, he scuffed up the pads of both his feet on the stone of the ledge so they'd be rougher and grip the stone better. Then he set his right foot on the robe again, found the same grip with his paw, and this time his foot bore his weight. He brought the other up quickly to balance himself and held there for a moment to make sure he wouldn't slip down again.

Carefully, he held on with both paws and one foot and brought his right foot up, searching for another place where it could hold on for a moment. He found it and repeated the process with his left foot, then his right paw, then his left paw, and then started all over again. At six inches each time, it felt as though Rodenta's crown barely crept closer to him, and every time he looked past the statue, he expected to see glimmers of dawn in the sky.

But the starlit sky remained dark, and the night remained cold, and presently Coryn found himself almost within reach of the shoulder. His paw extended out and closed around a more solid grip than he'd felt since leaving the ledge. He pulled himself up, managed to get a foot over to the upper arm of the statue, and then he could stand upright, where his nose was level with Rodenta's ear.

There indeed was a large gold medallion inside, as thick as his thumb and as wide as his paw. He had to find a grip with his left paw so that he could free his right to reach in and grasp it.

The metal was colder than the stone, and the seal was heavy when he lifted it. He pulled it carefully, imagining the seal slipping from his paw and falling a hundred feet to the street he was resolutely not looking at.

He did, however, have to look down the statue's robe to see the path of his descent. Could he do it with one paw holding the seal? Likely not. He would have to hold it in his jaw.

The thing felt even heavier with his mouth holding it, and he did not trust that it wouldn't slip on his teeth. So he had to keep his head tilted back as he worked his way back around to the center of the statue's back, and there, finally, he was able to slide down—slowly—and arrive back on the ledge.

The seal remained tightly between his teeth. Slowly he lowered his head and brought his paw up. It ached from the climb but still gripped the seal as his teeth let go. He had it. He'd done it. Now all that was left was to figure out how to use the seal to bargain for Clement's release.

He turned back toward the open window, and the warmth of

success fled him in an instant, leaving a chill shiver. Two-Claws climbed out of the window to stand on the ledge, his tail swaying.

"Ah," he said, his voice thick and a little slurred. "Tha' was a nice climb, pup. I thank ya for doin' the job f'me." He raised one paw to his head; Coryn couldn't smell blood out here, but there was a dark patch on the fur. "Not sure I'd be up f'rit right now."

"Stand aside," Coryn said with more bravery than he felt. "I'm taking the seal and going."

"Ha! Ha ha!" The rat laughed. "Cub's grown claws, 'e has. Careful, little'un, if I have to pick it off yer body down in the street, I will, but I'd prefer not to."

Coryn retreated to where he had the wall and statue behind him. Two-Claws advanced, grinning. "Takes more'n a knock on the head to keep me down. But you didn't kill me. Speaks to respect y'got, an' I 'preciate that."

If Coryn was going to grapple, having the seal in one paw was more of a disadvantage than he was going to be able to overcome. So he reached behind him and set it down behind a curve of Rodenta's tail, and then faced Two-Claws. "I won't let you take it," he said.

"Let's be reason'ble." The rat kept coming forward in a fighting stance, though his words were calm and honeyed. "You can't do aught wi'that. I c'n sell it, an' I'll give you your two gold and ten more besides."

"I want Clement's freedom."

"An' why? He stole it! He's in jail for it! That's the law, that's the right of it. You don't owe him a damn thing. He lied to you, took yer food an' shelter an'," his eyes flicked down to Coryn's groin, "prob'ly more. An' you want to reward him?" The rat took another step and his balance wavered. He steadied himself on the wall. "I'm more honest than he. I never lied t'you."

"You stole from me."

"I told you I was a thief!" Two-Claws stood only a body length from Coryn now. The wolf resisted the urge to retreat, aware of the seal behind him.

"Clement wants to start over. He wants to live with me," Coryn said.

"He tol' you what you wanted to hear. This adventure ends like t'other one did, but this time you might have gold in your pocket, not out of it."

"If I trust you."

The rat stopped and looked up, and his face was as honest as Coryn had seen it. Now the smell of blood floated in the breeze. "Trust me or trust that noble to let Clement go, them's your options. Me you know. Want me t'tell you about the noble? He'll take his seal, he'll thank you kindly, and then if yer lucky, he won't throw you in prison with yer sweetheart. Yer better off takin' my offer, an' on Rodenta I swear I'll bring you yer gold. In Her presence an' all. An' I tell you what, gold's the language these nobles understand. You'll have more luck gettin' Clem out of prison with ten gold than you would doin' the right thing. They don't care about justice. They care about gold."

Coryn wavered. The words were persuasive, and he knew from his dealings with Lord Barclaw that gold was important. But he thought, too, about Ki and Lucy, and he set his stance. "That's their business. I'm going to do what's right, and I trust that they will too."

"Ha! Still a foolish cub." With no more warning than that, Two-Claws lunged at him.

Coryn bent his knees, meeting the rat's charge square in his chest. He tried to keep his weight toward the wall, and Two-Claws was doing the same thing, so they ended up half-falling into the wall, their feet sliding precariously on the ledge as each tried to gain an advantage. "Please stop!" Coryn gasped out. "Why can't you let me have it?"

"Because," Two-Claws grunted, "you'd waste it. I'm the thief. I'm the one knows what to do, an' somethin' this valuable—"

The rat braced his feet and got between the wall and the wolf, and pushed Coryn away. Coryn staggered a step back and his foot touched the edge of the ledge; he panicked and dropped flat to the stone, clinging to it as best he could.

Taking advantage of the moment, Two-Claws sprang for the statue. Coryn rolled toward the wall and got to his feet in time to see the rat holding up the seal, his eyes glittering as brightly as the gold. "Such is the way of things, pup," he said. "An' now I bid you g'night."

He tucked the seal under one arm and swung himself over the ledge.

"No!" Coryn yelled, and threw himself across the stone, seizing the rat's paw that still clung to the ledge.

"Ey!" Two-Claws pulled, but he didn't have any leverage, and Coryn's grip was strong. The wolf seized the seal with his other paw, but the rat bent his arm and grabbed it as Coryn tried to pull it back.

"Let go!" Coryn growled through gritted teeth. "You're going to fall!"

"Not if," Two-Claws grunted, "I pull you over first."

But he didn't have the leverage to make good on that threat, and his only option was to let go of the seal. His teeth clenched and his eyes narrowed, and then he pulled himself up and sank his teeth into the wrist of Coryn's paw holding the seal.

Coryn yelped and let go. Two-Claws yanked the treasure back triumphantly, then turned his teeth to the paw still holding his wrist. Instinctively, Coryn pulled back from those sharp incisors, hauling the rat almost fully back onto the ledge.

Two-Claws twisted his paw and shoved, freeing himself and pushing Coryn back against the wall. The rat grinned widely.

"Lovely t'see you 'gain, pup," he said, and lowered one foot, looking for the support to begin his climb down.

Coryn, in a miasma of pain and anger, kicked out at that smug smile. The rat dodged, but with only one foot holding his weight, he couldn't completely avoid the blow, and Coryn's foot caught him on the cheek. He blinked; his paw slipped on the stone.

For a moment he hung there, his smile frozen, and then he clutched the seal to his chest and fell.

CHAPTER 12

For a moment, Coryn stood frozen on the ledge. He couldn't move, even as he expected Two-Claws to somehow climb back up into his view. And then a noise, an impact from a hundred feet below, made him jump. The sound was unmistakable.

Having been shaken out of his shock, Coryn knelt on the ledge and cautiously leaned out over the wall of the Cathedral. The body of the rat lay in his cream-colored tunic against the black of the street, a still blot on the ground.

Coryn stared until the height made him dizzy, and still the rat didn't move. What did he expect, he asked himself as he leaned back, that Two-Claws would survive a fall from that height onto a hard stone road?

Then he remembered that the rat had been holding the seal, the thing Coryn needed to recover to help Clement. He got to unsteady feet and lurched for the open window, tumbling through. He'd have to run down the stairs; that would be faster than climbing for sure, and even if his legs hadn't been tired, he wouldn't trust himself to climb down with the sense of urgency now bristling his fur out.

He got to the room, ran into the hallway and down the tight spiral stairs. His heart pounded and he kept urging himself to go faster, until he caught the edge of a step and lost his balance. His body flew out of his control and landed hard on his shoulder, then skidded down a few more steps. Instinctively he wrapped his arms around his head to protect it and tried to stop his fall with his feet, and after hitting the wall and falling several more steps, he slowed enough that he could get his footing again.

Breathing hard, he stood and braced himself against the wall. His shoulder and hip both hurt, and he'd jammed his toes against the stone when he tried to stop. The smell of blood came from his bitten wrist, but nothing seemed broken. He descended the next few steps cautiously and without difficulty.

Okay. Quickly but a little slower, he told himself. His foot hurt whenever he landed, but he ignored that as best he could. Again, the stair seemed interminable, but this time he smelled the smoke from the torch and knew when he was close to the bottom.

This time, nobody came out to confront him, so Coryn ran through the Cathedral to the front doors, where it took him a minute to figure out how to throw the lock and open the door. He slipped out and ran into the street, around the curve of the Cathedral, around to the Rodenta tower, and there saw a red-jacketed fox kneeling beside the prone form of the rat.

Two weasels stood together at a short remove from the body, but otherwise the street remained deserted. Coryn cursed, but there was nothing for it now but to go up to the fox. He planned what he would say as he approached, but all the words were driven out of his head as he looked down at what remained of Two-Claws.

The rat's eyes were closed. He'd landed on his back and no doubt several bones were broken, if not most of them, but only around one leg was there a pool of blood. If not for the impossible angle of that leg, at a casual glance, Two-Claws might simply be sleeping on the stones of the street.

Coryn didn't want to look any closer than that. The fox, who looked up as he approached, was holding the gold seal in one paw. "Stay back," he ordered.

"I know him." Coryn retreated a step.

The fox's ears came up. "Oh?"

"He climbed the Cathedral. I watched him. He uh, he went up there and then was climbing down when he slipped." Coryn pointed to the seal. "I think that's what he was fetching from the roof."

The fox looked up the wall of the Cathedral. "He climbed up there?"

"Aye."

"And came down with this?" He held up the seal.

Coryn nodded. "He didn't go up with it, so I guess that's what happened."

The fox narrowed his eyes. "You saw him fall?"

"Well—not really. But I heard it."

"And you only arrived here now?"

The wolf gulped. "Yes." Before the fox could ask another question, he asked, "Do you know Lox? He's a cougar, he's a guard here in the city. I know him. He'll know something about this." He pointed to the seal. "About that. I know who it belongs to."

"Calm down." The fox shook his head. "You'd better come along with me."

"Y-yes." Coryn looked down at Two-Claws again.

"Leave your friend," the guard ordered, standing. "He's not got anything more of value on him."

"He's not my..." Coryn trailed off. He didn't want to go with the guard; memories of being pulled to the station five years ago came back to him. The fox might well arrest him for being an accomplice of the thief. If he ran away now, the guard wouldn't chase him. But the seal would be returned to Lord Fardew, who would spare no thought for the thief in jail for stealing it. Clement needed him to be brave.

So he swallowed his fear and walked away from the Cathedral, away from the small body of the rat on the street in front of Rodenta's tower. The fox didn't speak to the weasel couple, nor to Coryn as they walked down the main street past three more cross streets, only seeing a few other people and lights in very few windows.

There were lights in the guard station's windows, and snoring came from the upstairs. The only other guard in the downstairs office, a squirrel, jumped up as Coryn entered the station behind the fox. "Who's this? What's your name?" He turned to the fox. "What's his name?"

"Ah..." The fox dropped the gold seal on the table in the middle of the room with a loud thunk, and the squirrel's eyes shot to the medallion.

"Ay! That's for us?" He squinted at Coryn. "We got to split it with him or did he steal it?"

"Neither," the fox said, and turned the seal over so the royal crest showed. "It's palace business. This fellow," he nodded back at Coryn, "says he knows the rat who had it."

"Where's the rat?"

"Dead." The fox sat himself down in one of the chairs. "You know a Lox? Cougar, guard?"

"Lox? Ell oh ex? Oh yeah!" The squirrel brightened.

The fox grinned at Coryn. "Spitty knows everyone."

"I'm Prix to you," the squirrel shot at Coryn, then returned his attention to the fox. "Aye, he's with station six, I think, want to go fetch him? Why?"

"This wolf," again the nod, "knows him."

"Who's he?" the squirrel asked, and turned to Coryn. "Who are you? What's your name? What happened to your arm?"

"I'm Coryn," he said, pulling his bleeding arm against his side and ignoring the question about it, "and that's Lord Fardew's seal. It was stolen weeks ago and Lox was trying to find it."

"Ay," the squirrel said. "Station six, they'd do palace business all right. How'd you come to know the fellow that took it?"

"He..." Coryn tried to think of how much of the story to tell. "He turned in another thief for it, but it turned out he was lying and only waiting for the guard to arrest that other fellow so he could get it himself. But I knew him and I followed him. I was going to get it back for Lord Fardew myself."

"You?" The squirrel laughed. "You a friend of Lord Fardew too?"

"He is a wolf," the fox pointed out, calm.

"I know a servant at the castle who knows his personal servant," Coryn said. "The one who got dismissed for letting the seal be stolen."

Both guards stared at him. "So?"

Coryn sighed. "I thought if the seal was returned, he could have his job back."

The squirrel paced, staring alternately at the seal and at Coryn. "Seems like you know an awful lot about this matter, huh? Maybe we should set you down, ask you to tell the whole thing start to finish? What d'you think about that, huh?"

Coryn sat down. "If you get Lox to come ask the questions, fine. He already knows most of it."

The squirrel snorted and then turned to the fox. "What you say, Martz? Want to run over to station six and wake up Lox?"

"No," the fox said, "but you should. You know him, I don't, and anyway I already went out today. It's your turn."

"This is part of the same thing you went out for," the squirrel argued. "It's related to the dead rat."

"But I went out," the fox, Martz, said, "and I came back, so my turn's over." He yawned. "I'll stay here with the wolf and you can go find that cougar."

"It's your turn still," the squirrel insisted, "and it's night out and you're better at night than I am."

The fox crossed his arms behind his head and leaned back, and didn't say anything.

Spitty, or Prix, stomped a foot. "Fine," he said, "fine, I'll go, and you, stay here and at least find out the wolf's name." He buttoned up his red jacket, huffed to the front door, and slammed it behind him when he left.

The fox turned his head lazily to Coryn. "What's your name?" he asked.

"Coryn."

"What happened to that arm?"

"Ah, tavern fight."

"You have anything to do with that thing being stolen?"

"No."

"Good. Don't go anywhere." And the fox closed his eyes, but kept his ears perked straight up.

It took a good long time before the squirrel returned with Lox, during which time Coryn tried to doze off, as Martz was doing, but failed. Every time he closed his eyes he saw the rat falling in slow motion, still smiling triumphantly even as the realization of his death came over him. Coryn had kicked out, he'd unbalanced Two-Claws. He'd killed him.

This is how you end up when you stray from the path. They're going to figure out that you murdered him. You're going to jail.

But the voice in his head mostly failed to penetrate his numbness. After all, the rat had threatened to murder him first, the rat had attacked him, the rat had stolen the seal (that Coryn had stolen).

And was that justification for murder? Canis said, "Give like to like," but threatening, fighting, and stealing were not the same as killing. And also, "If another has left the Path, do not leave the Path to follow them, for love or justice." There was no question that killing the rat was not part of Canis's Path. Two-Claws had never actually tried to kill Coryn. He'd said terrible words, aye, but as soon as he'd gotten the seal, he'd left. He wouldn't have harmed Coryn any longer if Coryn had let him go.

But Coryn had kicked out, and he couldn't even say why. He'd been angry in that moment, angry that the rat had won, angry that he'd gone to all that trouble and climbed the Cathedral, sucked the rat's cock, climbed the statue of Rodenta, fought Two-Claws, and at the end of it all he wasn't even going to get the seal and Clement would be left to die in jail.

It would've made more sense, wouldn't it, to have run down the stairs and met Two-Claws in the street? He almost certainly could have gotten to the bottom before the rat, and then they could've fought again on solid ground and Coryn might have won that one. Two-Claws would still be alive, and maybe Coryn wouldn't be in a guard station trying to figure out how he was going to get Clement free when he could barely stop thinking about a different rat.

Two-Claws had taken him in five years ago, had promised him a night of adventure and had delivered. If Coryn had been smarter about it, he wouldn't have ended up paying off a debt for five years. All the rat had done was abandon him; Coryn himself was the one who'd let the guard take him and who had promised his father stolen gold. His father was the one who hadn't even tried to stand up for his son, who had promised a debt that would kill him.

That's what that voice in his head was, the voice telling him to stay on the path. It was his father's memory. Well—staying on the path had been a strain that had killed his father, and straying from the path had led to Coryn killing a thief. So what was the right answer? On this, the voice was silent.

Because he couldn't sleep, he stared on the gold seal on the table. As hard as it was to focus on it without thinking about Two-Claws, he tried to move his mind forward. One of the things Two-Claws had said to him rang true, that the nobles would not care if someone was rotting in jail or not. That meant that once Lord Fardew got his seal back, Coryn wouldn't have much leverage, if any, to argue that Clement should be released.

So he'd need to make sure that Lox did something about it when he got here. He went over his story again to make sure it sounded reasonable. That meant that he had to think back to Two-Claws falling, over and over again, and imagine the different things he might have been feeling so he could describe the fall. He sighed and closed his eyes, because he might as well see the rat's final expression again if he had to think about the fall anyway. What was strange to him was that there'd been no fear in the rat's eyes. There'd been peace and triumph, as though even in falling to his death, he'd won.

When the door opened, the squirrel strode in. He looked around and went right to the seal on the table and picked it up, then looked suspiciously at Coryn as though the wolf might've somehow done something to it. "Martz," he said. "Martz!"

The fox didn't open his eyes. "I'm awake," he said.

A cougar followed Spitty into the room, his guard's uniform askew and done up with one button left open. Coryn jumped up as the cougar closed the door. "Lox," he said.

"Evening, Coryn." The cougar's eyes went to the seal on the table. "This is it, ay?"

"I guess so." Coryn hadn't had a chance to take a good look at the seal, but even in the light of the lanterns and no hundred-foot drop at his feet, he couldn't tell anything about it other than that a coat of arms adorned one side. He thought he remembered the royal seal on the other side, but other memories had taken precedence. He could no longer be sure of what he'd seen in the dim light of the obscured moon.

Lox picked up the seal and turned it over. The squirrel, watching, sucked in his breath but only said, "That the thing they're looking for? It looks like a royal seal but I never seen one before so I wouldn't know. It's gold sure enough, isn't it?"

"It looks like the seal." Lox turned to Coryn. "It looks like Lord Fardew will owe you a favor."

"Here now." The fox opened his eyes. "I'm the one found the body."

"Alan Masterson found the body," the squirrel chirped back. "He just came and told you 'bout it. Wolf here told you what it was an' who to fetch for it."

"Whose side you on?" Martz demanded. "We split any reward by shift anyway."

"Ooh that's right." The squirrel turned to Lox. "My partner there found it. Lord Fardew owes him a debt."

The cougar acknowledged this claim, or maybe dismissed it, with a nod, and turned to Coryn. "Why don't you tell me what happened to you tonight?"

His eyes flicked to Coryn's bloody arm. The wolf followed the glance and took a breath. "I ran into Two-Claws at a tavern and he was bragging about how he put one over on the guard. Some people didn't believe him and there was a fight. I got involved but he didn't see me." He held up his arm. "So I followed him afterwards and he went to the Cathedral. I had to stay back because he almost saw me a couple times. I was on the roof of a building, a shop or something, a couple streets away, but I could see him in the moonlight. He climbed up the tower to the statue of Rodenta, stayed there for a few minutes, and then he was starting to come down and he slipped and fell into the street. I got down off the roof, but it was hard to get down quickly and then I got turned around and went the wrong way, so by the time I got to the street, the guard," he gestured to the fox, "was already there."

Lox nodded. "Fox. What's your name?"

"Martz."

"Martz, what happened here?"

The fox yawned. "Alan Masterson, a weasel, came runnin' in, said someone fell off the Cathedral. It was my turn to go so I left Spitty here and went with Masterson. Sure enough, there was a rat in the street, dead. Mighta fallen. Mighta just been killed there. Lots of bones broke, anyway. He had that," he pointed to the seal, "in one paw. I'd just got it out when this wolf came runnin' up."

"Did you see where he came from?"

The fox flicked his ears. "Ah, no. Not every night you find a royal seal on a dead body. I was curious."

"Course he was," the squirrel, Spitty, put in. "Anyone would be, find a great gold treasure like that. An' he didn't keep it, he brought it back here so we could give it back. You tell Lord Fardew that."

"I'd expect guards to be honest." Lox's tone belied his words. He weighed the seal in his paw.

"This means Clement is innocent, right?" Coryn couldn't stop himself from bursting out with the plea. "Two-Claws knew where it was; he must have stolen it and blamed Clement so you'd arrest the wrong rat."

Lox narrowed his eyes, still staring at the seal. "That might be," he said slowly.

"But who gets the reward?" Spitty asked. "It's us what found it."

"I don't care about a reward," Coryn said quickly, "as long as Clement is released from prison. They can have the reward."

He gestured to the squirrel and fox, and Spitty responded. "See? Right honorable this one is. His story sounds fine to me, so let's release this Calumet from prison and get our reward from Lord Fardew, everyone's happy, seems to me, ey?"

The cougar looked up at Coryn. "This will be a difficult story to manage. The captain won't like that the rat played the guards like a lute. We might have to come up with a different story to tell the Lord. Do you think you can agree to that?"

"Would it get Clement out of jail?"

Lox exhaled. "I can't promise that. But I can't see another way it would be possible at all."

"Then aye," Coryn said, trying to contain the wagging of his tail. "I think I could, aye."

Because the sun had not yet risen, Lox told Coryn to go back to his inn and rest until someone came to fetch him. "I promise you," he said, "we will not forget about you."

The excitement of the evening had well worn off by this point, so Coryn was happy to comply. He stumbled back to the Four Quarters, found his room, closed the window, and fell into bed.

When he woke, the sun sat high in the sky, and his stomach complained loudly about how long it had been since he'd eaten. He rubbed his eyes clear and wandered out to the public-house to find it mostly empty.

There wasn't much food left, but the innkeeper scraped together a plate for him (at full price, of course). Coryn sat at one of the small outside tables, in view of the Four Quarters, and had barely started eating when the wolves from Tistunish he'd met the previous day came up to him. He didn't register their presence until they sat down.

"Did you try to go to the Cathedral this morning?" one of them said.

"We tried," the other chimed in. "But there was a guard at the door, and they said there would be no services today."

"No services! Can you believe it?" the first said.

"I'm sorry about that." Coryn's ears perked. "Did they say why?"

"No!" the first said, "but they told us that the Cathedral almost never closes."

"So," the second said, "this might be even more special."

"At least that's how we're looking at it."

Coryn nodded. "That's a good way of looking at it."

"And," the second said, "they told us it will be open this afternoon, so we can go in and walk around."

"That's something, anyway." Coryn went back to his breakfast.

"So we thought we'd let you know, and we're glad we saw you here."

"What were you doing this morning? Sleep late?"

He lifted his muzzle and for a moment considered telling them the truth. But only for a moment. "I did sleep late," he said. "I'm sorry to have missed you."

"As it turns out, you didn't miss anything."

"So of all the mornings to sleep in, this was a good one."

He smiled at them. "That's good to know."

"We'll leave you to your breakfast." The first one got up.

"But if you want to come over with us this afternoon..." The second one stood too.

"I'm sorry," Coryn said. "I've got appointments all afternoon. But I hope you have a wonderful time."

"We will." Their tails wagged as they walked back up to their room.

It was a few minutes later that Lox walked by, and Coryn

thought that it would have been very funny if the guard in his full uniform had come in to talk to him while the wolf couple were talking about the guards at the Cathedral.

He called out, and the cougar came to stand over his table. "You ready?"

Coryn looked down at the bread and cheese remaining on his plate. "Not quite."

"Well, hurry up. You've got an appointment at the guard station and then we're going to the palace."

"The palace?" Coryn shoved bread into his muzzle.

"Aye. We're going to return the seal and I thought you'd like to be part of it. I couldn't track down Lord Fardew's personal servant, I'm afraid, but if you have any idea where he is..." Coryn shook his head, and Lox said, "All right, then it'll be just you."

Coryn pushed cheese in after the bread and nodded. Lox sighed and sat down with him until he'd finished.

The visit to the station, which was across the river near the palace, consisted of Coryn retelling his story from the night before while Lox and the other cougar, the captain who'd come to Coryn's farm, listened, and a harried skunk wrote it all down. There were a couple points where Coryn faltered, but he pretended he was trying to find the right words, and neither the cougars nor the skunk remarked on it, if they even noticed.

When he'd finished, the skunk took the written statement and left the room. The captain turned to Lox and said, "Guard doesn't come off too well in this, do we? Took the true thief with us down to Deverin, caught the wrong fellow, imprisoned him, and it took this farmer to spot him?"

Lox cleared his throat. "But sir, didn't you tell me that you had your suspicions of Two-Claws the rat the whole time? The only way to get him to reveal where the seal was, you told me, was to make him think we suspected someone else, and then he'd be sure to go get it. But he's clever, so the guards couldn't watch him, and that's why I spent so much time with Coryn here on the way back from Deverin, telling him exactly how to follow the rat. And thanks to your good sense, we outsmarted one of the cleverest thieves in all of Divalia."

"Mmm." The older cougar stroked his whiskers. "When you put it like that, Lox, that sounds like a story Lord Fardew would appreciate hearing."

"I thought so, sir."

"Fine. I'll take the wolf and the others to the palace. Can you find him something nicer to wear?"

"Of course, sir." Lox nodded as the captain left the room without even looking at Coryn.

Coryn stood. It seemed they were going to accept his story, even though as he looked back on it, he could find several places where they might have pressed him. "I don't have much to spare for clothes."

"We're not going shopping." Lox beckoned him to a small storeroom in which two large chests held what looked like a jumble of different cloths and fabrics. "There. Let's see if anything in here fits you. You're about my size, I'd guess."

Coryn rummaged through one of the chests while Lox looked through the other. "What is all this?"

"Oh," the cougar said carelessly, "sometimes people leave possessions here and we hold onto them in case someone comes to claim them."

That seemed rather more altruistic than Coryn would have expected from the guard, and if it were true, why were they pawing through the unsorted, disorganized mess as though they were poor people on a rubbish heap? And why were they treating it as a place to find something for Coryn to wear? None of the clothing would have looked at home in the palace, but one or two of the pieces, especially the jackets, were nicer than anything Coryn owned.

At last they settled on a green jacket made of cotton, with lovely pale yellow trim around the collar and cuffs. Whoever had lost this would surely want it back, Coryn thought, and then as he was putting it on, he noticed a small dark red stain on the inside of the left breast, and guessed that the owner had probably lost more than the jacket.

As he dressed, he asked, "Why *did* you help me? You could've just taken the seal. I didn't even think about it until this morning."

The cougar smiled faintly. "Yes, those two who found it would have liked that, I'm certain." He studied his claws. "That sort of behavior happens often in the guard, despite what our charge is. I suppose..." Claws flexed all the way out, then back in. "When we talked on the road, I was impressed by how devout you are. The Cathedral means a lot to you, I could tell. And where Felis tells us to look to our family and be good providers, I know Canis speaks of the pack and extended family. And here was this rat, a thief even if he didn't steal the seal, but who'd made himself part of your pack. And you weren't abandoning him.

"Not to mention," he added as Coryn digested that, "that the guard doesn't come off too good no matter what the truth is. If he wasn't the thief, we arrested the wrong fellow; even if he was, you found the seal where none of us could. So." He spread his paws and his smile grew fuller. "I thought, what does it cost me to do a good deed?"

"It means a lot," Coryn said. "Thank you."

"Offer up a prayer for me next time you pray," Lox said, clapping him on the shoulder, "and we'll call it even."

The captain was waiting with Martz and Spitty out in the main room of the station. Both fox and squirrel had buttoned up their uniforms and looked quite sharp, and even in his new jacket, Coryn felt underdressed.

He bid good-bye to Lox and followed the three guards out of the station, down the street, and to the front entrance of the palace, where the captain barely spoke to the guards—the same bear guards who'd turned Coryn away the day before—as he led his group through. Bonto glared at Coryn, clearly recognizing him, but the wolf kept his head up as he walked past.

The captain's swift, assured pace through the palace's halls left Coryn little time to gawk at the people, the tapestries, the portraits, the stonework. They went up a different staircase, this one with a wolf statue at the base, and then down a hallway, past many private apartments with portraits outside their doors, to a large open room with great windows that looked out over the river and the Cathedral.

Waiting for them there were two people: a finely-dressed wolf in a deep blue doublet with gold buttons and fringed cuffs over matching blue trousers sat in a velvet-plush chair, and beside him stood a porcupine in a neatly-tailored outfit that was less flashy but no less expensive-looking. When they entered, the captain and the other guards bowed, so Coryn did too. Delicate, expensive scents tickled his nose, musky and sharp, rarer than the violets Lord Barclaw had sprinkled him with.

"Lord Fardew," the captain said, "it is my great privilege and honor to return to you the royal seal of your lordship, which the city guard recovered for you."

He held out a silk cloth-wrapped bundle. Lord Fardew took it and unfolded the cloth reverently to reveal the gold seal. For a moment, he simply stared down at it, then he let out a long breath and held it up to the sunlight so that it gleamed. "That should satisfy His Majesty, eh, Zinno?" He turned his muzzle toward the porcupine without taking his eyes from the seal.

"Indeed, sir. What a relief to see it safely back again." The porcupine bowed his head to the captain. "A tribute to the hard work of our city guards."

"Yes," the wolf said, turning back to the captain. "How did you find it?"

The captain cleared his throat. "As you know, sir, we at the sixth were working with all available guards to find it. We followed rumors of its theft to a particular rat who was well known to the guards. To make him feel confident, we pretended to be on the trail of another, but then we followed him to the Cathedral, where he had hidden the seal. Unfortunately, as he was climbing down after retrieving it, he slipped and fell, and perished when he struck the street. Our guards here," he indicated Martz and Spitty, "retrieved the seal and made sure that it was safe until it could be returned to you."

"Excellent work, Captain," Lord Fardew said. "And this wolf, why is he here?"

"Ah," the captain said, turning to look at Coryn. "He is a farmer who was known to the thief and was very helpful to our guards in finding and following him. The guards all felt that he should share in the recognition."

Share in it? Inwardly Coryn sputtered with indignation, but, he reminded himself, it didn't matter as long as he got Clement out of prison.

"There is praise to share, to be sure." Lord Fardew smiled. "You have spared me from embarrassment and perhaps worse, and I am grateful indeed. Do you think ten gold crowns for each of the four of you would be adequate thanks?"

"Yes sir!" "Oh aye!" the fox and squirrel said at the same time.

"Excellent." Lord Fardew turned to the porcupine. "Would you see to it, please?"

Coryn's mouth was dry. "Sir," he rasped out, and then, because the wolf didn't seem to have heard, "I beg your pardon, sir."

Lord Fardew looked at him curiously, ears askew. "What is it?"

he asked. "Is ten crowns not enough?" His voice held a faint hint of sarcasm, subtle enough that Coryn might have missed it except that he was familiar with the similarly subtle manners of Lord Barclaw.

"My lord," Coryn replied, "it is most generous indeed. But I would give it all back if you could help redress an injustice."

The wolf perked his ears. "An injustice, you say?"

"Aye." Coryn took a breath. "You see, when the captain told you they were on the trail of another, that other was a rat that the true thief said had stolen the seal. He is a friend of mine. As they, I mean the guard, wanted to do their jobs, of course, they arrested my friend, and he remains in jail today. The true thief wanted them to arrest him so that they wouldn't follow him anymore, but I warned them that the true thief was, er, the true thief." He was starting to get tripped up in pronouns. "The point is, the thief lied about my friend, and I would like him to be released from jail now that his innocence is proven."

Lord Fardew absorbed this and turned to the captain. "What say you?"

The cougar had been watching Coryn with a troubled expression, and now snapped his attention back to the lord. "Ah," the captain said, "well..."

They wouldn't want to release Clement, Coryn realized, and in that moment saw that his only hope was to threaten to contradict the captain's story in which the guard had planned everything out. "You arrested this rat, whom you knew to be innocent," Coryn said, "as a way to make the true thief reveal himself. Isn't that what you said happened?"

The cougar frowned at him. "Yes. It is true that the rat who is a friend of this wolf's is in jail."

"For the crime of stealing my seal?"

"Yes, sir." He drew out the words, slowly.

"Then surely if this other thief has been caught..." The wolf gestured in that way Lord Barclaw also did when he didn't want to have to finish his sentence because he expected Coryn to understand what he intended.

"Sir...this other rat is also a thief."

Coryn jumped in. "He has been living with me on my farm for the past month. I will take charge of him, and I promise to keep him out of Divalia. He won't come back into the city at all. He'll come live on the farm. He might have been a thief in the past, but he isn't now."

"Captain, that sounds reasonable to me." Lord Fardew gave a decisive nod. "Let the other rat out of jail, and he will be banished from the city into the custody of this wolf here. There. Justice is done."

"Sir," the captain said, but Lord Fardew cut him off.

"If this rat is innocent, he should be released to his friend. If he is a thief, well, then there will be one less thief in Divalia. Does that not make you happy?"

"Yes, sir." The cougar didn't look happy at all.

"And Zinno," Lord Fardew turned to the porcupine, "that will be only thirty gold from my account. See to it, if you would. And of course, none of you will speak of this."

"Of course, sir." The porcupine bowed as Lord Fardew rose, and the captain and guards stammered their agreements to silence. Coryn joined in, a little late.

"Once again, captain, my thanks to you and your men. You have rendered a great service to me and to the kingdom."

The captain bowed, so Coryn did too, and when he straightened, Lord Fardew had left the room.

"Captain," the porcupine said, "I trust I can send the thirty crowns to the sixth and they will reach the proper paws."

"Of course, thank you," the cougar said. Martz and Spitty exchanged glances but did not object.

"As for the release of the prisoner, I leave that to you." The porcupine made to leave the room.

"Sir," Coryn called. "Mister...Zinno?"

The porcupine turned, a half-smile on his face. "Just Zinno, or Master Steward if you prefer. My time is very valuable."

"Yes, sir, of course." Coryn half-bowed awkwardly. "I, ah, I have an appointment with Lord Barclaw this afternoon. Must I leave the palace and come all the way back in or can I go see him now?"

The steward's eyes widened. "You have business with another lord?"

"Aye."

"And you are a...farmer?"

"Lord Barclaw owns a debt—owned a debt that I incurred a long time ago."

"I see." The porcupine scratched his chin and then extended a paw, thick claws beckoning Coryn forward. "I'm headed in that direction. I'll escort you to Lord Barclaw's chambers."

"Thank you." Coryn half-bowed again.

"You don't need to bow to me." The porcupine sounded amused. "I've no royal blood. I just look after the interests of all those who do."

"All right. Oh, just a moment." Coryn turned to the cougar. "Captain, should I collect my friend tonight from the jail?"

"We'll bring him to the sixth district station," the captain said, eyeing the Steward. "Come find me there before sunset."

Coryn thanked him and then hurried after the porcupine, who moved very quickly through the palace corridors. "May I ask you something?" Coryn said when he caught up.

"As long as I can answer before we get there."

"Yes." Coryn rubbed his whiskers. "Lord Barclaw has taken a fancy to me and wants me to move to his lands. I don't think I want to."

"You don't think you want to?"

"I don't want to." Coryn said it more firmly, as they rounded a corner and the smell of wolves gave way to the smell of foxes. "But I don't know how to say no to him. He sent a servant to come fetch me once when I didn't keep an appointment, so I can't simply ignore him."

"Wait." The porcupine slowed. "He wants you to move to his land—whose land do you live on now?"

"Lord Deverin's."

"He sent his servants onto Lord Deverin's land?" Zinno's voice rose. "Do they have an understanding about you?"

"I—I'm not sure. I mean, he said something about asking Lord Deverin's steward to arrange suitors for my sister, but—"

Zinno was quiet for a moment, still walking. "My advice when a commoner has a disagreement with a Lord is that the Lord will always win, and the commoner will spare himself a good deal of trouble and misery if he acknowledges that and moves forward with that understanding. It is possible that Lord Deverin would allow Lord Barclaw to do what he wants; after all, they move larger pieces around on the board of government every day, and what is the life of a farmer? But...hm, hm." He stopped in the middle of the corridor and looked Coryn up and down. "Who else lives on the farm?"

"My sister and her daughter."

"Parents both joined the Circle? No other males?"

"None."

"I see." Zinno stroked down the quills at the back of his head. "You say Lord Barclaw fancies you."

"Aye."

"And you just gave up ten gold crowns to rescue a thief from prison."

Coryn shifted uncomfortably. "Aye."

The porcupine's smile widened. "A friend, you said."

Coryn nodded. "Close friend indeed, to be worth ten crowns. A child I could see being worth ten crowns, or...a wife." Coryn didn't say anything. "You and this thief aren't married?"

"No." Coryn splayed his ears and looked away.

The porcupine chuckled. "But maybe, in time?"

"Maybe."

"Can you read? Have you read any P. Zinsky books?"

"I can, but I don't know who that is."

Zinno chuckled. "If you've any coin to spare, go find Arcalli's bookshop and ask him for something by that name. P. Zinsky. I promise you won't regret it."

"All right." Coryn committed the name to his memory.

"And this thief won't remain behind on your land if you go to Lord Barclaw's, I wager. Not if you promised to take charge of him. You couldn't live happily on Lord Barclaw's land with him? The old bear won't have it?"

"Honestly," Coryn said, "I don't think he would care. He just wants me to come visit once a month or maybe twice a month. But..." I'm done with that part of my life.

Are you? Have you earned that?

Yes, he told the voice definitively. I have.

"But you don't want to be in that situation. All right." The porcupine shook his quills. "I have an idea. Come with me and follow my lead."

He started off again, and Coryn followed. "I appreciate your help, but...I thought your time was valuable."

"Oh," Zinno said, "I love my job, but sometimes it gets a little old being ordered around by lords and nobles all the time. It's rare I get a chance to put something right for a commoner, and after that nonsense the guards fed Lord Fardew—oh, don't worry, he believed every word of it—and the way you stood up for yourself, I've a mind to help you." He chuckled. "And it means a chance to put a quill in the old bear, which I confess is the stronger attraction for me."

"Thank you," Coryn said. "Ah, how exactly?"

"I am the Royal Steward," Zinno said, "so I have a good deal of experience in having lords and nobles do things for each other and to each other, and all I'm going to do is make sure that Lord Barclaw understands exactly what it means to have you move from a farm on Lord Deverin's land to a farm on his. It may come to nothing, in which case I apologize for getting your hopes up, and I recommend that you and your thief take his offer and put up with monthly visits—" Here he lowered his voice. "The lord is old, after all, and after he...no longer desires your company, you can sell the farm and go wherever you wish."

Coryn swallowed. "I hope your plan works."

"I do too." The porcupine flashed Coryn a smile. "It would speak well to my experience in this position." He stopped in front of a door, and Coryn recognized the portrait of Lord Barclaw. "We're here. Are you ready?"

When Coryn assented, Zinno knocked. Perroh answered the door and greeted them with mild surprise. "Steward Zinno," he said. "I hope Coryn did not trouble you overmuch."

"Not at all," the porcupine replied. "As it happened, he was in the palace for an unrelated matter and engaged me in conversation."

"I...see." Perroh looked back and forth between them. "I...thank you for accompanying him to Lord Barclaw's quarters."

"Yes." Zinno took a step forward, and when Perroh backed up, the porcupine continued on into the chambers. "Before I go...he made mention of a small matter that I thought I should discuss with Lord Barclaw. Is his lordship available?"

"He, er, is, but, ah." Perroh looked back toward the bedroom and then waved Zinno to the sitting-room. "If you would please wait here. Coryn, you can come back to—"

The skunk had turned toward the changing room, but Zinno interrupted him. "Oh, I think Coryn should be present for this conversation as well." He extended a paw and took Coryn's wrist. "Come, wait with me."

The sitting-room held two chairs big enough for a bear's bulk and a low chaise longue. Zinno sat on the chaise and so Coryn sat beside him, both leaning forward. The tunic over the porcupine's quills bulged out and Coryn supposed it would be uncomfortable for him to sit against a chair back.

When Lord Barclaw entered the room, it was with a robe loosely draped around his shoulders that concealed most of his body except for a line down his chest and stomach and sheath and half-hard cock. He glared at Zinno and Coryn and then sat heavily in one of the chairs, tugging the robe until one edge of it lay over his cock, technically hiding it but leaving the shape of it well visible. "Well," the bear said, "Master Steward, to what do I owe this intrusion?"

Zinno smiled, not visibly responding either to the snippy tone nor to the bear's state of undress, and said, "Good day, Lord Barclaw. I hope this is not too much of an imposition, but a matter has come to my attention. I would rather settle it here with you before I discuss it with Lord Deverin."

Barclaw squinted and reached inside his robe to scratch his balls, giving both Coryn and Zinno another good look at them. "Deverin? What's he got to do with anything?"

"Coryn here," Zinno gestured to him, "has told me that you've offered him a farm in your land."

The bear's eyes narrowed as he stared at Coryn. "What business is that of yours?"

"Well—"

Lord Barclaw interrupted Zinno. "And he shouldn't be talking to you about that anyway. That's between me and him.

Why are you talking to the palace steward? Why didn't you come directly here? That's what I ordered you to do."

Zinno put a paw on Coryn's knee. "As I said, Coryn was in the palace on an unrelated matter."

"What matter?" Lord Barclaw's tone turned peevish.

"He assisted the palace guard in finding a thief," Zinno said. "Quite a valuable service, in fact."

"When did you have time to do that?"

Once again, Zinno patted Coryn's knee, a signal to him to be quiet. "If you please, my lord, I do have many pressing issues to attend to today and I would like to get my answer from you. It will be very quick, and you will have time to talk to Coryn afterwards."

The bear heaved a sigh and turned his grudging attention to the porcupine. "Yes? Yes?"

"If you've offered him a farm to entice him to move to your land and away from Lord Deverin, then I'll have to inform Lord Deverin so he may have his exchequer determine what payment from you will be appropriate to offset the taxes you are removing from his land and adding to your own."

Lord Barclaw went very still. "What...payment?" he said finally.

"Oh, it's a usual thing, goes back to King Cadmur," Zinno said casually. "It's not invoked often, but in certain cases it may be. I assume you've talked to Lord Deverin about this matter?"

Coryn still didn't know where the steward was going with this conversation, unless he were trying to sow discord between the lords. He doubted very much that Lord Deverin would object to Lord Barclaw moving a farmer from his land. But when Lord Barclaw didn't answer, Zinno went on. "I have business with Lord Deverin later today, so I can ask him if you don't remember, m'lord."

The bear stirred and sat up straighter. "He hasn't moved yet," he snapped with a wave at Coryn. "I'll speak to Deverin after."

"Of course, of course." Zinno remained agreeable. "If you like, I can broach the matter with Lord Deverin. He'd likely come to me or the Exchequer to make the tax determination anyway."

"Er." Lord Barclaw seemed nonplused by this offer.

"I just wanted to confirm that you desperately want this wolf to be closer to you." Zinno took out a piece of parchment from his tunic. "I'm sure Lord Deverin won't object in that case. May I use your quill and ink? It will be easier if we write this down."

"I—" The bear's glance went to his desk, where several quills stood next to an inkpot that, if the dust on it was any indication, was probably bone-dry. "I never said 'desperately.' And why is there a tax burden? His farm isn't moving."

"No," Zinno said, "but you're leaving it in the care of a mother and daughter, with no father or husband or brother to work the land. The yield is sure to suffer. By contrast, you're bringing this able-bodied wolf to land of yours that is currently unworked, meaning there will be much more harvest to tax come next year."

"That's preposterous," the bear said. "I'm not—see here, this isn't about taxes and harvests."

"Oh, no, of course not." Zinno turned to Coryn. "I don't blame you at all for falling in love with him. He's lovely indeed. And if I had the means of a Lord at my disposal, why, I also might stir heaven and earth—"

"Hardly!" Lord Barclaw huffed, interrupting. "Heaven and Earth? And who made mention of love?"

Now Coryn was starting to see the strategy. He ventured a short statement. "My lord," he said, "you did see me yesterday and insist I return today, and accompany you to your castle."

"That—there is no 'love' there."

"No?" Coryn tried to look hurt.

"Of course not," Zinno put in smoothly. "How could a lord love a simple farmer? He's more like a favored mount, I suppose? One you like the feel of being astride?"

"Astride?" Lord Barclaw sputtered. "He has a gentle muzzle —this is not important. He's coming to my land because I wish it."

"Of course." Zinno got up and walked over to the desk. "Why does it matter what we call it? You don't want to spend another day apart from him." He lifted the top of the ink pot and sniffed it, then replaced the lid.

The bear stood, which caused his robe to fall open again. "Stop saying things I haven't said," he cried, and Coryn shrank back from that tone.

But Zinno merely turned with a half-smile still on his muzzle. "Forgive me, m'lord," he said, "but it appears I'm having trouble understanding. You have set aside a valuable farm on your land for this farmer, but you don't love him. You wish him to visit you every day you are in the palace and to accompany you back to your castle and remain close to you, yet you claim you are not desperate for his company. So far, all you have asserted is that you find his muzzle attractive, and while I will take your word for his skills, I cannot imagine that your lordship might not be just as satisfied by any of the courtiers I know live at Castle Barclaw. Perhaps you will be able to enlighten me so that I may communicate to Lord Deverin the exact urgency of your request?"

Lord Barclaw breathed heavily in and out. He looked from Coryn to Zinno and then back. "I want—I simply want—"

Coryn couldn't help noticing that the bear's erection had gone down all the way, mostly because as Lord Barclaw stood and took a step forward, his sheath was at Coryn's eye level.

"There's no shame in it," Zinno said. "You recall Lord March, some five or six years ago? He favored a servant girl from the Crossed Swords, brought her into the palace and everything. People are used to it."

For several seconds, Lord Barclaw stood and huffed. Then he rounded on Coryn, standing there with his belly hanging over his sheath, his balls dangling below them. His musk filled Coryn's nostrils. "Why did you come to the palace? I told you to come to the castle, not the Royal Palace."

"You seemed pleased to see me, my lord," Coryn said. "I only thought—"

"You only thought. You only thought." Lord Barclaw stomped back to his chair and then turned again, his robe sweeping around him. "You think you're so important. I decide what's important to me. You...farmer, you don't decide."

"No, my lord."

"All right, go. I no longer wish to give you my farm. I don't wish to see you again. I don't 'love' you and I am not desperate for your company." He strode toward the door, calling, "Perroh! See them out!"

When the door had closed behind them and they stood outside in the hallway, Coryn turned to Zinno and extended a paw. "Thank you," he said. "I've no idea how you did that."

The porcupine clasped his paw with a smile. "Of course you don't. You would have to have lived in the palace for most of your life, and have listened to the way the lords talk to and about each other, and you would have to remember that Lord March's nickname around the palace when he chased that serving girl was 'Guttercock,' and then besides you would have to be of a station not equal to the lords, but apart from them and answering only to a higher authority than them." He released Coryn's paw. "You rendered a great service today, not only to Lord Fardew but to the kingdom, and to me personally. I shudder imagining the horror I would have to endure if there were any trouble around Lord Fardew's succession. I suspect your role in it was greater than the captain told in his story, or he wouldn't have allowed you in the room at all. I'm pleased to do this trifle in exchange."

"It may be but a trifle to you, but..." Coryn rubbed at his eyes, finding them moist. "I can't—this is—" He gulped. "It's been five years since I felt this free. And what you consider a trifle, a small kindness, it means the world to me."

"I'm also something of a romantic," Zinno said lightly. "So go get your friend and leave this city, and if you value your life and your love, I'd advise you to return as infrequently as possible."

Coryn rubbed tears from his muzzle. "I'd like to do a kindness for you."

"Do as I said, then." The porcupine patted him on the shoulder. "Now, I'm pleased to have been of use to you, but do follow me quickly to the exit. I was not lying when I said I have a great deal of work still to attend to today."

"Yes," Coryn said. He took a deep breath and tried to collect himself. "I'm sorry."

"Don't be sorry." Zinno set off down the hallway. "I appreciate the honesty of your response, truth be told, and I'll sleep better tonight knowing I've done some real good for once. Not to mention, if I ever feel gloomy, I can always remember the old bear's tantrum to cheer me up."

"But," Coryn hurried to keep up, "you're the Royal Steward. Don't you do good work every day?"

The porcupine flashed him a smile. "Dear boy," he said. "I mean it. Leave this palace and city as soon as you can."

CHAPTER 13

The sixth district station was housed in a pale stone building, three stories, so stately that Coryn walked past it twice looking for something old and wooden like the station Martz had brought him back to. He only realized which building it was when he saw a red-jacketed guard come out of it.

He opened the door and walked into a gleaming lobby with a slick marble floor and gold-embossed wooden counter behind which a red-jacketed coyote and beaver stood talking to a tall bear. Against the back wall to his left sat three elegant chairs, their fine woodwork complemented with soft purple upholstery, and to his right, a plain wooden bench.

Both the coyote and beaver looked occupied, so he walked over to sit on one of the fancy chairs. He'd barely swept his tail out of the way when the coyote called to him. "Hey! Wolf!"

Coryn stood and took a step toward the counter, but the coyote pointed to the bench. "The chairs are for nobles. Wait there."

So Coryn walked over and sat on the far less comfortable bench and tried to guess which of the fancy doors leading deeper into the station Clement would come out of. Or maybe the staircase tucked away there to the left, the one he couldn't see anymore from the bench even when he craned his neck around.

He hoped Clement would be healthy. He hoped Clement would forgive him for what he'd done.

When he'd determined to secure the rat's freedom, foremost in his mind had been that he had to make amends for his action. Clement had been so kind to him in their last conversation that he'd never considered that the rat might hold a grudge against him. And yet, he'd loved his father, but the weight of the betrayal (as Coryn had seen it) had taken its toll on their relationship, compounded by the monthly payments and then Ki's failed marriage.

Coryn had never properly forgiven his father. Nearly two years ago now, he'd walked out into the fields when the old wolf hadn't come in for dinner, and in the fading light he'd seen the motionless grey form at the edge of a half-harvested barley field. He'd thought that death might ease the tension between them, as nothing else had, and in the moments he'd stood there and stared down at his father's body, he'd waited for forgiveness to come to him. He'd stood for long minutes and felt only emptiness and regret. Death hadn't erased the betrayal. Ki had cried, and Coryn had pretended that he'd done his crying out in the field, but all he could think about then was how his father would never be able to say or do anything to restore Coryn's faith in him.

Even now, thinking of his father brought mixed feelings of shame and anger, but no forgiveness. So how could he expect Clement to forgive him?

Deep breaths. Clement would forgive him because Coryn had tried to make amends. It would have been so easy to ride to Castle Barclaw and take the farm and tell himself that if

Clement didn't want to be in jail, he shouldn't have stolen a royal seal. Coryn wouldn't have done anything wrong by abandoning Clement, according to the law.

But neither had his father.

He wrung his paws together and took another breath. If Clement didn't forgive him then...then that would be that. He'd ride with the rat out of Divalia and then would bid him farewell, and he'd have to convince Ki of what he'd done without the rat as witness.

"You."

He looked up. The beaver was beckoning him forward. "What's your business here?"

Coryn stood and walked toward the counter. "I'm, ah, the captain said I was going to meet..." He swallowed and started again. "There's a prisoner, a rat, he's being released and I'm taking charge of him."

The beaver looked him up and down. "Course you are," he said. "Run along now before I put you in jail for the night."

"No," Coryn said. "Really. Ask the captain."

"Which captain?" The beaver seemed amused.

"The, ah, the cougar. Or ask Lox. He knows me."

The guard's smile faded at the name. He turned to the coyote, who was chatting with another guard who'd come in. "Ey. Tanic. Where's Lox?"

"Dunno," the coyote said. "Upstairs maybe. Who wants t'know?" He eyed Coryn and rubbed the white line of a scar down his cheek.

"This wolf says he's taking charge of a prisoner from a captain who's a cougar."

"Hah!" The coyote's laugh was loud and sharp. "An' I'm set to become Gaiavox next week. Fortune smiles on us all, ay?"

"He knows Lox."

"So? Lots of scum knows Lox. Lox ain't a captain." He

addressed Coryn. "How you know him? Tavern fight? He catch you in the palace?"

"He came down to my farm and we rode together back to Divalia," Coryn said.

The coyote scratched his scar again. Coryn's evenness seemed to rob him of the enjoyment of his teasing. "Captain Inx is in back," he said. "Likely that's the one you want." And he went back to chatting with the other guard as if Coryn had left the room.

The beaver stared at Coryn. When the wolf didn't move, he sighed. "Right," he said. "I'll see if Captain knows anything about this." He pointed back to the wooden bench and said, "Wait there," then turned and walked slowly back to a door behind the long counter.

So Coryn sat and waited. Several minutes later the door opened, and the cougar captain emerged with the beaver in tow. When the cougar's eyes lit on Coryn, he turned and said something to the beaver, who went back through the door while the captain came up to the counter and beckoned Coryn forward.

"We're keeping a description of this rat," he said without any greeting. "If he comes back to Divalia, he'll be arrested as soon as he sets foot inside the walls. We'll tell him that but make sure you tell him too. And we're informing Lord Deverin that we're releasing him into his land and that you're vouching for him."

"He won't steal anything else," Coryn said, though he wondered how much good a description would do, given that he'd mistaken the rat for someone else for weeks. "I promise."

The captain sniffed. "Don't make promises for others, pup. I guess you figure you can get some free work on your farm, but this type, he's lazy. He's not used to working. Maybe he'll last a few months, maybe a few years, but eventually he'll remember how easy it was to steal for a living and he'll go back to it. Mark my words."

You don't know him, Coryn wanted to say. You didn't see him throw himself into the farm. Maybe he just never had a family, never had someone to stick up for him and love him. But all he said was, "Yes, sir, thank you, sir," because in a few minutes it wouldn't matter at all what the captain thought.

The cougar looked him up and down. "All right," he said. "I've said my piece. Long as he's outside my city, I don't much care what happens to him."

"Yes, sir." Coryn's mouth was dry, but he got the words out. He couldn't keep his eyes away from the door the beaver had gone through.

When the beaver came back, a slight, dirty figure trailed behind him. Clement looked much the same as the last time Coryn had seen him, in the same torn tunic and with the same resigned expression, though when he stepped out into the large, bright room, that expression turned bewildered. Then he saw Coryn and he froze.

The beaver went a few more steps before noticing that Clement hadn't followed him, and then he reached back and grabbed the rat's tunic, pulling him forward. "C'mon," he rasped. "Almost think you'd want to go back to jail."

"No, sir," Clement said, and stumbled forward, not taking his eyes from Coryn. The rat mostly looked dazed as he navigated the space behind the counter and came to stand beside the captain.

The cougar didn't acknowledge him for a moment and then he inked a quill and pushed a paper over to him. "Make your mark there at the bottom," he instructed the rat, holding out the quill between two fingers.

Clement stared at the paper as though he'd never seen writing before. Coryn leaned over and said, "This says that you're being released. You'll come with me and you promise not to come back to Divalia after sundown today. All right?"

The "All right" meant as much "is that all right?" as "do you understand?" Clement nodded, then added a thick, "Yes," and Coryn couldn't tell which question he was answering. The rat took the quill and scribbled at the bottom of the parchment.

The captain took the quill back, again between two fingers, and stared at the parchment for a second, then unlatched the small door at the end of the counter. He pulled Clement across and urged him through it, then closed and latched it again. "I don't know what you've done to this wolf," he said, "but if I were you I'd be grateful to him to the end of your days. Don't let so much as a whisker or tail tip get out of line again, or even he won't be able to pull you out of the dark hole we'll throw you in."

"Yes, sir," Clement said. "Thank you, sir."

"Don't thank me. My choice? I'd rather see you behind bars for the rest of your life or at the end of a rope. Even if you didn't do this last thing, there's plenty you did do and it's only on account of you're promising to leave my city for good that I'm even considering this. Got enough vermin on the street without tossing them back once they're caught." He snorted and met Coryn's eye. "Already said to you what I had to say. Don't you forget it, mind. Now clear out of my station."

"Yes, sir," Coryn said, and Clement echoed him.

The rat moved slowly, so Coryn put an arm around his back and hurried him out into the street. The sun hung low and orange over the rooftops of Divalia, reflecting gleams off the stone roof of the palace and warming the red clay-tiled roofs along the street where the rat and wolf stood. People walked by them, though not as many as crowded the streets down by the market or the Cathedral.

Coryn didn't know whether to reach for Clement's paw or not. He couldn't stop looking at the rat, could barely believe that Clement was standing here right next to him, but the rat still looked dazed and didn't seem to want to meet his eye. Finally Coryn cleared his throat and said, "Ah, we should collect my things from the inn and get to the gate before sundown."

Clement nodded and now he did look up. "What's this about leaving the city forever?"

Coryn swallowed. "I had to say that to get you out of jail. They wouldn't have done it otherwise. I'm sorry, I—is there anything you want to get before we leave?"

"No. Mmm...perhaps there is, at that. Do we have time?"

"They said sunset." Now Coryn did take Clement's arm, and winced at how thin it felt. "I'm truly sorry. But I couldn't let you stay in jail."

"Why not?" The rat gave him a wan smile. "It's the fate of a thief. We enjoy the life until we're caught, then it's over. We all know it. I knew that last job would likely be the end of me, and it was."

"It's not the end of you," Coryn insisted. "You're coming back with me. It's the start of something new."

"It's the end of me as a thief." Clement took in a breath and let it out, and then turned and wrapped his other arm around Coryn. "I knew that. It's thanks to you that I have a new beginnin' to look to, an' I'm sorry, if I'm not sayin' the right things it's down to me not knowin' how to begin to repay a debt like this."

Coryn hugged the rat, tension melting away from him. "It's my fault you're there in the first place. I had to get you out. You—you forgive me for what I did?"

"Course I forgive you." The rat nuzzled his cheek. "Didn't have to go t'all the trouble of gettin' me out for that. I know why you did it. Question is: do you forgive yourself?"

"The question really is, will Ki forgive me?" Coryn gave the rat one last squeeze and then disengaged from the hug. "She kicked me out."

Clement raised his eyebrows and then looked at the sun.

"You can tell me 'bout it on the ride back. Time's short an' we best make the most of it."

So they went to gather Clement's things first, down the river nearly twenty minutes' walk to a neighborhood where the roofs were patched with oilcloth, where most walls were wood, and the few stone buildings showed rough patches and large holes where stones had been scavenged. Whether the smell rose from the river or the street Coryn couldn't tell, but it smelled of waste and rot with accents of the bitter tang of disease.

And yet, the people in this neighborhood, though missing patches of fur and teeth, joked and laughed with each other from the windows to the street. The atmosphere crackled with banter and insults, jokes and jabs, more than anywhere else in Divalia Coryn had been. The market had been close, perhaps, but even there the merchants' chatter had been more subdued, as they were preoccupied with their sales.

Here, a beaver mended pots on his front stoop while carrying on a conversation with a porcupine in the second story across the street; a weasel sat in her window mending a tunic and talking to a fox sitting on the street outside carving a little piece of wood.

But as they noticed Coryn with Clement, the chatter died down. Mouths closed and eyes tracked their progress down the street. Clement strode ahead unbothered, but Coryn curled his tail down and flattened his ears. He didn't need to be part of this community, but he hated being the reason they had to restrain their natural conversation.

Clement led Coryn to a small wooden house that smelled strongly of rat. "I'll just be a minute," he said. "I know yer supposed to guard me or what have you, but I'd feel better if you didn't come in."

"I trust you." Coryn leaned against the wall and eyed the sun. "We don't have a lot of time, though."

"This'll take but a minute. Thanks."

Clement disappeared into the house. A moment later, voices emerged through the door and window. Coryn folded his ears down but couldn't help hearing them.

A gruff, older male voice: "There you are. Jus' come strollin' back in."

Clement: "Came to say g'bye. I been kicked out of the city."

"Kicked out?" A female voice. "What fer?"

The older voice, whom Coryn supposed to be Clement's father: "Got caught stealin', no doubt. Knew he would."

"If he got caught," this could be Clement's mother or sister, "he'd be in jail."

"I was in jail," Clement said. "I was released because they did someone else for the thing I stole."

"If you's released," his father said, "you didn't steal it, and don't claim you did."

"I stole the royal seal of Lord Fardew." The words came out of Clement in a rush, as though he'd been both waiting to say them and dreading it. "I stole it right out of the palace and only three other people knew I did, and one of them turned me in. But then he got greedy and went and took it and they got him. Then they let me go."

"Ha. Ha!" His father's laugh made Coryn's ears fold down. "They never. You fucked off t'have a good time somewhere, no thought to what your ma'n'me might be eatin', now yer back with some river-wrote story about stealin' a royal seal."

"You're still alive, I see," Clement said flatly.

"No thanks t'you."

"I did steal it all the same," Clement said. "And I have to go before sundown. If you ever want me, send word to Doubleford and you'll find me. I'm sorry."

"Yer not sorry! You finally stiffened yer back enough to do what you been wantin' to for years!" his mother yelled.

"If he did steal it," his father laughed, "be just like him to fuck it so bad like that."

"Good-bye," Clement said.

"He'd steal somethin' priceless," his father said as the door opened, "an' get nothin' from it, no gold, no ransom, nothin'."

Clement came out and closed the door behind him, but his father kept going, shouting now, loudly enough that people around perked ears. "An' he comes back to brag about stealin' with nothin' but a story and then says he's done with his family, abandonin' us like trash."

"Why not just throw us in the river?" his mother joined in.

"Come on," Clement said. He clutched something in his paw. "I got what I need. Where's your Inn?"

"By the Cathedral," Coryn said. "The Four Quarters."

"Right." Clement led the way, along shortcuts and alleys that Coryn wouldn't have known, though he would have been able to find his way by following the spire of the Cathedral, visible anywhere in Divalia.

When they'd left Clement's old neighborhood behind, which took about two minutes of walking, Coryn ventured a question. "So...those were your parents?"

Clement nodded. They walked on together in silence, and then he said, "Might not make much sense t'you, with the nice family you got."

"I only got to know my mother for a little while," Coryn said, "and my father was—well, let's just say Ki kicked me out for being too much like him."

Clement gave him a look of interest. "I'll tell you the story on the way back," Coryn promised. "And I know it's not the same. My father was harsh because I didn't live up to his expectations, but he didn't say mean things to me most of the time." He paused. "He just...let me believe them."

"Ay." Clement sighed. "My ma and da didn't want me to be a

thief, but what else can I do? If I didn't bring home enough, they told me I was a failure. If I stole to put food on the table, I was a failure. So I stopped worryin' about what they said. I provided an' I got good at the thing I was good at. I found other folks what'd tell me I done good."

"But you wanted to say good-bye."

"Aye. They're the only family I got."

Coryn put a paw on the rat's shoulder. "Not anymore."

Clement smiled. "Thank you for that, but we both know it's not the same. Blood is blood."

"I know," Coryn said. "I meant it as much for me as for you."

At the Four Quarters, with the sun touching the rooftops of Divalia, Coryn hurried to gather all of his possessions together. "What happens if we don't make it out by sunset?" he asked Clement, scanning the room to make sure nothing was left behind.

"I don't expect they'll worry over a few minutes." Clement sniffed the air. "But best not try, eh?"

"No, I don't intend to." Coryn stared at the window, still half-open.

"Two-Claws was here." Clement said it guardedly. "Did you know, or was he looking through your things?"

"I know," Coryn said. He tried to think about how to tell him what had happened to the other rat. Would Clement care? Two-Claws had betrayed him, after all. "He's dead," he said plainly.

"Ha." Clement sniffed the air. "You might believe that, but that's a slippery one an' unless you seen the body yourself and felt it go cold..." His words trailed off as he saw Coryn's splayed ears. "You saw the body?"

"He fell from the Cathedral," Coryn said. "I saw it."

Clement sat down heavily. His ears drooped and his tail hung limply behind him as he stared down at his paws. "Taught me everythin' about thievin'. Showed me tricks, took me on jobs, told me 'bout easy marks."

"He betrayed you to the guards."

"I shouldn'ta told him about the seal. Didn't tell him where it was but I bragged about it. That was a thing he taught me: A good thief don't brag."

Clement had been punished for not following the rules of the person responsible for teaching him everything about the world, by that person. Who'd shown no remorse. "He bragged," Coryn protested. "He told you about the night with me."

"Bragged about the conquest," Clement said. "Not the theft. Ah well." He stood. "You'll tell me about it. Let's get out of this stinking city."

As they set out on the road south from Divalia, Coryn glanced at the horizon and could not make out even a sliver of the sun, but fortunately the guards had barely looked at them as they left, so if they'd been told to detain Clement after sunset— unlikely—they had ignored that request.

The rat sat behind him on Dandi, who was eager to run again after days in a stable. Coryn was briefly tempted to let him run throughout the night, but Clement's head kept falling to rest on his shoulder, and he himself wasn't sure how much longer he could stay awake. So he settled for getting out of sight of the walls of the city and then stopping at one of the many inns that dotted the road this close to the capital.

"The 'Almost There,' Clement read off the sign as Coryn came to a stop by the stable. "Wasn't there one called the 'On Your Way Home'?"

Coryn said, "This one looks the least crowded," and then he realized that Clement was making a joke, and he laughed.

"Good," Clement said. "I'm glad you can still laugh."

"Me?" In that moment, Coryn knew for sure that Clement

had forgiven him, and the relief extended his laugh a few seconds more.

"All right." The rat nudged his shoulder. "It wasn't that funny."

"Don't sell yourself short," Coryn told him. "It was pretty good."

They got a hearty dinner and then retired to their room. This inn, close to the city, offered only private rooms, but they were all small ones, barely larger than the two straw mattresses each one held. "This must be why it wasn't as crowded as the others," Coryn murmured, tossing his bag down on one of the mattresses.

"I don't care." Clement fell down onto the other mattress. "I haven't slept on anything this soft since…"

He trailed off and didn't look at Coryn. The wolf knelt down on his mattress facing Clement. "I'm sorry," he said. "I shouldn't have told the guards where you were."

"You were protecting your family," Clement said. He rolled over to stare up at the ceiling. "They would have found me anyway."

"I know." Coryn's ears flattened. "I know all the excuses. I'm saying: I'm sorry. Even with all that, I wish I hadn't done it." He took a breath and went on before Clement could answer. "Five years ago, when that thing happened with Two-Claws, my father turned me over to the guards the same way. It was the right thing to do, I suppose. But when he made our family pay that debt, it ruined my sister's marriage and it drove him to an early grave. And it was all my fault."

Now the rat turned. "Did he say that to you?"

Coryn scratched below one ear. "He didn't not say it."

"Your sister don't seem to pine after her marriage," Clement pointed out. "And someone might die any time. Who can say whether these things were because of what you did?"

"We definitely had less money because of what I did," Coryn said.

"Money can help," Clement said, "but it ain't all there is in life. What I'm sayin' is that maybe your father wasn't right."

"I know. I've been wondering that myself." Coryn sighed.

"I know you have."

He blinked up and met Clement's soft brown eyes. "You do?"

The rat nodded. "'Cause you've tried so hard to make up for turning me in."

The wolf's ears flattened again at the baldly stated reminder of his betrayal. Clement reached out and rested a thin paw on Coryn's knee. "I didn't know before, but after hearin' about how your father made you regret your mistake for five years and piled guilt on your back, it makes sense now. You turned me in, as he did you, and now you don't think that was right and you want to make up for it."

"I know I can't," Coryn said.

Clement's paw squeezed his knee. "Perhaps not, but you've got me my freedom. Far as I'm concerned, we're square. You might not feel that way now, and maybe not ever, but I promise you I don't resent you for what you did then, and I'm more'n a little in awe over what you did after. So we've talked about the first; why don't you lie down here and tell me all that's happened since we parted ways?"

So Coryn lay back, and with Clement curled up against his side, told the rat about seeing him in the custody of the guards, meeting Lox on the road, arriving in Divalia, looking around the Cathedral, his attempt to enter the palace and his meeting with Lord Barclaw, and then his encounter with Two-Claws and how he finally found the seal, though he called it, "the thing you hid," mindful of people who might be listening at doors in this public inn.

"So you found it." Clement's paw rested on Coryn's stomach and rubbed there. "Smart."

"I just followed your clues."

"And you climbed up the Cathedral. That was brave."

"I didn't manage to do it without being followed."

Clement laughed. "If you'd managed to lose Two-Claws, I'd bow at your feet an' insist you go back to Divalia to take up thievin' full time. That one's one of the best there is."

"Was," Coryn said.

"Right." Clement's paw stilled. "You told me. How'd it happen?"

Coryn told him about their fight and the other rat's fall. "I didn't quite believe it until I saw him on the street," he said.

Clement nodded. "He always said he was hard to kill, but I reckon dropping from the roof of the Cathedral would do it to anyone."

"I'm sorry," Coryn said. "He was your friend. Your mentor."

"Was." Clement pressed his nose into Coryn's neck. "Very much 'was.'"

"All right." Coryn exhaled. "I feel like that was my fault too. I kind of kicked him."

"Anyone who picks a fight on the top of the Cathedral knows it might end on the street," Clement said. "How did you get the seal back to the palace?"

"I had to talk to the guard who found his body..." Coryn told him that whole story as well. "And then I met you at the station and that's it," he said. "So many people helped me. Lox, the Steward...I was lucky."

Clement exhaled a warm breath into Coryn's neck fur, and then he pushed his paw under Coryn's tunic to rest in the wolf's stomach fur. "Made your own luck," he said. "I can't believe what you did for me."

Warmth closed Coryn's throat for a moment. He swallowed

and curled an arm around the rat's thin shoulders. "I owed it to you."

"I think you owed it to yourself," Clement said, and lifted his head to kiss the side of Coryn's muzzle, then his lips.

They kissed, while the rat's paw roamed around Coryn's stomach, and for a few seconds they stayed like that. Coryn promised himself that he would never forget how grateful he was to have the rat in his arms again, that he would never again take him for granted or push him away.

Clement pulled back from Coryn. "You risked a lot to save me, ey? I won't let you down, promise. Swear by Rodenta."

"You don't owe me anything," Coryn told him. "But I want you to stay with me. As long as you want to."

"I want to right now." Clement touched his nose to Coryn's. "Y'know, my dad said I got nothin' from stealin' the thing, but...I think I got somethin' better'n gold, somethin' I'd never expected."

There were no more words after that, but there didn't need to be. Clement pulled Coryn's tunic off, and then removed his own while Coryn pushed his trousers down. When he pulled the rat against him, fur to fur, Coryn's paws roamed over dirt clumps and skin that felt tighter over the rat's bones than he remembered. Even the fur seemed thinner somehow under his fingers.

But Clement held him with the same strength and the same warmth he remembered, and so Coryn didn't say anything, even though he thought to himself that it was his fault. He made himself feel every inch of Clement's fur as his paws traveled down the bony shoulders, across the ridge of the rat's spine, down to the angular points of his hips, and around his rear and thighs. Then the rat's fingers found Coryn's sheath, gave it some gentle strokes, and those thoughts of guilt receded. He closed his paw around the rat's sheath and held it as the warm cock extended out into his paw.

"Got any oil, perchance?" Clement murmured some moments later, his fingers teasing Coryn's very full erection.

"Actually, I do."

The rat smiled. "That confident about rescuin' me, were you?"

"No," Coryn admitted, panting a little. "It's just that Ki kicked me out, so I took all my possessions."

The rat's ears flicked back. "Well," he said, "one thing at a time, ey?"

So Coryn got the oil and applied it under his tail as the rat slicked up his cock, a little ritual that already calmed him with its familiarity and the certainty of what was about to come next. When it did, when Clement pressed up behind him and that warmth made its way inside him, Coryn relaxed. In the familiar rhythms of sex, even here in this small room in an inn outside Divalia, Coryn felt secure and safe, that he had at least made things right enough to be here, with someone he loved, who loved him too.

* * *

If Coryn had had his way, they would've taken a full week to make the trip back to Doubleford, enjoying the crisp early winter weather, the smell of the fallen leaves, and the cold nights that made them press together more closely. Even the rain was nice, bringing out Clement's scent and his own, and they did lie in bed that first morning waiting for the steady rainfall beating at the window to subside, warm together with the outside chill at the edges of their perception, a morning in which Coryn was happier than he could remember being in a very long time.

If they'd been on Elly, perhaps they could have taken that much time, but Dandi insisted on running as fast as Coryn would let him, and sometimes faster. Though this did send cold wind knifing into Coryn's ears and eyes and nose, it also made Clement cling to him tightly, so there was at least a little benefit to it.

On the third day of their trip, with the sun high in the sky, they reached Aryss's farm. This time the old wolf was inside with his wife, but came out when Coryn rode up, shading his eyes against the sun. "Ah," he said. "Was wondering when you'd be back."

"I'm sorry it wasn't sooner. I got detained in Divalia."

"Brought back someone from there too, I see. Good day." Aryss raised a paw in greeting and then peered at Clement. "Is that the rat who was living on your farm the past month?"

Coryn dismounted and held up a paw for Clement, but the rat slid off Dandi's back without assistance. "It is."

Aryss took a long look at Clement, sniffed the air, and then said, "Thanks for returning Dandi. He give you any trouble?"

"No." Coryn patted the mount's scaly shoulder. "Unless you call it 'trouble' to run too fast."

"Can be." Aryss took the reins. "Much obliged to you for giving him some exercise."

"You're sure I can't give you anything for his use?"

The old wolf shook his head. "No coin necessary, but you and the rat can come over for a bit of wine and tell me the story of this trip someday if you want to repay me."

Coryn turned to Clement, who returned his gaze and smiled. "'Smostly your story," he said.

"Someday, then," Coryn said to Aryss. "There may be things we'd prefer you keep to yourself."

"That's fine," Aryss said. "We have an old stove out in the barn. We can fire it up and sit out there."

"Oh, I didn't mean—"

"Course," Clement interrupted, stepping forward. "Sounds lovely."

"Right." Aryss nodded. "Safe journey home, then."

"Thanks." Coryn embraced the other wolf.

Clement gave a little half-bow. "Much obliged," he said.

As they set out on the walk back to Coryn's farm—Ki's farm, now, he supposed—Clement glanced back at Aryss's farmhouse. "That was the wolf what sucked you off while I was in the cart, ey?"

"Aye." Coryn's ears warmed.

"Reckon he wants more than just a story from our muzzles maybe. Or to use his own."

"Maybe. I didn't realize that when he said it, but I wouldn't be surprised."

"You trust him?"

"He was a friend of my father's, but he's always been my friend too. I do."

"Right then. Might make for a fun evening." Clement grinned at him.

Coryn wasn't sure he was ready for that, but his tail was wagging at Aryss's acceptance of Clement. "Maybe we can live in his barn if Ki doesn't take me back."

"She'll take me back," Clement said confidently, "so if she don't take you back, you can live in your stables with me."

When Coryn turned to look at him, the rat was grinning, waiting for Coryn to laugh along. When he did, Clement joined him, and put a paw across his shoulders. "There you are. It'll be fine. Ki'll be reasonable for Lucy's sake if nothing else, and if she isn't, then it ain't the end of the world. I'll stick by you 'cause I got to."

"Aye," Coryn said. "Pretty clever of me to have the royal

guard make you remain at my side. Much easier than simply asking you."

"Ah, well, see, if y'ask, never know what answer y'might get. Guards are more reliable." Clement squinted. "Figure we should go back an' kiss in front of the gates once a year just to prove to 'em that I'm still behavin'?"

"I'm sure I'll want to go back to the city someday," Coryn said, "but right now I'd be happy to stay on the farm with you and Ki and Lucy for the rest of my days."

"You've got a lot of days left." Clement looked away ahead of them. "Plenty of time to change your mind."

"I've already lived a lot of days," Coryn replied. "Pretty sure I know my mind. It was exhilarating to climb the Cathedral five years ago. And a few days ago. But I've got the memories now and I don't need to go live them again. There's a lot in Divalia but there's also plenty to do here in Doubleford. There's the chicken coop to build and the fields to plant, soon enough, and teaching Lucy to do all of this. And then in a few years she's going to be courted and we'll have to figure that all out, and I think the barley wine we make could be better, I want to talk to people about that."

Clement laughed. "Got enough to keep you busy, then. Can't say I won't miss the city m'self, but the last few weeks here I learned a couple things about me. Like I like quiet. Not always, but...sometimes. An' with the right company."

"I like the rain, too," Coryn said. "And it hasn't snowed here but just wait. Lots to do then. Clear the road, clear the roofs, make sure none of our neighbors are snowed in or need food. Most folks can fend for themselves but every winter there's someone who didn't plan well."

"I'd like to meet more of the people around." Clement scanned the road. "Everyone's been welcoming. Course, lots of that is cause they know you."

"I used to talk to more of the people around here." Coryn followed Clement's gaze down the road that led to the little town of Doubleford. "Growing up, I mean. I ran for errands to the town, over to other farms, sometimes all the way over to Radbridge. But after..." He paused, and Clement nodded understanding. "We didn't go around as much. I was ashamed of it and Father...maybe he was too. He stopped sending me places and stopped going himself, so I didn't go either. Then when Ki's husband left—he was the one who was going to take over the farm—we all kept to ourselves." It felt good to talk now that he could tell the whole story. "As Lucy grows up, Ki's been sending her around to meet other cubs, but I hung back. I didn't want people to know I was still paying off that debt. I didn't even really talk to Aryss and Lokyl again, not properly, until a year or so ago."

Clement nodded. "One way or another," he said, "it'll be a new start."

"I hope so."

They walked on side by side down the road, cold under their feet though the breeze was light and the sun warm. Around them, the trees reached bare branches up to the blue sky, their leaves already decaying on the ground. The winter air here had a particular familiar smell, the smell not just of the decaying leaves but the faint whiff of fermenting barley, which carried farther when the grass and leaves had died, and the musky scent of mounts along the road, and below everything, faint and pervasive as the hum of insects, the smell of other wolves, all the families that lived around here who had shed their fur into the air and planted their paws and their lives in the soil.

He belonged here, not in Divalia and not in Barclaw's land. That farm might have been his in name, and someday he might have felt comfortable there, but this place, this land, he was part of it and there was something special about being here. His father might have been wrong about many things, but he had been right about that.

Clement was a product of Divalia; did he feel the same about the city? Maybe, but he'd also lived here already, and he was getting used to it. If Coryn had to move somewhere else, it would help to have someone there, part of a family, who would make him feel at home.

He would do his best to make Clement feel at home, part of their pack.

They approached the trail that led down to the farm. Coryn paused to look down, and Clement stopped with him. "It'll be okay," he said.

"I know." Coryn took a breath.

"Y'know," Clement said. "If you'd asked, I'da said yes too."

Coryn turned to look into the rat's smile, and then impulsively kissed him.

The farm appeared still from a distance, but when they descended the shallow hill and crossed the muddy track that led over to the stables, the door flew open, and Lucy stood in it. She stared at them, nose lifted, but the breeze was blowing her scent toward them, so it took a few more steps before she called out, "Uncle Coryn!" and ran toward him.

He knelt in the mud and held his arms out, and she leapt into them, wrapping him in a tight hug. "Did you come back to visit? Mommy said you might."

"I hope to stay for a while," he said. "But I'll talk to your mother about that." Ki appeared in the doorway, surveyed the situation, and her ears went up and eyes widened. She walked slowly toward them.

Only then did Lucy notice who Coryn's companion was. "Clement?" she asked, and then disengaged from her uncle to fling herself at the rat. "It *is* you!" she shrieked, throwing her arms around him. "I'm so glad you came back! How did you get away from the guards? Did you escape? Did you jump into the river and swim away? Don't worry, you can stay here."

Coryn got to his feet, keeping his eyes on Ki. Her ears had swiveled out to a neutral position and her tail swished behind her. She walked slowly forward and stopped ten feet from the pair of them. "I hope this doesn't mean we'll have guards here at the farm again," she said, her eyes on Coryn.

Only then did Lucy disengage from Clement. "I thought of a better hiding place than the roof," she said. "There's a big rock over by the spring with space under it and you can hide there. Once I hid under there and Mommy didn't know where I was even though she came down to the spring and called me. I kept very quiet."

Coryn smiled at the memory; Ki had been worried until Lucy had reappeared, very pleased with herself. But Ki wasn't smiling. Her eyes stayed fixed on Coryn's.

"No," he said. "No guards. Clem's been released."

"It's all down to Coryn," Clement said. "He's petitioned Rodenta herself and his prayers was answered, just like the Cantors tell us they will be."

Ki's eyebrows rose. She didn't look away from Coryn. "What happened?"

"They caught someone else with the thing they thought he stole," Coryn said. "So I went to the guard and asked for him to be released and they did."

"It's a wee bit more complicated than that." Clement laughed. "I'm not allowed back in Divalia an' I have to stay near Coryn here so he can supervise my reformed character. Also, Coryn's leavin' out some of the best parts, but aye, that's the short of it."

Coryn licked his lips. "I know what I did was wrong," he said, "but I worked hard to put it right. I think that's a valuable lesson for Lucy to learn too, don't you?" When Ki didn't answer, he said,

"I gave up the place Lord Barclaw offered me. I don't have anywhere to go but here, but if you don't want me here, then I guess Clement and I can look to get hired on at a farm near here. Or not so near here."

Lucy squealed. "You can't go!" She clung to his leg. "Mommy, you said Uncle Coryn did something bad, but if he said he's sorry, isn't that enough? You told me if I did something bad and I was sorry and fixed it that you'd forgive me."

Finally, Ki cracked a smile. "Father never tried to put right what he'd done wrong," she said. "I don't know if he ever really understood why it was wrong. It was hard for us for a long time, and it wasn't until he died that I understood it myself, not really. While he was with us, I would talk myself into believing he was in the right. I knew you were unhappy," she said to Coryn, "but I told myself that you'd made a mistake and he'd corrected it so you'd never make a mistake like that again."

Clement chuckled. "Wait 'til you hear the whole story," he said with a wink. "There are...similarities."

"It wasn't a mistake this time," Coryn said. "I did what I had to do to fix the mistake."

"I felt bad after you left," Ki admitted. "It was hard enough for me to see Father in that way, but once I managed it I thought you should have managed it as well. But you didn't, and maybe it's harder for you."

"I see it," Coryn said, a touch snappier than he wanted to. "I'm the one he was disappointed in, you know."

"I know." Ki reached her arms out. "What I mean is, I'm sorry. We should be helping each other through this. In a way, throwing you out was as bad as what he did. So...welcome home?"

He smiled and pulled her into a hug, tail wagging, breathing in her familiar scent that was as much a part of his life as the scents of barley, grass, mud, and mounts. "I'm happy to be home," he said.

Lucy, still attached to his leg, looked up. "But you and Clement will have to go live in the stables because Mommy told me I could have your upstairs room in the house."

* * *

They sat in front of the fire that night, Lucy in Ki's lap, Clement and Coryn with their arms around each other. The chicken dinner sat warm in Coryn's stomach, the smell lingering in the air below the smoke of the fire that dominated the room. He had just finished telling a truncated, sanitized version of his story for Lucy and Ki's benefit, which had left Lucy round-eyed and agog, and Ki impressed, though she tried to hide it. "They told us to get out of the city by sunset," he said, "so Clement and I gathered up a few things and rode Dandi out of there."

"How was Dandi?" Lucy wanted to know. "Was he better than Elly?"

"He was faster but also didn't listen as well." Coryn smiled.

"I'm glad you didn't fall off the Cathedral," Ki said.

Coryn gave her a look and a nod that told her he would fill in the rest of the story later. "So am I."

"Me too," Lucy announced. "Cause then you wouldn't be here and probably Clement wouldn't either."

"Quite right, m'dear," Clement said. "If not for your uncle, I'd still be in that cold stone cell probably starving."

"Don't they feed you in prison?" Lucy asked. "Was it very horrible?"

"Extremely," Clement assured her. "Do all you can to keep away from that place."

"She will." Ki folded her arms over her cub protectively. "But we shouldn't dwell on that now."

"No," Coryn agreed. "I'm glad we're all here and we can put that—all that, all of this—in the past where it belongs."

"Can't ever leave the past behind," Clement said, resting his head on Coryn's shoulder. "Life ain't a river that carries away all the things as they happen. It's a house, an' all your past just stays in the house. You might push it up into a room and lock the door, but it's still there. Got to deal with it sooner or later." He shrugged. "Or maybe you don't, maybe you go to Canis, and she opens all the doors to your house an' goes through all your things like a taxer, askin' the value of each one and whatnot."

Coryn didn't know what to say to that, and Ki didn't either, so it was Lucy who spoke up first. "What's a 'taxer'?"

"You know that wolf who comes to look at our fields and storehouses twice a year?" Ki asked.

Lucy thought. Coryn grinned. "The one your mother calls the 'bloodsucker'?"

"Oh!" The cub perked up. "He's a taxer?"

"Yes. He comes to look at what we have and decide how much we have to give Lord Deverin."

"I don't like taxers," Lucy said. "I don't think Canis is a taxer."

"No, perhaps not," Clement said with a smile. "What do you think Canis is?"

Lucy thought about that. "I think Canis is like a mommy, but for all of us. She takes care of us and tells us when we're bad but she helps us get better."

"That's nice," Ki said, nuzzling Lucy's ears. "I like that, too."

"I think Clement's right about the house, though," Coryn said. "Like our house has all these things in it from our whole lives. Sometimes we don't think about them for years, but other times we look at them every day."

"Like those chairs that Father made," Ki said.

"He made a lot of this house," Coryn agreed. "And we have to live in it."

"But that doesn't mean we have to do all the same things he did."

"No." Canis taught that the shadow of the father lies always over the path of the cub, Coryn knew, but that didn't mean that the path was entirely in shadow. Sometimes it took a shadow to show you how to walk in the light. "We just have to keep doing the best we can."

"Sounds good t'me." Clement kissed Coryn's ear, making the wolf's tail wag contentedly. "Figure we should go do our best out in the stable?"

"You don't really have to sleep in the stable." Lucy's tone made it clear that Ki had told her to say this. "If you don't want to."

"You're a big cub," Coryn said. "You can have the upstairs room. Clement and I can sleep out in the stable for now, and maybe we can start to build another room onto the house."

Ki smiled broadly. "That sounds like a lovely project for the winter."

Clement didn't say anything, but his arm tightened around Coryn's. As his head nestled into the crook of the wolf's neck, Coryn thought about the four of them, living here on this farm. He couldn't see the Great Cathedral from here, but he didn't need to. The mystery and adventure and romance it promised lay here against his side, and his heart filled, not with longing, but with gratitude.

ABOUT THE AUTHOR

Kyell Gold has won thirteen Ursa Major awards and a Cóyotl Award for his stories and novels, and his acclaimed novel "Out of Position" co-won the Rainbow Award for Best Gay Novel of 2009. He helped create RAWR, the first residential furry writing workshop, and has instructed at each of its sessions through 2022.

He lives in California, loves to travel and dine out with his partners (when possible), and can be seen at furry conventions around the world. More information about him and his books is available at http://www.kyellgold.com.

twitter.com/KyellGold
patreon.com/kyellgold

ABOUT THE ARTIST

Sara "Caribou" Miles is a long time artist of anthropomorphics and other oddities. She has created numerous book covers throughout the years, including ones for the Volle series of stories set in this same universe. She can be found at most major furry conventions and online at caribouink.com. She currently shares her home with her partner and many 4-legged friends in the mysterious woods of New England.

twitter.com/Caribouink
instagram.com/caribouink31

ALSO BY KYELL GOLD

Love Match

Love Match (vol. 1, 2008-2010) — Rocky arrives in the States from Africa and navigates the treacherous worlds of professional tennis and high school.

Love Match (vol. 2, 2010-2012) — Rocky begins his professional career, at the cost of his family and romantic relationships.

Love Match (vol. 3, 2013-2015) — As his career trends upward, Rocky's romantic life becomes less stable.

Out of Position (Dev and Lee)

Out of Position – Dev the football player and Lee the gay activist discover how to navigate their relationship. *(mature readers)*

Isolation Play – The continuing story of Dev and Lee, as they contend with family and friends in their search for acceptance. *(mature readers)*

Divisions – As Dev's team fights to make the playoffs, Lee fights to keep his sense of self. *(mature readers)*

Uncovered – The playoffs are here, and Dev needs his focus more than ever. So when Lee becomes too distracting, something has to give. *(mature readers)*

Over Time – Dev and Lee try to plan their future while dealing with crises all around them. *(mature readers)*

Ty Game — Dev's teammate Ty navigates an arranged marriage while also falling in love. *(mature readers)*

Tales of the Firebirds — A collection of stories exploring the lives of some of the other characters from the Out of Position series. *(mature readers)*

Titles – In the two weeks leading up to Dev's third try at a championship, Dev and Lee face new challenges and changes in their lives. *(mature readers)*

Dangerous Spirits

Green Fairy – A gay high school senior struggling through his final year finds a strange old book that changes his dreams and his life.

Red Devil – A gay fox who fled his abusive family in Siberia seeks help from a ghost who demands he give up his gay lifestyle.

Black Angel – A young otter struggles to understand her sexuality as her friends prepare for post-high school life and dreams of women in other times plague her.

Argaea

Volle – The story of how Volle came to Tephos, a spy masquerading as a noble, and the first adventure he had there. *(mature readers)*

The Prisoner's Release and Other Stories – The story of how Volle escaped from prison, and the story of what happened after, plus two other stories following characters from "Volle." *(mature readers)*

Pendant of Fortune – Volle returns to Tephos to defend his honor, but soon finds himself fighting for much more. *(mature readers)*

Shadow of the Father – Volle's son, Yilon, must travel to the far-off land he is meant to rule, but he will have to fight treachery to take the lordship. *(mature readers)*

Weasel Presents – Five short stories from the land of Argaea, including "Helfer's Busy Day" and "Yilon's Journal." *(mature readers)*

Return from Divalia — Years after a night of adventure ruined his life, a young wolf gets a chance at redemption. *(mature readers)*

Forester Universe

Waterways – The full story of Kory's journey to understand himself and what it means to be gay. *(mature readers)*

Bridges – Hayward seems content to set up pairs of his friends. But what does he really need for himself? *(mature readers)*

Science Friction – Vaxy never took sex seriously, until he found out the professor he was sleeping with was married... *(mature readers)*

Winter Games – Sierra Snowpaw was an unsure high school student when someone he thought was a friend changed his life. Now he's fifteen years older and still looking for answers. *(mature readers)*

The Mysterious Affair of Giles – A servant in a British manor house tries to solve a murder.

Dude, Where's My Fox? – Lonnie chases down a fox he hooked up with at a party as a way to get over his breakup. *(mature readers)*

Dude, Where's My Pack? — Lonnie tries to navigate relationships old and new. *(mature readers)*

Losing My Religion – On tour with his R.E.M. cover band, Jackson mentors the new guy in the band as his own life falls apart. *(mature readers)*

The Time He Desires — A Muslim immigrant struggles with the betrayal of his son and the dissolution of his marriage, as well as his own long-past trauma.

Camouflage — When Danilo is sent 500 years into the past, he must choose between safety in an unfamiliar world and his own sense of what is right. *(mature readers)*

Other Books

The Silver Circle – Valerie thought the old hunter was crazy when he warned her about werewolves—until she met one.

In the Doghouse of Justice – Seven stories of superheroes and their not-so-super relationships. *(mature readers)*

Twelve Sides — Twelve short stories about side characters from the above books. *(mature readers)*

Do You Need Help? — Writing advice for furry (and non-furry) writers.